The New Jedi Order faces triumph and disaster as the Galactic Alliance battles back from the edge of defeat . . .

Books published by The Random House Publishing Group
are available at quantity discounts on bulk purchases for
premium, educational, fund-raising, and special sales use.
For details, please call 1-800-733-3000.

STAR WARS

THE NEW JEDI ORDER

FORCE HERETIC III
REUNION

SEAN WILLIAMS
AND
SHANE DIX

BALLANTINE BOOKS • NEW YORK

A Del Rey® Book
Published by The Random House Publishing Group

www.starwars.com
www.delreydigital.com

ISBN 0-345-42872-2

Manufactured in the United States of America

First Edition: July 2003

OPM   10 9 8 7 6 5 4 3 2 1

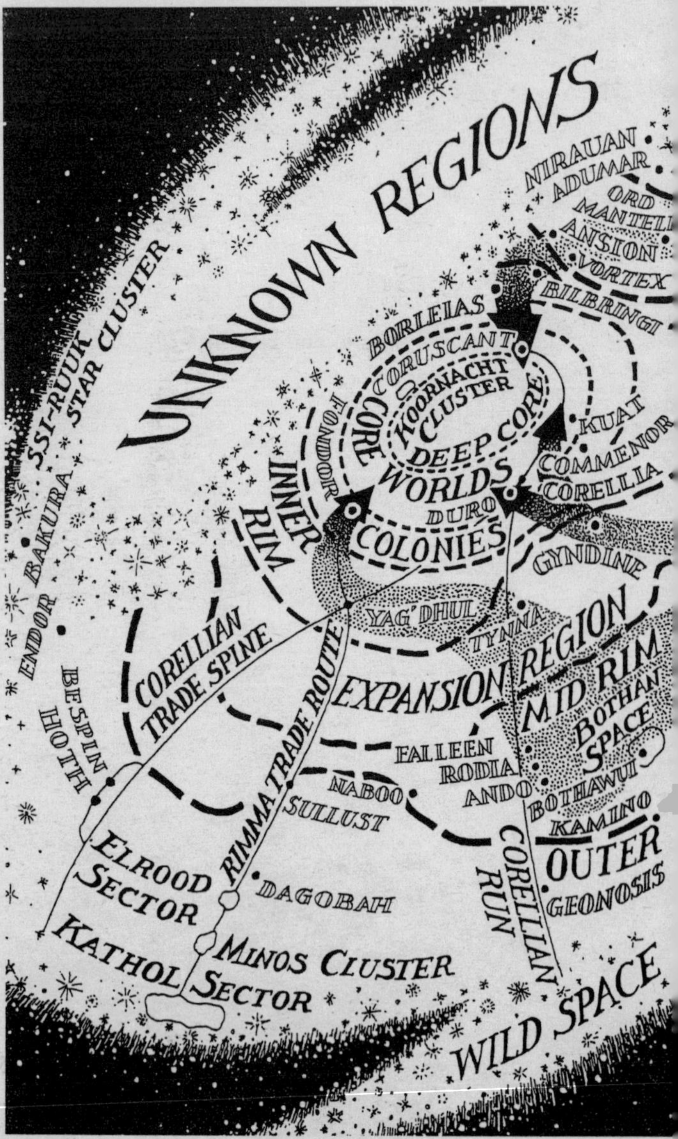

UNKNOWN REGIONS
NIRAUAN
ADUMAR
ORD
ANSION
VORTEX
BORLEIAS
CORUSCANT
CORE
KOORNACHT CLUSTER
DEEP CORE
WORLDS
FONDOR
INNER RIM
KUAT
COMMENOR
CORELLIA
DURO
COLONIES
GYNDINE
SSI-RUUK STAR CLUSTER
BAKURA
ENDOR
YAG'DHUL
TYNNA
CORELLIAN TRADE SPINE
RIMMA TRADE ROUTE
EXPANSION REGION
MID RIM
BOTHAN SPACE
BESPIN
HOTH
FALLEEN
RODIA
ANDO
NABOO
SULLUST
BOTHAWUI
KAMINO
OUTER
GEONOSIS
CORELLIAN RUN
ELROOD SECTOR
DAGOBAH
MINOS CLUSTER
KATHOL SECTOR
WILD SPACE

TINGEL ARM
EMPIRE
BELKADAN
HELSKA
BASTION
DUBRILLION
DANTOOINE
BIMMIEL
ORD BINIR
AGAMAR
DATHOMIR
ITHOR
YAVIN
MERIDIAN SECTOR
CORPORATE SECTOR
WAYLAND
MYRKR
OBROA-SKAI
OSSUS
TION CLUSTER
HAPES CLUSTER
CRON DRIFT
KASHYYYK
BIMMISAARI
KUBINDI
KESSEL
HUTT SPACE
YLESIA
NAL HUTTA
RIM
GAMORR

THE STAR WARS NOVELS TIMELINE

6.5-7.5 YEARS AFTER STAR WARS: A New Hope

X-Wing:
Rogue Squadron
Wedge's Gamble
The Krytos Trap
The Bacta War
Wraith Squadron
Iron Fist
Solo Command

8 *YEARS AFTER STAR WARS: A New Hope*

The Courtship of Princess Leia
A Forest Apart
Tatooine Ghost

9 *YEARS AFTER STAR WARS: A New Hope*

The Thrawn Trilogy:
Heir to the Empire
Dark Force Rising
The Last Command

X-Wing: Isard's Revenge

11 *YEARS AFTER STAR WARS: A New Hope*

I, Jedi

The Jedi Academy Trilogy:
Jedi Search
Dark Apprentice
Champions of the Force

12-13 *YEARS AFTER STAR WARS: A New Hope*

Children of the Jedi
Darksaber
Planet of Twilight
X-Wing: Starfighters of Adumar

14 *YEARS AFTER STAR WARS: A New Hope*

The Crystal Star

16-17 *YEARS AFTER STAR WARS: A New Hope*

The Black Fleet Crisis Trilogy:
Before the Storm
Shield of Lies
Tyrant's Test

17 *YEARS AFTER STAR WARS: A New Hope*

18 *YEARS AFTER STAR WARS: A New Hope*

The Corellian Trilogy:
Ambush at Corellia
Assault at Selonia
Showdown at Centerpoint

19 *YEARS AFTER STAR WARS: A New Hope*

The Hand of Thrawn Duology:
Specter of the Past
Vision of the Future

22 *YEARS AFTER STAR WARS: A New Hope*

Junior Jedi Knights series

23-24 *YEARS AFTER STAR WARS: A New Hope*

Young Jedi Knights series

25-30 YEARS AFTER STAR WARS: A New Hope

The New Jedi Order:
Vector Prime
Dark Tide I: Onslaught
Dark Tide II: Ruin
Agents of Chaos I: Hero's Trial
Agents of Chaos II: Jedi Eclipse
Balance Point
Recovery
Edge of Victory I: Conquest
Edge of Victory II: Rebirth
Star by Star
Dark Journey
Enemy Lines I: Rebel Dream
Enemy Lines II: Rebel Stand
Traitor
Destiny's Way
Ylesia
Force Heretic I: Remnant
Force Heretic II: Refugee
Force Heretic III: Reunion

ACKNOWLEDGMENTS

Thanks to the all-important support team that made this journey so much more interesting and enjoyable than we dared expect: Kirsty Brooks, Ginjer Buchanan, Chris Cerasi, Leland Chee, Richard Curtis, Nydia Dix, Sam Dix, Nick Hess, Christopher McElroy, the Mount Lawley Mafia, Ryan Pope, Michael Potts, the SA Writers' Center, Kim Selling, Sue Rostoni, Stephanie Smith, and Walter Jon Williams. We would particularly like to single out Greg Keyes, Jim Luceno, and Shelly Shapiro for helping (with apparently boundless patience) tie so many threads together. From a continent that sometimes feels far, far away indeed, ta muchly.

DRAMATIS PERSONAE

Arien Yage; captain, *Widowmaker* (female human)
B'shith Vorrik; commander (male Yuuzhan Vong)
C-3PO; protocol droid
Danni Quee; scientist (female human)
Droma; former acquaintance of Han Solo (male Ryn)
Gilad Pellaeon; Imperial Grand Admiral (male human)
Han Solo; captain, *Millennium Falcon* (male human)
Jacen Solo; Jedi Knight (male human)
Jagged Fel; Chiss squadron (male human)
Jaina Solo; Jedi Knight, Twin Suns Squadron (female
        human)
Jabitha; Magister of Zonama Sekot (female Ferroan)
Kunra; former warrior (male Yuuzhan Vong)
Leia Organa Solo; former New Republic diplomat
        (female human)
Luke Skywalker; Jedi Master (male human)
Mara Jade Skywalker; Jedi Master (female human)
Ngaaluh; priestess of the deception sect (female
        Yuuzhan Vong)
Nom Anor; former executor (male Yuuzhan Vong)
R2-D2; astromech droid
Saba Sebatyne; Jedi Knight (female Barabel)
Shimrra; Supreme Overlord (male Yuuzhan Vong)
Shoon-mi Esh; Shamed One (male Yuuzhan Vong)
Soron Hegerty; Imperial biologist (female human)

Tahiri Veila; Jedi Knight (female human)
Todra Mayn; captain, *Pride of Selonia* (female human)
Tekli; Jedi healer (female Chadra-Fan)

THE NEW JEDI ORDER

FORCE HERETIC III
REUNION

PROLOGUE

Neither moved; neither spoke. They stared unflinchingly into each other's eyes.

Surrounding her, hidden by shadows, Tahiri could sense an alien landscape. She could tell from its pull that it was big, yet at the same time not large enough to contain the two of them. She wanted to look down and see it, to understand this strange and disturbing ambiguity, but she couldn't afford to do so, not even for a second—for a second was all it would take to lose her purchase on this precarious balance of power. One blink of an eye and she could be dispelled into the darkness altogether, never to return—and she had no intention of ever allowing that to happen. This world was hers, and she would remain like this for as long as it took to ensure that it *stayed* hers. It was just a matter of time. All she had to do was be patient, be *strong*.

Soon, she told herself. *It will all be over soon. Just another moment . . .*

But that moment seemed as long as the blackness around her was deep. It was a moment that stretched back to the explosion that had first given birth to the universe, and forward to the time when eternity would turn all the suns cold. It didn't matter, though. She would endure a thousand such moments to ensure that the world below did not fall to Riina.

Yes, that was it. Riina: the other girl's name. She

1

wanted to destroy Tahiri and take the world from her. Tahiri could feel the girl's intentions as though they were her own.

I will not succumb, she thought determinedly. *I am Tahiri Veila; I am a Jedi Knight!*

And I am Riina of Domain Kwaad, the girl said in response. *I shall not succumb, either.*

With that, Tahiri's mirror image finally moved: her hand went to her side and removed the lightsaber from her belt.

A lightsaber, Tahiri thought, *not an amphistaff.* Riina wanted everything she had, and she fought with everything Tahiri had, too.

The light from the blade revealed something of their surroundings. To one side there was a dry and rocky ground that stretched out forever, and to the other there was a chasm of terrible blackness, an emptiness that pulled at Tahiri, drew her to the edge of the precipice upon which she stood. She could tell from Riina's fearful gaze that this same emptiness was tugging at her, also. One wrong move and either of them could fall into an embrace of eternal nothingness, leaving the darkened world to the other.

The notion renewed her resolve, and with a snap and a hiss that echoed throughout the landscape she activated her own lightsaber.

The two advanced slowly toward one another until the two bubbles of light from their lightsabers touched and they were standing face to face. Then, in unison, the two blades rose into the air and came down sharply at the other's head. They connected in midair with a deadly crackle, sending sparks arcing into the darkness . . .

PART ONE

INFILTRATION

Han Solo fought the urge to wipe a droplet of sweat from his brow, knowing that such a gesture would be seen as a sign of nervousness, and thus give the others a clue as to what he was holding.

"What's it to be, Solo?"

Han went for a stall, his second in as many minutes. "Let me get this straight. It wasn't enough that you guys got tired of using integers—or that you weren't satisfied with just using real numbers, either. You had to start messing with imaginary and transreal numbers as well."

The larval-stage Ruurian bounty hunter's face was locked in a sneer. "Do you have a problem with that?"

"Why should there be a problem?"

"Then get on with it!"

One corner of Han's mouth curled up into a half grin. His opponents were starting to lose their patience. That could work to his advantage.

"So you're saying that we can use *any* arithmetic operation we like. We can divide, subtract, multiply—"

"I know what you're doing," growled a bad-tempered Givin, its skeletal jaw clicking impatiently against its upper "lip." Given its species' predilection for mathematics, Han imagined that it was the Givin who was responsible for the changed rules. "You can't bluff us, Solo."

"Perhaps the great Han Solo has lost his edge." The

fourth player, Talien, a Yarkora with numerous gold rings dangling from each enormous nostril, uttered a contemptuous snort.

Han glanced down at the chip-cards in his hand. "Or perhaps it's just that my math is a little rusty."

He laid the cards on the table, resigning himself to winning the strangest game of sabacc he'd ever played. The three $^3\sqrt{23}$ chips that the last round had dealt him stared up at the ceiling in staves, flasks, and coins. His decision to ditch the idiot card and take a chance on fate had paid off.

"Read 'em and weep," Han said, leaning back into his chair. "Or whatever it is you guys do around here."

"A cubic sabacc?" The Ruurian's red eyes glittered dangerously in the bar's dim and smoky light as it glared at Han. "That's not possible!"

"It's not impossible," the Givin snarled. "Just extremely unlikely."

"Solo, if you're taking us for a ride, I swear—" the Yarkora began.

"Hey!" Han exclaimed, standing up and stabbing a finger at Talien's enormous nose. "You scanned me on the way in. If I'd had a skifter on me, you'd've known about it."

The Givin's bony mouthplates ground together in frustration. "Skifter or no skifter, Solo, I still say it's safer to believe in human nature than the kind of luck you're claiming."

"Come off it, Ren. You're saying I cheated in a game I didn't even know existed until I docked here a couple of days ago?" He snorted derisively. "You're giving me a lot more credit than I deserve."

"That's *all* the credit you'll be getting," the Ruurian muttered, reaching forward with one of its many arms to scoop up the chips.

Han grabbed the junction between the alien's two uppermost body parts and twisted sharply—not enough to do any damage, but certainly enough to make the Ruurian think twice. "You touch my winnings, and then you'll see just how much of my edge I've lost."

Chairs scraped across the stony floor as the other two players backed away from the sabacc table. Shouts sounded in a dozen different tongues around the room. The Thorny Toe maintained a strict no-weapons policy, but that didn't mean that fights couldn't be lethal. And as far as the patrons of the Thorny Toe were concerned, the more violent the altercation, the better the entertainment value.

"Overrated muck hauler!" the Ruurian grunted, wriggling its lengthy body in an attempt get free. Han struggled to hang on, while at the same time trying to keep the alien at arm's length. Each of the Ruurian's body segments possessed a set of limbs that clutched at him with hostile intent.

"Who you calling overrated?" Han muttered, tightening his grip. Although low in mass, the alien could bend in places Han couldn't, making it difficult to maintain the upper hand. The Ruurian hitched its back end under the table and managed to tip him off balance. As he went down, a dozen sharp-tipped digits swarmed up his legs and chest, looking for soft spots. Tiny, razor-sharp mandibles snapped at his nose. The audience cheered, goading the antagonists on.

Just as he was beginning to think he'd taken on more than he could handle, two rough, three-fingered hands grabbed both him and the Ruurian, hauling them off the ground and separating them in midair.

"Enough!"

Han recognized the guttural accent of a Whiphid and instantly ceased trying to kick his way out of the creature's grasp. He knew better than to fight a Whiphid. Their claw and tusks were as mean as their temperament.

"He's a cheat!" the Ruurian whined, snapping at Han with its nether mandibles.

The Whiphid shook the alien so hard Han swore he heard its exoskeleton rattle. "This bar isn't crooked!"

"That's what I've been trying to tell them," Han said, offering a self-satisfied smirk. "I beat them fair and square!"

The Whiphid dropped them both roughly to the floor, then pointed one of its claws accusingly at Han. "The boss wants to see you."

A flash of uncertainty cooled any joy he might have taken from the victory.

"Not before I collect my winnings," he said, climbing to his feet. He stepped resolutely to the table.

"You have five standard seconds," the bouncer said.

Han needed only two. Using his shirt as a catchall, he scooped the credits off the table. The Ruurian looked on balefully, emitting a soft growl that only those in its immediate vicinity would have heard.

"You know, Talien, folks like you give sabacc players a bad name." Han couldn't resist taking the opportunity to gloat as he packed his winnings safely in his pockets. "Back in my day—"

"Spare us the glory speech." Talien made no attempt to stop Han from walking off with the winnings, but glared at him menacingly. "Save it for your kids. Maybe they'll be impressed by the once-great Han Solo."

"Why, you—" Unreasoning anger rose in him, but before he could react, the bouncer caught him by the back of his jacket and tugged him away.

"Enough, I said!" The Whiphid lifted Han into the air again as though he were a child. Suspended, helpless, Han could only force his anger down and ignore the jeers of the other patrons as he was unceremoniously "escorted" from the bar.

"You humans are always causing trouble," the Whiphid grumbled once they'd passed through a door to the back of the Thorny Toe and Han had been lowered to the ground once more. "If I had a credit for every time I've bounced one of you out of here, I'd have made it back to Toola years ago."

"You see many strangers through here, then?" Han asked, straightening his jacket.

The Whiphid looked at him suspiciously. "Why? You looking for someone?"

"No; just curious." He shut up, then, not wanting to draw any more attention to himself than he already had.

The alien took him up a flight of stairs and deposited him in an empty room containing little more than a padded green couch and a water dispenser. Han assumed it was an antechamber adjoining the bar owner's office. He sat himself down on the couch and was startled when a voice issued into the room from unseen speakers.

"Han Solo, eh?" The voice's sex, species, and accent were heavily disguised, but the speaker seemed amused underneath the camouflage. "You're a long way from home."

"Well, you know me," Han bluffed. "Never been one to sit on my hands."

A strange noise issued from the hidden speakers. It might have been a laugh. "But you've always been one for gambling," the voice returned, more soberly. "It's good to see that nothing's changed."

Han frowned at the familiarity. He desperately tried to think whom he had known in the past who might have ended up owning a bar on Onadax, one of the dingiest worlds the Minos Cluster had to offer, and whether he— or she—might hold a grudge against him.

"You get your thrills where you can," he said, stalling again.

"I'd like to ask you a few questions, if I may."

Han shrugged, giving in but feigning nonchalance all the same. "Fire away."

"Who sent you?"

"No one sent me."

"Why are you here?"

"I'm just passing through. Is that a crime in these parts?"

"Where are you headed?"

"Nelfrus, in the Elrood sector."

"You must be going the long way around, then."

"You can't be too careful these days. The Vong—"

"Are everywhere," the voice interrupted. "Yes, I know. But they're not here."

"Which is why I thought I'd come this way."

After a slight pause, the voice continued: "Are you here alone?"

"What difference does that make?"

"Perhaps none. *Millennium Falcon* has been on Onadax two standard days, one day longer than a Galactic Alliance frigate that docked here yesterday. Am I to assume that there is no relation between this craft and your own?"

"You can assume what you like," Han said. "But that frigate doesn't have anything to do with me. What did you say its name was?"

"I didn't. It's *Pride of Selonia*."

He made a show of thinking about the name. "Sounds familiar. You think it might be someone looking for me?"

"Or perhaps the other way around."

"I'm just here for the scenery," Han lied. He jingled the credits in his pocket. "And whatever else I can pick up on the way."

At this, the faceless bar owner did laugh. Onadax was a sooty, inhospitable world, not dense enough to harbor metals of any value, poorly placed even with respect to other worlds in the sector, and too small and ancient to possess any noteworthy geography. Its only saving graces were its lack of a policing authority and a relaxed attitude toward documentation of all kinds.

Just because the government turned a blind eye to who passed through, though, didn't mean that the locals were stupid.

"Okay," Han said, scanning the blank walls and ceiling, wishing there were some reference point on which he could focus his attention. "Let's stop playing games. You're right. I *am* looking for someone. Maybe you can help me."

"Why should I?"

"Because I'm asking nicely. Do you get many Ryn through here?"

"No more than usual," the voice said. "Lift up any dirty rock in the galaxy and you'll find a family living under it. Your taste in friends must have gone downhill if that's who you're after."

"Not just any Ryn." Han fumbled, not for the first time, for the right way to describe the Ryn he was seeking. "Just one that was supposed to meet me here on Onadax. He hasn't shown, so I'm looking for him."

"In a bar?"

"It's not as if Onadax has much else to offer."

The voice chuckled again. "You're looking in the wrong place, Solo."

"That sounds suspiciously like a brush-off. I swear, it's nothing underhanded."

"From you, those words take on a whole new meaning."

"I'll even pay, if that's what you want."

"If that's what you think I want, then I fear you're definitely in the wrong place—and at the wrong time."

The Whiphid guarding the door stirred.

"So it would seem," Han said. "Look, I'm racking my brain here trying to work out where we've met before. Can't you give me a name to help me out a little?"

There was no reply.

"What've you got to lose?" Han said. "You obviously know me—"

He stopped when the Whiphid's clawed hand came down on his back and began to drag him away. "At least give me a clue!"

The Whiphid hauled him out of the audience chamber and back down to the barroom. Clearly, the interview was over, and no protest from Han was about to be considered.

"Is he always this friendly?" he asked the bouncer. He amended that to a hopeful "She?" when the question wasn't answered.

The Whiphid collected Han in its powerful grasp once again and hoisted his feet from the floor.

The bouncer forced its way through the crowd. Laughter and applause followed them, turning to cries of annoyance as Han's head rammed into something's foul-smelling midriff and sent a jug of ale splashing across the floor. Recriminations flew, which the bouncer ignored.

"I think you'll find my seat was over that way," Han said, pointing hopefully in the direction of the sabacc table where he'd been playing.

The Whiphid ignored him as well, propping him upright none too gently at the door. There was no question that Han was being told—not asked—to leave the premises.

He smiled, taking a hundred-credit chip from his pocket and slipping it to the alien bouncer.

"For your trouble," he said.

"For yours," was the response as he was forcibly ejected into the street.

"What sort of dive is this, anyway?" Han protested to the closed door as he picked himself up and dusted himself down once more. His shoulder was tender where he'd hit the ground, and the bouncer's claws had left a few tears in his jacket. Still, it could have been worse. At least he'd made it out with his winnings.

His comlink buzzed as he limped down the seedy back alley that housed the Thorny Toe. He pulled the comlink out of his pocket, knowing before he'd answered the call that it was Leia on the other end.

"You're out?" Her voice was faint, but her concern was obvious.

"And in one piece. The bar staff aren't as tough as their jamming fields suggested they might be."

"Did you find anything?"

"Nothing useful, although I'm guessing there's more going on here than meets the eye."

"There always is." Leia hesitated. "Is that fighting I hear?"

Han glanced behind him. The ruckus inside the bar was getting nastier by the second.

"My exit was none too subtle," he said, picking up the pace.

"Start making your way back, then. It's not safe out there, Han."

"On my way now."

"I'd advise against stopping somewhere else en route, even if it does allay suspicions."

Han smiled to himself. In the old days, he would've been tempted. But the choice between Leia and a seedy dive was getting easier every year. "Will do."

The secure channel closed with a soft click. Han's smile ebbed as behind him the fight spilled noisily out into the street. He hurriedly rejoined the stream of barhoppers cruising the settlement's main thoroughfare, the grilling he'd received at the Thorny Toe still nagging at him. That the owner of the bar had known him didn't bother him so much; after all, the Solo name had spread across the galaxy and back again, especially in the quasi-legal circles to which he'd once belonged. But the complete stonewalling regarding the Ryn *did* bother him. His other sources hadn't known anything, but at least they had been up front about it. Dumb ignorance was totally different to silence.

Han rubbed his shoulder and hurried back to the *Falcon*, hoping Jaina had had better luck on the other side of town.

Luke Skywalker gripped the sides of his seat as *Jade Shadow* emerged roughly from hyperspace. The bulkheads groaned under the strain, while containers of stored goods in the passenger bay could be heard crashing to the floor. Deeper into the ship could be heard the beeping and tweetling of an anxious R2-D2.

"What was that?" he asked his wife beside him in the pilot's seat, when the disturbance had passed.

Mara was already flicking switches and checking monitors, giving her ship a quick once-over. "A hole the size of a Star Destroyer just opened up in front of us."

Every hyperspace jump they'd made in the last couple of weeks had been fraught with danger and uncertainty. Not even with the detailed maps of the Chiss Expansionary Defense Fleet to guide them could they account for every hyperspatial anomaly. But if anyone could find a way through the rips and reefs on the other side of known space, it was Mara. He had nothing but confidence in his wife to get them to their destination.

Luke examined the boards before him. "Let's just hope *Widowmaker* is okay."

Lights flickered across the displays, and a new blip appeared on the scopes—shakily at first, but steadying.

"Here she is now," Mara said.

Seconds later, the voice of Captain Arien Yage sounded

over the comm. "How about a warning or something next time?"

Luke smiled to himself at the captain's comment. "Sorry about that, Arien. If we could give you a heads-up, you know we would."

"No problem. We got out in one piece, and that's the main thing."

The frigate was locked on *Jade Shadow*'s navicomputer and would mirror every move Mara made through the shoals of the Unknown Regions, but there was no way to communicate through hyperspace and therefore no way to warn of any sudden exits.

"This is getting annoying," Mara muttered after doing checks on her displays. "I can't work out what I'm doing wrong."

Luke was just as confused. Three times they'd tried and failed to jump the last parsec to where the empty system of Klasse Ephemora lay. There—so Jacen had deduced on Csilla, and so all evidence supported—they would find the living world of Zonama Sekot. But it felt to Luke as though something were keeping them out. Mara assured him that it wasn't like that: the hyperspace anomalies were a natural phenomenon; they didn't do anything *consciously*. Nevertheless, it was uncanny how there seemed to be so many of them around this particular point in space.

"Maybe it's because of the anomalies that Zonama Sekot came here in the first place," Luke suggested. "It's safe in here, after all. Once it got in, it could be reasonably sure no one else would bother trying."

"Well, the Chiss probes managed to get in," Mara said. "And if they can do it, then so can I."

Luke sent a wave of reassurance to his wife, buoying up the flagging confidence that simmered just beneath her show of determination. She was a much better navigator than an astromech, and—while it was pointless speculating on the capabilities of a world-sized intelligence like Zonama Sekot—he was sure she could match its flying abilities any day.

"It could be dark matter," Soron Hegerty said from behind them. The elderly professor of comparative religions—a specialist on exotic alien life—had come forward from the passenger bay, steadying herself with one frail hand against the transparent canopy covering the cockpit.

Luke faced her. "Do you think so, Doctor?"

"Perhaps," Hegerty said. She paused a moment, obviously trying to think of a way to condense all her studies on the subject into a few words. "Dark matter interacts only gravitationally with the rest of the universe. It pools into clumps like ordinary matter, forming clusters and galaxies similar to the one we inhabit. Some scientists believe our galaxy to be surrounded by a halo of such galaxies—completely invisible to the eye, but there nonetheless.

"Danni and I were talking about this just yesterday," she went on. "She wonders if such an invisible clump might explain the hyperspace disturbance in the Unknown Regions. A dark matter cluster could be in the process of colliding with our galaxy right now, passing invisibly through it, detectable only by its gravity. Clusters aren't uniform in density: they have dust lanes and empty bubbles—and stars, of course. The uneven distribution of dark matter might account for the difficulty we've had charting this region from the 'real' universe. It all comes down to a collision with another galaxy we can't even see—a collision taking place over billions and billions of years."

Hegerty looked through the forward screens, eyes glittering as though in wonder at the invisible worlds she imagined.

Mara brushed a strand of red hair back from her face. "That's all very interesting, Doctor. Can we chart the dark matter somehow and work out how hyperspace is folded around here?"

Hegerty returned from infinity with a shrug. "Theoretically, perhaps. You'd need some sort of large-scale gravity detector, and a means of working out exactly how dark matter influences hyperspace."

"So it doesn't actually help us right now?"

Hegerty shook her head. "I just wanted you to know that you're dealing with a changeable phenomenon. If Zonama Sekot can detect the gravitational passage of dark matter through our galaxy, it might have located a bubble that was about to close. If it put itself inside this bubble, and the dark matter walls slammed shut around it, it could guarantee its safety. Nothing would be able to get through until the dark matter shifted and the bubble opened again."

Luke could tell from Mara's expression that she didn't like this idea at all.

"If you're right, this bubble must be big enough to enclose an entire star system," she said. "I don't believe something that big would be totally seamless. There has to be a way in—and a way out, too. If I were a living planet on the run, there's no way I'd lock myself in anywhere. There *has* to be a way."

Luke put a soothing hand on her arm. "I suggest you rest first, my love. You're not going to get anywhere when you're frustrated like this."

Mara was about to argue the point, but then something softened behind her eyes and she sagged back into her seat. "You're right, of course. I guess I'm just in a hurry to get on with it. The sooner we find Zonama Sekot, the sooner we can go home."

Luke sympathized with that feeling all too well. Ben,

their son, was a long way away, hidden in the Maw with the other Jedi children, safe from the Yuuzhan Vong. The last holos they'd received had revived an ache that was never far away. The boy was growing up without his parents, just as Luke had grown up without his. It was necessary, but not ideal.

With Mara's approval, he ordered a rest stop. Deep in the star-spangled blackness of the Unknown Regions, the mission came to a temporary halt.

Jag Fel sat by Tahiri's bed, staring curiously at the young girl for what must have been the tenth time in two hours. Her brow was drenched with sweat and needed to be wiped frequently. Her hands gripped tightly at the sheets on which she lay. Every now and then she made a strange mewling noise, which sounded to Jag almost like a suppressed scream.

Jaina had wanted to make sure that someone was at Tahiri's bedside at all times, in case she woke up.

It was Jag's shift. He just hoped it wouldn't be on his watch that Tahiri opened her eyes—because if it *was* Riina who emerged, he knew he would do whatever was necessary for the safety of all concerned.

Jag was startled out of his brooding by the buzz of the comlink. Captain Mayn of the *Selonia* had installed a compact communications rig in Tahiri's room so that whoever was on watch could keep in touch with events elsewhere. He answered it before the noise could disturb her.

He found himself in the middle of a joint conversation between Jaina and her parents.

"Something fishy is definitely going on," Jaina was saying.

"At the Thorny Toe?" That was Han, speaking from the bridge of the *Falcon*. He sounded slightly out of breath. "I thought so, too. The guy I spoke to—whoever it was—is definitely up to something."

"Not that," Jaina said. "The cubic sabacc gives it away. It's too unlikely. Someone let you win."

"What about that famous Solo luck?"

"No one's *that* lucky, Dad. Face it: someone didn't want you snooping around. Rigging the table to make it look like you cheated would have been easier than trying to expel you by force for no good reason. It's the only explanation."

Her father reluctantly conceded her point. "It's possible, I guess."

"That still doesn't tell us who's behind it." Leia's unease wasn't so easily assuaged. "The bar owner is clearly involved. He's either warning us off or looking for an edge of his own. Either way, we know that we should go back."

"What about you, Jaina?" Jag broke in. "Did you find anything?"

She made an exasperated noise. "If I'd been stonewalled I'd count myself as lucky. I haven't found a whiff of the Ryn anywhere, and I'm not likely to, now."

"Not now that they're onto us," Han said gloomily.

"Worse. There's some sort of disturbance out here. A brawl of some kind, and it's spreading." For the first time, Jag noted the sound of the city behind her voice. He could hear shouting and what sounded like transparisteel shattering. "Law enforcement is nonexistent here, of course, so it's getting nasty very quickly."

"How far are you from the *Falcon*?" Leia asked.

"A dozen blocks, but it's getting tougher by the minute. Wait a second."

Jaina's end of the conversation went silent for a minute. Jag was prepared to wait it out with the others, but Captain Mayn's voice came over the comm.

"We've got something of a situation here," she said. "Dock security is warning of a riot breaking out across the city. There's a mob on our way, apparently."

That accorded with the sounds Jag at heard at Jaina's end.

"Any word on what caused it?" Leia asked.

"None as such. There are rumors of an incident somewhere in the city. They say that a Galactic Alliance agent attempted to infiltrate a secure compound and has made off with a fortune."

"We have no agents here that I know of," Leia said.

"Apart from us," Han put in.

"Sorry," Jaina said, coming back onto the line. "Got caught in a traffic snarl. The way to the *Falcon* is blocked. I'm going to try for the *Selonia* instead."

Jaina's footsteps were hurried over the comlink. Jag could hear the concern in Leia's voice as she said, "Hurry, but be careful. Someone might be trying to whip up resentment against us."

"Why?"

"Let's wonder about that later," Han said. "Just get back safely."

Jag echoed that sentiment wholeheartedly as Jaina's channel went silent. "Sounds to me like someone's covering their tracks," he said to those remaining on the line.

"You and me both, Jag," Han said. "And if Jaina wasn't out there in the middle of it, I'd happily leave them to it."

"That's probably our best course of action," Leia said. "We've been looking for the Ryn and haven't found them. They've had plenty of opportunities to look us up and haven't. I'm starting to think that we've been wasting our time."

Han uttered a grunt that could have been one of agreement.

"I'll prepare for liftoff," said Mayn, ever the pragmatist. "We'll be away the moment she's on board, if that's what you decide."

"Should I ready Twin Suns?" Jag asked.

"Not necessary, Jag," Leia said. "We can handle the Onadax defense grid long enough to get away, if it comes to that."

"I'll wait here then." He nodded stiffly. "Thanks for keeping me posted."

"Stand by," Mayn said.

With a slight hiss of static, the line closed.

Jag resisted the impulse to pace. He hated being confined to medical quarters while Jaina put herself at risk out in the city, but there was nothing he could do about it. Orders were orders, and his Chiss training left him no option but to obey. All he could do was wait for Mayn or somebody else to update him.

Tahiri stirred on the bed beside him, issuing another of her strange, strained sounds.

Hurry up, Jaina, he thought as he mopped the girl's brow. *Hurry back to me . . .*

Jacen frowned and tried again.

"Mon Calamari Communications Control, this is Farmboy One. Come in, MCCC. I repeat, this is Farmboy One. Please respond."

Silence.

He sighed as he leaned tiredly back into his chair. While Luke and Mara rested, Jacen was in charge of *Jade Shadow*. Sensing a familiar wistfulness in his uncle and aunt, he had decided to report to the new capital, looking for an update on his cousin Ben. His failure to raise Mon Calamari troubled him, even though he knew there was probably a perfectly logical explanation. Communications with the Unknown Regions weren't ideal; all transmissions were routed through a bottleneck on the edge of the Outer Rim. That bottleneck had never closed before, but that didn't mean it wasn't possible.

Before jumping to conclusions, though, Jacen had wanted to test every alternative hypothesis. *Jade Shadow*'s comm systems were working perfectly well at short range; several conversations with the *Widowmaker* proved that. And when he'd changed his target and tried to hail the CEDF network, the crisp precise tones of a Chiss comm officer answered immediately, so it was clear that the subspace transmitters were still working, too.

"MCCC, this is Farmboy One," he continued. "This is an emergency. We require an immediate response!"

When there was still no reply after a couple of minutes, he decided the fault *had* to lie in one of the relay bases between the Unknown Regions and the rest of the galaxy. There was no other possibility that he could think of.

"What's the emergency?"

Jacen turned to see Danni silhouetted in the doorway. "We're out of blue milk," he lied. He didn't want to alarm anyone until he'd had a chance to speak to his uncle. "You know how cranky Mara gets when she doesn't get a proper breakfast."

She moved around to take position in the copilot's seat beside him.

"There is no denying that you are an amazing Jedi, Jacen Solo, but you are a terrible liar."

Jacen smiled. For all the new understanding of the Force he had received under Vergere's tutelage, all the skill as a Jedi he'd amassed over the years spent fighting the Yuuzhan Vong, Danni could see right through him.

"I can't raise Mon Cal," he said, his expression becoming more serious. "There seems to be some sort of break in transmission between here and there."

"What sort of break?"

"It's hard to tell from this end. I do know, though, that

if we can't contact Mon Cal, we won't be able to tell them what we find here."

"*If* we find anything. There are no guarantees, Jacen."

"You saw the data—"

"I did, and I agree with you. I'm just trying to encourage debate in your own thoughts." Danni's curly blond hair framed her head like a halo, glowing in the instrument lights, and her green eyes seemed to bore into his. "I feel your tension, Jacen. You're humming like an overloaded shield. What if we *don't* find anything, or it's not what you're hoping for? That's what you're thinking, isn't it? Underneath everything else, that's what really bothers you."

He nodded. That fear was running at the back of his mind, a steady rhythm constantly unsettling him, encouraging him to overreact. "Perhaps you're right," he said. "I guess we're not completely cut off. We can still reach Csilla. Maybe I should check with them to see if they can get through to Mon Cal. If not, they can keep trying while we go ahead with our mission."

Her smile broadened. "Sometimes all we need to do is get the thoughts that trouble us out of our head and into the open where we can see them more clearly."

She reached out to pat him reassuringly on the shoulder, but her hand never fell. Something powerful and strange rolled through him. Jacen pulled away from her, thinking at first that what he was feeling must somehow have had something to do with her. But the sensation persisted, and her expression echoed his alarm.

"You can feel that?" Whatever it was, it was getting stronger—and it was coming through the Force.

Danni nodded, covering both ears with the flats of her palms. "What *is* it?"

"I don't know." His head was starting to vibrate like a bell. He turned to the displays ahead of him, searching for information. "But I intend to find out."

* * *

Saba started awake from a deep sleep feeling as though someone were trying to crack open her skull. She called out in alarm, flailing wildly at the empty air before realizing where she was: resting up against the wall in one of *Jade Shadow*'s crew quarters. She'd closed her eyes to meditate when Mara had announced the mission had stalled, and she must have fallen asleep.

No alarms were ringing; she couldn't smell panic pheromones in the air; everything seemed completely normal—except for the fact that the crack in her skull seemed to be widening . . .

She sat up with a growl, sharp teeth clenched in a tight zigzag line. Her eyes peered out from under heavy, knotted brows. She focused upon a spot on her bed, desperately trying to concentrate on who or what was causing the intense discomfort.

Find the pain, she told herself. *Trace it back to your attacker!*

She breathed deeply through her nostrils and sought to find her inner calm, the still center of her being. It had taken her years to overcome the natural instincts of her species, and in times of stress—when every cell wanted to slash and tear instead of contemplate and respond with careful forethought—the urges were particularly hard to suppress. But she was strong, and determined.

The Force came to her bidding with familiar ease, flooding her with energy that swept the tiredness and confusion away. And with it, too, came the knowledge that what she was feeling was coming through the Force itself, as though something very large and powerful had been disturbed nearby.

Through the discomfort of such intense feelings, she felt the first glimmerings of excitement. It could be only one thing!

Saba hurried forward through the ship. She could tell

that the others gathered there shared her excitement. Master Skywalker, Mara, Jacen, Tekli, Danni—they could all feel it! On a ship full of Force-sensitives, it was impossible to hide something as powerful as this. Only Soron Hegerty seemed immune, asleep as she was in one of the cabins.

R2-D2 tootled as Saba went past. She tapped the droid's shining dome, but didn't stop. The smell of human uncertainty emanating from the fore of the ship was strong, and Saba breathed through her mouth to ensure her thoughts remained clear and focused.

"—can't be sure at this range," Mara was saying, addressing the others standing around in the passenger bay. "It could be anything. Massive psychic disturbances occur for all sorts of reasons."

Master Skywalker nodded. "She's right, Jacen. When Alderaan was destroyed by the Death Star, Obi-Wan felt it from a great distance."

"I know, but this is *close*," Jacen insisted, his voice thick with excitement. "I can *feel* it. What else could it be?"

Saba could sense the others wanting to believe but remaining reluctant to gamble on the young Jedi's hunch.

"Jacen iz right," she said, the words emerging in a rough approximation of Basic from her stress-tightened throat. "Zonama Sekot criez out in the void."

The Jedi Master faced her. "But why?"

"It feelz . . . distressed." The pained looks on the faces before her showed that they felt it, too. It was impossible to keep out.

"Almost frightened," Danni ventured, hugging herself. "But angry, too."

"Okay, suppose it *is* Zonama Sekot," Mara said. "What then? Do we attempt to contact it?"

"That depends on whether you think you can follow this signal to its source."

The red-haired woman frowned. "It's possible, but

I'm not sure I like the idea of turning up uninvited. This thing sounds agitated as it is. Barging in there might only antagonize it further."

"Maybe," her husband replied, "but I think that turning up and *showing* it our intentions rather than trying to explain them from a distance is the better option." He turned to the Barabel. "Jacen, Saba—you're our life-sensitives. What do you think?"

Jacen looked uncertain.

"I can no more read this mind than I could the entire contentz of the Chiss library," Saba told Luke, her tail tapping restlessly against her right ankle.

"Won't going closer make the situation worse, though?" Danni asked.

Master Skywalker looked uncertain. "All I'm sure of is that this our best shot at getting where we want to go. If we ignore it, we might never get another one."

Mara inhaled deeply. "Okay, then let's do it while we still can."

Luke reopened the line to the captain of the *Widowmaker*. "Arien, I want you to lock onto our navicomputer and prepare for immediate departure. We've got a lead, and if our hunch is right we'll soon be exactly where we need to be. We don't know what we might be getting into, so be prepared."

"Ready when you are," came the immediate reply. "Yage out."

Luke looked around the cockpit at the nervous faces watching him. "Maybe we should meld," he said. "Pooling our concentration might make it easier for Mara to trace the source."

Danni had had only limited experience with the Jedi practice of mind-melding, but she nodded along with the others. Saba began the familiar exercises with a series of deep breaths. She felt the life-sparks of those around her, glowing like embers in a white-hot furnace. The strength of the signal was such that it almost totally blanketed them. But she concentrated, bringing them steadily into focus, and slowly their thoughts joined in a tight embrace.

Mara's mind danced with hyperspace coordinates, instrument panels, and other space flight paraphernalia. Saba added her perceptions of the distant world-mind to the mix of thoughts and impressions gathering around Mara. Danni offered the clearest knowledge of astronomical forces. Saba imagined herself on the dark, red-lit world of Barab I, prowling low for shenbit bonecrushers, every sense keen. Zonama Sekot wasn't the same thing as a flesh-rending giant lizard, but the principle was the same. They were hunting, and she was a *good* hunter . . .

Mara took everything she was given and plotted a course. *Jade Shadow*'s hyperdrive roared into life, and Saba felt the familiar sensation of lights streaking past them and falling behind as the strange topology of hyperspace enfolded them.

Here the territory belonged to Mara. Even with the Force to guide them, the way was tortuous and fraught with danger. *Jade Shadow* did her best to follow the path laid down for her, with the *Widowmaker* firmly in tow, but almost immediately she encountered the same barrier she had earlier. With a sickening wrench she was dumped back into realspace, only slightly closer to Klasse Ephemora than she had been before.

Mara didn't give up. The signal from the distant mind was as strong as ever. Saba concentrated on it, feeling out the insubstantial pathways between it and them. There was nothing but vacuum in the way, she told herself. Crossing that vacuum should be as easy as leaping across a room. Her tail quivered with effort as she imagined that hyperspace leap in detail.

Jade Shadow jumped again. The hull vibrated as Mara plunged the ship headlong through the strange spaces surrounding their objective. Saba received impressions of incomprehensible shadows sweeping by, bizarre n-dimensional membranes reluctantly unfolding to let them pass. She didn't know what they were or where they came from, but it seemed for a time as though Mara was making progress. They were getting closer—they had to be!

Then, rattling like an old freighter, they were dumped back into realspace. They stopped long enough to check on the *Widowmaker*. The frigate limped from hyperspace seconds after *Jade Shadow*.

"Is the *Widowmaker* holding up?" Mara asked.

"It's seen worse," the Imperial captain assured her. "I imagine she'll keep going long after we give up."

Satisfied, Luke gathered the Jedi minds around him for another try.

"I think we can do it this time," he encouraged them. "Mara was right when she said before that there had to be a way in. All we have to do is find it."

Grimly determined, they tightened the meld and tried again. Saba felt herself dissolving in the confusing sensations passing through and around her as hyperspace folded around them. The pull of Zonama Sekot was stronger than ever, and growing stronger with each passing second. She felt as though she were drowning in the massive outpouring of emotions, a mote of sand caught in a dust storm, swept up on a rising surge, unable to control where it took her.

For a timeless moment, she completely lost all sense of herself. She was subsumed, absorbed, erased. The hunt consumed her. All her attention was focused on her quarry—on tracking it, finding it, *catching* it . . .

Then, abruptly, something changed. She didn't know what it was, but the thoughts changed in pitch. It was as if they'd reached the eye of a storm. Energy still swirled around them, but at the center there was a kind of peaceful balance. Saba felt her thoughts regain a sense of normality, joining up again in a single coherent stream. They had emerged from hyperspace once more, only this time the screens were alive with data: there was a sun blazing on one, a gas giant looming on another. A faint green-blue speck hung in the center of a third screen—and it was to this that her senses clung. Green meant chlorophyll; blue meant water. If a world was ever to live, it had to have both.

Zonama Sekot!

But as the view zoomed in closer, she saw yellow and bright red clouds blossoming as energy weapons flashed and flared around the atmosphere. Thin-hulled spaceships burst open under the influence of stupendous forces, casting countless lives into the harsh vacuum of space.

And that wasn't all. What Saba saw behind the space battle was completely beyond her experience. Bright feathery ribbons trailed from the planet's poles like liberated coronas. Fleeting sprites danced in the upper atmosphere, sending towering flashes of energy spiking far above. Massive sheets of lightning swept around the equator, gathering speed until they joined in a smooth ring; then, with a piercing crack, they lashed out and up like a whip of pure energy. Magnetic field fluxes measured by *Jade Shadow* accompanied what appeared to be tractor beam effects on scales Saba had never imagined possible.

Zonama Sekot's attackers were obviously Yuuzhan Vong vessels: two mid-size cruiser analogs and countless numbers of coralskippers. But they weren't the only ships in the air. Among them darted and wove tiny points of light like no ships Saba had ever seen before. Every one was different; every one was beautiful; every one was deadly.

Zonama Sekot was fighting back!

Anger blazed—ugly in its ferocity, devastating in its

efficacy—and with it came a return of the storm. Saba barely had time to wonder what would happen when the mind they'd been seeking finally noticed *them*, when a wall of psychic energy struck them, tossing them into oblivion.

"Spare me, Master! Spare me!"

Supreme Overlord Shimrra gazed down with cold contempt at the squirming thing at his feet. The Shamed One had been tortured and beaten, but still she hadn't broken. If the godlike ruler of the Yuuzhan Vong found this puzzling, he didn't let it show.

"Spare you?" he said, slowly pacing around the prostrate figure. "Why? So you can continue to pollute my chambers with your false protestations of innocence?"

"Not false, Lord! You must believe me."

"You dare to tell me what *I* must do?" Shimrra snarled.

The object of his ire quivered piteously. "Forgive my ignorance! If I knew the answers to the questions you ask, I would surely tell you!"

"But you *do* know. You are a pawn of the vile sect that dares follow the *Jeedai*."

"Master, I swear by—"

"Spare me oaths to your infidel gods. I will hear no more of your foul lies." Shimrra gestured imperiously, and the Shamed One was dragged away. The charnel pits where the heretics were taken for dishonorable execution had been working day and night in recent times. A swarm of ravenous yargh'un—toothy rodents as long as a Shamed One's leg—devoured the victims in swift order. Crippled, their limbs broken prior to being tossed to their doom, those found guilty of heresy were shown no mercy, nor afforded any honor in the manner of their death.

"Destroy the yargh'un," Shimrra ordered of the guards who had stepped forward to do his will.

The guards stopped in their tracks, confused by the Supreme One's command. "Master?"

"The beasts have been defiled by heretical blood," he said. "Take them from the pit and have them burned."

"What shall we do with this one, Master?" The guards indicated the Shamed One quailing between them.

"Deal with it as you normally would. Break its legs and throw it into the pit." Shimrra ascended his throne, climbing heavily across pulsating hau polyps. "It can die slowly of starvation and thirst, like an animal. Its body will stay where it lies to serve as an example of what will happen to anyone who dares allow this heresy to propagate. There will be no easy deaths for those who turn their backs on the gods."

The guards obeyed Shimrra's will with grim determination, ignoring the plaintive cries of the condemned. The cries turned to shrieks as all hope fled, then faded to distant wails as the Shamed One was dragged away from the throne room.

Shimrra waited until the last echo had passed before speaking again.

"You do well, Ngaaluh. Once again your investigations have exposed the enemy within."

The slender priestess bowed deeply. "I am honored by your acknowledgment, Supreme One."

"You find success where many others have failed." Shimrra's baleful gaze scanned the faces of the priests, shapers, warriors, and intendants who had been assembled for the interrogation. "We must be ever watchful to ensure that the roots of heresy spread no farther than they already have. More than that: we must actively seek out nests of perfidy and find their source."

Assent came loudly and without hesitation.

"Be assured, Great One," said High Perfect Drathul, senior intendant of Yuuzhan'tar, "that we are making every effort to arrest this terrible tide."

"Your will—the will of the gods—is not to be denied," seconded Warmaster Nas Choka, cutting the air with his ceremonial tsaisi. "We will not rest until the last heretic lies crushed beneath our soles!"

"Nor would I expect anything less," the Supreme Overlord said. "In fact, henceforth anything short of enthusiasm for the heresy's eradication will be regarded as collaboration. And collaboration will be punishable in the same fashion as treachery. Is that understood?"

The echoes of the Supreme Overlord's pronouncement rumbled around the throne room, and all who heard it bowed solemnly in agreement.

"You will continue this work, Ngaaluh," Shimrra intoned. "I cannot personally oversee every interrogation and execution, yet it is my misfortune to be the one responsible for upholding all that the gods have entrusted to us. I am therefore glad to have someone in whom I can place my trust. Go forth and find me more bodies for the yargh'un pit. When it is full, I will build another, and another, until the curse of this foul heresy is erased from the galaxy once and for all, and the gods favor us again."

"Yes, Supreme One." Ngaaluh's bow was even deeper than her first.

The Supreme Overlord shifted in his throne and stared dispassionately over the heads of his minions. "Leave me now. I have much to contemplate."

One by one the members of Shimrra's court filed out of the chamber. The priestess Ngaaluh was among the last to leave. She turned to glance back at Shimrra, giving the villip beacon she carried a final glimpse of the Supreme Overlord, seated atop his throne.

To Nom Anor, watching the events on a villip choir far away, deep beneath Yuuzhan'tar's surface, Shimrra looked isolated yet undiminished. The Supreme Overlord's power and confidence was evident in his straight-backed pos-

ture and the indifference with which he dismissed his
court. The ruler of the galaxy had weathered many
storms in his time and, judging by the glaring determination of his stare, planned to weather many more.

Nom Anor's smile, previously broad and triumphant,
slipped at the sight. His gnarled hands curled into fists as
he paced back and forth across his audience chamber—
the sixth he'd occupied in as many weeks. The transmission from Ngaaluh ended as she crossed the security
perimeter of Shimrra's throne room.

"Another success," Kunra murmured. The disgraced
warrior, Nom Anor's adviser in all matters nonreligious,
slouched by the door, to all appearances perfectly relaxed. But Nom Anor knew better; Kunra was alert for
trouble, listening intently to everything taking place on
either side of the door. "We've gained a great deal of
valuable intelligence since Ngaaluh joined us. She is in-
strumental in our growing influence."

Nom Anor nodded distractedly. As though his silence
were a challenge, Kunra persisted in his enthusiasm.

"Not only does Shimrra find a traitor close to his
throne, but then he fails to extricate a confession from
her! Did you see the look on his face? He is frightened
of us!"

"I find it difficult to watch." Shoon-mi appeared from
the shadows beside the Prophet's stately chair with a
bowl of water Nom Anor had requested. The Shamed
One was dressed in a faded priest's robe and wore his
scarless face with something akin to pride. His expression, however, was forever glum, and seemed to become
increasingly so with each passing day.

Nom Anor understood his religious adviser's concern
perfectly. "In all of us lurks a residual loyalty to the old
ways, Shoon-mi. Sometimes even the truth finds it difficult to erase the programming of a lifetime."

"That's not what I meant, Master." Shoon-mi looked almost sullen. "I'm referring to Eckla of Domain Shoolb."

Nom Anor stared blankly at Shoon-mi for a few moments before comprehension dawned: Eckla was the Shamed One who had just been sentenced to death in Shimrra's chamber.

"Yes, of course," he said. "Her sacrifice was a noble one, and did not go unnoticed." The words flowed smoothly, covering the fact that Eckla of Domain Shoolb had ceased being of interest to Nom Anor as soon as the risk of her betraying him was no longer an issue. "She will be remembered as a martyr to our cause."

"One of many, now."

Nom Anor's instincts urged him to reprimand the impudent nobody daring to rebuke him, but he forced himself to speak calmly. "The way to liberation is long and hard, Shoon-mi. We all knew this when we joined, and we would all do the same as Eckla if our time came."

"Without hesitation, Master." Shoon-mi made all the appropriate gestures, but still a hint of defiance remained in his tone. "I remind each new novitiate that pain is often the only reward of faithfulness. Few seem deterred."

"At least something lies beyond the pain," Nom Anor reminded him, feeding his assistant the spiritual fodder he craved. "The *Jeedai* promise a new life, whereas the old brings nothing but death and servitude. Freedom is worth the risk of pain, don't you think?"

"Yes, Master."

With nothing more to add, Shoon-mi bowed his way out of the audience chamber. Nom Anor could have used his advice on forthcoming novitiate selections, but he let the Shamed One go for now. Had he cared at all about the life of Eckla of Domain Shoolb, he, too, might have needed some time alone to think.

He gestured for Kunra to shut the door. He felt restless, unnerved. If Ngaaluh's infiltration of Shimrra's court was so successful, why didn't he feel satisfaction? Why couldn't he be like Kunra, and blithely accept that Shimrra was feeling the full effect of the heresy undermining his authority?

"Tell me about the ones you're training in this region," he said tiredly, when he was certain the room was secure. "What progress have you made?"

"I have selected three of the more adept recruits, without Shoon-mi's knowledge." The disgraced warrior moved from his position by the door toward Nom Anor. The confident ease of his movements revealed that he had grown to enjoy his position as lackey-cum-chief-lieutenant for the Prophet. "Each shows the right balance of fanaticism and stupidity for the task. I'll let them fight among themselves to see which is successful."

"Literally fight?" Blood sports didn't fit in with the Jedi Heresy, but Nom Anor knew that Kunra had a dark, rough edge that might go that far.

Kunra shook his head. "The successful applicants must be able to meet the stare of Shimrra's lackeys unflinchingly, yet without resorting to violence. They will take their first steps toward true defiance against each other. The first to strike a blow will be the first to be dismissed."

"And by dismissed you mean—"

Kunra nodded. "Eliminated."

Nom Anor nodded, satisfied. There were many conflicting demands made of an organization such as his. The first was finding ways to spread the heresy through conduits that had never been designed to act efficiently or reliably. The Shamed Ones had always gossiped, but did so with no concern for accuracy and were safe only under the assumption that no one higher up cared to listen. For the heresy to be effective, distortions had to be kept to a minimum. And now that higher ranks *were* listening, precautions had to be taken to ensure that the message couldn't be traced. These two objectives were frequently contradictory, and Nom Anor relied on his two assistants to balance them, with or without each other's knowledge.

So if Shoon-mi was responsible for ensuring the spread of the word, Kunra, then, was there to plug the leaks. He and a small, handpicked team of what Nom Anor thought of as "spiritual police" worked secretly to tie up any loose threads that threatened to unravel the entire fabric of the scheme. His work was made easier by the fact that disappearances were assumed to be the work of higher echelons getting close to the sources of the heresy. Each surgical elimination had the added effect of heightening paranoia and, arguably, making his role less essential.

But as the network expanded, and exponentially more mouths began spouting the Jedi tenets, the risks multiplied. Sometimes Nom Anor woke in the middle of the night, sweating with panic at the thought that even now, despite all his precautions, Shimrra was closing in.

"Good work," he said, praising Kunra as he would a trained pet. He didn't need to earn Kunra's loyalty; he had purchased it simply by sparing the ex-warrior's life. "But don't bore me with the details. Just make sure you have a candidate ready in three days. I wish to move on. This skulking in the dark is not something I care to make a habit of."

Kunra bowed briefly. As with Shoon-mi, there was a certain amount of defiance in the gesture, but Nom Anor could accept it from Kunra. The ex-warrior needed spirit to carry out his tasks effectively. Shoon-mi just needed obedience.

"Leave me now. I wish to think."

Kunra strode from the room, shutting the door behind him. Tiredly, Nom Anor leaned over to the bowl of water at his side so that he could wash his face. Things were going well, yes: the heresy was spreading, and a constant moving from place to place ensured that Shimrra was still no closer to catching him. That wasn't enough, though, and it never would be. The heresy had been from its conception a means of restoring himself to power. Every step he took had to advance that cause, or it was a step backward. The question that ever nagged at him, though, was: power over whom? Was being the leader of a scruffy army of Shamed Ones and misfits sufficient?

He froze, staring down at the reflection in the bowl of water. It was haggard and grimy as a consequence of living in the foul subterranean dwellings of Yuuzhan'tar, and its eyes were full of doubt. It looked like a stranger.

With a frustrated snarl he dashed the bowl of water to the floor.

Kunra was wrong. Shimrra wasn't frightened at all. Not once had he shown a flicker of fear. Anger, yes, but not fear. The heresy was a hindrance, not a threat. And the Prophet? The king of a dungeon might be a king, but he was still living in a dungeon.

It was well beyond time, Nom Anor told himself, feeling better even as he came to the conclusion, that he started exercising some real power . . .

On the *Falcon*, tempers were flaring.

"We *can't* leave yet," Han insisted. "Not until we know Jaina's all right."

"She's safe, Han. You know that. She's on her way back to the *Selonia*." Leia felt confined in the tiny cockpit and had to resist the urge to storm out. C-3PO was lurking in the access way, looking back and forth between Han and herself as he followed the heated exchange. "By staying here, you're putting us at risk."

Through sensors on the ship's hull she could hear the baying of the mob that had converged on the *Falcon*'s landing field. Only the halfhearted efforts of dock security had kept them at bay.

"So what?" he argued. "We can defend ourselves."

"It doesn't help the cause if we go around stirring up trouble, Han! We're supposed to be spreading a peaceful message, not unrest."

Han rubbed at his temple as though he had a headache. On the screens before him were views of the cordon around the *Falcon*'s dock, along with various patches from local feeds.

"What about the Ryn?" he asked more calmly.

She didn't have an answer ready for that. Her thoughts had been focused on Jaina, too. But she supposed that was a consideration. Back on Bakura, Goure had sent them to Onadax on the pretext that another Ryn would meet them there. Thus far, still, there had been nothing.

"I don't know," she said. "Maybe Goure got it wrong. Or perhaps things changed here between the message he received and us arriving. The Ryn network is slow, re-member. Maybe—"

"Wait." He waved her quiet. "Did you hear that?"

Leia listened, but heard nothing. She put a hand on his shoulder, lightly patting his taut muscles. If her husband wanted to find a reason to delay, he was going to have to do better than that.

"I really think it's time we went somewhere safer, Han. Captain Todra can look after herself, and Jaina won't be much longer. I can feel her getting closer."

He glanced at her, and with a sigh relented.

"All right," he said, flicking switches. "But we're only going to low orbit. If they so much as *think* about hurt-ing her, I want to be able to—"

"Jaina can handle herself," Leia interrupted, suppress-ing a smile.

A furious pounding from the belly of the ship brought the discussion to a halt.

"I *thought* I heard something." Han flicked further switches as Leia dropped into the seat beside him. He scanned through various security cam angles while she brought the retractable repeating blaster to life.

Through one of the cams they saw a gangly figure banging on the belly hatch with a hefty metal rod. The alien's face was obscured by a fogged-up visor, but apart from this there was nothing overtly suspicious or threatening about him or her. The cheap enviro-suit the stranger was wearing was too flimsy to have concealed any weapon.

"I doubt security would send someone looking like that to do their dirty work," Leia said. "Do you?"

Han shook his head dubiously. "Fire a warning shot. That'll fix him."

"That might not be such a good idea, Han. It could be taken as a sign of aggression."

"It's *intended* to be a sign of aggression, Leia," he shot back. "And if he doesn't stop banging on the *Falcon* like that, I'm going to get a whole lot more aggressive, too."

"But he just seems to be trying to get our attention, Han."

"Yeah, and look what he's doing to the paint job in the process!"

"I'm not firing, Han." She sat back in her chair with her arms folded resolutely across her chest.

He looked at her for a moment, then rolled his eyes. With an annoyed grunt he heaved himself out of the pilot's seat and headed off down the corridor, muttering something about "mutiny" under his breath.

Leia continued with the preflight warm-up he'd started, all the while keeping one eye on the belly cam covering the ramp.

With a clunk and a whir it opened wide enough to allow Han to bellow a warning to the insistent alien. Leia watched the animated exchange between the two of them, although she couldn't read lips well enough to work out exactly what was being said. Whatever it was, though, it resulted in the alien briefly lifting his mask, which in turn prompted a look of stunned amazement from Han.

She didn't see the alien's face, so it came as a complete surprise when Han lowered the ramp the rest of the way and gestured for the alien to come aboard. He did so, tossing to the ground the metallic rod with which he'd been banging the ship. And as she watched the alien climb the ramp, Leia couldn't quash a rising sense of unease in her stomach.

"*Jade Shadow,* please respond!"

Captain Mayn's voice dragged Luke out of what felt like a very deep pit. The world was shaking around him, and a roaring sound filled his ears. Somewhere beyond the haze caused by the intense mental attack, he could feel Saba, Danni, and Tekli nearby, all out cold. Jacen's mind was bright and conscious, already reaching out to the others. Farther away, but still in *Jade Shadow*, he could sense Soron Hegerty, sleeping heavily. And beside him, his wife, wrestling with the controls.

"We're kind of busy right now, Captain," she said. Her voice sounded calm, but Luke could tell from her thoughts that she was also suffering the aftereffects of the attack. "We'll get back to you the first chance we get, okay?"

Before the *Widowmaker* could respond, Mara switched off the comm unit so there would be no more interruptions. The normally simple task of landing her ship was clearly taking a lot of concentration.

"Where—?" Luke started, but his throat was too dry to get the words out. Pulling himself upright in his seat, he cleared his throat with a cough and tried again. "Where are we?"

"Coming in to land," she replied, not taking her eyes from the controls.

Through the cockpit's canopy, Luke could see the lush vegetation of the planet below. To the far south he noticed vast areas of cleared land—possibly the same scarring from the Yuuzhan Vong attacks Vergere had described, or perhaps lasting aftereffects of so many jumps through hyperspace, during its flight through the Unknown Regions. From far above, there was no way to tell.

He glanced at his wife. The bags under her eyes were heavy and dark. "Are you all right?"

"I guess," she said distractedly.

"What happened?"

"I'm not sure. It felt like a Force punch—only a hundred times more powerful. Whatever it was, it managed to knock out everyone on this ship—and *keep* them unconscious, too."

"But not yourself?"

Mara shrugged. "One minute I'm out like the rest of you; the next I'm awake and listening to Jacen take instructions over the comm."

"Jacen?"

"He woke first. He thinks it was Zonama Sekot that knocked us out and woke him up later, but it was definitely someone on the surface who gave him coordinates and an approach corridor. He'd just finished explaining that he wasn't the best person to pilot the ship when I woke up. That'd be the planet too, I guess. When I told them I would need to confer with you, the people on the ground said that wasn't an option. Given what the *Shadow*'s recordings show, I didn't think arguing with them was the most sensible thing to do."

"What do you mean?"

She looked over to him, and this time there was more than just exhaustion in her eyes: there was a hint of nervousness as well. "Take a look for yourself," she said, flipping a switch to begin the playback of the recording.

"This was taken just before I was roused, after we came into the system."

Luke turned to the monitor and viewed the footage *Jade Shadow*'s instruments had managed to capture while the crew was insensate. It showed the Yuuzhan Vong ships he had glimpsed on their arrival, along with the spectacular pyrotechnic display put on by the planet. He had forgotten about the battle in the confusion of waking up, but seeing it again brought it all back. His surprise at seeing the Yuuzhan Vong in orbit above the living planet was total.

He watched with awe as the alien ships fell back under the local defense forces. The battle was intense. Although the Yuuzhan Vong force was small, it almost held its own against the planetary defenses—almost. But eventually the alien ships broke under the relentless resistance and scattered. Zonama Sekot's defenders hunted down the fleeing ships and destroyed them one by one.

When the recording had finished, Luke turned back to Mara. She was piloting her ship through the last stages of descent.

"Are there any left?" He didn't need to elaborate.

"All destroyed, as far as I can tell. There's a lot of static. We were on the fringes but still affected."

"Why didn't we end up like them?" he asked.

Mara glanced at him sidelong as she brought the repulsors on-line. "I have no idea, Luke."

"Perhaps it read our minds and realized we didn't mean it any harm," Luke thought out loud. "And it woke Jacen first because of his natural affinity for unusual minds."

"There's only one way to know for sure," Mara said. "That's to talk to the natives."

"And I guess that's what we're about to do." In the main screen, heavily forested land ballooned up toward them. "Maybe they can tell us what the Yuuzhan Vong were doing here in the first place."

"We know they've sent missions into the Unknown Regions. The Chiss told us that before we left Csilla. This must be one of those missions."

"I guess—but I can't believe they just stumbled across Zonama Sekot. We had a hard enough time finding it on purpose."

"There might be more of them, then, and they might have been poking around in here longer."

Luke nodded, although his questions were far from answered. "That makes twice they've found it now, that we know of," he said. "It's almost as though they're actively looking for it . . ."

Jade Shadow set down perfectly in a broad, grassy field surrounded on all sides by steep forest walls. Flicking switches, Mara killed the engines and settled back into her seat.

"Welcome to Zonama Sekot," Jacen said from behind them.

Luke half-turned to study his nephew. Jacen's eyes were fixed on the view through the cockpit's massive, transparisteel canopy. On the surface of the planet outside, life swirled though the branches of the trees in a variety of colors and forms.

"Where exactly are we?" Luke asked.

"If you want a name, I can't help you," Jacen said. "Whoever I spoke to gave me detailed coordinates for this landing field, then left us alone. But we're somewhere in the southern hemisphere."

Mara gestured to a topographic display that indicated their precise location. "If what Vergere told you is true, all of this was destroyed by the Yuuzhan Vong the last time they were here, sixty years ago."

Jacen nodded. Luke could understand the note of

incredulity in Mara's voice. There was no evidence whatsoever of the destruction that had been inflicted upon the planet, apart from the odd, cleared patch visible from orbit. Zonama Sekot had managed to heal itself.

"Did they say anything else? Anything at all?"

Jacen shook his head. "Only for us to land, and to keep the *Widowmaker* in orbit, where it won't be harmed."

"I presume Arien experienced the same thing we did."

"Actually, no," Mara said. "They were completely unaffected. Some of the crew suffered headaches and spacesickness, but nothing more serious than that. It's almost as though the Force punch was aimed solely at us."

"Us because *Jade Shadow* arrived first," Luke asked, "or us because we're Jedi?"

He could tell that Mara was about to protest that she knew as little as he did when something caught their attention outside. Stepping out from a narrow gap in the trees were two individuals. Both were tall and thin, with icy, pale blue skin and wide gold-black eyes. The male's hair was a deep black, while the woman's swept back in a wave of pure white. Their jaws looked strong, their expressions stern. They wore robelike garments consisting of wide sheets of fabric falling from their shoulders in overlapping streams, all in shades of green and gray.

They came to a halt a safe distance from *Jade Shadow*, staring at the yacht with their hands clasped in front of them as though waiting for Luke, Mara, and Jacen to step out.

"Well," Luke said, glancing at his wife, "here are the natives."

"Their expressions don't look too inviting, do they?" Mara said, standing.

Jacen went to leave the cockpit, but Luke took his arm. "I'd rather you waited here with Artoo to keep an eye on the others."

Jacen looked for a second as though he might argue.

The stubby droid tootled encouragingly, and the look passed. "That makes sense, I guess. Just call if you need help."

"Don't worry," Mara said, squeezing his hand as they passed through to the air lock. Together she and Luke made their way past the others—Tekli, Saba, and Danni sprawled unconscious on the floor of the passenger bay—to the rear of the ship and the exit hatch. Mara keyed the air lock open and waved Luke through. He stepped down the egress ramp, stopping at the bottom in the knee-high grass to take lungfuls of Zonama Sekot's invigorating air. He closed his eyes for a second, enjoying the feel of the cool breeze on his skin.

We're actually here, he thought. It would take more than a less-than-friendly welcome to dull that sense of achievement.

He opened his eyes when Mara came up beside him. Her expression reflected an amazement similar to his own. The sky was a vibrant blue, and a fitful wind stirred the flat, wide-bladed grass about their feet. Small clouds scudded overhead, partially obscuring the broad, reddish face of Mobus, the giant world around which Zonama Sekot orbited. The system's primary was halfway up the sky and twenty degrees away from the gas giant.

Another deep breath swept the last lingering feeling of doubt away. This place was real, and it smelled like life itself. There was a powerful potential in the Force trembling behind everything, as though a psychic thunderstorm were about to burst. Was that the mind of Zonama Sekot? Luke wondered. Was that what Vergere had felt when the living planet had become conscious, all those years ago? Even on Ithor, he had never felt fauna and flora blend so effortlessly into such a magnificent whole.

He put his ruminations aside when the two strangers approached.

"Who are you?" the woman demanded.

"My name is Luke Skywalker," he said. "And this is my wife, Mara. We'd like to thank you for welcoming us—"

"You're *not* welcome," the male said sharply.

Mara frowned. "But weren't you the ones that gave us the coordinates to—?"

"We were ordered to do so," the woman cut in.

"Yours is the first vessel to land on Zonama in more than fifty years," the man added. "Sekot has willed it, and so we obey."

With poor grace, Luke noted.

"You speak the names *Zonama* and *Sekot* as though they were separate things," he said. "Why is that?"

"Sekot is the mind," the man said.

"Zonama is the planet," the woman concluded.

"Then you are the Zonamans?" Luke asked.

"We are Ferroans," said a voice from behind Luke. He turned to find himself facing a blue-skinned woman dressed similarly to the others, except her garments were entirely black.

Mara had spun around, surprised, and dropped into a defensive stance.

The corners of the woman's mouth turned up into a slight smile. "Forgive me for startling you." Her hands came up in the universal gesture of peace. "I mean you no harm. I am the Magister. I stand between Zonama and Sekot."

Mara relaxed slightly. Luke studied the new arrival with wary fascination. He couldn't tell exactly how old she was. Her pale blue skin was wrinkled, but her hair was thick and black, tied in a tight ponytail that hung to her hips. She radiated an incredible vitality that he would have expected from a much younger person. Her Force-signature was odd, too—as if he were viewing it through a rain-coated viewport.

There was no denying that she was in charge, though. The other Ferroans backed reverentially away and bowed their heads.

"Then I take it that you are the one we need to speak with," Luke said.

"If you have anything to say, then yes, your words should be directed to me."

Luke nodded as he took a step toward the Magister. "We need to discuss the aliens you were recently fighting." He indicated the sky with a glance. "We know them as the Yuuzhan Vong, but in the past I believe you have referred to them as the Far Outsiders."

The Magister's face tilted, an expression of fascination spreading across it. "How do you know that?"

"A Jedi Knight who once visited here told her story to my nephew."

"You speak of Vergere, then," the woman said, nodding. "We remember her well. And fondly."

Some of Mara's uncertainty ebbed at the open mention of the other Jedi's name. "You do?"

"Her story is well known to us. She drew the Far Outsiders away, for a time—long enough for us to prepare for a second assault. We are capable of defending ourselves now, as you have seen."

Luke nodded. "The demonstration we witnessed was impressive, to say the least."

"A demonstration implies it was put on for your benefit," the male Ferroan said. His tone made it quite clear that it had not been at all.

"Now, Rowel," the Magister cautioned gently. "These are our guests."

"No, Magister," the other woman said. "These are intruders. They don't belong here. We should send them away immediately and forget about them."

"Denial solves nothing, Darak." There was no acrimony in the Magister's words, nor any hint of reproach.

"We have tried to forget about the universe at large, but have clearly failed in this. In the space of a single day we have encountered two species who sought to find us. Our denial of them did little to deter them."

"But Magister," said the woman, Darak, "they bring with them violent changes! We have lived in peace for decades, and suddenly the skies are filled with the fire of war!"

"That is so," Luke said. "And I fear there may be more to come."

"You bring ill tidings then," Rowel said, glaring balefully at him.

"It is always so with these Jedi Knights," Darak added.

"Wait," Luke said, forestalling Mara's defensive rebuttal. "Did you say *Knights*? Have you had other Jedi Knights here, apart from Vergere?"

"We have entertained more than one over the years, yes." The Magister glanced reprovingly at the other Ferroans. "In the past, the Jedi Knights proved to be our friends, our allies. Why should that not be so now?"

"We should be cautious," Darak advised. "We are but one world against millions."

"No one is immune," Luke said. "You cannot hide from what is coming. Today's events prove that. It's a hard truth, but it *is* truth we bring, not lies."

The regal woman studied the two humans before her with a piercing gaze.

"I would very much like the chance to speak with your nephew, to exchange with him our memories of Vergere."

"Send them away!" Darak hissed. "Don't listen to them!"

The Magister laughed loudly at this. "Really, my friends. You go too far." To Luke and Mara, she continued: "I beg you to forgive their disrespect. Their apprehensions are not unjustified. We have seen unstable times in the past—especially during the Crossings, when we searched for a new home. Those times were hard on everyone. There were terrible upheavals: deaths, famine, plagues." A fleeting sadness crossed the Magister's lined face. "There have been no visitors to Zonama for many years. We live in peace, and now conflict has returned to us. We are understandably concerned."

Luke nodded. "As are we. The presence of the Far Outsiders here was unexpected, and is of grave concern. This is one of the many things we must talk about, and soon."

"It shall be so," the Magister said, a stern glance at Darak and Rowel indicating that she would brook no disagreement. "The others may attend, too," she added. "They wake even as we speak."

"You will need to come with us, then," the male Ferroan said.

"Where to?" Mara asked, eyes narrowing.

"To our village," Darak said. "That's where the meeting place is."

"Okay," Mara said. "Tell us where it is and I'll fly us there myself."

"That's not possible," Rowel said. "Your vessel cannot come."

"And how do you intend to stop me from—?"

"I don't." Rowel pointed to *Jade Shadow.* "Sekot has already taken care of it."

Mara's protest died on her lips as she glanced at her ship. The grass her yacht was resting on, along with vines that had crept unnoticed from the surrounding undergrowth, had invaded the ship, entwining around its landing struts. Green fronds peeked out of apertures and vents all along the underside, indicating that the intrusion was extensive throughout the ship.

Mara reacted defensively, purely on instinct. She took two steps toward the ship, activating her lightsaber. The bright energy blade cut a glowing line through the crystal clarity of the day, promising a swift and indiscriminate pruning.

Luke caught her by the arm before she could take a swing. "Easy, Mara," he said gently. He leaned in close to her as he guided the blade down to her side, whispering into the red hair covering her ear, "If Sekot can do this to the ship, it can certainly do it to us, as well. You can't hope to fight a planet, my love."

He was already reaching out for Jacen inside the ship and, seeing that his nephew was unharmed, he sent Mara his reassurance. She relaxed in his grip, removing her thumb from the activation stud of her weapon and killing the blade. Nevertheless, she was clearly not happy with the situation. Nor could he blame her. Sekot had attacked her ship and made her a prisoner on the planet. It didn't sit well with him, either; however, he was prepared to ride it out.

"Magister—" he started, but stopped upon realizing she was gone. He hadn't noticed her leaving, but she was nowhere to be seen. Her unusual Force presence lingered on the wind, as though part of her were still around. That faded into nothing even as he clutched at it, trying to follow it. It was almost as though she had literally dissolved into thin air.

"If you are going to come with us," Rowel said, "then we leave now."

"Thank you," he said, recovering in order to reply as courteously as he could. If the Ferroans were trying to provoke them in any way, they would be disappointed. "But if we're not permitted to take *Jade Shadow*, then how are we to get anywhere?"

The Ferroan pointed at a path visible at the edge of the

landing field. "We walk, of course," Darak said with a faint smirk.

Jaina reached *Pride of Selonia*'s dock seconds before the mob. The journey through the streets of Onadax had been arduous, and fraught with danger. Several times she'd had to double back to avoid either fires or a fight with the locals. Whoever had stirred up the city had done a frighteningly thorough job.

At the entrance to the dock, two guards barred her way.

"We have orders to detain anyone attempting to enter this vessel," said one, a swarthy Selonian.

"Orders from whom?" she responded, acutely conscious of the mob baying at her heels. "For what reason?"

"That's not your concern. If you could just step this way—"

This way, his mind revealed, led to a pair of stun cuffs and a blow to the head.

"You don't need to hold me," she said, taking his will and bending it. "I'm exempt from the orders you've been given."

"We don't need to hold her," the Selonian told the other guard. "She's exempt."

Jaina smiled winningly. "Perhaps I should move through now; I'm sure you have better things to do than stand around chatting."

"Move on through, please. We can't stand around chatting all day."

The guards parted, allowing her access to the *Selonia*. She hurried up the ramp to the ship's wide air lock and keyed in the appropriate security code. Before she had finished, however, the panel hissed open.

"We've been waiting for you," said Selwin Markota, Captain Mayn's second in command. He waved her inside. "We're ready to lift off."

The clamor of the mob behind her rose a notch as it reached the docks. "That would be good idea."

Exhaustion rushed through her as Markota hurried through the corridors of the frigate. A solid man with receding hair, he was an excellent administrator, ever dependable in a crisis. That he was walking so briskly confirmed their circumstances were urgent. Gravity shifted minutely beneath her feet as the frigate left Onadax behind.

"What about my parents? Did they get away okay?"

"They're in orbit, waiting for you to call."

"Any sign of pursuit?"

"Not so far. My gut feeling is that this was a warning. Someone wanted us out of the way, but didn't necessarily want us dead."

She nodded, absorbing the information. "The riots were real enough to me."

"I'm sure they are. Onadax, like most illegal communities, is a tinderbox ready to go up at the slightest spark." Markota cast a baleful glance over his shoulder. "We picked up some local news traffic not long ago. Someone posted a bulletin concerning the agent we supposedly sent. Eyewitness accounts describe a person leaving the supposed scene of the incident, an hour or two ago. That person matches Han's description."

Jaina thought of her father's telling of the incident at the Thorny Toe. It certainly hadn't sounded severe enough to start a riot. But Han Solo's capacity for understatement was as legendary as his luck.

Markota stopped outside the medical suite that Tahiri had been assigned. "They're waiting for you in here."

The first thing she saw when she entered the suite was Jag, rising from his seat with an expression of relief on his face. He was across the room in an instant, his big hands first touching her hair, then falling to her shoulder, which he gripped firmly but warmly.

"When we lifted off and I hadn't heard—" He fell into an awkward silence, as though embarrassed. "I'm glad you're okay," he finished.

Smiling, she touched his cheek lightly with the back of her hand.

"I'm glad, too," she said.

He moved aside, then, to allow her into the suite properly. With a single glance she took in Tahiri on the bed, pale and comatose, in exactly the same position she'd been in since Bakura. Numerous tubes and monitors snaked under the sheet covering her, monitoring and meeting all her body's needs. Her eyelids were red, and her lips were cracked and dry.

"Sorry to interrupt the moment," came her father's voice from the room's comm unit.

"Dad?" she said, surprised. "I hadn't realized there was a line open to you! Is Mom there with you?"

"I'm here, Jaina," her mother said.

"It's great to hear your voices," she said.

"The feeling's mutual, sweetheart," Han said.

Jaina sat on the edge of Tahiri's bed, taking the girl's hand loosely into her own. "Sorry things didn't go as planned."

"That depends," Leia said.

"On what?" she asked. "Did you find anything about the Ryn?"

Jaina's father seemed oddly hesitant to answer that question. "Not exactly."

"What does that mean?"

"Well, we heard from *someone*, but it wasn't who we expected."

Jaina sighed, too tired to play games. "Can someone please tell me what's going on?"

"We picked up a passenger as we were leaving Onadax," Han explained. "Someone who said he was trying to escape the riots. We haven't had much chance to talk to him since we took him aboard, but I'm guessing he's not the one we're looking for."

"He's the right species," Leia added, "but doesn't know much about what's going on."

"And who is *he*, exactly?"

"He's Droma," came a distinctly Ryn voice over the comm. "It's nice to speak to you again, Jaina."

Jaina's eyes widened in surprise. "It's good to hear your voice," she managed.

"Hey, I told you to wait in the hold," she heard her father say.

"What, you think I'm going to take your secrets and sell them to the Vong or something?" The Ryn blew a rapid, lamenting tune from the chitinous, flutelike nose sported by the members of his species. Its sound came clearly down the comm. "Don't be so paranoid."

"This has got nothing to do with paranoia! It's to do with *privacy*."

Their voices slowly faded into the background, culminating in a tired sigh from Leia—as though having the two of them on board together was already proving too exhausting for her.

"As soon as we're in orbit, I'm coming across, Mom."

"Personally I think you're better off where you are. But, if you feel you have to, then I'll let your father know you're coming."

Jacen helped Danni up from the floor of the passenger bay. He waited a moment as she rubbed a dull fog from her eyes. Nearby, his uncle knelt by Saba and Tekli, gently rousing them.

"Welcome back," Jacen said.

"How—?" Danni started groggily. "How long was I out?"

"A few hours," he said.

"We're here?"

He smiled broadly. "Yes, we're here, Danni. Come see for yourself."

Seeing that she was still feeling vague and disoriented, he steadied her as she made her way to the rear of the ship to where the exit hatch hung invitingly open. Before he'd taken one step down the egress ramp, he felt his breath taken from his lungs at the sight outside.

Knee-high grass swayed in a serene breeze beneath a magnificent deep blue sky. The air was filled with a fine down—possibly pollen from numerous flowering plants scattered about the area. Jacen breathed in deeply, savoring the thousand exotic scents and enjoying the slight giddiness the fragrances caused in him.

We made it, he thought as he descended the ramp and set foot on the planet's soil. *We're actually on Zonama Sekot.*

After a dozen steps through the grass, he stopped to let her look up at the multicolored globe of Mobus suspended in the sky above, resembling a mighty, baleful eye bulging down upon them.

"Incredible, isn't it?" he said softly.

"I don't know what impresses me most," she said. "The view, or the fact that we're actually standing on a sentient planet."

"Don't worry," he said, "I'm sure the locals will manage to dampen your excitement a little."

"The locals—?" For the first time she noticed the two tall figures standing some distance away to their left, quietly conferring with one another. "Why? What's wrong with them?"

"Let's just say they're not particularly overjoyed to see us," another voice said. They both turned to see Mara, striding toward them across the grass.

"What exactly happened?" Danni asked. "Did *they* knock us out?"

Together, Mara and Jacen explained the situation as

best they could. They told her of the space battle and the Yuuzhan Vong expedition, *Jade Shadow*'s descent to the surface of Zonama Sekot, Luke and Mara's encounter with the Ferroans and the Magister, and the imprisonment of the ship. On hearing this part, Danni went to examine the verdant fronds that had crept up the landing struts of *Jade Shadow*, confirming Mara's assertion that they weren't going to leave anytime soon. There was a ferocious vitality surging through the leaves; cut one and three more would undoubtedly grow in its wake.

"What about the *Widowmaker*?" Danni asked.

"The other vessel will come to no harm as long as it remains in orbit," came the voice of one of the Ferroans from behind. Jacen turned to see the two wading through the tall grass toward them.

"But how did you do this?" Jacen felt Danni reach out with her growing perception of the Force to taste the world around them. She felt what he did: no mind, no thoughts; just a constant pressure—similar to what a body would feel at great depths in an ocean, only mental rather than physical. "By the Force?"

"Sekot has many defenses," the male Ferroan said unhelpfully.

A groan in the direction of *Jade Shadow* announced the arrival of Soron Hegerty, assisted by Luke and closely followed by Tekli. Saba wasn't far behind; the Barabel's expression was suitably awestruck as the shock of displacement slowly faded. Saba's hand rested on the lightsaber at her hip while her gaze constantly scanned the tree lines around them. It was clear that the hunter in her was not going to be distracted by the splendor and magnificence of her surroundings.

"It is time," the female Ferroan said. "We have a long walk ahead of us."

"Why?" Danni asked. "Where are we going?"

"We'll explain on the way," Luke said.

"Are the treez of your forest safe?" Saba asked.

"They are not trees," the woman said. "They're called boras, and they make up the tampasi. They will harm you only if you attempt to harm them."

Without another word, the two Ferroans set off across the field, their pace suggesting that either the visitors keep up or they would get left behind.

Jacen's uncle turned to the Chadra-Fan. "Tekli, would you mind staying here and keeping an eye on *Jade Shadow*?"

The diminutive Jedi bowed her head in acknowledgment. "Of course, Master Skywalker."

"We'll keep our comlinks open at all times," Luke assured her.

Tekli bowed once more and then returned to *Jade Shadow*.

Luke faced the others. "Is everyone ready?"

"I don't think we have much choice," Jacen said, gesturing to the two Ferroans receding into the distance. "They'll be disappearing over the horizon if we don't get after them soon."

"Like I said," Mara muttered as she headed off in the wake of their escorts. "Real friendly."

Jaina listened with interest to Droma's simple story. Her parents had already heard it, but listened again with unflagging interest. Jaina received the distinct impression that Leia was almost hoping for an inconsistency to arise.

After rescuing his sister at Fondor, Droma and his family had drifted from place to place, as was their custom. The encroaching front of the Yuuzhan Vong kept them moving at first toward the Core, then into the outer regions of the galaxy, seeking safer climes. There they encountered fierce parochialism, anti-Jedi sentiments, civil war, and other signs of collapsing infrastructure. It was all his family could do just to keep their collective heads above water.

"Then we heard about the Ryn network." Droma's tail whipped and coiled as he paced the *Falcon*'s main hold as if it were an extra hand, gesticulating to emphasize certain points of his speech. "We knew of the Great River, but we weren't qualified as resistance fighters or idealists. We're just travelers, with our own unique skills. The thought of using those skills to gather and disseminate information as we traveled seemed so obvious, and I'm not surprised it took one of us to think of it. A great, galactic enterprise the Ryn could finally be part of! It seemed almost too good to be true."

"We've only met two from this network so far," Jaina said. "There was one on Galantos, who saved us from a Peace Brigade trap, and Goure on Bakura who sent us here. He said that—"

"That someone would be waiting for you," Droma interrupted, nodding. "That sounds like them."

Jaina looked questioningly at her father, who just shrugged. "He does this. It takes some getting used to."

She looked back at the Ryn. "Are you able to tell us anything that might help us find the Ryn we were supposed to meet here?"

Droma shrugged. "I can't tell you much more than I already have. I came here to apply on behalf of my family. We wanted to become part of the network ourselves; we want to give something back to the people who helped us on Duro, without compromising what it means to be a Ryn. I don't care what people think of us; I don't want to be a hero. I just wanted to try to keep the clan safe, you know? I figure the more friends we have, the safer we are. If the ceiling's about to come down on us all, I'd like to have some company."

"So what happened?" Jaina asked.

Droma made a disappointed noise, deep in his throat.

"They heard me out, but said they had no vacancies in the organization at this time—at least not where we were stationed. I said we'd be prepared to move to somewhere we *were* needed, but they weren't interested."

"Would you be able—" Leia started.

"To identify the boss Ryn?" Droma finished, shaking his mane of wiry hair doubtfully. "He's about as shy as they come. And for good reason, too. It certainly sounds like he and his network have been helpful to you and other people in recent times, and the Yuuzhan Vong aren't going to like that very much."

Jaina frowned. "So you can't tell us any more about them?"

"I would if I could, believe me. You helped me out, getting me off Onadax like that. It was about to get real ugly down there."

"You don't know anything about that, I suppose," Leia said. Her expression was one of acceptance, as though she finally believed the Ryn's story, but there were still numerous holes to fill. "It looked to us like someone was pulling up stumps and getting rid of the evidence."

"Evidence of what?"

"The network, I presume."

Droma shrugged again. "Sorry, but it's no business of mine. I'm just here for the ride. If you could drop me off somewhere in the Juvex sector, though, I'd be extremely grateful. I can work my way back to the others from there."

"If we're going that way, sure," said Han.

"What do you mean, 'if'?"

"Truth is, we don't really know where we're heading next," Han said.

Droma was looking at them as though they were speaking Gamorrean. "What about Esfandia?" he asked. "You're going there, right? And Juvex is on the way."

"Esfandia?" Han repeated, frowning.

"Esfandia is one of two small communications centers on the other side of the galaxy," Leia said. "It services the Outer Rim. There used to be only one, Generis, but another was brought on-line at the beginning of the war."

"Why would we go there?" Jaina asked.

"You don't know what's happened?" Droma appeared genuinely shocked.

"No," Jaina said. "What *has* happened?"

"It's only something I overheard while I was being interviewed," he said, shifting uncomfortably in his seat. "A message came through while I was there. They mentioned something about the head Ryn not wanting to do anything about it, though, because he figured you guys would have already heard about it through official channels."

All eyes remained on Droma, waiting for him to explain.

"You seriously don't know what I'm talking about?"

Jaina took a step toward him. "No, we don't—and if you're so good at reading what people are going to say, then you'll know that I'm about to—"

"Jaina," her mother cautioned.

Droma chuckled at this, glancing at Han. "I see she's inherited the Solo temper."

"You can't even begin to imagine," Han said.

The Ryn turned from Han back to Jaina. "Generis has been destroyed by the Yuuzhan Vong, and Esfandia is under attack."

"When?" Jaina asked,

"Yesterday, I think."

"What has this got to do with us?" Han asked. "I know these sort of stations. If it's Outer Rim, it's probably automated, maybe staffed by a token crew to keep things maintained. If the Yuuzhan Vong have attacked it, it's already lost."

Leia shook her head. "Cal Omas beefed up the defenses there before we left. It might still be holding on."

"And what if it isn't?" Han asked. "Does it really matter if we lose contact with part of the Outer Rim?"

"It's not just any part of the Outer Rim," Leia said. "Generis and Esfandia are the only relay centers we have servicing the Unknown Regions. Every communications signal to and from the Chiss goes through there. Take them out and you effectively put the Unknown Regions out of contact."

There was a moment's silence as the implications suddenly sank in.

They'd been walking for more than two standard hours in virtual silence. Darak and Rowel, their Ferroan guides, stayed for the most part ahead of Jacen and the others, rarely bothering to check that their guests were keeping up with them.

This wasn't necessarily a problem. There was more than enough to see. The tampasi was vigorous and rich with life. The trunk of each boras was a miniature ecosystem, supporting dozens of species of plants and fungi, which in turn provided homes and food for brightly colored insects. These insects became prey for lizards and arachnids, which were eaten by birds or larger animals still. Everywhere Jacen looked, he had the feeling that a tiny universe had, just that second, stopped in the middle of furious motion, and would start up again the moment he glanced away.

Danni had complained that it didn't make sense that they should have landed *Jade Shadow* so far away from their destination, but Darak had said that their ship was not permitted in the airspace around any inhabited area; it could interfere with the carefully balanced ecosystem of the planet.

That Jacen could understand. There was only so much

wonder he could take, though. His curiosity piqued by something his uncle had told him, he quickened his pace to bring himself alongside Darak. She didn't turn to acknowledge him in any way, nor slow her pace.

"My uncle tells me that you remember Vergere," he said.

"Your uncle is mistaken," she said, keeping her gaze fixed on the path ahead. "I was a child when she and the other Jedi came to Zonama, and my settlement half a world away."

The other Jedi . . . Jacen felt the tug of this revelation like a physical force.

"Your people, then," he persisted. "You know of her. You've heard stories."

"Stories, yes. Bedtime stories for children."

He didn't let the Ferroan's frosty tone deter him. "I'm not sure whether you know it or not, but the Jedi were almost wiped out about fifty years ago. The ones who came here when you were a child would have been trained in the old ways. If we could learn more about them—"

"Not all were trained," Rowel put in. "One was an apprentice. Strong in his fashion, but unrefined."

"What happened to them here?"

"We are guides," Darak said sourly, "not historians."

"I know, but surely—"

He stopped when a shadow passed over them. Glancing up into the upper reaches of the boras, Jacen looked just in time to see something large and dark pass overhead. It didn't stay in view long enough for him to make out exactly what it was.

The others had stopped also and were gazing upward. Darak and Rowel continued on unconcerned.

"What was that?" Jacen asked.

"A kybo," Rowel called back. "Their fields are nearby."

"Are they dangerous?" Mara asked.

"Hardly," the woman said. "They're airships."

Moments later they emerged from the dense tampasi into a clearing that was twice the size of the one in which *Jade Shadow* had landed. Hovering just above the ground were half a dozen enormous manta-shaped dirigibles. Of roughly the same proportions as *Millennium Falcon*, but at least three times larger, they cast deep shadows across the meadow. Each kybo had five slender lines anchoring it to gnarled roots that protruded from the ground, holding it taut against the gently tugging winds that blew across the vast, grassy area. Beneath each hung a single bullet-shaped gondola with two bone-colored fans protruding from the rear.

Higher up, drifting over the tops of the enormous boras, Jacen could see a further three of the airships, as well as another one at the far end of the field coming in to land. Decorated in long, sweeping stripes of purple and orange across rough white skin, the crafts stood out against the lush green backdrop of the tampasi.

Working around the area were thirty or more Ferroans, some carrying baskets, some working on gondolas, others securing lines. They all looked incredibly industrious.

"Couldn't we have traveled to your village in one of these?" Danni asked.

The two Ferroans were already meters away from her after she'd stopped to take in the sight.

Darak stopped to answer her. "These airships are not transports," she said. "They're harvesters. They are used to collect produce from the tops of the boras."

Luke, Mara, Saba, and Soron emerged from the tree line together, all looking in wonder at the spectacle around and above them. They moved as a group over to where one man was working on repairs to a gondola that was lying on the grass on its side. The accompanying dirigible floated directly overhead, its anchor lines creaking as the great balloonlike structure moved in the wind.

Jacen felt confident stepping beneath the massive dirigible. From where he stood, he could see that it was composed of dozens of smaller bladders full of gas, each separated by thin membranes. For the craft to crash, a majority of those bladders would have to fail simultaneously, an eventuality too unlikely to worry about.

Inside the gondola was dark and dank. From the sunlight available he could make out benches for sitting on as well as a number of large baskets woven from vines, obviously for the harvested fruit. The sides were moist and ribbed, and he couldn't help thinking that to sit in one would have been like riding in the belly of a giant whaladon.

"Are you the pilot?" Luke asked.

"My name is Kroj'b," the man said. "I am her companion."

"Companion?" Mara said.

The man smiled, revealing an expanse of healthy white teeth. "We have a symbiotic relationship," he explained. "I care for her and she cares for me."

Jacen realized only then that the dirigible wasn't just a balloon; it was a living creature.

"What do you call her?" he asked.

The man smiled.

"Her name is Elegance Enshrined," he said, as though pleased to be asked.

Jacen nodded thoughtfully. "It's a good name; I like it."

"Your approval is neither sought nor required," Rowel said from nearby. "You must come now. We still have a long way to go, and Darak will not wait."

In the distance, the female Ferroan could be seen nearing the distant line of boras. Rowel turned and moved in her direction also, seemingly unconcerned whether the others followed. As much as he would have liked to have stayed and talked some more to this kybo's "companion," Jacen knew that they had to comply with Rowel's and Darak's wishes if they were to ever reach their destination.

He and the others continued with their trek, with Danni coming up alongside Jacen.

"It's all so amazing, isn't it?" she said. "There seems to be life in everything around us. Everywhere we look!"

Jacen nodded, watching one of the kyboes skimming the tops of distant boras. "It makes me feel very small," he whispered as they wound their way alongside the massive boras trunks. Strangely, though, that thought didn't bother him at all.

Back on *Pride of Selonia*, Jaina sat beside Tahiri through the long jump across the galaxy. While Jag stretched his wings at the head of Twin Suns Squadron, she kept an eye on her friend's progress. Although by medical definition Tahiri's condition was supposed to be stable, Jaina wasn't convinced. Outwardly the girl appeared okay, but below the surface Jaina sensed a terrible psychic disturbance that was only getting worse with time.

"Can't you feel it?" she asked Dantos Vigos, the *Selonia*'s chief medical officer, a Duros with long, solemn features. Tahiri's skin was waxy and pale, and the scars on her forehead continued to burn. The self-inflicted ones on her arms had all but disappeared. "It's as though there's a fire blazing inside her."

Vigos shook his head as he studied the girl's vital signs. "She doesn't seem to be running a fever."

"I'm not talking about her body; I'm talking about *her*."

Vigos stared at her, his eyes filled with puzzlement. He was a highly trained doctor with at least two decades of combat experience under his belt, and he wasn't the type to turn his back on any relevant information that might help a patient. But clearly he was unable to grasp what Jaina was trying to tell him now.

"I'm afraid she's going to run out of fuel," Jaina mused softly, not really talking to him anymore. "What happens then?"

She wished she had Uncle Luke or Master Cilghal with her. They'd know what to do, she was sure. This wasn't her field of expertise; this wasn't an enemy that could be squared up to and beaten down. What tactics was she supposed to use against an enemy that was trying to take over her friend's mind? An enemy that came from within that thought it had as much right to that mind as Tahiri herself?

"Jaina?"

She looked up, realizing the doctor had asked her something.

"I said, is there anything I can get you?"

Jaina shook her head. Vigos patted her shoulder sympathetically and returned to his duties, leaving her once more alone in the room with Tahiri. As much as she'd have liked him to stay and do *something* to help her friend, she knew that in reality there was nothing anyone could do except stand around and watch her decline.

No, Jaina thought resolutely. She wasn't about to let that happen. She refused to just sit holding Tahiri's hand while the girl battled futilely against her inner demons. That was as good as giving up, letting Riina win. Jaina had never before abandoned a friend in need, and she wasn't about to start now.

The only question was: what could *she* do about it? Tahiri might be losing a battle, but it was one she'd been fighting for years. Unknown to anyone, she had been maintaining a delicate rearguard action against the Yuuzhan Vong personality thought expunged on Yavin 4. Only now were the cracks beginning to show. If Jaina intervened, the facade might crumble completely, leaving Tahiri exposed. It could be just as dangerous as sitting back and doing nothing.

There was no way for Jaina to contact the *Falcon* or Twin Suns Squadron for advice, either. While they were in hyperspace, it was up to her and her alone. She sat for more than an hour weighing up the possibilities—few though they were—all the while holding Tahiri's hand, feeling the Force ever so slowly ebb from the young girl.

I don't care what her vital signs say, she thought. *She's slipping away. I can* feel *it.*

"What's our ETA?" she asked Captain Mayn via the room's comlink.

"Two hours until we're within sensor range of Esfandia," came the reply. "We're running on schedule, if that's what you're asking."

Two hours, Jaina thought. That could be easily long enough to make a difference.

She closed her eyes, concentrating on forming the mind-meld that the younger Jedi Knights used to share strength in battle. If Tahiri was losing the fight, perhaps all she needed was a little reinforcement . . .

Tahiri felt something sweep over her, as though a deep-ocean wave had just rolled by. She didn't dare look around, though, for fear of giving Riina the advantage in their duel. Her world consisted of nothing but those green eyes and the harsh humming of two lightsabers striking at each other in imperfect synch. Fatigue ground painfully at every muscle in her body, but she wasn't about to give in. She was determined not to allow her place in this world to be usurped.

Parry.

But something had changed, and now primal instincts were whispering to her, warning of the dangers that this change would bring. She couldn't afford to allow herself to let her guard down. Whatever that deep-ocean wave had brought with it, she had to regard it as a threat.

Lunge, parry.

Did you feel that?

Although the voice came from her assailant, it reminded her too much of her own voice.

I felt it, she replied, stepping to one side as Riina's lightsaber swung past.

Do you know what it is?

Tahiri sensed Riina's uncertainty, and her hands gripped her pommel a little tighter.

No, she said, taking the lightsaber in both hands and bringing it down toward Riina's head.

Riina blocked it easily, as though she'd been expecting it. The lightsabers remained locked, crackling menacingly in the quiet. Then Riina leaned in closer with a nervous half smile, and her green eyes fixed Tahiri through the glow of her weapon.

Something's coming, she whispered.

Tahiri desperately wanted to look around. She felt as though the small of her back was on fire. A hole burned there from the stare of an unnamed something that was gradually drawing nearer. But how could she fight it if she took her eyes from Riina?

Backpedal, block, sweep.

Riina leapt away, lightsaber poised defensively.

We could fight it together, she said.

Tahiri's body went cold as suspicion flushed through her. *Why should I want to do that?*

It's either that or stand here while it picks us off—first one, then the other. It would be as easy as hunting scherkil hla.

Tahiri's mind supplied her with an image of squat, flightless birds bred as a protein source on Yuuzhan Vong worldships. She forced it back down; such images, such thoughts, did not belong here.

Stab, deflect.

She fought hard, fending off not just the lightsaber, but also her suspicions. Ally herself with Riina? That was tantamount to giving in! She'd been subsumed once by the alien personality, and only Anakin's intervention had saved her. She couldn't count on him a second time, since he was—

Her mind balked at the word as it rang through her like a funeral bell tolling:

Dead.

Anakin couldn't help her now, or ever. There could be no escaping this simple truth. She was on her own.

Slice, duck, swing.

A voice called out to her, carried on the dark wind that blew from the shadowed lands around them. It called her name, but stretched out over many agonized and tormented seconds, as though it were coming to her from far, far away . . .

Did you hear that? she asked Riina, beginning to feel truly frightened.

I heard it. Riina's voice was colored with relief. *It's calling* you. *It doesn't want me.*

Why me? Tahiri demanded angrily, slashing viciously at Riina three times in quick succession. *Why not you?*

I don't know. Riina's amusement was touched with uncertainty. She retreated with a jump that took her five meters away from Tahiri.

But you know it'll come for you afterward.

Kick, advance.

At least I won't have you at my back to worry about when it does!

Again the voice boomed out of the shadows, sounding like the first rumble of a mighty wave crashing along the shore.

It's not honorable to keep your back turned to an enemy in a fight, Riina said. *Nor practical.*

I can only face one enemy at a time, Tahiri responded, forcing Riina away with a series of aggressive blows. She moved like she'd never moved before, dazzling herself with the grace and power of her strokes. She was like Anakin, filled with the Force, burning up in a white and brilliant fire.

The image brought with it memories, and the memories in turn brought emotions that she'd rather forget. She attacked again, even more viciously than before. But in the end, all she succeeded in doing was to force her and Riina into another deadlock. Eye to eye, barely centimeters apart, lightsabers crossed between them, they stared at each other, frozen.

The voice called her name again, and this time it sounded much closer—so close that she could almost feel breath on her neck!

Without thinking, she turned to look. Darkness shrouded the world around her and Riina like fog, but to one side it was parting, and pale light shone through the gap.

No! I won't let you kill us!

Riina flung Tahiri away from her and ran into the fog. Startled, Tahiri fell to the ground, but in one bound was up again, chasing Riina, following her frantic footsteps. Whatever was coming for her out of the darkness, she didn't want to face it without knowing exactly where Riina was.

And what she was afraid of.

I won't let you kill us . . .

Riina's words haunted her as she ran through the darkness, her name echoing once more from behind her.

Leia literally took a backseat during the flight to Esfandia. Trying to compete with her husband and Droma was too exhausting, and, ultimately, pointless. At times it seemed their affinity wasn't entirely amicable, but it was perfectly natural. They'd hardly stopped talking since the Ryn had come aboard. Bringing each other up to date on events since they'd parted at Fondor, they covered everything from sneaky tactics to Anakin's death. After the latter, Droma had left the bridge for a while, to sing a plaintive lay in a language Leia didn't understand, but then he'd returned with a story about one of his exploits in the Senex sector. The tale was as tall as a Bolenian hill-spinner, but it served its purpose by easing the pall of melancholy that had engulfed the *Falcon*.

"So they started taking apart the tanker module," Han was saying now, relating one of his own stories to Droma, his mood far removed from the grief that had consumed him earlier.

"Which you said was filled with liquid hydrogen."

"Yeah, but destroying the tanker didn't stop the hydrogen. If anything, it spread out a little, exactly as planned."

"Why?" Droma asked, frowning. "Hydrogen won't burn without oxygen."

"That's what Goldenrod said. That's the trouble with droids: no imagination. As our shields failed, I told Leia and Jacen to punch holes through the cruiser's hull with our quads. Before I could tell those scarheads to eat ions, there was more than enough oxygen for the hydrogen to react with. The cruiser went up so fast we had a tough time dodging the pieces. After that, it was just a matter of getting out of there. The few skips we left behind weren't putting up much of a fight."

"Understandably. I hear Vong skips are useless once they're cut off from their yammosks."

"Well, they're not completely useless," Han said, "but it does give you an advantage."

Droma shrugged. "Speaking of yammosks, I've heard some stories about them that would make your tail stand on end!"

Leia listened to the banter but offered nothing toward the conversation. Instead, she concentrated on the information Droma had provided them: communications had indeed been lost with the Unknown Regions. The destruction of the base on Generis and the attack on Esfandia appeared to be the source of the disruption. A free-floating proto-world, Esfandia had long since cut free from whatever star had given birth to it, but still had enough radioactivity bubbling in its core to sustain a liquid atmosphere. It wasn't the most hospitable of places, but it didn't need to be. A skeleton crew of about a dozen people, mainly technicians, normally inhabited the relay outpost, which had been hastily converted from a scientific station at the beginning of the war with the Yuuzhan Vong. Since Luke's mission had entered the Unknown Regions, the Galactic Alliance's military presence around Esfandia had been upgraded to two squadrons of X-wings and a frigate by the name of *Corellian Way*. What had happened to those forces was unknown. The relay staff only had time to broadcast a message alerting their superiors on Mon Calamari that they were under attack by the Yuuzhan Vong before all communications had been lost.

That wasn't necessarily a sure sign of disaster. The relay base was designed to resist such attacks. Imperial AT-AT technology had been adapted to the cold soup of Esfandia's environment, creating a giant, mechanical, crablike construction capable of moving from place to place at a slow but steady pace. Such mobility was an advantage, given that most of the world was studded with receivers sensitive enough to detect transmissions from deep in the Unknown Regions. The base was designed to circumnavigate the globe, maintaining the receivers, while the technicians remained safely inside. That the ability to move made it easier to hide when attacked was a bonus.

The base, therefore, could have simply gone to ground, tucked away in a crevasse or under the thick silt of the atmospheric soup. If it could be found, it could be reactivated. Assuming, of course, that the Yuuzhan Vong hadn't found it first and destroyed it for good.

Leia sent her thoughts outward, far beyond her location in hyperspace, beyond Esfandia and whatever awaited them there, to her brother, Luke. The last message Cal Omas had received from him suggested he'd found a promising lead and was setting off to investigate. He hadn't specified what that lead consisted of or where he was headed, and now there was no way they would know unless they repaired the communications outage. Leia had no doubt that, were anything terrible to happen to him, then she would know about it. She would *feel* it, just as she had in the past. Nevertheless, she was concerned. So much was invested in his mission—personally, and on a galactic scale—that if something were to go wrong, it would be a disaster of unimaginable proportions.

The conversation between her husband and his old friend shifted as the *Falcon*'s console began to beep and flash, announcing that they were nearing their destination.

"Right on the nose," Han said proudly, flipping switches in readiness for the return to realspace.

"And we didn't even have to get out and push," Droma said dryly.

"Yeah, that's real amusing," Han returned without smiling. "Now you want to move your funny, fuzzed-up self out of that chair so Leia can come forward and help me?"

"No, that's all right, Han," she said as Droma began to stand. "I'm sure Droma can manage."

She couldn't say that she was enjoying the break from routine, but it was interesting to watch Han's interaction with the Ryn. Memories of the terrible time when Han had pulled away from her while grieving for Chewbacca still stung, but only Droma had witnessed how low Han had really sunk back then. If having the Ryn aboard did remind Han of those painful times, he certainly wasn't letting it show.

"You remember how to operate the copilot's board?"

Han asked Droma without looking up from what he was doing.

"Follow orders, and curse when something goes wrong," Droma replied with a smile. "Which it invariably does."

Han affected an indignant expression on behalf of his beloved freighter. "Hey, she may be old—"

"But she's still got it where it counts, right?" Droma said.

"What have I told you about doing that?" Han said irritably.

Droma laughed. "Anyway, it's not the age of the ship that worries me," he said, flicking a couple of switches of his own. "It's the age of the pilot I'm more concerned about."

The navicomputer bleeped, cutting off any retort Han might have been about to offer. Both faced the front just as the sweeping streaks of hyperspace dissolved into a cold and distant starscape. There was no primary to dim the stars with its glare; the nearest inhabited system in this section of the Mid Rim was more than ten light-years away, and the nearest star of any kind was half that distance. There was nothing for trillions of kilometers but space dust, and the tiny bauble that was the lonely world of Esfandia.

Or so it *should* have been. As *Pride of Selonia* along with Twin Suns Squadron emerged from hyperspace alongside the *Falcon*, Droma's eyes checked the sensor console for the orphaned planet. The *Falcon*'s sensor suite was still ahead of standard tech, and it soon acquired the target. It was covered with thick clouds, and glowed a burnt orange in artificial colors that looked wrong to Leia's eyes until she realized what was missing: because Esfandia had no sun, its sole source of heat lay at its core. And with no orbit to follow, that meant it would have no seasons, either—which in turn meant no icy poles, and no broiling equator. It would be the same temperature all over.

Closer scans, however, revealed that not to be entirely the case. There were at least six hot spots on the hemisphere facing them, and even as they watched, another blossomed into life.

Droma zoomed in closer to examine the cause.

"Aerial bombardment," he said. "Someone's dropping mines from orbit."

"They're taking out the sensors," Leia said. "The Yuuzhan Vong are still here!"

Han's eyes darted across the displays in front of him. "I've got a strong presence in close orbit. Seven capital vessels, nine cruisers. Not many skips detached, though. No sign of the local defenses, or the reinforcements from Mon Cal."

"I think I can guess why not, too," Droma commented.

Leia knew exactly what he meant. The Yuuzhan Vong force in orbit over Esfandia was enormous by any standard. Against the two squadrons and one frigate Esfandia had possessed, plus the two squadrons Mon Calamari had dispatched to investigate, it was almost obscene. *Overkill* didn't cover it.

"I thought the Vong's resources were stretched," Droma said.

Han just grunted. A crackle of information flowed across newly reopened communications lines. Captain Mayn and Jag were looking for instructions.

"Tell them to hold off for a moment," Leia ordered. "We can't go in like this. It'd be suicide."

Han turned in his seat to face her. "We can't just leave, Leia."

She nodded in agreement. "The relay base must still be down there, otherwise the Yuuzhan Vong wouldn't be wasting time taking out the sensors. Without the base, none of it would work."

"So what are we going to do?" Han asked. "They're going to see us any second."

Leia stood to look over Han's shoulder, placing a hand gently on his neck. The Yuuzhan Vong forces were formidable. "If we can get past the capital ships, we might be able to make it down into the atmosphere and find the base before they do."

"Then what?" Droma asked. "We'd be in exactly the same position as the base. It would just be a matter of time before they find us."

She could feel her frustration mounting as a solution to the dilemma failed to present itself. If they had to abandon Esfandia, they might still be able to jury-rig another relay base elsewhere that would allow them to reestablish contact with Mon Calamari.

She shook her head irritably. It would still mean leaving innocents here on Esfandia to die, and the thought of that simply made her feel ill, reminding her as it did of the time back on Gyndine, where so many had to be abandoned to a cruel fate.

There has to be another way, she thought.

Almost in answer to the thought, a bleeping sounded from the sensor suite, announcing hyperspace emissions from the far side of the planet.

"Incoming," Droma announced, his tail wrapped around the base of his chair, gently twitching.

"That's all we need," Han muttered. "Maybe it's time we bid a hasty retreat, after all."

"Hold on." Leia switched vantage points to look over Droma's shoulder. "I don't think they're Yuuzhan Vong. Broadcast an emergency on the Imperial codes."

"Imperial—?" Han started, but clammed up at a glance at the scanner display. The corner of his mouth curled up into a grin as he sent off the coded transmission. "Well, I never thought I'd be glad to see a Star Destroyer."

Not just one of them, Leia noted. Two of the massive

vessels were lumbering out of hyperspace over Esfandia, fully equipped with support vessels and TIE fighters already streaming from launching bays. The way they swooped in to engage the Yuuzhan Vong filled her with an immediate sense of optimism and kinship.

She didn't immediately recognize the markings on the Star Destroyers, but judging by the blast scoring and other minor damage, it looked like they'd both recently seen combat.

The *Falcon*'s comm bleeped, and Han quickly answered it. It was Grand Admiral Pellaeon.

"I should have known I'd find the *Millennium Falcon* here," he said. "You're always at the heart of trouble."

Leia felt a smile creep across her face. "It's good to hear from you, Gilad."

"As it is you, Princess," he said.

"That's not *Chimaera* you're flying," Han put in. "It looks too old."

"It's *Right to Rule*," Pellaeon said. "One of the oldest in the fleet. We've been chasing this sorry bunch halfway across the galaxy, trying to restrict the amount of damage they inflict. We lost them at the last jump, which is why we've only just arrived. Our intelligence data on your remote stations is sadly out of date."

"Not as good as theirs, obviously," Leia said.

"We're here to try to turn our luck around now."

"I'm glad to hear it."

"Are you joining us?"

"We're at your command, Admiral." Leia said.

"I'll have targets for you shortly. Commander Ansween will relay them to you." Then, almost as an afterthought, the Grand Admiral added: "Nice to be fighting beside you finally, Captain Solo."

Han looked up at Leia when the line closed a moment later. "We're taking orders from an Imperial now?"

"Things have changed," she said. Her heart was telling her that Pellaeon could be trusted, and the Force was telling her the same thing. "He's defending a Galactic Alliance asset. Think how strange that must feel to *him*."

Han chuckled ruefully. "I guess. It's just that I've never been one for taking orders—from *anyone*. I hope this newfound camaraderie between us isn't going to make him think that's about to change."

Leia smiled at her husband; one hand fondly massaged his neck. "I'm sure Pellaeon's fully aware of that, Han."

The comm unit crackled back to life, this time with a female voice—obviously the commander whom the Grand Admiral had mentioned.

"Your primary target is the destroyer *Kur-hashan*," she said. A flood of charts and other data accompanied the message on the *Falcon*'s monitors. "This is a yammosk-bearing vessel. Secondary targets are support vessels. Engage at will. *Right to Rule* out."

Han punched a course into the navicomputer. "You got that, *Selonia*?"

"Loud and clear," came back the voice of Captain Mayn.

"Jag?"

"Twin Suns awaits your orders, Captain," Jag said. He sounded calm and controlled, but underneath the cool exterior Leia knew he was primed and ready for combat.

"Are we about to do what I think we're about to do?" Droma asked, somewhat nervously.

"You're the one always second-guessing everyone," Han replied. "You tell us."

"It doesn't take much foresight to know we're still outnumbered. While it's nice that we have company and all, it still only makes two Star Destroyers against sixteen of the big uglies."

"I know," Han said, a wide, familiar grin settling onto his face. "It makes it so much more interesting when the odds are stacked against you, don't you think?"

PART TWO

CONFRONTATION

Blood. That was the first thing Nom Anor noticed as he emerged from the warrens under Yuuzhan'tar: not the sudden sharpness of light, or the wind, or even the towering remains of the planet's previous rulers. It was the smell of blood, thick and heavy on the air.

He breathed in deeply, and smiled to himself.

The Prophet and his entourage were on the move again. Nom Anor, Shoon-mi, and Kunra all accompanied Ngaaluh as she supposedly spearheaded an investigation into religious corruption in the renamed Vishtu sector of Yuuzhan'tar. Officials at all levels eased her passage. Her sudden notoriety had preceded her: who better than a priestess of the deception sect to uncover deception among the higher ranks?

Ngaaluh brought with her an extensive entourage of her own, all unaware that she was in fact the servant of the corruptor, and that the corruptor himself moved among them. It was the perfect cover. Nom Anor, under heavy disguise, had taken the persona of a lowly worker, the next rung up from a Shamed One. It was his job to supervise the care of the baggage-vrrips, massive six-legged bovine creatures bred purely to haul heavy loads from place to place. The goods in Ngaaluh's case consisted solely of records, plus five prisoners for interrogation. Nom Anor had overseen the selection of these prisoners. They consisted of would-be heretics: a handful who had proven too unreliable or mentally unstable to be of any use to him or the cause. Nom Anor, in his guise as the Prophet Yu'shaa, had fed them very specific lies. Allowed to think that the Prophet had accepted them, these five had been sent out to spread a perverted version of the word of Yu'shaa. Ngaaluh's spies—still faithful to Shimrra, and believing they were doing the will of the Supreme Commander—had caught them in due course. Interrogation would reveal terrible secrets about Vishtu sector and the various officials who oversaw it. Thus they did the work of Nom Anor by unwittingly spreading misinformation.

"Halt!"

Nom Anor whipped his vrrips into line as Ngaaluh's caravan approached the entrance to Vishtu's command enclave. The clumsy entourage staggered to a halt in a cloud of dust. Bugs swarmed around them, getting under hoods and into clothes, driven mad by the smell of blood. Two warriors guarded the entrance, grotesquely armored and scarred in imaginative ways. One of them growled for authorization, and Ngaaluh's chief underling presented it for inspection. Security was tight. Ngaaluh watched from an ornate seat on the back of the largest vrrip as one of the guards checked and double-checked her authenticity. Her expression was one of weariness—appropriate for the moment, thought Nom Anor, and probably quite genuine, too. The journey had been long and tiring, even from the comfort of Ngaaluh's seat.

The guard expressed dissatisfaction with the authorization, much to Nom Anor's surprise. It was the one thing about the entourage that was unquestionably genuine. An argument broke out between the underling and the guard, and Nom Anor craned to overhear what was being said. Had the guards somehow learned of the Prophet's imminent arrival and stepped up their vigilance?

Nom Anor caught the eye of Kunra, in the disguise of the caravan's junior vrrip handler. He was unrecognizable beneath a mask of blasted tissue, heavily scarred as though from extensive, nonritual burns. The ex-warrior nodded and tightened his grip on the long, rigid whip that all vrrip handlers carried.

Before Nom Anor could edge closer, a mailed, thorny hand struck him across the face. "This does not concern you, worker," snarled the second guard, whom Nom Anor had not noticed circling the caravan. "Do not interfere in the matters of your superiors!"

Nom Anor kept his head low, partly as an act of obeisance, but also to hide any damage that might have occurred to the masquer hiding his real face. He also didn't want the guards to see the anger he could feel burning in his chest—an anger and loathing that would have surely given him away as something other than a lackey from the worker caste.

He had to contain his emotions. For all intents and purposes, he *was* a lackey, and given that station he could expect to be kicked and beaten at the whim of those above him.

He gritted his teeth and mumbled something suitably obsequious. The warrior guard grunted and walked away.

"Are you all right?" Kunra whispered when the guards were out of earshot.

Nom Anor straightened and checked his features. His masquer was intact. "I've had worse," he said, staring balefully after the guards.

That was true enough. Working up the ranks of executors had been a long and painful process; he had received as many beatings as he'd given. Working closely with the pain-loving Shimrra and his coterie of sadomasochistic warlords had kept him treading a tightrope between influence and agony, never knowing when he might find himself tipping onto the wrong side.

The thought warmed him that he would one day return every single one of those indignities on those who had administered them. None would be spared. Every slight along that path to revenge only fueled his determination, from the lowliest guard to the high prefect himself . . .

Finally the guards called out for the gates to be opened, pacified by their brief exercise of authority. Massive muscles strained under the effort of opening the way ahead of Ngaaluh. The once artificial door had long since been replaced by a swarbrik, a sturdy organism that, if attacked, could excrete a highly toxic gas and regenerate its tissues at a heightened rate. It groaned as its keepers poked and prodded it into activity, slowly obeying their commands and allowing the caravan through.

Nom Anor cracked his long whip, and the vrrips grumbled into life. Their giant haunches rocked from side to side, and Nom Anor forced himself to concentrate on his hefty charges. He didn't have time to appreciate the moment as the giant arch crept over him, and the road's dusty scent subtly changed to give way to more exotic spices. For a minute or more, his concerns were focused solely upon the vrrips and his job. It was important, he knew, not to arouse any further suspicions. To those observing him, he was a worker, nothing more; no one should suspect for a second that he was anything more than a lowly vrrip handler, shamed into submission.

Ngaaluh's expression didn't change once, not even as they passed a wide, dark pool where it seemed the swarbrik itself was bleeding. The creature was sick, weeping from a dozen breaches in its thickened hide. Nom Anor could see no obvious cause of the illness. It was just another of the many small ways in which the World Brain was still malfunctioning on the surface of Yuuzhan'tar.

His smile returned beneath the masquer. Perhaps, he

thought, there were advantages to living underground after all.

Jag didn't waste time questioning his orders; he was just glad to be out of hyperspace. While Pellaeon forced a wedge between the planet and the Yuuzhan Vong to prevent further bombardment, Jag drove the squadron he shared with Jaina like an arrow at the warship *Kur-hashan*.

"Twin Two, take Six and Eight around the left flank. Three, take the right with Five and Seven. The rest of you, with me."

Twins Four and Nine pirouetted neatly to create a V-shape with Jag in the middle, moving in perfect synchronicity. He was beginning to forget which pilots were Chiss and which were Galactic Alliance in origin; they'd spent enough time fighting together to have become one. To a casual observer, the clawcraft and X-wings may have looked different, but the ships in their crosshairs were the same.

The Yuuzhan Vong were just waking up to the fact they were under attack from two sides. *Kur-hashan*'s coral arms seemed to erupt, dispensing coralskippers like seeds to the galactic winds. The flat ovoid yorik-vec assault cruisers—fast but low in firepower—swept around the grotesquely organic capital vessel to engage the attackers. *Pride of Selonia* powered in to meet them, laser cannons blazing.

The normally dark environment of Esfandia was soon shattered by the almost stroboscopic effect of all the ships' weapons firing, while screaming engines cast cometlike sprays of energy across the starscape, bringing a false dawn to all sides of the planet. Faster, furious specks darted by the thousands between the artificial and organic behemoths turning to battle. With his sensors turned to maximum just to enable him to see the planet, the light flashing around him soon overwhelmed Jag. It was as if he were seeing the universe from a completely different scale, with the larger ships appearing as quasars and the smaller vessels swirling around them taking the role of galactic clusters—all sped up so that trillions of years of motion was compressed into seconds.

A skip erupted into fire off to Jag's starboard, dragging him from his reverie. He silently chided himself; idle thoughts like that were dangerous in combat.

"You want to watch yourself there, boss."

The voice belonged to the Y-wing pilot whom Twin Suns Squadron had recruited from Bakura. She'd proven more than capable in combat in the fight against the Ssi-ruuk, and had volunteered to help fill some of the empty spots created since the mission had begun. The pilot had jumped at the opportunity—and with the skip that had been about to attack him now a boiling mass in his wake, Jag was glad she had.

"Thanks, Nine," he said, swinging his reticle around to target another coralskipper. "That one must have crept up on me."

"There's another on your tail, One," said Four, retro-ing heavily to pass under the Yuuzhan Vong fighter that Jag hadn't noticed coming in from behind. He pulled him-self into a tight spiral and came out on a completely dif-ferent heading, seeing spots from acceleration. He ramped his inertial dampener up a notch and fired at a skip that flashed by with alarming suddenness. His shot was casu-ally soaked up by a dovin basal. The coralskipper tail-ing him, however, wasn't so fortunate; it disappeared in a stuttering flash from his rear screen. He felt his claw-craft shudder slightly from the shock wave of the nearby explosion.

"Much appreciated, Four."

"You'd do the same for me," the Chiss pilot returned.

"Count on it," he said.

Ordinarily, Jag would never have permitted such casual banter among his pilots. The Chiss were taught discipline before they could crawl. But he'd found that, in this instance, with the squadron's mix of Galactic Alliance and Chiss pilots, a small amount of informality helped everyone come together and function effectively as a team in the most trying of circumstances—such as now, at three-quarters strength, and grossly outnumbered besides.

"Don't take any chances," he ordered his pilots. "We're here to protect the *Selonia*. Besides the *Falcon*, we're all that stands between it and *Kur-hashan*."

"Copy, One," came back Three, currently harassing a blastboat analog many times its size. "Where *is* the *Falcon*, anyway?"

Jag scanned the displays before him, looking for the distinctive disk-shaped freighter. It wasn't immediately visible, and he didn't have time to look for it, as the Yuuzhan Vong resistance suddenly stiffened and he found himself in the middle of what seemed like three firefights at once. A grin formed on his face as he put aside thoughts of the squadron in favor of his own survival. To Jag, there was nothing quite as satisfying as confronting a worthy adversary. Until now, the Yuuzhan Vong fleet had seemed disorganized, almost dispirited, and his pilots had managed to pick them out of the sky with relative ease. But there seemed to be some spirit returning to their attack. The advantage of surprise was well and truly gone.

His mind instinctively probed at his enemy's weaknesses as he flew, juking and firing whenever a target appeared before him. If Pellaeon had been following the Yuuzhan Vong force before them, then that suggested it was the remains of the fleet that attacked Bastion and Borosk in Imperial Space. Partial or total, it didn't matter: the Yuuzhan Vong had suffered heavy losses and, if

Jag had learned anything from watching the Galactic Alliance fight, there would have been a significant reduction in the yammosk-per-fighter ratio. Alliance pilots seemed to have an instinct instilled in them: to go for the head whenever possible. Destroy the decision-making part of an organism, and victory will soon follow.

Well, he thought, wherever the head was in this particular battle, it had obviously decided to fight back. Coralskippers flew in sheets like rain upon the attacking forces, delivering through sheer numbers what tactics alone could not. Galactic Alliance versatility beat Yuuzhan Vong methods most times in a one-to-one fight, and Esfandia was no different. The longer it stayed ten-to-one, though, the less confident Jag was inclined to feel.

Yet the shift in emphasis on behalf of the yammosks had one beneficial side effect: while the focus of the Yuuzhan Vong was on the skies above Esfandia, little or no attention was paid to what was happening below. And it was only then, as Jag turned his attention briefly downward to note that the Yuuzhan Vong bombardment of the planet had ceased, that he located *Millennium Falcon*. She was slipping unnoticed into the turgid, roiled-up mess that was Esfandia's atmosphere.

Jag had just enough time to wonder what Han and Leia were doing before the warship *Kur-hashan* cut off his view of the planet, blinding him with violent splashes of energy.

Whatever they're up to, he thought as he rolled his craft away from the incoming fire, *I'm sure I'll find out soon enough . . .*

When Ngaaluh was settled in her rooms, Nom Anor and his entourage slipped away. Their places were taken by three Shamed Ones who served the Prophet, so their absence would not be noticed. That their appearances dif-

fered from Nom Anor and his advisers didn't matter—
Shamed Ones were rarely looked upon with any scrutiny.

Deep under the priestess's quarters, accessible only
by a secret passageway and passwords, were a series of
basements that had been transformed from the infidels'
boxy tastes to something more organic; not even the Jedi
philosophy could convince a Yuuzhan Vong to live in a
lifeless coffin. Nom Anor inspected the new audience
chambers and found them satisfactory. They were aus-
tere and secure, the only ostentatious element being the
chair he insisted upon, placed on a podium so that during his sermons he would be visible to all. The Prophet's
role at the center of the heresy was crucial, and it was important to play it convincingly. Or so he told Shoon-mi.
His enjoyment of the sense of power it gave him he kept
carefully hidden.

After a hasty meal of raw hawk-bat, Nom Anor retired
to a private chamber to work on the heresy. The Jedi philosophy spreading among his minions was an evolving
thing, requiring constant fine-tuning—especially with the
Jedi Knights' continued resistance to Shimrra's attempts
to have them purged from the galaxy. But it was important that the faithful be restrained from acting too pre-
cipitously when things appeared to be going well, just as
it was for them to be given encouragement following any
setback. There was a constant need to balance conflicting factions and agendas, needs and objectives.

The minions he left in his wake played a key role in
translating his will into action. Some had been chosen by
Shoon-mi for their fanatical dedication to the Prophet, others by Kunra for their clearheadedness. Others Nom Anor
himself had selected, seeing in them a keen understanding of the philosophy itself. These subordinate Prophets
served as direct substitutes for the Prophet Yu'shaa, for
it simply wasn't possible to be everywhere at once, and
there were so many questions, so many things the heretics

wanted to know. What were the movement's goals, beyond obtaining freedom for the Shamed Ones? Was displacing Shimrra atop the Supreme Overlord's throne a goal of the movement if Shimrra refused to accept their demands? Would the Jedi Heresy replace the Great Doctrine as blueprint for the destiny of the Yuuzhan Vong? Where did the old gods and ways fit in?

Nom Anor was wearying of such questions, but he knew that in them lay his only chance of survival, let alone advancement. Spurned by Shimrra, he had no other way to attain power than through the tenets of the Jedi Heresy. That he didn't believe in them himself didn't matter in the slightest. That those below him did—with the assistance of the subordinate Prophets—was all that mattered, wherever those beliefs took them.

He wasn't certain if the work he ordered would result in freedom for the Shamed Ones, even as a sideline. He was simply using the movement to hurt those who had hurt him, via terrorism, political assassination, theft, and other means. He had been trained in covert activism; although his skills had mainly been used to attack the infidels, they could just as easily be turned against those of his own kind.

Sometimes, late at night, he wondered what the future held for him. What lay in store for the skulking yet all-pervasive figure of Nom Anor? Would the Jedi Heresy succeed in returning him to an honored place in society, along with the Shamed Ones? Would he become lost behind the mask of Yu'shaa the Prophet, trapped by the very robes he had adopted as a means of escape?

Ngaaluh joined him when she was able, to discuss recent developments on the surface. The priestess was clean and smelled of incense, but she was clearly exhausted by a busy day, by maintaining her pretence with flawless diligence.

"I hear word from Shimrra's court," she said, sinking

into a chair opposite Nom Anor with a weary sigh. "High Priest Jakan has assured His Dire Majesty that the fall of the heresy is imminent."

"Either he is overly confident or he is a fool, then," Nom Anor said, unmasked. Ngaaluh knew who "Yu'shaa" really was, but that didn't assail her belief in the Prophet. Her faith in the heresy was so complete that she had no difficulties believing it could seduce even an old scoundrel like the ex-executor.

Ngaaluh nodded. "He *is* a fool. The heresy is too entrenched to be crushed solely by optimism and good intentions. But he has plans."

Nom Anor smiled at this. He toyed with a coufee while they talked, slicing thin wafers off a twig of waxwood and popping them one by one into his mouth. "How does Jakan intend to do away with me this time?"

"He is petitioning for a total ban on access to the lower levels. Once all authorized personnel have been evacuated, he proposes to release a plague of wild spinerays into the tunnels. Shapers will increase their mobility, fecundity, and appetite, so they will breed and kill, breed and kill. Jakan predicts that anything living down here will be destroyed within a matter of weeks."

Nom Anor laughed out loud at the naïveté of the plan. "And who does he think will destroy the spinerays when this is accomplished? Who will stop them from escaping to the upper levels? The fool would throw the egg out with the afterbirth if Shimrra let him."

"Another plan concerned pumping corrosive gas into the tunnels," Ngaaluh said. "This failed on the grounds that the gas could eat into the foundations and bring the planet's surface down around us."

Nom Anor laughed again. "I daresay some would have found this an acceptable risk, nonetheless." He nodded thoughtfully as he slipped another slice of waxwood into his mouth. "It is good they are desperate. It shows we must be worrying them."

"I believe so, Master. The strength and rightness of our convictions undermines every move they attempt against us. They cannot destroy us."

"But that doesn't mean they won't continue to try."

Ngaaluh bowed her head. "This is true, Master. And I will stop them as best I can."

"How goes our plan?" Nom Anor asked, taking the opportunity to change the subject to one of immediate concern. "Have you inveigled yourself within the corridors of the intendant Ash'ett?"

"I have." She nodded, sending shadows across her angular features. "He is exactly as you said he was: greedy and self-serving. He mouths platitudes to the old gods and curses the Jedi, but would follow neither, given the choice. He is his own creature."

His own creature, Nom Anor echoed to himself. They were well-chosen words, and would have served as a good description of himself, too, had she but known the truth.

"You agree, then, that he must fall?"

She nodded. "With him out of the way, there will be room for someone sympathetic to our cause. I will place the ones we have prepared in his staff, and guarantee his destruction."

"Excellent." He nodded sagely, inwardly crowing with delight. Prefect Ash'ett was an old rival, someone who had shown no compunction when it came to squashing those around him in order to advance himself—Nom Anor among them. Like many of his old rivals, Ash'ett had risen to power on Yuuzhan'tar, taking territory and glory as the opportunities arose during the fall of the infidel empire. Such power should have been Nom Anor's. Ash'ett's time of reckoning was long overdue, and would come with interest.

"I have identified another unworthy," Nom Anor said. "When we are done here, we will move to Gileng, where a certain Drosh Khalii has grown fat on the profits of war for too long."

Ngaaluh nodded again, her eyes gleaming in the yellow lichen torch. If she was daunted by the thought of having another target to consider before this one had been eliminated, she didn't say.

"The hard work of revolution goes ever on," Nom Anor said.

"We are making progress, Master."

"Indeed." He resisted the urge to ask *Where to?* "Do you have anything else to report?"

"Yes, Master."

"Tell me, then," he said, offering Ngaaluh a slice of waxwood. The priestess accepted it but didn't place it in her mouth straight away.

"I hear whispers in the court, Master," she said.

"That is not uncommon. At any given time, there might be hundreds of rumors crossing the galaxy."

"The name of the Unknown Regions, as the *Jeedai* call them, recurs in these rumors. The missions they speak of, however, seem unrelated to the Chiss. Their focus is on something entirely different."

"Which is?"

"I'm not sure, Master. There are few details beyond what I have told you."

"Gossip," Nom Anor said, dismissing the news with a wave of his hand. "Idle chatter among the ruling classes as they seek to deflect blame from themselves. I've seen it a thousand times before."

"As have I, Master—but these whispers persist. Something is afoot. The enemies of Shimrra are restless."

"Well, if so, perhaps we can use them to our advantage." Anything distracting Shimrra from the heretics was a potential boon.

Ngaaluh slipped a piece of the waxwood between her tattooed lips. "There is a rumor I heard from a very reliable source of a mission newly returned from the Unknown Regions. The mission had been gone an extremely long time, and its commander was surprised on his return to find that many of his commanding officers had been replaced."

Not surprising, Nom Anor thought. The life expectancy of the warriors decreased the closer one got to the top.

"Go on," he said, hoping the story would soon get interesting.

"The commander, one Ekh'm Val, sought an audience with the Supreme Overlord himself. He boasted of finding the lost world of Zonama Sekot."

"Zonama Sekot?" Nom Anor frowned. "But the living planet is nothing more than a legend."

"Not if this Ekh'm Val is to be believed."

"What happened when he spoke to Shimrra?"

"I don't know," Ngaaluh said, leaning in close, her eyes glittering. "That I haven't heard. Commander Val appears to have disappeared."

"Really?" Nom Anor was mildly intrigued now; he couldn't tell why Ngaaluh was telling him this, but the story was an interesting diversion. "Perhaps he was lying and paid the price for it."

"Perhaps," she conceded. "But the rumor persists. There may be truth behind it."

"Do you think it is important?"

"My instincts tell me to listen. The *Jeedai* teach that we should trust those instincts."

Nom Anor almost rolled his eye. "By all means listen, then—and report back to me if you learn anything of importance."

"Of course, Master. I am your obedient servant."

Ngaaluh smoothed her robe and waited for him to speak.

He took pity on her and tossed her a compliment as Shimrra might have tossed the yargh'un a heretic for a snack.

"You're doing excellent work, Ngaaluh. Your skill at deception is admirable."

Ngaaluh snorted. "It's all I can do to not cry out my rage against the atrocities that Shimrra commits upon the truth."

"Your perseverance does us all proud."

The priestess paused, turning the remaining waxwood between her callused fingers. "It is hard at times," she said.

"You should rest," Nom Anor said. Ngaaluh looked exhausted, physically as well as spiritually. He, too, felt the need for stillness. While nights, per se, might not have technically existed in the depths of Yuuzhan'tar, he still had to listen to his biological rhythms. "Go back to your chambers, before you're missed, and get some sleep."

Ngaaluh nodded and rose painfully to her feet. "Our struggle goes well. I have hope that we will achieve our goals soon."

He only nodded encouragingly, hiding his weariness behind a careworn smile. "Go, now, my friend."

Ngaaluh bowed again and left the room. Barely had she gone when a soft knocking issued from the door.

He sighed. "Yes?" he called, expecting it to be Kunra to advise him of the successful deployment of the fake heretics.

The guard outside opened the door to admit Shoon-mi. The Shamed One peered cautiously into the room.

"Forgive me, Master, for visiting you at this late hour."

Nom Anor irritably waved away his lackey's concern. "What is it?"

"I was wondering if there was anything I can get you, Master."

"If there was, don't you think I would have called you?"

Shoon-mi nodded as he took a step into the room. "It's just that you didn't call for your evening meal. I thought that—"

"I wasn't hungry, Shoon-mi; it's as simple as that. I had work to attend to."

Shoon-mi executed a pious bow. "Forgive me, Master. I had only your well-being at heart."

"It's appreciated," he said. "But now I really must rest."

"As you wish, Master." Shoon-mi bowed a third time, and went to leave. As he was approaching the door, he turned back as though he had forgotten something. "I have taken the liberty of taking your masquer to have it refreshed."

"My masquer?" Nom Anor looked around at where it normally hung with the others on stalks by his bed. Sure enough, the skin and features of the Prophet were missing. "Very well. It was starting to look a little shabby. Good thinking, Shoon-mi."

"I shall have it returned to you in the morning, Master, in time for your first audience."

Fatigue rushed through Nom Anor at the thought of resuming his usual routine so soon. Being outside had reminded him of how far he had fallen. He may have risen on the back of the rising tide of heretics, but there was still a long way to go before he could walk freely in the natural world.

"I'm sorry, Master," Shoon-mi said. "I am babbling while you should be resting. Are you certain that there is nothing I can assist you with before you retire?"

Nom Anor shook his head, waving his religious adviser away. "I promise you that I will call should I need anything, Shoon-mi."

With that the Shamed One bowed one last time and left.

The door clicked shut again, and Nom Anor threw the heavy bolt across to ensure he had no more interruptions. Outside, he thought he could hear voices whispering—Shoon-mi and Kunra, rapid and emphatic, as though arguing—but he didn't have the energy to listen in to the conversation. *Let them fight among themselves,* he thought, reclining on the bed with a chorus of creaking sinews. *At least it keeps them occupied.*

Exhaustion carried him quickly into sleep, and once there he dreamed of a man with a face more scarred than any he'd seen before, flayed and salted and left to fester. The nose was an open wound, and the mouth a jagged and lipless mess. Incongruously, two red mqaaq'it implants stared out at him from where eyes should have been, giving the visage an air of authority.

The image snarled at him—and Nom Anor awoke to the realization that the face was his own reflection, but the eyes belonged to Shimrra. He shuddered on his narrow bed and pulled the covers tighter around him. Sleep, however, had fled, and he lay huddled in silence until dawn broke, far above, and duty once more called.

"Almost there," Han said, dipping the *Falcon*'s nose a little deeper into the turbulent soup that was Esfandia's atmosphere. The freighter's chassis shuddered under the extra forces she was being asked to bear. She was riding the dense, frigid gases she encountered with all the grace of a ronto.

Leia clutched the sides of her rattling seat to prevent herself from being thrown to the floor, mentally keeping her fingers crossed the whole time. In the copilot's position, she did what she could to assist Han in the "splashdown," as he'd called it. She'd never entered such a dense atmosphere before, outside a gas giant. The situation was compounded by the fact that the heat of the *Falcon* alone tended to make the bitterly cold, liquid air explode in new and turbulent ways around them as they plummeted groundward, not to mention the various hot spots left by the Yuuzhan Vong bombardment. She doubted Esfandia had experienced such an input of energy for millennia.

"We're almost there." Han kept up the litany of small encouragements, although Leia suspected he was talking to the ship herself rather than her passengers.

They had made it past the Yuuzhan Vong fleet easily enough; in the heat of the moment, one battered old freighter feigning a death roll would never warrant too much attention. From there it was just a matter of getting under cover without displaying too many course changes.

"This is definitely one of your crazier ideas," Droma said from behind them, clutching both their seats for safety's sake. "If it's at all possible, you've actually become more reckless since last I saw you."

"I'm getting us through this, aren't I?" Han said, returning his attention to the task at hand.

"This far, yes," Droma said. He pointed to the viewport. "But that's a whole lot of murk to be lost in."

"We have a radar survey of the surface of the planet," Han said calmly. "It's not as if we're going to run into a mountain or anything."

"So all we have to do is find the station; is that it?"

Han looked back at the Ryn, obviously detecting his friend's sarcasm. "Something like that, yeah."

"Before someone sees the *Falcon* on their scanners and drops a bomb on us," Droma said.

"Or we lead them to the station ourselves," Leia added, following up on the Ryn's point. The *Millennium Falcon*'s engines would stand out like a nova in the planet's cold atmosphere.

Han dismissed their concerns with a brief snort. "Look, all we have to do is release a couple of concussion missiles along the way. Their heat signatures will confuse the readings from orbit, right? Besides, the Vong mines have already stirred things up down here. Hot air rises, remember. Get us deep enough and the upper layers will cover us quite nicely."

"Are you sure?" Droma asked.

"I'd bet my life on it."

"And mine." The Ryn tooted mournfully. "That's the problem."

"Hey, trust me, okay?" The ship glided forward in silence for a few seconds before he added, "I know what I'm doing."

Leia clutched her seat even tighter, having heard those words from her husband all too often in the past. Han usually *did* know what he was doing, but the ride was rarely an easy one.

"Now," Han muttered, "where do you suppose we should start looking?"

Leia peered ahead and saw nothing but blackness. Through a low-light enhancement algorithm on the displays she saw a featureless orange fog. The radar map, taken on a quick pass before dropping into the soup, suggested they were crossing what resembled a vast arterial basin. But that wasn't possible; water had never flowed on Esfandia, except within the communications base. These icy depths knew no life and, should the bubble of hospitality within the *Falcon* be breached, it would kill them as soon as—

Leia jumped as something loomed out of the darkness, visible only as a bright orange splotch on the enhanced display and shaped like a large, quivering flower. It was gone before she had a chance to make out exactly what it was.

"What was that?" Droma asked, sounding as startled as Leia had been.

"I don't know," Han said. "And I'm not about to go

back to find out." He arbitrarily set a reference grid over the barren landscape, steering the freighter across it. "There's a series of deep channels just east of here. I'm cutting our velocity and altitude to take a closer look. When we reach the edge, Leia, I want you to send out a missile to cover our tracks, okay?"

"How many concussion missiles do we have?" Droma asked. "It could take us forever to find this thing."

Han shrugged. "It's a small world."

"It's not *that* small. And remember, what makes it easier for us to find them makes it easier for the Yuuzhan Vong to find us."

"Then we'd better get started, hadn't we?" Han said. He swung the *Falcon* over a steep rise, then flattened out. "Ready with that missile, sweetheart?"

Leia was. On the radar map ahead she saw a sharp drop approaching. Targeting the orange void behind her and putting the missile on a timer fuse, she let it fly just as the *Falcon* dipped her nose and dived deeper into the frigid atmosphere. The missile shot off into the distance, its boiling wake a gently curving arc leading nowhere.

Han hugged the canyon wall as closely as he could while they fell. Leia caught sight of two more of the odd flower-shaped objects whipping by and wondered what they might be. Pockets of gas? Crystal agglomerates? Clumps of the local equivalent of amoebas, perhaps? Whatever they were, they were exceedingly delicate. In the rear view she saw nothing but wisps left after the *Falcon* had passed, and the fierce burn of the freighter's engines soon evaporated even those.

The bottom of the canyon came with surprising suddenness. One moment they were diving nose-first, the next Han had swung the *Falcon* around level. There was little change to the forward view.

"Cutting main drive," Han announced. His voice

seemed unnecessarily loud in the almost deathly quiet of the cockpit. "Dropping back to repulsors."

Leia kept her eyes on the sensors as the *Falcon* cruised through the depths, but there was little to see. The canyon floor was darker and more barren than before. The ambient temperature had risen, although it was still very cold. The surface of Esfandia was a strange and alien place that was unlikely to ever see the stars. Its stony ground could have been composed of frozen carbon dioxide, and was twisted into peculiar shapes that were so fragile that they would have probably been disturbed by a single ray of sunlight.

"Can anyone see anything out there?"

Han made a show of peering out the forward viewport, squinting as though this would somehow make the blackness outside easier to penetrate.

"Nothing," Droma said softly. "How big is this base meant to be, anyway?"

"Fifty meters across," Leia said, "not counting its legs."

"So if it was here, it'd certainly stand out. We might not be able to see it, but we'd definitely get a solid *ping* off its hull."

Leia nodded. "Even if it was buried, we'd spot it from up close."

"Then I guess it's not here." Han scrolled through the radar map. "At least not in this canyon." His finger indicated a much larger network south of their present position. "I propose we surface and try this one here. Unless anyone has any better ideas."

A sense of futility welled up inside Leia. She couldn't begin to imagine the number of possible hiding places there could be on Esfandia for something like a communications base. There were hundreds of canyons, and probably a thousand times more fissures it could have slipped into. They could search for months and not find it.

"Maybe we'll get lucky," she said, more for her own sake than anyone else's.

"Hold it," Droma said. She looked around to the Ryn, waiting for him to continue. His head was cocked in a manner suggesting that he was intently listening to some faint and far-off sound. "There's something . . ."

"What is it?" Leia pressed.

"Are we scanning comm frequencies?"

"Across the dial," Han said. "Why?"

"Turn up the gain. Listen."

When Han did as he was instructed, a faint whistling became audible. At first Leia thought it was just random noise, but a closer inspection revealed it to be chopped up into discrete fragments, almost like a—

"That sounds like a digital transmission," Han said, finishing the thought for her.

"Could it be the base?" Leia asked, mystified.

"I'm not sure," Han said. "I can't get a fix on it. The signal seems to be coming from several places at once. We must be getting echoes off the canyon walls."

"It *is* a signal, though, right?" Droma asked.

Leia listened for a few seconds longer, then shrugged. "I don't recognize the protocol. Han?"

Han shook his head. "It's all Kubazian to me. Where's Goldenrod? He might be able to translate."

"He shut himself down during the trip," Droma said. "He's sitting there in the main hold with those Noghri bodyguards of yours. The three of them aren't really much for conversation, are they?"

"Well, don't just stand there jabbering," Han said. "Make yourself useful and go wake him up. And don't feel the need to be too gentle, either. He should know better than to be snoozing at a time like this."

On the contrary, Leia thought. The droid knew only too well that trouble would be awaiting them when they arrived at Esfandia. It invariably was. She couldn't blame him for wanting to opt out every now and then.

Alone for a second, she turned to Han. "Do you really think this is going to work?"

"It's worth a try. While everyone is distracted upstairs, it might be the only chance we get. All it will take is for us to get lucky once. And if those signals *are* from them, then—"

He was interrupted by a tap on his shoulder. Droma leaned past Leia and Han to point at a telemetry display.

"I think you should see this," the Ryn whistled.

The display contained an image of the flickering, furious web of the space battle above, followed as much as was possible from the *Falcon*'s viewpoint. The view showed two wedge-shaped fighter groups darting in different directions away from the Yuuzhan Vong fleet. Imperial forces engaged with one of them, but couldn't prevent them from reaching the atmosphere. Both groups of Yuuzhan Vong fighters dipped under the fog and disappeared.

"Looks like we've got company," Han said.

Leia wasn't surprised. It was only a matter of time before the Yuuzhan Vong tried the same tactic as they had.

"Why can't things ever be easy, Leia? Just for once it would be nice if things went the way they're supposed to."

Leia smiled. "Even if they did, Han, I'm sure it would just make you all the more suspicious."

Everything around Saba burned with a bright, potent vitality. With each lungful of air she took, she could feel the life force of the planet diffuse into her blood and spread to all the cells in her body. The cycle of life and death was in constant play in the tampasi all around her. Iridescent insects glided from branch to branch overhead, seeking pollen from the giant drooping flowers that grew there. Every now and then she would see gangly, six-legged creatures leap out from the cover of the fat leaves to snatch at these insects with unnaturally long and glistening tongues. These in turn were eaten by translucent, long-feathered birds that appeared and disappeared in bright flashes among the boras, their shrill calls echoing throughout the tampasi whenever they successfully managed to catch one of their prey.

She couldn't get enough of it, no matter how deeply she inhaled. She wanted to ingest the whole world and become one with it. Soron Hegerty walked alongside her, talking about the Ssither, a saurian race the biologist had studied many years ago, but Saba barely heard a word. Only as a strange darkness fell over them did she stir from her reverent daze.

She looked up, expecting to see another airship passing overhead, but even as she did so she knew that this couldn't be the explanation. This darkness was too complete—as though night had abruptly fallen across the world.

"What iz it?" Saba asked. The others were all gazing up in obvious concern.

"It's Mobus," Soron Hegerty said. "We've fallen into its shadow."

Saba understood. She didn't need to see the gas giant in the sky above to know that the sun had slipped behind it as Zonama Sekot continued on its orbit around the giant world. The animal life on the living world, however, didn't know the difference between sunset and eclipse.

"We call it Sanctuary," Rowel said. His gold-black gaze was on Luke, glittering in the sudden twilight.

Again Saba nodded, understanding the Ferroan's misgivings. The people of Zonama Sekot had searched long and hard for somewhere to feel safe. They had found it, finally, and now it had been invaded again. How would that feel?

They walked on through the tampasi, chilled by the unnatural darkness, as hushed as the world around them. Despite the gloom, their progress wasn't impeded in any way. The lower branches of the boras sprang to life with a million flickering lights cast by insects nesting there. The greenish bioluminescence illuminated the tampasi floor with a soft, pale light that allowed them to see where they were going. New creatures stirred as ones accustomed to daylight retired for the duration of the eclipse. Saba held her breath as an entirely new ecosystem woke around her.

The sun returned as the ground party approached a Ferroan village an hour later. Voices rose around her, and it was with no small sense of sadness that Saba realized that they had reached the end of their journey through the tampasi.

"It's hard to imagine that boras could grow as tall as they have in such a short time," Jacen was saying to one of their Ferroan guides as they entered the village. "Where I come from, trees like this would take thousands of years to grow."

Rowel glanced at him, his brow pressed down in confusion. "Why would your world take so long to yield its treasures?" he asked. "What is the point in holding back from your inhabitants if it means that most would never get the chance to appreciate your beauty?"

Jacen smiled at this, and Saba sissed softly to herself. To Rowel, worlds were thinking, living things, not just places to live. What most people would consider normal might seem odd to him.

Darak led them to a ring of brown, mushroomlike habitats clustered around the base of a nearby boras. Each habitat had a central pillar that rose two stories high, and was capped with a roof that bulged out and then down until it touched ground. The texture of the walls was rough and flexible, almost rubbery, and the doorways and windows were rounded as though grown rather than cut.

Grown, Saba thought, with the faintest of misgivings. After so long dealing with the organic technology of the Yuuzhan Vong, anything that worked on a similar principle automatically triggered a negative reaction.

Darak led them to the largest habitat and waved them inside.

"We will meet in one hour," she said. "At sunset."

Without another word, Darak and Rowel withdrew, leaving the visitors to make themselves at home.

The ground floor contained a number of seating mats scattered about in casual orderliness, along with several tables containing bowls and plates piled high with foodstuffs. The second floor grew out of the central stalk and was accessible by a spiny spiral staircase.

"Fascinating," Hegerty said, marveling at the habitat's architecture.

Saba's stomach growled; she stepped over to one of the tables and dipped a claw into a bowl of an off-white paste. She cautiously sniffed at it before tasting.

"Well?" Danni asked, coming up beside her. "What's it like?"

"Not obviously poizoned," she said.

"I think if any harm was intended for us," Mara said, "then it would have happened before now."

"Mara's right," Luke said. "They could have killed us while we slept on *Jade Shadow* if they'd wanted to."

Danni reached into another bowl, this one containing green nutlike pellets. She tasted one, nodding with surprised satisfaction to the others.

"It's good," she said, trying some of the other foods.

Jacen, Mara, and Hegerty joined them at the table. Only Luke stood to one side, looking out the window.

"It's clear that things have changed since Vergere was

last here," the Jedi Master said after a moment. "We'll need to be on our toes. I suggest we use this time to prepare ourselves for the meeting."

While she agreed with Luke, Saba found it difficult to emulate the Jedi Master's calm. They were on Zonama Sekot! How could she just push that fact to the back of her mind and ignore it? She could feel the living world around her; incomprehensible thoughts washed over her like ocean currents. They had reached the place Vergere had sent them to find, a planet that could well prove to be the key to ending the war with the Yuuzhan Vong.

That the Yuuzhan Vong had also located the living planet, however, didn't bode well. They had successfully achieved their goal—only to find not solace from their concerns, but rather more problems. At least, she thought, they weren't prisoners. The door hung invitingly open, and there were no guards outside. This seemed strangely at odds with the distrust the Ferroans had displayed since the Jedi Knights had arrived. Then again, perhaps security wasn't that much of an issue when you were on a planet that could keep a watch on everything for you . . .

Jacen was about to try some more of the food when he noticed three childlike faces with wide eyes peering around the entrance to the habitat at him. They disappeared with a giggle as soon as they saw him looking back at them.

"Nice to see that not all of the Ferroans hold us in contempt," Mara said at his shoulder.

He was about to agree with her when Saba uttered a low, perplexed growl. She was standing off to one side, staring out of one of the windows.

"Saba?" Mara said. "What is it?"

The Barabel shook her head uncertainly. "This one

feels Sekot not just on the surface of this world, but beneath it, too."

"I've been wondering about that also," Jacen said. "I'm sensing life below us as well as around and above us."

"You mean in subterranean chambers?" Mara asked.

Jacen shook his head. "In the rock itself."

"That's not as crazy as it might sound," Danni said around a mouthful of berries. "Some species of bacteria can survive a long way underground—kilometers, even. If Sekot arises out of the biological matrix covering the planet, then it seems reasonable that the life *inside* it contributes, too."

"Which might explain the planetary defense systems we saw in action," Jacen said.

"How, exactly?" Hegerty asked.

"Well, Vergere talked about biological factories making spaceships and other things," he said. "Sekot clearly found ways to use the technology the Ferroans brought with them when they colonized this world, before it became conscious. Since then, it's gone even farther. If life has spread down into the crust, and perhaps even deeper, then Sekot could conceivably manipulate the planet on a grand scale."

"You mean like building a couple of immense hyperdrives," Hegerty said.

"That," Jacen said, "but also holding the surface together during long jumps—or bending magnetic field lines at will. Jumping in and out of systems must have been fairly traumatic; without something to keep heavy radiation and gravitational effects at bay, the surface of the planet could have been totally sterilized."

"What I want to know," Mara said, "is where Sekot actually came from. If life on this scale can evolve naturally, then why isn't *every* planet talking back?"

There was no easy answer to that question.

"Perhaps there's something special about the Ferroans," Hegerty suggested.

"I'm not picking up anything radically different about them," Luke said. The Jedi Master opened his eyes, looking at each of them in turn. "They're naturally attuned to the life fields around them, but not symbiotically. That would happen to anyone born and raised in an environment as strong in the Force as Zonama Sekot."

"Perhaps it was just a random mutation," Danni said. "If the odds are against something like this happening, then that might explain why it's only happened the once."

Luke nodded thoughtfully. "It's possible. I'm sure the Magister will be able to tell us more."

Jacen hoped so. When it came to Zonama Sekot, there were too many unknown factors for his liking.

"Looks like you've made a friend," Mara said, her voice whispering close to his ear.

"What do you mean?" he asked.

She indicated the entrance with a nod. Turning, he saw that one of the little girls had returned and was staring in at him again. When she saw him look at her, she waved shyly and then quickly ducked out of sight with another giggle. Smiling, he went over to the doorway and looked around outside for her.

The girl was standing near the base of a boras, ready to flee if she had to.

"What happened to your friends?" he asked.

"They're scared," she said.

"There's no need to be," he said. He extended his open hands in a *no-weapons* gesture. "See?"

She pointed at his belt. "What about your lightsaber?"

Jacen was surprised by the girl's knowledge of the weapon, but he tried not to let it show. "You know about these?"

The girl nodded.

"And do you also know that I'm a Jedi?"

Another nod. "The older ones tell stories about the Jedi."

"What do these stories say?"

She hesitated, looking around in a manner that suggested she was worried she might be seen talking to him.

"What color is yours?" she asked.

"Color?" Then, realizing: "Oh, my lightsaber? Would you like to see it?"

She shook her head in a definite no. "They're dangerous!"

"Not in the right hands," he said. "I would never hurt you, or anyone here."

She wasn't convinced. "Jedi Knights have other ways to hurt."

"What do you mean?"

"Anakin killed the Blood Carver without a lightsaber."

That pulled Jacen up with a start, and for a few seconds he didn't know what to say.

Anakin killed the Blood Carver without a lightsaber.

The words sounded strange, no matter how many times he rolled them about in his head. How could his brother have ever come to Zonama Sekot without Jacen knowing? There was only one possible answer, and for a joyous moment Jacen entertained the hope that Anakin had somehow managed to manifest himself here in ghostly form—as had his uncle's teachers, Master Kenobi and . . .

Then the hope died as a cold feeling blossomed in his gut.

Anakin killed the Blood Carver . . .

"Tell me," he said, trying to keep the urgency out of his voice, the fear of what the truth might be. "What was the name of the other Jedi, who came here with Anakin?"

"Obi-Wan. Obi-Wan Kenobi."

The child looked at Jacen as though he were an idiot, and he wondered if that was exactly how he *should* feel.

"Tescia!"

A woman's voice rang out, and the girl jumped back with a guilty start.

"Tescia, what are you doing? I told you to stay away from there!"

With a fearful look, the girl fled, leaving Jacen standing alone in the doorway.

He watched as the girl disappeared into one of the habitats with her mother urging her on. Then, with a heavy heart and a sense of foreboding, he returned inside to relate what to the others he'd just heard.

Gilad Pellaeon surveyed the battle from the bridge of *Right to Rule*. It was going as well as could be expected. The chunk of the retreating Yuuzhan Vong fleet that he'd been chasing from Imperial Space had stumbled across Generis with eager destructiveness. He had been unsure what their intentions were until he consulted old intelligence reports and learned that Generis was a relay base for communications between the Unknown Regions and the Core. Given the Chiss's isolationist stance, it had never been targeted for sabotage by the Empire. Taken by surprise, there had been little the Imperial forces could do for the relay base. Generis had fallen, and the Yuuzhan Vong had moved immediately on to Esfandia, to repeat the insult.

Pellaeon didn't consider it anything more than that. The commander in charge of the retreat, B'shith Vorrik, wasn't a sophisticated strategist. There was little chance of a trap, or of there being a higher purpose to his strategy. The fact that Luke Skywalker had disappeared into the Unknown Regions on a secret mission just weeks earlier couldn't possibly be connected to the attack. How could Vorrik possibly know of the mission? And if someone higher up *did* know about it, why should they even care?

Pellaeon smiled to himself as the battle ebbed and flowed around him. The answer to the last question was probably the key to the mystery—if indeed there was one. Whatever Skywalker was up to, it was either totally irrelevant or absolutely integral to *everything*. There was no chance of anything in between, he was sure.

And in the meantime lay the opportunity to return the insult . . .

"Watch the northern flank," he instructed one of his senior officers, indicating a section of the battlefield where the Yuuzhan Vong were managing to regroup. "Get a yammosk jammer in there now. I want that entire side as chaotic as possible."

He was under no illusions that they would win. All they had to do was hurt Vorrik long enough to make him reconsider his attack, and/or rescue the hardware and crew aboard the relay station. If they were alive down there, then he would make sure they were found. He wasn't about to pull back until he knew for certain one way or the other.

Pellaeon frowned, still concerned by the northern flank. Despite a large injection of TIE fighters and energy fire, the Yuuzhan Vong persisted in gathering there. He didn't know what it was they were up to, but he did know he wanted it stopped.

"Put me through to Leia Organa Solo."

"I'm afraid *Millennium Falcon* has dropped off our screens, sir."

"Destroyed?" He wasn't sure what he disbelieved more: that such a thing could happen, or that he'd failed to notice it.

"Gone to ground in the atmosphere, sir. Or so we suspect. It was last seen descending toward the southern pole."

This would have placed the *Falcon* on the side of the planet farthest from where the fighting was most intense, and therefore in the best position to be overlooked. He nodded, satisfied with the assumption that the Princess and her rough-and-ready husband had plans of their own.

"Get me the commander of the Galactic Alliance frigate instead."

Within seconds, a flickering, colorless hologram of Captain Todra Mayn stood before him.

"Your orders, Admiral?"

A certain stiffness to the woman's voice assured him that past enmities between the New Republic and the Empire hadn't been completely forgotten. But she wasn't obstructing him, and that was the main thing.

"I have a mission for your strike group," he said. "Can you spare three fighters?"

She looked reluctantly at the displays before her. "We will if required to, sir."

"But you don't wish to?" he asked.

A flicker of uncertainty passed across her face. "To be honest, sir, we're doing some damage on that warship. With just half a squadron to watch our back, I'm not sure we'd be able to effectively keep up the attack."

"Don't worry," he said. "I'll make sure you get backup."

Pellaeon gestured to an aide and instructed her to assign a full TIE squadron to *Pride of Selonia*. Then he returned his attention to Mayn.

"So, Captain, do you think Galactic Alliance, Chiss, and Empire can work together?"

"I guess we'll find out soon enough, sir," she said. "I'll instruct Colonel Fel to take his orders directly from you."

"Very good. Carry on, Captain."

The woman nodded a little less stiffly than before, and the transmission ended.

Pellaeon turned back to the fighting.

"Connect me to Colonel Fel," he instructed his aide.

"Twin One," came the almost instantaneous reply.

"Colonel, I have a mission for three of your best pilots," he said. "The northern flank is proving resistant to our tactics. I'd like you to reinforce the message we're trying to deliver."

"Yes, sir."

"There's a yammosk in there somewhere. We haven't been able to get close enough to find it yet, but we're working on it. When we do locate it, I'd like you to keep it distracted. I want it out of the picture."

"Understood, sir." There was a slight pause. "Any further instructions, Admiral?"

"Such as?"

"Approach vectors, rendezvous coordinates, attack runs—"

Pellaeon smiled. "Why don't you just surprise me, Colonel?"

Jag frowned behind the controls of his clawcraft.

"*Surprise* you, sir?"

For a moment, Jag swore the Admiral was chuckling—but that simply couldn't be possible. Grand Admiral Pellaeon—who had served under Thrawn, and who had almost single-handedly prevented the Imperial Remnant from flying apart in a thousand fragments—was not renowned for his sense of humor.

"Do you have a problem with that, Colonel?"

"No, sir. I just—"

"Then carry out your orders. We don't have time to debate the matter."

The line fell silent, and Jag was left shaking his head. *Surprise me.*

Those two words were anathema to everything he'd been taught at the Chiss academy, and that the Imperials to a lesser degree espoused. Not only was it dangerous to identify personally with one's role in a battle, but an orderly, coordinated offensive was the only way to ensure that such a large operation could work effectively. Let every pilot go rogue and follow his instincts, and the battle would quickly degenerate into chaos.

But it wasn't every pilot, he told himself.

Surprise me.

It was a challenge. His response wouldn't prove just his own worth, but the worth of the Alliance and the Chiss forces as well.

The legendary Grand Admiral Pellaeon had asked him for a *surprise*. He had an idea where to start:

What would Jaina *do?*

He pondered this while he got the basics out of the way, informing Captain Mayn of his decision to leave Twin Suns in Twin Seven's capable hands. She confirmed her new role with a simple affirmative. With Twins Four and Eight trailing him, Jag swept away from the dogfights taking place in the vicinity of the *Selonia*.

Telemetry flowed in from the Imperial forces. They were fighting on numerous fronts simultaneously, doing their best to keep the Yuuzhan Vong distracted from the relay base below. A large amount of wreckage—ranging from microscopic dust fragments in boiling clouds to drifting hulks, their biological systems spewing fluids and sweeping the space around them with strange gravitational storms as their dovin basals expired—had accumulated in the space around Esfandia. Some of it was already falling into the atmosphere, slashing the dark, icy sky with brilliant streaks. Jag only hoped the *Falcon* knew well enough to keep its head down.

Surprise me.

A Yuuzhan Vong corvette and a cruiser analog, hugging the planet jealously in a low orbit, dominated the northern flank. Presumably the yammosk was in one of those two ships. Swarms of coralskippers were gathering to them like nanja flies to a thawing corpse. Outnumbered four to one, Imperial TIE fighters did their best to keep the alien warriors from gaining a foothold. Once they got themselves organized, Pellaeon's second Star Destroyer, *Relentless*, would become vulnerable on that side, as would the planet itself and the relay base with it. As it was, Pellaeon was only just managing to hang on and avoid the Yuuzhan Vong pinning him down, and ending the battle once and for all. And if the relay base was taken out, the battle itself would become altogether meaningless.

Jag could see the importance of securing that section of the battleground. But sending three fighters against a cruiser, a corvette, and countless fighters was madness of the first order. What was he supposed to do? Ram the cruiser? He'd be lucky to get past the dovin basals! And even if he did, what would the momentum of one small starfighter do against a ship of that size?

What would Jaina do? he asked himself again, forcing himself to think laterally.

Then, unexpectedly, a creeping sense of unreality spread over him. An idea had formed in his mind. A crazy and reckless idea that seemed perfectly fitting. It certainly wasn't the sort of tactic he'd have normally employed. It was, for all intents and purposes, *surprising*.

"Jocell," he called to Twin Four, deliberately dropping the formalities now that it was just the three of them. "You in the mood to pick a fight?"

"Not sure exactly what you mean by that, sir," she replied uneasily. "But I'm always ready."

"Not just any fight." He scanned the region around the northern flank. There: a dead gunship, drifting like a

lost asteroid, its biological systems slowly dying. Half
the ship was black with fire; the other half radiated heat by
the terawatt out into the sunless vacuum, chilling rapidly
in the process. It was moving in an elliptical orbit that
would take it in the direction he wanted. He nudged his
vector minutely closer to it, and his wingmates obedi-
ently, and unquestioningly, followed.

"Now all we need are some skips."

"I take it you have something in mind, sir?" asked Enton Adelmaa'j in Twin Eight.

"I do," he replied. He couldn't quite believe it himself,
so there was no point in attempting to explain it to them
just yet. "Behave as normal, and don't be surprised if I go
into a spin for no reason. Just cover me, okay? Make
sure nothing picks me off while I'm playing dead."

"What if you *are* dead? How will we tell the
difference?"

"In the long run, I think you'll know."

He quickly double-checked the calculations. Yes, this
could work. He wasn't used to relying on chance, but he
was prepared to make an exception here, and the idea of
that gave him an unaccountable thrill. Not just because
he would be surprising Pellaeon, either: it was also because he was surprising himself.

As he angled his flight toward a knot of coralskippers
harrying a nearby Imperial squadron, he sent his thoughts
out to Jaina. He wasn't Force-sensitive and he doubted
she could hear him, but he was sure she'd understand.

Wish me luck, Jaina.

Then, gunning his engines, he swooped in to attack.

Jaina struggled through blackness. She had never experienced a mind-meld like this before. It was as though
she were trying to swim through mud. The normally
bright center of Tahiri's mind was muffled and distant,
buried.

"Tahiri?" She called her friend's name as she searched for that bright center. Occasional flashes of memory and emotions lunged out of the blackness, startling her. She saw two figures dueling in a place that looked disturbingly familiar, glimpsed as though on a fogged screen. Then she saw those figures running, possibly hunting, lightsabers slicing bright swaths through the fetid air. The light they cast confirmed her first impressions. Even with the prominence of shadows around them, she could tell where they were: it was the worldship around Myrkr; it was the place where Anakin was killed.

Vast statues loomed over them, offering razor-tipped tentacles in return for devotion; deep shadows hid hints of voxynlike monsters, and the air stank of death and grief. The moment she'd melded with Tahiri's mind and stepped into the young Jedi's private torment, Jaina had been inundated with memories of the pain she'd felt when Anakin had died, and the grief she had endured afterward. The inner landscape reflected all of these dark emotions back at her; every craggy shadow seemed to emanate all manner of negative emotion: grief, anger, fear, betrayal, loneliness . . .

These were all things she couldn't allow herself to be distracted by, though. She had to stay focused, to help as she could. She could play no role in whatever fantasy Tahiri was embroiled in, but she could offer strength.

As another image flashed through the darkness, though, she wondered whom exactly she was giving strength *to*.

Tahiri's scarred, grim-faced mirror image had murder in her eyes. Although Jaina knew it to be Riina whom Tahiri was fighting, or hunting, she kept seeing Tahiri. The only way to separate them was by the hand that held the lightsaber: in the real world Tahiri was left-handed, while Riina held hers in her right hand.

"Tahiri? Can you hear me?"

Jaina wanted Tahiri to know that she wasn't alone; that help was at hand if she needed it.

Grishna br'rok ukul-hai, a voice snarled in her mind. *Hrrl osam'ga akren hu—akri vushta.*

"I don't understand," Jaina said into the void.

An image came of Tahiri's face lunging out of the darkness, eyes glaring with hate. She flinched. Not for the first time, Jaina wondered if she was out of her depth. Psychic healing was Master Cilghal's field, not hers. Her intentions were good, but that wasn't enough.

I think it's time to get out of here, she thought.

When she attempted to break the meld, however, she found that she couldn't. The illusion of the worldship seemed to close in around her like the walls of a cage, and she realized with alarm that she was trapped.

Ash'nagh vruckuul urukh, mocked the voice of Riina from the shadows. *Esh tiiri ahnakh!*

Jaina saw an image of Tahiri hunting her shadow flashing out of the void. Jaina quelled a sense of dread and frustration rising in her. There had to be something she could do. She just hoped she could find it in time . . .

Luke's thoughts should have been clear when the time came for the meeting with the Magister, but instead they were an untidy tangle. Ever since Jacen had told him about his encounter with the young Ferroan girl, that was all he'd been able to think about.

Anakin killed the Blood Carver without a lightsaber . . .

He could understand Jacen's initial confusion. At first he, too, had assumed that Tescia had meant Anakin Solo. But he knew that wasn't possible. Luke's youngest nephew had never come to the Unknown Regions, and he certainly couldn't have kept his encounter with a living planet a secret if he had. No, the girl had clearly been referring to Luke's father. Before Zonama Sekot had vanished into the Unknown Regions, Anakin Skywalker must have come here—and he'd come with Obi-Wan Kenobi. Why they had done so, though, Luke couldn't imagine. To look for Vergere, perhaps? In search of the same thing she'd been after: the planet's biological technology? And what had happened to them here? What did it mean that the boy had killed a Blood Carver without using a lightsaber? That he had used the power of the dark side?

Without more information, it was all just speculation. Nevertheless, he found it difficult to turn his thoughts away from the matter. His mind was still spinning with possibilities when Darak and Rowel finally came to inform them all that it was time.

Luke took a deep, calming breath and let himself be led with the others from the habitat. Night had fallen, turning the tampasi into a vast, starless space that chattered with half-heard rustlings and strange calls from unseen animals. The only light came from balls of bioluminescence balancing atop slender stalks. Standing a meter taller than Luke, they cast a bright greenish glow across the undergrowth. A double row of these lightstalks led a path around the bulk of a nearby tree, a path that Darak and Rowel took them along without ceremony or conversation. Far above, where they'd been tethered for the night, the massive shapes of the kyboes shifted restlessly in their sleep.

The light-stalk path wound through the trees for several hundred meters before culminating in a large, bowl-shaped depression. There, gathered in a circle, a dozen Ferroans awaited them. Standing in the center of these was the black-robed figure of the Magister. She bowed her black-maned head respectfully as they entered the natural amphitheater. The Ferroans—four men and eight women—offered no such gesture; they just stared at the visitors with undisguised suspicion and hostility.

Darak and Rowel guided the group to the center of the

depression, then stepped back to stand symbolically at the end of the path that had brought them there. The Ferroans now surrounded them: to leave the meeting place they would have to break the circle.

When all was still, the Magister spoke.

"Once again the Jedi come to us," she said. Her voice was soft, like a cool breeze on a hot night, but it carried clearly to those gathered around her. "As always, you bring more questions than answers."

"We are here to answer those questions," Luke said, wondering why the Magister looked different. Her presence in the Force was strong, but much more muted than it had been on the landing field. The impression nagged at him, even as he put it aside to concentrate on the conversation. "There are many we would ask of you, too."

She inclined her head slightly, then straightened. "There are some among the council who would have me ask Sekot to send you away immediately. You come to us, by your own admission, as harbingers of doom. I have heard it said that you are more than that; that you bring a direct and deliberate threat to us and to our way of life."

"What do you mean?" Jacen asked. "We haven't made any threats. We mean no harm."

"Three times, now, we have had to defend ourselves," the Magister explained, "and each time Jedi were present. You cannot blame us for wondering: is it the circumstances that attract you, or are the circumstances a result of your visits?"

"Magister," Luke said, "if these attacks upon you are in any way connected to our being here, then I assure you it is unintentional on our part. The Far Outsiders arrived before us; we had no idea they would be here until we arrived. Their presence here is a mystery to us. Perhaps we can solve it together, if you allow us to."

"How would you have us do that?"

"We begin by talking. As I have said before, we are here to discuss our common enemy—the ones we refer to as Yuuzhan Vong. It is a long story, but perhaps in its telling you will come to see the truth of what I say—and the sincerity of our intentions."

The Magister pondered this for a long moment. Again Luke sensed a fundamental difference between their first meeting and the present. Where before she had been curious about the Jedi, welcoming them cheerfully and openly, now she seemed wary and protective. He wondered what had changed her mind.

Her gaze swept the visitors gathered before her. With a slight nod, she seemed to come to a decision. Her legs folded beneath her and she sank gracefully to the ground. Her robe pooled around her on the soft undergrowth.

"My name is Jabitha," she said. "We shall hear your story." She indicated for Luke and the others to likewise sit upon the grass. The other Ferroans, perhaps pointedly, remained standing. "Sekot invites you to talk freely."

Luke took a deep breath, and began. He started from the time the Yuuzhan Vong had first come to the attention of the New Republic on Belkadan, when Danni Quee had witnessed the launch of their invasion. The grim progression of the war was burned in his mind: from Sernpidal, where Chewbacca died, to Helska 4, Dubrillion, Destrillion, Dantooine, Bimmiel, Garqi, Ithor, Obroa-skai, Ord Mantell, Gyndine, Tynna, Fondor and its shipyards; Kalarba, Nal Hutta, Nar Shadaa, Sriluur, Druckenwell, Rodia, Falleen, Kubindi, Duro; the Jedi academy lost with Yavin 4, Ando, Myrkyr, where Anakin Solo fell, and Coruscant, the capital, where for a while all hope seemed lost.

He talked about the hundreds of billions of deaths across the galaxy, trying to capture in words how it felt to watch everything he had loved slip away—not just the government he'd helped form from the ashes of the Empire, but also the principles on which it had been based. As the Senate had dissolved into bureaucracy and corruption during the last days on Coruscant, he had seen former allies turn against each other, driven by fear and self-preservation—but in the end only hastening the Yuuzhan Vong's steady march.

He talked about biological technologies, and the Yuuzhan Vong's philosophy of pain and sacrifice. He described worlds succumbing to insidious growths, free people plucked from their homes and turned into blaster fodder, spies sent to disrupt the peace by spreading lies about those encouraging the survivors to band together against the enemy. He talked of desperation and of genocide, of plans to end the oppression that were rooted in the very same evils, of the Jedi's hope to find a middle ground, to keep the people of the Galactic Alliance free of the stain of mass murder. He spoke of his love for Ben, and his hope that his son might one day grow to know a peaceful life in a galaxy in which war was not the norm.

"What does this have to do with Zonama Sekot?" the Magister, Jabitha, asked when Luke had finished. "What is it that brings you here, so far from your home, from your war?"

Jacen took up the thread of the story to answer her question.

"We have come here because my teacher, Vergere, advised that the answer to our problems might lie on Zonama Sekot." He described their mission to find the living planet through the Unknown Regions, not omitting the defense of the Empire or the tense internal conflict in the Chiss territories. He followed their path through the Chiss library, tracing legends and folktales of the wandering planet. He successfully evoked the despair they'd felt when it seemed that the living world might slip through their fingers, despite their best efforts. The realization that Zonama Sekot might be masquerading as a moon rather than an independent planet, he told Jabitha, had been the key to resolving the mystery. The location finally found, they'd set off immediately from Csilla to find their objective.

At the conclusion of his speech, Jabitha frowned, confused, and shook her head. "But this still does not explain why you are here. In what way did Vergere expect us to be able to help you?"

"That's what we're here to find out," Mara said. Luke could feel her impatience kept carefully in check. The attitude of the Ferroans had rankled her from the start, but he trusted her not to say anything precipitous.

"We are but one world with a small population," Jabitha said. "What can we do against this invading horde you have described? Our strength lies in defense, not offense."

"That may be so," Danni said, "but if we'd had your defenses at our disposal in the first place, we may have stood a better chance of repelling the Yuuzhan Vong at the borders of the galaxy."

The Magister's frown deepened. "Your words make it sound as though Zonama Sekot is all-powerful. But this is not so. Although it did once manage to repel the Far Outsiders, it was not without suffering major damage to itself. The attack traumatized it greatly. Our defenses are not impenetrable." She looked down at her feet, then back at Luke. "You should know that the conflict you witnessed has also scarred Sekot deeply, mentally if not physically. The appearance of the Far Outsiders came as a terrible shock. Sekot was not anticipating them; there was no reason to suspect that they were nearby. They tried to study us without being noticed, but our sensors are acute. Sekot's defenses were activated, and the Far Outsiders took that as an aggressive reaction. They, too, reacted defensively. It is not clear who struck the first blow. The conflict was sparked by fear and uncertainty, as many conflicts are. We do not wish to be party to another such conflict."

"I understand," Luke said, although there was much about the situation that remained mysterious. He had assumed that the Yuuzhan Vong had opened fire on the living planet, as they had once before. "We would not want to place Sekot in any more peril than it already faces. But you must be aware that you are in peril already. The Yuuzhan Vong have stumbled across Zonama Sekot twice now, on different sides of the galaxy. They are not so many that this could have happened by chance." Although he lacked hard evidence to back up the claim, Luke pressed on with the point. "They must be looking for you—and they will keep looking until they find you again. If so much as one ship survived the fleet that found you this time, they will descend upon you en masse, and you won't be able to defend yourselves."

The Ferroans shifted restlessly, unnerved by the image, but Jabitha didn't flinch from it.

"And what would you have us do?" the Magister asked Luke. "You speak of consciences, of right and wrong, and of the horrors perpetrated upon you and the galaxy by the Far Outsiders. You speak of their wish for genocide. And yet, do you not wish the same for them? Do you not wish *them* removed from the galaxy as they wish you?"

"Absolutely not," Luke said. "We have, in fact, fought hard to prevent just such an outcome," he added, the horror of the Alpha Red virus still fresh in his mind.

"The Yuuzhan Vong aren't all warriors," Jacen said. "They are women and children, too. They are slaves, and outcasts, and scientists, and workers. They have as much right to life as we do. There is no question about that."

"Then why have you come here? What possible help can we give you?"

"We must work together to find that out," Luke said.

"*Must?*" Jabitha echoed. "It is true that all have a right to life. It is also true that everyone must decide what to do with it. Sekot chose to distance itself from the rest of the galaxy when our attempts to trade peacefully were met by aggression and suspicion. We have suffered greatly to find peace. Why must we suffer again on behalf of those who do not have the fortitude to free themselves?"

"Because the living Force requires it," Jacen said.

Jabitha's eyes flashed at Jacen. "What is that? *You* dare presume to speak for the Force?"

Silence fell around the amphitheater. The air was thick with tension. Luke could feel the situation rapidly slipping from their control. In the hope of rekindling the welcome they had first received from the Magister, he decided to try another tack.

"You say that you have been attacked three times," he said. "We know of two instances, both perpetrated by the Yuuzhan Vong. Were they behind the third, too?"

"No," the Magister said. "That force consisted of forces of the Republic, led by a Commander Tarkin."

Luke's eyebrows raised slightly. *That* was a name from the past he recognized only too well. "Is that when you fled? When you went into hiding?"

"Yes."

"And that was the same time the Jedi were last here?" he persisted. "After Vergere's visit?"

"Yes."

Luke detected a slight softening of Jabitha's expression. That was the encouragement he had been hoping for.

"Tell me about them," he said. "Tell me about Anakin Skywalker and Obi-Wan Kenobi."

The silence seemed to stretch forever. It felt to Luke as though everyone had stopped breathing. Even the soft night breeze rustling through the branches above seemed to stop.

"They came looking for Vergere," Jabitha said eventually. "And they came out of curiosity, wondering at the living ships we once sold to a select few. Under the guise of clienthood, they passed a testing ritual designed to see if they were suitable for partnership with one of our ships. The youngest, Anakin, was a mystery to us all. Normally, during the ritual, three or so seed-partners would bond with the client to form the basis of a new ship. Anakin drew *twelve* to him. His ship was a thing of beauty." Jabitha paused, her gaze distant as though recalling long-forgotten times. "The Force shone brightly in Anakin. He was, briefly, my friend."

A strange feeling crawled into Luke's stomach. "You met him?"

"He saved my life," she answered. "And he revealed to me the truth about my father."

The words that Jacen had told him about the Blood Carver once again echoed in Luke's mind.

"There was a Blood Carver," he prompted.

"An assassin sent to kill Anakin," Jabitha explained, nodding. "He used me to gain leverage over Anakin, and Anakin became very angry. He killed with the strength of his mind. Until that moment, we had not known that such things were possible."

"They are possible," Luke said, ignoring the emotions pouring through him at the revelations concerning his father, "but killing out of anger is wrong. The power of the dark side is seductive and dangerous. The Jedi have never countenanced its use."

"Yet Anakin used it."

Luke tried to find the words that might easiest convey

Anakin Skywalker's fate. "It came at a cost," he said after some reflection.

Her gaze focused on him, sharp as a Tusken Raider's gaderffii. "You are his son, aren't you? And I don't just mean that because you share the same name. He is *in* you." She faced Jacen. "And you, too."

"He was my grandfather," Jacen said; Luke just nodded.

"Sekot recognized the echoes of my friend in you both when you came here. That is in part why you were allowed to land. But you dismiss Anakin's actions as though they were an aberration, a mistake. We do not remember them that way. He loved our world, and we will not allow anything you say to damn his memory."

"The dark side is the dark side," Mara pronounced. "If you'd met Luke's father when he was older, you wouldn't be so quick to defend him."

"That Anakin did what he did out of good is more important to us than the means he chose. He was a *child*, and you will not damn him for that here. He *saved* me."

Luke countered her defensiveness with a calming gesture. "It is true that I once abhorred all my father stood for, but I have not held such thoughts in a long time. You see, he saved me, too, when the Emperor, his Sith Master, tried to kill me. I no longer wish his spirit ill will; his name lived on through my family, who found no shame in it. I would count a friend of Anakin Skywalker a friend of mine, were I permitted to." He held Jabitha's gaze without flinching. "But the shadow of Darth Vader, the man he became when he embraced the dark side, still hangs heavily over us. We have fought long and hard to free ourselves from his oppression—and we will not succumb to the same mistake he made in order to fight the Yuuzhan Vong. That would make a mockery of everything my father stood for, at the beginning and end of his life."

Jabitha bowed her head in acknowledgment of his

short speech, but whether he'd convinced her or not was uncertain.

"It is late," she said. "You have had a long journey and must be tired. If you will allow us, we will provide you with shelter for the night."

Luke felt disheartened. "Does that mean that our discussions are at an end?"

"I need time to talk with the council." Jabitha indicated the ring of stony-faced Ferroans standing around them. "We will take into consideration all that has been said here this night and decide whether or not there is anything more to discuss."

"Then I advise you to consider very carefully," Mara said. "The Yuuzhan Vong don't keep treaties, and they don't take prisoners. If they do overrun this galaxy, then they will ultimately destroy you, too. No matter how powerful Sekot thinks it is, no matter how far it runs, it won't be able to hold them off forever. And it'll be too late then to look for allies, because we'll all be dead."

"My wife's words are blunt, but truthful," Luke said. "If you have any doubts about the Yuuzhan Vong's motives, we can show you the history of the war in more detail."

"That won't be necessary," Jabitha said. "We feel that we understand the nature of your foe well enough." The Magister's expression was one of great weariness, and again Luke was struck by how different she seemed from their first meeting. Then she had been vital and energetic; now she looked tired, drained.

"We will talk again in the morning," she said, standing and indicating that they should, too.

With a gesture, Darak and Rowel stepped back, offering an exit from the circle. Luke would have liked to say more, but he knew that to push now would be to jeopardize their chances with the Magister. So he inclined his head slightly in a tight, polite bow and led the way from the natural amphitheater. The others followed suit. Once they were clear of the circle, the Ferroans silently closed up behind them. Looking back, Luke saw Jabitha standing again in the middle, her eyes seeing worlds he doubted he could even hope to comprehend.

Tahiri rocked back on her heels as her mirror image abruptly spun around and confronted her.

It's here!

What is?

The shadow!

Tahiri looked around her, but could see nothing. She and Riina were momentarily united by their mutual fear of the thing that had come for them. Tahiri felt her strength leach out of her at the thought of coming face to face with it. She was tired of fighting. If she let go now, she might finally join Anakin in another world, another life. And perhaps in that other life he could find a way to forgive her . . .

You could help me fight it, Riina whispered close to her ear. *Stand and help me kill it.*

How? . . . Tahiri started, but didn't know how to finish the question.

You fought before, Riina said. *You held your own against me. You are strong.*

Tahiri shook her head. She wasn't a warrior at heart. She'd tried to be one once, but it had cost her the one thing she'd truly loved. It had cost her Anakin; it had cost her a *family.*

I was never strong enough to destroy you, she said. *I could only bury you.*

You weren't trying to destroy me, Riina said. *You were trying to destroy yourself.*

Tahiri wanted to deny the accusation. But the scars on her arm burned in support of Riina's argument.

And you know I can never let you do that, Riina said.

Why not? Tahiri asked, her face flushing with shame.

Because I don't want to die with you.

But you're already dead! You are a cold and cruel death that constantly sits inside me!

And you are the cold death that envelops me, Riina responded, her words in Tahiri's ear as rough as a sandstorm. *We are bound together, you and I. This is a fate we must accept.*

I accept nothing!

Riina stepped up to Tahiri, her footsteps sounding loud in the hollow silence that had descended around them.

Don't you think I would give you the death you desire if I could? Riina said. *But we are bound together. You must see that! I could no more live in this body without you than you could without me. I cannot give you death without embracing it myself—and I am not ready to do that!*

Tahiri felt her world shifting around her. She wanted the words to refute Riina's claim, but in the end there were none.

This can't be happening, was all she could manage in way of a defense.

It is, Riina said. *And you must accept it.*

Tahiri shook her head. *I can't.*

Then you leave me no choice.

Riina took two steps back and raised her lightsaber horizontally in front of her. Tahiri tensed in anticipation of a blow that never came. Instead, Riina's blade flashed upward, spinning high into the blackness and casting a bright blue light across the surrounding ruins, causing shadows to dance around them. Openmouthed, Tahiri followed the lightsaber's flight in fearful silence.

As the blade came down again, Riina reached out to catch it. Tahiri could tell straight away that the Yuuzhan

Vong girl had misjudged the descent, but she seemed incapable of calling out to warn her. She just stood mutely watching on as the bright blue blade slashed Riina's hand and then clattered to the floor.

Then, from somewhere far away, almost smothered by a terrible, blinding pain, Tahiri heard herself scream.

C-3PO cocked his golden head.

"You hear that?" Han asked.

"Of course, sir," the droid said. "The signal is quite clear."

"We haven't been able to locate a source yet; the atmosphere appears to be carrying it a long way, and spreading it out in the process. But the important thing is, can you translate it? And don't bother telling me how many languages you speak. The only person in the room who hasn't already heard that spiel a thousand times is Droma, and he's not easily impressed."

"As you wish, sir."

Leia suppressed a half smile as C-3PO nodded stiffly. The warbling transmission issued from the cockpit speakers with liquid clarity. *Millennium Falcon*'s audio scrubbers had managed to remove much of the background hiss, along with the increasing electromagnetic noise from the battle taking place above the planet. If C-3PO couldn't translate it, no one could.

While the droid was busy with this task, Han angled the *Falcon* up and over a ridge, diving deep into another trench. Droma, in the copilot's seat, fired a concussion missile at a distant mountain, in the hope that the resulting explosion would cover their tracks. Thus far there had been no attempt to interfere with their progress across the surface of Esfandia, so they had to assume that the tactic had thus far worked.

But there had been no sign of the relay base, either. Wherever it was, it had dug in deep and wasn't moving.

"The transmission appears to be in a very strange form of trinary machine language," C-3PO said, his glowing photoreceptors gazing off into distant semantic landscapes. "The grammar is inconsistent, and the vocabulary quite peculiar. I am quite certain, though, that this is the source language."

"Is it coming from the relay base?" Han asked over his shoulder.

"I don't think that's terribly likely, sir," the droid said. "Not unless it has taken to talking to itself."

"There's more than one signal?" Leia asked.

"I have identified at least seventeen."

"*Seventeen?*" Han repeated. "That's impossible."

"They could be decoys," Droma suggested, "laid out across the surface to misdirect the search."

"What's the point of that if you can't find a single decoy? The way the atmosphere spreads these frequencies, we'd be lucky to bump into *one* by accident."

Droma shrugged. "It'd keep us busy, though. And the Yuuzhan Vong."

Leia thought of the strange, flowerlike formations the *Falcon* had passed through earlier, and an uneasy thought suddenly occurred to her . . .

"These transmissions," she said. "Are they all using an identical variation on that trinary code?"

"No, Mistress. Each transmissions source has its own unique variation."

"What's the point of that?" Han said.

Leia waved him silent. "And what are they talking about, exactly?"

"It's difficult to say with any precision. Some of the nouns are unfamiliar to me, and the modifiers have mutated in ways that defy—"

"Your best guess will do," Han interrupted.

"There seems to be a lot of talk about the battle," the

droid returned after listening to the signals for a few seconds. "The atmospheric disturbances are severe in some areas, and it would appear that the local flora has suffered catastrophic damage."

"Did you say *flora*?"

"Indeed, sir. The ecosystem of this world is another major topic of conversation, particularly among those whose food supplies have been threatened."

"Food supplies—?" Han glanced at the forward viewport. It was black and lifeless outside. Even using enhanced vision, the surface showed no obvious signs of any biological activity. "Are you saying that the things making these signals are *alive*?"

"Why, yes, sir. I had assumed you already suspected this."

"But how is that possible in an environment like this?"

"Life has been found before in atmospheres of similar constitution, sir," C-3PO lectured. "It could have evolved here in the planet's early days, when the heat from the core was much more intense. Single-celled lifeforms could easily have evolved, perhaps larger organisms also."

"But you're talking intelligent life," Han protested. "Things that can *talk*!"

"Indeed, sir. It is also possible that these life-forms are not indigenous to Esfandia."

"They could have been imported here?" Leia asked. "Where from?"

"From wherever it was they evolved, Princess."

Han raised his hands in frustration. He looked at Droma as though for support.

"I guess it makes sense," the Ryn said. "If life was going to exist here, it would have to be scattered; a low-energy world couldn't support too dense a population. They would have to use a form of communication that could reach long distances, and comm frequencies give them that."

"But *trinary* code?"

"I think someone taught them to speak that way," Leia said.

Han's eyes narrowed thoughtfully. "Someone on the relay team?"

"Past, if not present. The language has had time to change, after all." She turned to C-3PO. "Do you think we could communicate with these creatures?"

"I can see no reason why not, Princess. We know the frequencies upon which they communicate, and I am fluent in an approximate version of their language."

He leaned forward to speak into the communicator.

"Low power only," Han said, letting the droid through. "And if they can't tell us anything about the relay base, we're not going to sit here and chat. We're not the only ones listening."

C-3PO performed the droid equivalent of clearing his throat, then warbled a series of strange, fluting tones into Esfandia's dense atmosphere. Leia tried to discern a pattern to it, but it was pointless. To her ears it sounded like three deranged flutists bickering over which melody to play.

When it was done, C-3PO straightened in satisfaction.

"I have broadcast a request for information on the location of the vrgrlmrl."

"Verger-*what*?" Han said.

"Vrgrlmrl: the relay base," C-3PO repeated casually, the burbling phrase rolling effortlessly from his vocal box. "If they reply, we will know—"

He paused as a stronger signal from the comm filled the cabin.

"Oh, my," the droid said, looking almost anxiously to the others around him. "I fear something got lost in translation. They misunderstood my request for information as an invitation."

"An invitation to what?" Han asked.

"I'm not sure. But if I may try again, sir, I might—"

"Spare us the details," Han said. "Just get them talking."

C-3PO burbled out another string of nonsensical sounds. The reply was immediate, although this time it was as if multiple voices had joined the conversation. And if before it had sounded like three flutists bickering, now it sounded like the entire orchestra had gotten involved in the argument.

Droma had his hands over his ears in a vain attempt to keep the cacophony out. "I haven't heard anything like this since I attended a benefit for a tone-deaf Pa'lowick— and boy, those guys could wail."

"Are you getting anything useful?" Han asked, rapping on C-3PO's bronzed casing.

The droid broke off his conversation. "Indeed, sir. For the most part the Brrbrlpp, as they call themselves, are a sociable species, and are happy to talk. They are familiar with the relay base, but will not reveal its location until they are certain we mean it no harm."

"Well, then, what are you waiting for? Reassure them, already."

"I have already done so, sir, but I'm afraid it will take more than that to convince them." C-3PO hesitated, looking to each person in the cockpit.

"What is it, Threepio?" Leia asked.

"Well, Princess, it seems that in the eyes of the Brrbrlpp, we are murderers and therefore untrustworthy."

"Murderers?" Han rasped. "We're not the ones bombarding their planet. We're trying to stop it!"

"It's not the bombardment that concerns them, sir. They claim that we have killed fifteen of their people since we arrived."

"What? When are we supposed to have done that?"

"They say that the voices of their friends were silenced when we crossed their paths."

With a sickening sensation, Leia thought again of the strange flower shapes that had brushed by the *Falcon*, dissolving in the freighter's turbulent, superheated wake.

"Stop the engines," she told her husband.

"What? Leia, you can't be—"

"Do it, Han," she insisted. "Switch off the repulsors—*everything*. Do it now before we kill someone else!"

Han complied, although it was clear from the expression on his face he didn't understand why. The *Falcon* settled slowly to the bottom of the trench, and when a quiet had washed over the ship, Leia explained her theory of what these aliens were.

"We didn't know," Han said, pale-faced at the idea of having inadvertently killed so many intelligent beings. "Tell them that, Threepio. Explain to them that there was no way we *could* have known."

"I will try, sir, but I don't think it will make much difference to their feelings toward us."

"There has to be something we can say to change their minds."

Leia put a hand on her husband's shoulder as, out of the darkness, one of the flower shapes drifted toward them. Now that she could see it properly, she saw how its edges rippled to provide motion, moving it through the atmosphere. A ring of photosensors studded its interior, along with radial lines of swirling cilia. Behind the cilia, through the creature's semitransparent flesh, she could see a complicated skeleton keeping the alien's "petals" rigid, as well as gently pulsing darker patches that might have been internal organs. And behind all that, tapering off into the distance, was a long, whiplike tail.

There was no sense of up or down, or of a face, and yet she knew it was watching them.

"Can they hurt us?" Droma whispered, as though worried the creature might overhear him.

"I doubt it," Han said, but he didn't sound confident.

Leia felt a faint rippling through the Force as a second alien joined the first. It was in turn quickly joined by a third. There was no doubt now that they were alive. More came, wafting in on the heavy currents of Esfandia's atmosphere, until the ship was surrounded by a ring of mysterious flowers.

We killed their friends, she thought bitterly to herself. *We killed their family.*

Somehow she didn't think that *sorry* was about to make up for that.

Saba smelled the thunderstorm long before she heard it. Her sensitive nostrils twitched at the moisture on the air, filtered through the tampasi and redolent with spores and sap. Within minutes she could hear rain sweeping across the treetops, driven at a sharp angle by powerful, gusting winds. Before long she could hear the sound of the water escaping the boras leaves high above and trickling down in streams to the ground.

The Ferroans had provided their guests with rolled-up sleeping pads and thick, coarse blankets. Following a light supper, Jacen, Danni, and Mara had decided to take advantage of the situation and rest, while Master Skywalker and Doctor Hegerty stayed up to talk. Saba stayed awake, also, despite being tired. She still didn't completely trust their hosts, and wanted to keep watch for the others. She remained on her pad the entire time, with eyes closed and ears opened, listening to everything happening around her—including the conversation between Master Skywalker and Hegerty.

"—mentioned the Potentium to Jacen," Master Skywalker was saying. "She didn't give him many details, though, and I've never heard of it. Have you?"

"No," the elderly human scholar replied. "But mind you, the study of the Force isn't really my field."

"What about the Ferroans, then? Is there anything about them you think I should know?"

"Well, I'm sure you've noticed their intolerance toward us," the doctor said. "Not that I can blame their suspicion. They've been contacted by strangers six times that we know of: three times by Jedi, including us; twice by the Yuuzhan Vong; and once by Tarkin and his Old Republic forces. Three times they've been attacked, and each time it happened, the Jedi were there. Once you could forget; twice you could forgive; but *three times*?"

"I know what you mean," Luke said. "I can't blame them, either, for thinking that way. But it's our job to change their minds. Otherwise this whole quest will have been a waste of time."

Rain crackled gently on the roof of the mushroomlike habitat, although inside was warm and dry. Saba could feel faint tendrils of life trickling through its capillaries. It seemed to like the rain, and much of the warmth was generated as a result of the pleasure it felt.

They talked further, but Saba was finding herself more and more seduced by exhaustion and the notion of sleep. Nearby she could make out the restive breathing of those sleeping around her, and she found herself soothed by the rhythm along with the rain on the rooftop. She fought the sleep for a moment longer, feeling that perhaps she should continue to keep alert for the others. But then, Master Skywalker was still awake, and he was more than able to keep an eye out for everyone's well-being. There really was no reason to stay alert . . .

Jag took the shot on his port shields and stuttered his engines as though he'd been hit. His clawcraft went into a wild tumble, careening dangerously across the battlefield. Stars slewed around him in a disorienting tangle, and he had to rely on his instincts in ways rarely called upon to make sure he was heading in the right direction. Only when the scarred bulk of the dead gunship loomed vertiginously over him did he kill the illusion—and then just for a split second.

Everything depended on him being able to convince those that saw him that his "death roll" was genuine, while at the same time maintaining enough control over his ship to ensure he wasn't actually killed.

A fraction of a second before colliding with the gunship, he fired his laser cannons. The resulting explosion boiled yorik coral in a great plume from the gunship, enveloping him in fire and debris. For a brief moment, he was actually cushioned by the blast—a situation he had initially feared might be untenable, until he checked the rating on his shields and found that they could take it. Inertial dampeners soaked up his residual momentum and brought him and his clawcraft to a creaking halt deep within the hull of the ruined gunship.

It had been a rough ride, and it took him a minute to get himself back together and make sure everything was still in one piece. His shields were recharging, the body of his starfighter was still rigid, and his weapons systems were still working. So far, so good.

The view through his forward canopy was like something he'd expect to find at the heart of a sun. The impact had unleashed a lot of energy on the dying gunship's interior, energy it wasn't designed ever to see. Molten decking bubbled against his shields, burning in what little atmosphere remained in the leaky hulk. Organic components released noxious fumes as they decomposed in the extraordinary heat. Jag imagined a plume of debris and particles spewing from the hole he'd left in the gunship's side. At least he hoped there was; that had been the plan, anyway.

He clicked his communicator. Unwilling to risk revealing his survival until the time was right, he had explained his proposal to Jocell and Adelmaa'j and told them how to respond should the first stage work out. His one click would tell them he'd survived. Thankfully, he immediately received two clicks in return, which meant that everything had gone according to plan on the outside, too: the Yuuzhan Vong had bought the illusion of his destruction. He exhaled heavily in relief, and instantly felt one knot of tension dissolve in his gut. It was time to work on the others.

He searched the wreckage with radar and other instruments. As far as he could tell, it was empty of life, but not completely dead yet. The spine of the ship was still transmitting data, although the "brain" of the living craft was dead and the various limbs it had once coordinated were disconnected. Patches of the yorik coral that comprised the hull would live for some time yet, even if, as a whole, it was beyond hope. And in places, surviving off scraps of nutrients and energy sources circulating irregularly through the infrastructure, were five clusters of dovin basals, the miniature black-hole generators that the Yuuzhan Vong used for propulsion, defense, and attack.

Jag nodded to himself, pleased with the situation.

He fired up his engines again. The clawcraft shifted in the wreckage, then settled as his shields got a better grip. He slowly upped the power, relying on the fighter's instruments—possibly scrambled by the impact—to tell him where he was going. No further clicks came from his wingmates, so he had to assume everything was still going according to plan. He pushed the engines to their maximum power before, gradually, creakingly, the ruined gunship began to accelerate.

Another two clicks from the outside confirmed that his reaction wake was being camouflaged by the vapor plume. Anyone studying the gunship's wreckage would simply assume that its interior was aflame and disregard it.

Hopefully there were too many other things to worry about—the Star Destroyers, the Imperial squadrons, and the two pesky Galactic Alliance fighters nipping at anything that seemed to be paying too close attention. And while they were busy with that, Jag could get started on the next stage of his plan.

Using the laser cannon as a surgeon would wield a vibroscalpel, he began to sculpt the interior of the gunship. Taking great care to avoid the weight-bearing stanchions against which his starfighter pressed, he cut great chunks out of the spaces around him and let them fall back into the exhaust plume. Relatively speaking, the thrust his starfighter could apply to the gunship was small, since the gunship massed many times more than his engine was used to propelling. He couldn't do anything about thrust, but he could affect the mass he was pushing against. By eating away at the gunship from the inside and letting the pieces tumble back into the wake, he could gradually increase the effect his clawcraft's engine was having. And that this inert wreck was suddenly accelerating across the skies of Esfandia wouldn't necessarily arouse the Yuuzhan Vong's suspicions. In large space battles, active debris was a common and occasionally dangerous hazard.

Another two clicks confirmed that he was on course and, as yet, unnoticed. His engines were redlining, but he figured they could sustain the effort for the ten minutes required of them. While the battle swirled around him, he moved the hulk slowly but surely to the northern flank. The attention of his cutting lasers encroached, meter by meter, to the hull. Red-hot wreckage boiled and burned around him, and every now and then he would come across a lifeless body that he had to force himself to ignore, and carry on. Each one he came across reminded him just how crazy this plan of his really was.

If it caught the Yuuzhan Vong off guard, he told himself, if only for a second, then it would all be worthwhile.

* * *

"Admiral, Twin One appears to be intending to ram that ruined gunship!"

Pellaeon's gaze didn't shift from the display to look at the officer standing beside him. "I can see what he's doing, Commander."

"But sir, the Yuuzhan Vong have collision avoidance systems at least as good as ours. They're not about to let wreckage drift into their ships. If they suspect the gunship is to be used as a ram, they'll simply blow it out of the sky! What could he possibly hope to achieve by doing this?"

"He hopes to surprise me, of course. And *them* in the process."

Despite his belief in the young Jagged Fel's abilities, Pellaeon couldn't help but feel some apprehension. He'd wanted something solid and disconcerting from the Chiss pilot, certainly, but he hadn't expected quite so dramatic a response as this.

Meanwhile, the disposition of the battle hadn't changed. The Yuuzhan Vong still outnumbered the Imperial and Galactic Alliance forces, and they were still amassing their forces in the northern flank. The alien corvette and cruiser had managed to repel all attempts to place a yammosk jammer between them. That remained a potential flashpoint. If it ignited, Esfandia might return to Yuuzhan Vong control.

But he was determined not to let that happen on his watch. He'd sooner ram the Yuuzhan Vong warships himself than allow that.

"Any sign of the *Falcon* yet?" he asked his aide.

"No, sir. It must still be down in the atmosphere."

He wondered whether he should send reinforcements down to the surface. The Galactic Alliance forces hadn't done so, but that was probably because they simply didn't have the resources to spare. His last conversation with Captain Mayn had ended on a notably cool note; perhaps an offer to assist would help bridge the gap.

His aide soon had her on the line, and he explained the situation as clearly as he could without spelling out every detail. He never entrusted confidential information to any sort of broadcast medium, no matter how secure the line was thought to be.

"So if you need any assistance in that regard," he concluded, "I'd be only too happy to offer."

Mayn was shaking her head before he'd finished. "Thanks, Admiral, but that won't be necessary. We received a low-power coded transmission from the *Falcon* a short time ago ordering us to deter any further incursions into the planet's atmosphere as a matter of some urgency. I was about to pass it on to you, in fact, when you called."

Pellaeon absorbed this. It didn't sound like a simple *everything's-under-control-no-help-required* instruction. One didn't normally issue orders requesting urgent inaction without good reason.

"Do they know about the Vong patrols scouting the planet?" he asked.

"I advised them of that myself."

"And they still don't want anyone to watch their back while they're down there?"

"They were quite specific about that."

"Did they offer any explanation as to why?"

"No, sir. The message was brief. They simply said they would explain in due course, when their location was less sensitive."

"What *is* their location?"

"That I don't know, sir," Captain Mayn replied expressionlessly. "The signal was too diffuse and brief to obtain a precise lock on—which I assume was the intention."

Pellaeon frowned. Did Captain Mayn really not know, or was she holding out on the information per instructions from her superiors? It seemed reasonable to assume that the *Falcon* was looking for the relay team. That wasn't a problem in itself. He simply hated being left in the dark.

"Thank you, Captain," he said, no longer caring to soften his tone in the interest of public relations. "In future, please keep me promptly informed of any such developments."

"Understood, sir."

The Galactic Alliance captain signed off, and Pellaeon turned away from the screen to consider what she had and hadn't told him. Part of him wondered if he was naive in assuming that he could trust this group of Galactic Alliance forces in the same way that Luke Skywalker and his associates had proved that they could be trusted. Yes, Leia Organa Solo was Luke's twin sister, but she'd been trained in the art of politics—and politicians had too many fingers in too many pies to be taken at face value . . .

"Admiral?"

At the sound of his aide's voice, he turned from his disquieting thoughts. "What is it?"

"I have a text message from Colonel Fel, sir, relayed through Twin Nine."

"What does he say?"

"He says: 'Get ready.' "

Pellaeon glanced at the displays showing the northern flank. The gutted gunship's path was a dotted line passing between the two major targets in that region. The Chiss pilot was clearly going to miss both ships by a healthy margin.

Any reply Pellaeon might have sent went untransmitted as, on the screen before them, the gutted gunship suddenly exploded.

* * *

"That was risky, Leia," Han said when the message to *Pride of Selonia* had been dispatched. "The transmission could be traced."

Leia folded her arms and shivered, unable to take her eyes off the screen in which the aliens C-3PO called *Brrbrlpp* had gathered. "I know, but we can't take the risk that any more of them will die. It's not acceptable."

"There are Yuuzhan Vong down here, don't forget," Droma put in. His tail twitched restlessly where it dangled over the edge of his chair.

"I haven't forgotten," she said tightly. "I just haven't decided what to do about them yet."

A strange new warbling came over the comm.

"The Brrbrlpp say that there are many hot bodies on Esfandia now," C-3PO translated. "They're doing what they can to protect their people, but without knowing where the next target will be, it's impossible to keep them all safe."

Leia could appreciate the problem all too well. There was only one possible solution, but she didn't particularly like it. It all boiled down to the question of what was more important: the relay base and communications with the Unknown Regions, or the lives of an alien species that got caught in the middle of a war.

"We can't stay down here indefinitely," Han pointed out.

"But we can't *go* anywhere, either," Droma said. "Not while those aliens are out there."

He indicated the ring of flowerlike aliens floating around the ship in mute appeal. The moment they engaged the *Falcon*'s drives, they would be swept away like Geonosians in a hurricane.

"I'm aware of all this," Leia said irritably. She tried not to take her frustration out on her companions, but it was hard not to when all her thoughts kept coming back to the same conclusion.

"Telemetry," Han said. Screens in front of the copilot's station flickered with data coming down from the *Selonia*. "Increased traffic in this area. The scarheads must've picked up the edges of our transmission."

"If we keep low, they won't see us, right?" Droma looked at both of them hopefully.

"Yes, but we're not about to do that," Leia said. "We have to send another message."

Han didn't look happy with her suggestion. "I don't think that's a good idea.

"If we do that, Leia, they'll spot us for sure."

"That's partly the idea."

Understanding dawned behind her husband's eyes. "Okay, but what about them?" He indicated the waiting aliens.

"How far can we extend the shields?"

"A fair distance. Why?"

"Can we create a separate pocket?"

"Not without serious modifications."

"But you could do it?" Leia felt disappointment mounting on top of her frustration.

"I guess."

"Good." She was only marginally reassured. Her plan would save the Brrbrlpp in the short term, but might end up killing them all in the long run. "I don't think we have an alternative," she said.

Han nodded as he turned away to begin hitting switches. "Then let's get started."

Droma was looking from Han to Leia with increasing puzzlement. "I don't suppose either of you would care to let me in on what's going on."

"It's simple," Leia said. "We're going to draw the Yuuzhan Vong here by sending another transmission."

Droma's bushy gray eyebrows shot up. "Not before

dropping me at the nearest thing that passes for a bar on this planet, I trust?"

Leia ignored the glib remark. "It's the only thing we can do. They know something's in the area, since they picked up the fringes of our last message. But they'll assume it came from the relay base; that's all they're aware is down here. They'll instantly converge on us, wanting to take us out."

"And that's a good thing—why?"

Droma looked to Han for support, but didn't get it.

"Listen," Han said, "we tell the *Selonia* to look for a convergence in our location, right? When the Yuuzhan Vong are all in one spot, they'll make the perfect target. The big beam weapons on one of those Star Destroyers should be able to make quite a mess out of them."

"Not to mention us, of course."

"Not if they aim right. We'll be cold, presenting as small a target as possible."

"What about the locals?"

"Hopefully they'll be tucked nice and safe under our shields," Han said. "Look, just relax, Droma, and stop your whining. Leia knows what's she doing."

"She married you, didn't she?" the Ryn muttered with a shake of his head. "That's not what I'd call a particularly good track record."

Leia turned away from the two and faced C-3PO, not interested in her husband's response to the Ryn. "Three-pio, advise the—" She stopped, unable to get her tongue around the pronunciation of the aliens' name. "Just tell *them* that they should come as close as possible to the *Falcon* and that they're to stay there until we tell them otherwise."

"As you wish, Princess."

"Tell them also to get anyone in the area as far away as possible. Things are about to get extremely messy around here, and I don't want anyone else getting hurt."

C-3PO relayed the message in burbling, singsong tones. A reply came in several stages, with the droid explaining key features of the plan that were beyond the aliens' experiences.

"They will do as you instruct," he said eventually, "although there are some concerns that they might be taken hostage. They ask us to be particularly careful of the nesting plains nearby."

"*Nesting* plains?" Han rolled his eyes. "That's just terrific. As if we don't have enough to worry about."

"What does it look like?" Leia asked.

"It consists of a series of caves and tunnels beneath the surface in which the female Brrbrlpp lay their eggs for the males to fertilize. They are private places, warmed from the heat of the core."

"And the fact that one of them is so near to us might explain why there are so many of those aliens around here," Leia mused aloud.

"Exactly, Mistress. If we had come down in the open plains, there would have been almost no one around."

"Well, we can't move now," Han said.

"Tell them we'll be as careful as possible," Leia said. "That's the best we can do."

C-3PO relayed her reassurance, while Leia came to terms with the difficulty of what she'd set out for herself. As things stood, the *Falcon* was a stationary object that the Yuuzhan Vong looking for the relay base could easily use for target practice. It could neither flee nor return fire, for fear of hurting the fragile locals. Add to that the nearby nesting area, and the fact they still had no idea where the relay base was, and it was beginning to look like they'd taken on more than they could handle.

"The message is on its way," Han said. "I've adjusted the shields."

Leia glanced at the screen and noted that the ring of

Brrbrlpp had contracted around the old freighter. "Then all we can do now is wait, I guess."

"And hope they're not too busy up there to rescue us," Droma said, his eyes drifting nervously to the ceiling.

For this one's home . . .

Saba's eyes snapped open. She sat bolt upright, heart racing and scales shifting in anticipation. She took a couple of deep and calming breaths, but the residue of the dream still troubled her. The burning planet, the anger, the slaveship, the torpedoes . . . She had relived the terrible images of Barab I's destruction too many times over the last few months, as well as the guilt that accompanied the dream.

For this one's people . . .

She shook her head to lose the dream and the emotions it brought. It was unlikely that she'd ever lose the dream completely; what had happened that day would haunt her for the rest of her life.

She sighed heavily to herself, and looked idly about the dark room. It was still nighttime, and everyone was asleep. The only sounds she could hear were breathing and the rain's continued pitter-patter on the rooftop. For all intents and purposes, everything seemed normal. And yet . . .

Her scales stiffened again, this time in apprehension. Something was wrong. She reached out around her with the Force, trying to isolate the unease she was feeling. She could sense her fellow Jedi Knights, could feel the mixed life signals of the airships and various Ferroans nearby, could feel—

She stopped, realizing what it was that troubled her— something so subtle that a human might have missed it. It wasn't what was there, but rather what wasn't. There was no longer the faint touch of the habitat's life force; it was *dead*.

With her senses tingling, she threw back her blanket
and made to stand. Halfway to her feet, however, something heavy and suffocating dropped down on her from
above and pushed her back to the ground.

She roared to wake the others. Her lightsaber flared
into life beneath the confines of whatever it was that was
holding her down. She slashed once, twice, and felt the
weight fall away. She forced her arms and head through
the hole she'd sliced, just as something hard and heavy
swung at her out of the shadows, cracking her across the
skull. She fell back with a grunt. Pain from the blow
seared down one side of her face.

She fought back, feverishly willing herself to move.
Someone had obviously killed the habitat and brought it
down upon them. Then, as each of them struggled to climb
out, the attackers would strike them as they emerged. It
was almost too easy. But clearly, these assailants didn't
know what they were dealing with. A Jedi Knight wasn't
so easily overcome; and four Jedi Knights was a force to
be reckoned with . . .

"Saba!"

The voice belonged to Soron Hegerty, and from the
doctor's tone, Saba knew she was in trouble.

She tried to break free to help the doctor, and was
struck again by the blunt weapon. This time she was
ready, though, and managed to deflect the blow so that
it only struck her shoulder. Her attacker let out a yelp of
fright as Saba pulled herself to her feet and raised her
lightsaber to strike back. From the glow of her blade, as
well as the reflected light from the gas giant Mobus, she
was finally able to make him out. He was a Ferroan male
of medium height and build, and his expression was one
of determination undercut with panic—a panic she knew
she could use to her advantage. She faced her attacker
squarely, roaring as loud as she could and raising her

lightsaber as though to strike. He took one look at her sharp teeth and claws, dropped his weapon, and fled.

She turned to where Hegerty struggled with three other black-clad Ferroans. There were more of them scurrying around on the folds of the collapsed habitat, but Saba ignored them. Master Skywalker and the others could look after themselves; it was Dr. Hegerty who needed her help the most right then. The Jedi Master was weaving through the rain, cutting the others free while staving off his attackers. Hegerty, her cries now muffled, was being dragged rapidly away.

Saba took off at a run, her tail pointing behind her in an arrow-straight counterbalance to the lightsaber in her hand. One of the kidnappers tripped just as Saba reached them, lightsaber cutting a hissing swath through the rain. The one who'd fallen scrambled backward through the mud, while the others turned to face her. There was fear in their eyes, but they held their ground. Two held heavy clubs like the one that had almost knocked her out before. The third pointed something at her that looked like a thin, twisted tree root, with a startlingly acute crystal point at its tip. Before she had time to wonder at its purpose, a miniature bolt of lightning arced toward her.

It grounded safely in her lightsaber, which she'd swung to intercept it with liquid ease.

"This one will not allow a friend to be harmed," she said, revealing her teeth in a menacing snarl.

The one with the tree root weapon lowered his aim, uncertainty overtaking his resolve, while the one on the ground scrabbled for purchase in the mud. The third kidnapper, the one actually holding the doctor, unceremoniously dropped his hostage. She fell into the mud with a grunt of both pain and indignation. Then all three were gone, running in different directions into the shadows.

Saba resisted the urge to chase after them. Instead, she

reached down with one clawed hand to help the doctor to her feet.

"Thank you," the scholar gasped, wiping water and dirt from her face. Her gray hair hung limply and was streaked with mud. "As soon as the roof came down on us, they were right there ready to cut me free. I thought they'd come to rescue me at first, until they clubbed me." She rubbed at her head. "Why should they want me, though?"

Saba knew. *Go for the weakest of the herd.* It was the first rule of predation, and in this case the weakest would have been those who weren't fighters. And that meant . . .

"We must get back to the otherz," she said, hurriedly leading the way.

They returned to find Luke and Mara arguing with a group of Ferroans who had come out to see what all the commotion was about. They seemed genuinely surprised, but not above taking affront at Mara's suggestion that they'd been in any way negligent.

"Are you suggesting we would *sanction* such behavior?" Rowel protested.

"All I know is that we were attacked," Mara said. "And you assured us we'd be safe."

"I thought Jedi could look after themselves," Darak sneered.

"The fact that we're standing here now shows that we can," Mara defended quickly, "despite the cowardly attack by your people! They waited for the habitat to collapse before doing anything!"

"Habitats don't just collapse," Darak said.

"Whoever planned this attack," Master Skywalker said, "obviously rigged it earlier."

Rowel looked exasperated. "But I still don't see who would do such a thing!"

"I don't care who," Mara said. "I just want them found."

"In this rain?" Rowel said. "They could have gone in a dozen different directions. You'll never find them now."

"We have to try," Jacen said, stepping into the conversation with a grim expression. To Master Skywalker and Mara he said, "She's gone."

"*Who* is gone?" Darak asked.

Go for the weakest of the herd . . .

"Danni Quee," Saba said. "They took Danni."

Jacen looked at her and nodded. "And I intend to find her before they get too far."

"Jacen, wait—" Mara tried to catch her nephew's shoulder as he started off into the darkness, but he shrugged her hand aside and continued on his way without further comment.

"This one will keep him safe," Saba reassured Mara. With a two-legged leap, she took after Jacen, hunting the moment . . .

Pellaeon's aide gasped as the decoy gunship blew up with Jag Fel inside it. The admiral noted other signs of surprise and distress across the wide bridge of *Right to Rule*. The fortunes of Soontir's son had captured more attention than he'd expected. To see them so suddenly dashed was a shock even to him.

He turned to his aide, opening his mouth to issue an order and recall all fighters from the northern flank. Before any words had passed his lips, however, something strange happened. The destroyed gunship had broken into several large chunks, with numerous smaller fragments boiling into vacuum. Two of the larger chunks were heading for the cruiser. Another, the largest, was tumbling toward the corvette. The fragments were large enough and had enough relative velocity to inflict considerable damage, if they hit, but as Pellaeon watched, the equivalent of collision avoidance systems came into play around the two ships. A gout of plasma fire lashed out at the first of the fragments to approach the cruiser.

Instead of blowing the wreckage into even smaller fragments, however, the vicious bolt of plasma was sucked away into nothing.

"What—?" Pellaeon stared at the screen in disbelief. Even when another plasma burst failed to destroy the rapidly approaching wreckage, he still didn't understand what was happening. Only as the corvette began firing on the piece tumbling toward it did he finally realize it: the plasma fire was being absorbed by dovin basals lingering on the fragments of the gunship's hull!

And with that realization, the rest of Jag Fel's plan fell into place for him.

"All fighters in the northern flank," he ordered his aide, "concentrate on those two targets! Divert *all* firepower to the weak spots!"

The aide frowned. "What weak spots, sir?"

"*Those* weak spots!" He indicated the sudden blossoming of energy as the first gunship fragment hit the Yuuzhan Vong cruiser. He leaned back in satisfaction as his orders were relayed and fighters converged on the damaged ship, intending to add not just insult to injury, but violent destruction as well.

Jag rode the wild tumbling of the third fragment as it arrowed toward the Yuuzhan Vong corvette hanging alongside the damaged cruiser. The Yuuzhan Vong were quick; he had to give them that. They were already concentrating their fire on his ride, hoping to overload the lingering dovin basals and blow the threat into a million pieces. When their shots cut through the debris enough to impact on his shields, he retaliated, knowing that the move would take them by surprise. A lethal piece of debris was bad enough; that it would return fire would have been completely unexpected.

His shots had the required effect. The Yuuzhan Vong gunners were distracted long enough for the gunship fragment to hit the corvette's hull. Just before the collision, Jag made sure the fragment was between him and the corvette; nevertheless, the impact was intense enough to almost buckle his shields. The shock wave from the resulting explosion caused him to black out for a moment, and when he came to again he found himself immersed in a white-hot ball of gas and debris. Repeating the tactic he'd employed in the gunship, he fired his way out of the impact point, tunneling deep into the heart of the corvette.

He didn't know how far he would get before his shields overloaded, but he was determined to do as much damage as he could before then. Since Yuuzhan Vong warriors were trained to fight to the death, opportunities to explore the interiors of their ships came rarely, and he had no idea where the equivalents of power generators or drives might be situated. He simply angled inward and backward along the craft's major axes, figuring that the most sensitive material would probably be kept there. He knew that it would be impossible to trigger an explosion like the one that had torn the gunship apart, but he figured it was worth trying.

Burning debris roiled around him, enclosing him in an extended, fiery bubble. The plasma effectively cut him off from the universe outside, stopping even the clicks from his wingmates getting through. Whether his maneuver had been sufficient for Pellaeon to turn the tide in the northern flank, he wouldn't know until he was out. He only hoped he wouldn't be met with a wall of coralskippers when he emerged. That would certainly bring an ignominious end to his daring plan.

Is this what you would have done, Jaina? he wondered. *Would you have gone this far?*

He kept on firing until his laser cannons threatened to melt and his shields were on the verge of collapse. In case he needed those systems on the way out, he rested them while he rotated his fighter around its center of gravity and prepared to retrace his steps. The view behind was the same as in front: nothing but boiling debris and the red-hot outlines of load-bearing structures, now deformed and sagging. A shudder rolled through the corvette, but he couldn't tell if it was a result of his actions or from elsewhere. For all he knew, the ship might have been on the brink of exploding, or it could have simply been changing course.

Gunning his engines and keeping a close eye on the instruments, he powered his way back through the burning ship. Occasionally, great clumps of anti-reactant foam clogged his path, and he was forced to burn his way through, starting new fires in the process.

As he neared the outer hull, he picked up the speed. The impact site of the gunship wreckage gave him more room to maneuver, and a greater feeling of exposure, too. Inside, he'd been relatively safe. Once outside again, he would come under the targeting system of every weapon on the corvette's hull—along with the targeting reticles of every skip within firing distance. The faster he came out, the better.

White heat faded to blue streaked with yellow, then orange, and finally red. Then abruptly there was nothing ahead of him but stars. He put his shields to maximum behind him and pushed the throttle as far as it would go. Burned black from nose to stern, his starfighter shot out of the burning ship like a particle discharged from the business end of a charric. He fought to keep his damaged stabilizers under control and ignored a blast of noise from his comm. Until he was certain he had his clawcraft under control, he didn't have time to look around.

When he did, he was amazed to find that his plan appeared to have worked. The corvette was in serious trouble, burning in too many places to count and looking like it could break up at any moment. Dozens of Imperial fighters were pounding it without relief. Nearby, the cruiser was coming under similar attack. The places where the gunship fragments had hit were targets for repeated combat runs, leaving them gaping and vulnerable. The holes vented gases and bodies in huge clouds, making navigation dangerous for Yuuzhan Vong and Imperial alike. Any chance of the northern flank becoming a focus for resistance now seemed very remote.

"Jag! You made it!"

The greeting burst out of his comm like a miniature explosion, closely followed by an X-wing swooping in from his right.

"Nice to hear your voice, Enton," he replied. "How's everything out here?"

"Much improved now, sir." This came from Twin Sun Four, settling into position off his port side. "I think you've shown those Imps a thing or two."

I certainly hope so, he thought as he continued to guide his battered starfighter out of the thick of things.

"Congratulations on a job well done, Colonel Fel." The voice of the Grand Admiral from the comm broke across his thoughts. "Consider me . . . surprised."

"I hope I managed to make a difference, sir."

"Oh, that you did," the Grand Admiral said. "It's becoming obvious that neither we nor the Yuuzhan Vong are going to control the planet. I'd expect a stalemate to form anytime now: us on one side, them on the other. I doubt that anyone will be getting any closer than low orbit. That should allow the ground crew time to find the base, at least."

"Have we heard anything from them, sir?"

"Not that I'm aware," Pellaeon said. "Although you might want to check with Captain Mayn. Tell her that if there's anything I need to hear, she knows where to find me."

Jag frowned, sensing something in Pellaeon's tone but not sure what it was—and certain it wasn't any of his business. "I'll contact her immediately, sir."

"I'd consider doing more than that," the admiral said. "You're going to need more than just a wire brush to get rid of that scoring."

Jag smiled as he turned his clawcraft around for *Pride of Selonia*. He had no idea how badly crisped he'd gotten inside the gunship and the cruiser, but if the admiral had taken time to comment on it, it must be bad.

He checked in with Captain Mayn, who ordered him back in no uncertain terms. There was a heavy strain in her voice, as though she was deeply worried about something.

"We haven't heard from the *Falcon*," she explained when he asked. "A garbled transmission came through a short time ago, but we couldn't decipher it. We suspect the Yuuzhan Vong are jamming transmissions from the surface."

"That's not good," Jag said. "They could be calling for help. Is there any way we can get down there?"

"No. And don't even think about trying, Colonel. You're not going anywhere until we check out your ship."

"Don't worry, Captain," he said. "I think one crazy stunt is enough for one day."

As he arced around the *Selonia* and moved into position to dock, he asked the question that had been on his mind since he'd emerged from the belly of the alien corvette.

"Captain, is Jaina there?"

There was a long pause. When Mayn returned, her voice was more strained than ever, and Jag knew that this was the source of the woman's anxiety.

"It might be easier to talk about that when you dock," Mayn said.

Jag felt an icy nausea squeeze his stomach. "Is something wrong?"

"To be honest, Colonel, we don't *know*. None of us here is a Jedi, so we have no idea if her condition is normal or not."

"*What* condition?"

Even over the crackling comm, he heard Captain Mayn take a deep breath. "She's unconscious; possibly in a coma, Dantos says. We don't know exactly when it happened, and we don't know when she's likely to snap out of it—if she snaps out of it at all. I'm sorry, Colonel; I wish I could offer you better news. But the fact is, we just can't reach her."

We can't reach her. Captain Mayn's words seemed to echo in Jag's ears. As he jockeyed his clawcraft around to the docking bays, he asked, "When did this happen? Where did you find her?"

"In Tahiri's room," Mayn answered. "She's been like that since we arrived."

Jag nodded, his jaw tightening. He'd known the answer before asking the question. That didn't make hearing it any better, though.

He gripped the controls of his clawcraft tightly as he carefully brought it in to dock, even though his every instinct urged him to hurry.

"Are you still there, Colonel?" he heard Mayn ask after a few seconds.

But he didn't have time to reply; he was too busy clambering from his cockpit. As soon as his feet hit the ground, he was running through the corridors, heading for Tahiri's room.

* * *

The area surrounding Shimrra's palace had undergone considerable change since Nom Anor's expulsion. Bioengineered life-forms extruded from the walls, floors, and ceilings of buildings as they slowly ate their way through the lifeless constructs of the planet's previous occupants, fashioning them into immense new extensions to house the Supreme Overlord's vast number of servants, executors, and other support staff.

There was no mistaking the palace itself. A worldship standing on one end, it rose like a majestic mountain from the ruins of the old world. It was a thing of awesome beauty and intimidating splendor with its mighty rainbow-edged wings stretching out across Yuuzhan'tar for all to see.

The exterior of the inner sanctum, Shimrra's private chambers, had been heavily decorated with slender, curving spikes that reached for the sky as though to snatch at the clouds. The number of entrances had been reduced—possibly in response to failed attempts by the heresy to get inside—and each one was now protected by heavy security.

Still, the priestess Ngaaluh had no difficulty smuggling a villip inside, with which to spy on proceedings. Cleverly incorporated into elaborate robes and ornamentation, it saw what was taking place with perfect clarity. Nom Anor, on the receiving end of its transmissions, saw, too.

A full court had gathered to hear the priestess's report on the Vishtu region. Nom Anor recognized many of the faces gathered before the Supreme Overlord. Many were ones he had himself served with. The others were recent additions, replacements for those lost in action or killed for failing their master. They watched proceedings with keen, cautious eyes, knowing that opportunities for advancement would be frequent in such an environment, but that risks were concomitantly high.

Then, of course, there was Lord Shimrra himself. Nom Anor felt an immediate adrenaline rush the moment his eyes fell upon the Supreme Overlord. It was easy to forget, when bathed in the rhetoric of the heresy, how striking Shimrra was—how gloriously *wrathful*. Every fiber of Shimrra's being screamed out in torment, tortured by the very garments he wore. He radiated psychic distress on every frequency—yet beneath that there burned a cold, implacable surety of purpose. He was like a natural force whose very presence demanded attention, and it took all of Nom Anor's will just to lower his gaze.

". . . resources provided by Prefect Ash'ett proved barely adequate for my investigation." Ngaaluh's report droned on, giving details in abundance, but offering no real information. "I was forced to procure my own means. And what I found was disturbing to an extreme. Numerous cells of heretic movements have formed in the consul's staff at all levels of seniority. It is clear, Great Lord, that the situation warrants serious scrutiny."

A flurry of whispers circulated around the throne room. High Prefect Drathul looked particularly concerned. As head of the intendant caste on Yuuzhan'tar, Prefect Ash'ett fell under his governance. Any stain on Vishtu would inevitably reflect on him.

"I find this disturbing," Shimrra rumbled from on high. His grotesquely magnificent throne towered over the penitents gathered before him, yet he did not seem dwarfed by it. Darkness and power radiated from him in waves. "Once again, Ngaaluh, you display unflinching bravery in bringing such news to my attention."

Another whisper; the Supreme Overlord had killed many underlings for delivering better news.

The priestess bowed low, unfazed. "It is my duty, Great One. I do not shirk from it."

"You have evidence, I presume?"

Ngaaluh snapped her fingers. Guards brought forth five prisoners in cages made of coral and sinew that formed a natural shell, through which numerous perforations admitted air. The cages unfolded with a gentle pressure on the outer spinal ridge, and the five prisoners tumbled out. They whimpered and cried as they struggled awkwardly to their knees, but none of them pleaded for mercy.

"These were apprehended in the act of spreading the word of the Prophet," Ngaaluh explained, perfectly truthfully. "They all work for Prefect Ash'ett."

The prisoners were pushed facedown onto the floor by Shimrra's swarthy bodyguards. They squirmed and wriggled, but were unable to escape. Bound by blorash jelly at wrists and ankles, the deformed creatures looked hideous in the face of Shimrra's imperial perfection. Everything the Supreme Overlord had, the prisoners lacked. There was beauty in pain and ugliness; Nom Anor had forgotten just how splendid it could be.

"You," Shimrra said, gesturing at one of the prisoners at random with a single long, clawed finger. "Are you a servant of the *Jeedai*?"

"With every breath," the prisoner gasped, knowing he was sealing his death sentence with those words. His eyes were wild with hatred and rebellion, but trembling limbs betrayed his fear.

"You do not fear the gods, then."

"No."

"Do you fear me?"

"No."

"What do you want?"

"Our freedom and our honor!"

The court hissed to hear the heresy spoken so brazenly in the very heart of the Yuuzhan Vong empire. All, including Nom Anor, expected Shimrra to enact an immediate and terrible revenge on the source of such a foul challenge—but the Supreme Overlord, as he so often did, surprised them all.

"Interesting." Shimrra's voice was measured, almost bored, as though they were discussing nothing more than fleet movements in a distant part of the galaxy. "It is as you have stated it, Ngaaluh. Tell me, do the *Jeedai* instruct these heretics personally, or do they direct them through another?"

The prisoner interrupted before Ngaaluh could answer. "I obey my conscience; I obey the Prophet!"

Nom Anor cursed. That wasn't what the fool was supposed to say!

"My personal opinion is that Ash'ett is involved," the priestess said, recovering quickly and getting the correct message across.

"But you have no *direct* evidence?"

"In time, I will provide it."

"That won't be necessary." Shimrra turned his attention back to the prisoners. "Throw them to the yargh'un pit. Their screams of torment will provide a pleasing ambience during my communion with the gods. And while you're about it, bring me Prefect Ash'ett."

"It would be good to hear his side of the story, Lord," High Prefect Drathul said as the heretics were dragged away. "I am certain that he can prove his innocence. He is a loyal and faithful servant—"

Shimrra silenced him with a gesture. "Whether Prefect Ash'ett is corrupt or not," he said, "the fact is that he has allowed the heresy a foothold in his affairs. That is not acceptable. He must be reminded of the consequences of laxity—as must everyone in a position of responsibility. I want every member of his immediate family executed in the yargh'un pit. If they offer resistance, execute everyone in his entire domain and install another in Vishtu sector. A confession will not be required; suspicion alone is enough. This is the price of laxity that all will suffer if the heresy is not wiped out."

The orders provoked gasps from the audience. Its severity was extreme, even for Shimrra. Prefect Drathul's face went a sickly shade of gray, Warmaster Nas Choka grinned a predator's smile at the fate of the intendants he despised, and Nom Anor, far away, cackled gleefully.

"I am weary of this pointless aggravation," Shimrra said. His every word and act was calculated to antagonize, to bludgeon those beneath into obedience. Not just the acts of gross violence, but the sweeping red gaze, the glistening teeth, the lazy pacing of a predator at the top of the food chain. "If there were a chance that these worthless animals could achieve their goal, then I might admire their determination, their loyalty to a cause. That their cause is utterly farcical wouldn't detract from the respect they would deserve, simply for attempting to rise above their station." Shimrra sneered mightily, triumphantly, at the terrified faces of those watching him. "But they are inevitably doomed. Their cause is hopeless and their deaths will bring them no honor. The gods spurn them as abominations. I will not suffer them, or anyone tainted by them, to live."

Nom Anor was delighted. His betrayal of Ash'ett had reaped unexpected rewards. Shimrra was obviously hoping to send a clear warning to all caste members while at the same time weeding out suspicious domains. From now on, suspicion alone was enough, and failure to fight the heretics couldn't be blamed on underlings. What that meant for the heretics, though, wasn't disaster. It gave Nom Anor an even more potent weapon. With just a word from Ngaaluh, Shimrra could be made to destroy whole swaths of his loyal supporters. It was perfect!

Ngaaluh, glorious queen of deception, was the first to recover from the Supreme Overlord's pronouncement.

"Your will, Great One, is the will of the gods," she said, bowing low. "We obey you utterly and without question."

The others in Shimrra's court had no choice but to follow suit, echoing her bow and her words with murmured praises of their own. High Prefect Drathul had looked for a moment as though he might protest, but Shimrra's warning was clear. Those who spoke out against punishment for heresy risked being labeled heretical themselves. Drathul's eyesacks were inflamed and black as he stooped to offer his loyalty to the Supreme Overlord.

Yet when he looked at Ngaaluh, his expression was free of hatred. Nom Anor looked for any sign of resentment at how Ash'ett—and by association all of the intendants—had been implicated in the heresy, but he saw nothing but resignation. That surprised him. It wasn't like Drathul to simply roll over and accept his fate.

The moment passed, and Ngaaluh moved back to allow other penitents to speak.

The conversation moved on to other troubles on the surface. A field of lambents had overheated and caught fire, disturbing harvesting on the far side of the planet. Lungworms from the district of Bluudon had developed the noxious habit of emitting hydrogen sulfide instead of life-giving oxygen. Two flocks of massive transport envelopers had gone wild on separate occasions, sending local communities into a panic until the beasts were contained. All could be traced to the ongoing malfunctions of the dhuryam controlling the transformation of Yuuzhan'tar. The new master shaper, Yal Phaath, had yet to find a solution to the problem.

Meanwhile, two thousand kilometers away, a cell of heretics had successfully infiltrated a coralskipper farming crew and slipped parasites into the feeding lines. Half-grown pods had exploded all over the shipyard, setting off others and creating a chain reaction that undid an entire year's work. The damage couldn't be hidden; even from orbit the destruction was obvious. It was the pro-Jedi movement's third major strike in a week. Nom Anor rubbed his hands together. While he wasn't responsible for the disruption of the World Brain, that didn't stop him taking credit for it. Word was quickly spreading: *anywhere* could be next. His power was growing by the day. Nothing could stop him now . . .

Wet leaves slapped at Jacen's face as he ran through the tampasi. Despite their size and weight, he didn't let them impede his progress; he just kept running, allowing the Force to guide him in his search for Danni.

He could sense her somewhere up ahead, but the reading was vague and distorted, as though something was interfering with the Force. But if he concentrated he could detect the young scientist's life signs, and was able to at least get some idea of which way they were taking her.

Leaping over fallen logs, ducking heavier branches, Jacen hurried through the dense undergrowth. The ground cover was so thick he couldn't see where to put his feet, and on more than one occasion he stumbled when the ground dropped out from beneath him. The rain fell in a heavy mist all around, plastering his hair and clothes to his skin and blurring his vision. It was all irrelevant. All that mattered was reaching Danni and making sure no harm came to her. He stayed focused on her spark in the Force and continued to push himself harder and faster through the vegetation.

Without warning, he burst out of a dense knot of ferns and onto a narrow path. He turned to follow it, knowing instinctively that this was how the Ferroans had made such speedy progress. Moving steadily along the path, he cast his mind out into the Force again to check the area.

He found Danni's spark—faint and flickering, but there nonetheless. He couldn't detect Saba, though—whom he had sensed following some time ago—nor hear her movement in the tampasi around him. He didn't have time to dwell on it. He had to stay focused . . .

His pace quickened, feet splashing noisily on the wet ground. He could tell that he was closing in fast, and this goaded him on. He could sense the kidnappers now, also: five in all, each with a certain calm to their thoughts. They were relaxed, exuding a confidence that came from the belief that they had gotten away with their crime— along with the fact that they were being joined by other conspirators.

Yes, thought Jacen, reaching out farther into the Force. There they were now. The two groups were coming together in a clearing up ahead, greeting one another with laughter and congratulatory handshakes, none of them exhibiting the slightest hint of fear or concern.

Removing his lightsaber from his belt, he increased his pace even more. The kidnappers were so close now that he could hear their voices just off in the distance, could even see faint movements through the gaps between the mighty boras that stood between them and himself.

If you've hurt her in any way . . .

Using the fallen trunk of a boras as a springboard, Jacen leapt into the small clearing where the kidnappers were gathered, somersaulting in the air as he went and igniting his lightsaber at the same time. When his feet touched the ground he was already in a defensive stance, ready to deflect the three bolts of energy that spat from the tips of the kidnappers' lightning rods harmlessly into the ground.

He raised his lightsaber above his head, poised in a double-handed pose to strike if anyone came too close. The kidnappers froze, and an uneasy silence fell over the clearing.

He looked down at Danni lying on a stretcher made from two thick branches with a crisscrossing of vines in between. He couldn't tell whether she was all right, but she didn't seem to be moving at all, and that didn't bode well.

"We're prepared to fight," one of the kidnappers said, stepping forward. The weapon in his hand trembled uneasily.

Looking around at the startled conspirators, he could see from their faces and postures that they weren't experienced fighters, and he had no doubts that he could take them all on with little effort. But that wasn't what he wanted. That wasn't who he was. There had to be a peaceful way of resolving this and getting Danni back safely . . .

"You can't win," another said with marginally more confidence. "It's fifteen against one."

Jacen was about to lower his weapon and try another tack when an ear-piercing roar broke the rainy quiet. A dark shape leapt out of the trees as Jacen had and dropped heavily into the clearing. Saba's lightsaber sliced through the air, turning the rain to steam with a menacing hiss.

"Fifteen against two," she snarled.

Half the kidnappers fled in panic at the sight of the mighty Barabel, not even attempting to put up a fight. Seven remained, all clustered around the stretcher, putting themselves between Jacen and Saba and their hostage. Five of them raised their clubs, ready to fight, while the other two flashed their gnarled lightning rods.

"Wait!" Jacen called out over the rain. If he was going to defuse this situation, he knew it would have to be now. "Please, just lower your weapons!"

Heads turned to him as he deactivated his lightsaber and returned it to his belt. He raised both hands defenselessly in the air.

"Do you really want to die here tonight?" he asked the Ferroans.

"You're the ones outnumbered, Jedi!" one of the kidnappers spat.

Jacen extended his will through the Force toward the lightning rod in the man's hand. With a small gesture, he pulled the weapon to himself. The Ferroan glanced down at his empty hands, then up at Jacen, surprise fighting with panic in his eyes as he took a nervous step back.

"Looks can be deceptive," Jacen said, dropping the weapon to the ground.

Caught between the snarling ferocity of a Barabel and Jacen's calm confidence, the group tightened their grip on their remaining weapons and moved in threateningly close to Danni.

Jacen stepped forward, one hand upraised, keen to stay any violent acts they might intend. "There has to be another way."

"Such as?" asked the one whose weapon had just been confiscated.

"We could try talking," Jacen said. "Perhaps if you told us why you're doing this, we might be able to work things out without violence."

"I don't trust them," said another of the Ferroans, a woman with black hair and round features. "I don't trust *any* outsiders!"

"There's no reason to be frightened of us," Jacen said. It was the truth, of course, but he pushed the words anyway into the more receptive parts of their minds to reassure them.

"We're not frightened of you," the woman snarled. "We just don't want you here!"

"But we *are* here," Jacen said. "And we're here by Sekot's invitation."

"Then Sekot is wrong," the first man said. "As Senshi says, it's—"

"Quiet!" snapped one of the kidnappers at the back, a narrow-eyed man whose hair came to a sharp widow's peak above his forehead. "Tell them nothing!"

Jacen thought quickly. This "Senshi" who had been mentioned was obviously someone of influence in their conspiracy—perhaps even their leader. This was the person he needed to be speaking to, rather than wasting time arguing in the rain. As easy as it would have been to rescue Danni now and return to camp, he knew that in the long run this wouldn't solve anything. The problem wouldn't have been dealt with, which meant further attempts on their lives would be made. This needed to be resolved *now*.

"You came looking for hostages," he said, "and you're returning with one. But three would be better, don't you think?"

"What are you saying?" the woman asked, frowning.

"I'm saying that we don't need to fight." He indicated Saba, who still had her lightsaber raised and at the ready. "Saba and I will accompany you, as prisoners, so that we can talk this out properly with Senshi."

"I still don't trust them," the woman said. She spoke to the other Ferroans, but her eyes flitted back and forth between Jacen and Saba.

"If you fight, you'll lose," Jacen said simply. "And possibly even die. But my way nobody has to die, and you get to return to Senshi with more hostages than he or she could have hoped for." Jacen put the weight of the Force behind the suggestion, trying again to breach the barrier of their minds. He felt the words find purchase in their thoughts—especially the mind of the man at the back whose comment had silenced everyone. "You know it makes sense."

The man nodded slowly. "It *does* make sense," he agreed.

The woman at the front turned on him, the look on

her face one of perplexity and anger. "Have you gone mad, Tourou? We can't take them to Senshi! They'll kill him for sure!"

"Nobody's going to kill anyone," Jacen assured her. "Here, look." He unclipped the lightsaber from his belt and tossed it to her. "You can hold my weapon for me, if my word's not enough."

The woman stared at the lightsaber pommel with something akin to horror—as though shocked to be given it, but terrified of what it might do.

Jacen nodded at Saba, who, after an initial hesitation, deactivated her blade and tossed it to the man Jacen had disarmed. If she was unnerved by Jacen's decision, she didn't show it. She was a picture of impassivity, awaiting further instruction.

"Very well," Tourou said. He gestured, and the group broke apart. Two came cautiously around Jacen's side to stop him from getting away, while another two did the same with Saba. "Pick up the stretcher," Tourou ordered his two new captives. "You'll carry your friend. That way you won't be in any position to try anything."

Jacen did as his captors told him, taking the rear handles while Saba took the front ones. Her tail swished agitatedly, flicking the puddles of water on the ground. Then they were moving again through the tampasi, with three Ferroans leading the way and four at the back.

Jacen looked down at Danni's limp form on the stretcher. Her clothes were soaked and muddy, and there was a bruise on the side of her head that looked quite nasty. Hopefully she would wake up soon; if she did, a larger degree of his uneasiness would be laid to rest, and he could concentrate on settling the grievances of the rebellious Ferroans. For now, though, he concentrated on walking, as well as trying to send his uncle some reassurance that they were okay. But he found it difficult to reach through the Force, and the farther they went into the tampasi, the fainter the life signals of the others back at the Ferroan camp became. Not for the first time since leaving them behind at the settlement, he wished he'd brought a comlink with him so that he could have at least let them know what was happening. Saba, he presumed, would have left hers behind, also, probably under the collapsed habitat with all the other gear. With nothing but the clothing they were wearing, they were both grossly unprepared for a mission that would take them farther away from their friends.

If I handle this correctly, he thought, *then maybe we won't be away for long . . .*

As they walked, Saba glanced over her shoulder and said, "This one hopez you know what you are doing."

He shook his head. "Not really. But it's uncertainty that make life so interesting, don't you think?"

Saba didn't smile at his attempted levity. She just returned her gaze to the path ahead and continued walking in silence.

Tahiri's scream was like a cold knife to Jaina's heart. She felt the darkness flex around her. Sudden, striking emotions stabbed at her from all directions: fear, pain, surprise, hurt. There was no way to separate them, and no way she could offer succor.

Then an image came to her of Riina crouched before Tahiri, blood dripping in a steady stream from a wound in her hand. Tahiri dropped, too, clutching her own arm. Her blue-white lightsaber fell from her hand, leaving a broad, black scorch mark as it hit the ground.

Jaina was confused for a long moment as to what had happened. In a previous memory-image she had seen the two women confront each other. Something had happened, and Riina had been injured. Now Tahiri appeared to be injured, too. Was their mental dueling finally drawing blood?

Tahiri, are you all right? Sithspawn! You have to hear me!

Jaina rattled at the confines of her mental cell. As before, Tahiri's mind was in no hurry to let her out, and she was unwilling to force the issue for fear of doing more damage. There was no one outside who could help, and she wasn't certain that her presence here was irrelevant. If she couldn't get out, then something wanted her there, even if both Tahiri and Riina appeared to be ignoring her for the moment.

Jaina had seen enough of the fight to know that Riina fought with all the skills of an alien warrior plus Tahiri's mastery of the Force. The ferocity of a Yuuzhan Vong combined with the skills of a Jedi would make Riina a formidable enemy if she ever took over Tahiri's body. More than ever, Jaina knew she couldn't let the Yuuzhan Vong girl win this battle. Jaina's mind urged Tahiri to get up.

A memory flash showed both women stirring. Blood shone blackly in the blue light. Only then did Jaina realize that Tahiri had inexplicably incurred exactly the same injury as Riina, but on the opposite arm.

Realization flashed like lightning in her mind. Tahiri and Riina were mirror images fighting each other to the death. What one did to the other, they did to themselves. If Tahiri defeated Riina, then she would defeat herself in the process. Neither could win!

There was a brief but intense moment in which Tahiri and Riina seemed to be arguing with each other without using words—as though some kind of communication was taking place on an altogether higher plane, one that Jaina was not privy to. Then, in unison, two sets of green eyes turned to look into the darkness.

The memory-image faded, but for a terrible second Jaina knew that they were talking about her. She felt definitely threatened by the double stare.

Another image. Both girls had risen to their feet, each releasing the wounds they'd been nursing. Their bloodied hands reached for their lightsabers. Both weapons flew through the air into their hands, the blades leaving identical, shining streaks of light through the dark.

Anakin is dead. Tahiri's voice came clearly from the darkness. The grief caught in her throat on the last word. *I cannot bring him back.*

The terrible, never-forgotten sadness rose in Jaina again, made all the more terrible in this nightmarish setting. She pushed it back and concentrated on sending Tahiri feelings of love and assurance.

I've run for too long. Tahiri advanced with her lightsaber raised. Riina matched her step by step. *It's time I faced my fears.*

Jaina tensed, unsure what she could do.

As though from a great distance, she thought she heard Jag's voice calling to her.

I love you, Jaina, the voice whispered over the darkened landscape. *Please come back to me . . .*

It was an illusion, she knew, a product of wishful thinking. Jag may have felt such sentiments, but he'd never actually *say* them. But just the thought of him saying such things was enough to give her the strength she needed.

Face your fears, Tahiri, she told the shadowy world around her.

The dreamscape began to tremble, as though about to dissolve away.

"Krel os'a. Hmi va ta!"

The darkness firmed at the sound of the harsh alien voice, and the dream tightened once again.

Leia held on as the shock wave from another near miss rattled the *Falcon*'s bulkheads. C-3PO's stiff arms went up in the air as he squawked in alarm.

"Oh, my," he exclaimed. "I do believe that's the closest one yet. It's only a matter of time before one hits home, and then I'm afraid we'll all be done for."

"Keep it down, Goldenrod," Han bellowed from a service hatch in the ship's belly. "The Ryn are easily jinxed, you know."

"Only in ships like this," Droma fired back. The two of them were hastily working on the shield generator power couplings, hoping to gain a few extra points of efficiency.

"There's nothing wrong with the *Falcon*," Han said as his head emerged from the service hatch. "Hand me that hydroclamp, will you?"

Droma shook his head as he passed Han the requested tool. "This must be the stupidest plan I've ever heard."

"Which part?" Leia asked wryly.

"All of it! But especially *this*. The only thing keeping us alive right now are the shields. If we accidentally shut them down while we're tinkering with them—"

"We're not going to shut them down," Han grumbled.

"And your confidence comes from having done this kind of thing so many times before?"

Droma's dig prompted Han to stick his head out from the hatch again and point the clamp at the Ryn.

"Hey, just because I've never actually done this before doesn't mean I couldn't do it anytime I wanted."

"So why haven't you?"

"Because I haven't needed to!" He looked to Leia, who was leaning against the door arch, and said, "Take him back to the cockpit, will you?"

Then he disappeared again into the hatch.

C-3PO turned to Leia in despair. "We're doomed," he keened.

"And take Goldenrod with you!" Han called out.

"Where are they, Princess?" the droid asked, seemingly oblivious to Han's annoyance. "Surely they should have been here by now?"

Leia shook her head, not having an answer for him. Therein lay the problem. They'd sent the message to Captain Mayn asking for help, but so far there'd been no reply—nor any sign of the help they'd requested. She was beginning to have one of Han's "bad feelings." But she didn't say anything; it would have only upset C-3PO further, which in turn would have annoyed Han.

"Try that, Leia!" her husband called.

She quickly returned to the cockpit and attempted to up the shield strength. It did increase, but only slightly. "Getting there," she called back.

Her husband appeared through the cockpit entrance a few seconds later, dropping heavily into the seat next to her and fiddling with the controls as he tried to wring every last megajoule out of the shield generators.

"Come on, girl," he muttered under his breath. "Show us what—"

A violent explosion from somewhere disconcertingly close suddenly thundered around the cabin, almost throwing them from their seats. Out in the corridor she heard the clattering sounds of C-3PO falling over, followed by another plaintive cry. Han furiously punched controls with one hand while clinging on to the console with the other.

"Doomed, I tell you," they heard C-3PO moan.

Droma entered the cockpit. "I'm with the droid on this. The only thing in our favor right now is that the Vong don't know our exact whereabouts. But if they keep shelling the area like this—"

"Your concerns have been duly noted," Han said. "In the meantime, though, why don't you go back there and have a game of dejarik with Cakhmain and Meewalh or something." Then, louder, "Threepio? How are our hangers-on out there? They're a lot more fragile than we are."

The droid waddled into the cockpit and proceeded to warble a message to the Brrbrlpp huddled in the *Falcon*'s protective shield. In the aft screen, they could be seen clustered together, the edges of their flowerlike bodies all touching to form one large, quivering mass.

"The Brrbrlpp assure me that they are managing well enough," C-3PO reported after the aliens had replied. "But they fear—as I and Master Droma do—that it will only be a matter of time before destruction befalls us. They would like to know if we have any other plans."

"Do they really think we'd be sitting here like this if we did?" Han said irritably.

"Just tell them we're working on it, Threepio," Leia said.

The droid relayed the message while Leia sat back in her seat to try and think of a plan that might get them out of their predicament.

"I think the time has come to move," Droma said bluntly.

"We can't move," Han said. "We'll melt our guests."

"They're going to be melted anyway when those shields fail—and then we'll all die."

Han nodded. "Drawing the fire of the Yuuzhan Vong seemed a good idea at the time, but it kind of relied on those upstairs getting our message."

"Maybe they did get it and just can't do anything about it right now," Leia said. "Who knows what might be happening up there."

"Can we use repulsors?" Droma asked.

"We might get a kilometer or two," Han replied, "but we'll still be in the blast range—and we're just as likely to be hit moving as staying still."

"Then what about letting our passengers go and blasting out of here once they're clear? That way we can draw fire away from them and fight back at the same time."

"But how many will be killed on the way?" Leia said. "And how many Yuuzhan Vong will be waiting for us?"

"Okay, then how about digging in?" Droma pressed. "The ground is really just cold sludge here. A good, hot blast would probably melt a sizable hole into—"

"Yeah, and would stand out like a huge target for any Vong passing over us." Han shook his head. "Sorry, pal. The same argument stands against sending another message for help: once those scarheads detect it, they'd be onto us in a flash. No, I think we've gone and dug ourselves into a—"

He stopped. *A grave,* Leia knew he'd been about to say, but the words were too close to the truth. A cold, dark grave on the edge of the known galaxy, with no possible way out.

Leia shook her head, frustrated. There *had* to be another solution—a way that didn't involve killing any more innocent locals, or ending up in a worse position than before!

"I suppose faking surrender is not an option," Droma offered.

"That doesn't work with the Vong anymore," Han said. "They're wise to that game."

The Ryn nodded and looked at the floor, his tail dropping limply behind him. Outside, the pounding of Esfandia rolled on like thunder, sometimes close, other times farther away. Whenever the floor beneath her shook, Leia tensed, each time expecting the shields to fail around them. The only other sound was the burbling of the planet's indigenous life-forms, issuing softly from the speaker.

"Well, then," Droma said, "seeing as we have no way out, there's something I should probably tell you."

"Excuse me," C-3PO interrupted, his photoreceptors glowing. "I think the Brrbrlpp may have the solution to our problem."

Han turned in his seat. "They do?"

"Yes, sir. The Brrbrlpp suggest that we take shelter in their nearby nesting area. It is underground, and easily large enough to fit our vessel. Or so they say."

"Why now?" Han interrupted, his expression one of annoyance and exasperation.

"Sir?"

"Why are they suggesting this now? Why didn't it occur to them before? They have a love for dramatic irony or something?"

"I don't believe so, sir," C-3PO answered, unaware of Han's sarcasm. "It would appear, though, that we have earned their trust. Protecting these few at great risk to our own lives has demonstrated that our past wrongs were clearly committed out of ignorance, not malice."

Han turned to Leia. "What do you think?"

"Can we get there on repulsors alone?" she asked the droid.

"The Brrbrlpp assure us that the nesting area is only a short distance away."

"Then—"

Her reply was cut off by another explosion, this one so close that it felt as though the entire world was breaking in two. The lights went out for a couple of seconds, then returned, flickering. Leia's ears rang as Han checked the instruments.

"One more like that and we're done for," he said.

"I don't know about you guys," Droma said, collecting himself from the floor, "but I think the locals' suggestion sounds wonderful."

Leia nodded at C-3PO. "Let's do it."

C-3PO conversed with the Brrbrlpp for a moment.

"They will move to the front and guide us. We are to travel in the direction they indicate."

Han nodded as the wafting aliens propelled themselves to the fore of the *Falcon*'s missile tubes. There they arranged themselves into a line pointing ahead and slightly to starboard.

Han fired up the repulsors and lifted the ship from Esfandia's surface. Dense air swirled around them, but the Brrbrlpp didn't appear disturbed. Protected within the shields, their ride would have been as smooth as it was for those inside the ship. Even when Han nudged the ship forward, their position with respect to the hull remained unchanged.

As the freighter turned to starboard, the line of Brrbrlpp straightened. Han took them gently through the murk, around a knobby protuberance that bulged out of the ground and vanished high above them, like a mountain. They dipped into a crater left behind by one of the Yuuzhan Vong's missiles, and out again, across an undulating plain. From their slightly higher perspective, they could see numerous bright flashes in the distance that revealed the continuing Yuuzhan Vong bombardment. It was disturbingly thorough. It was only a matter of time before one of those missiles got lucky.

"Is it much farther?" Han asked, obviously sharing Leia's concern. She felt more exposed moving around than they had been in hiding.

"We should be there at any moment," C-3PO reported.

"Does anyone else feel as though we're exchanging one tomb for another?" Droma asked. "What if the good guys lost the fight up in orbit and we're stuck down here forever? All the Vong will have to do then is wait us out."

"I don't like the look of this," Han muttered, his eyes darting nervously across the console before him. Several blips had appeared on the edge of the long-range scanners, dodging the bombardment sites. They traveled in formation at first, but then split up in different directions and zigzagged across the scope.

"They're sweeping the area at close range," Han said.

"Guess they got tired of trying to flush us out with bombs alone," Droma said, "and have decided to do the dirty work themselves."

Han nodded. "We're not going to be able to hide like this for much longer."

"Excuse me, sir, but the Brrbrlpp are changing direction." C-3PO pointed at the line of aliens guiding them across Esfandia, which was now angling down instead of forward.

"I don't understand," Han said, sweeping the forward cam across the stony surface. "I don't see anything. No caves, no tunnels, no—"

A red light began to flash on the scanners.

"Whatever we're supposed to be seeing, Han," Leia said, "I'd work it out fast if I were you. That's a coral-skipper heading our way."

"Ask them what we're supposed to do, will you, Threepio?" Han guided the *Falcon* down as far as he could go.

A wall of gray dirt and rounded pebbles confronted them. Further warbling was exchanged between C-3PO and the aliens as the droid tried to impress upon the Brrbrlpp the urgency of the situation.

"Hurry it up, Threepio," Han muttered anxiously. "We don't have all day!"

"We don't even have a minute," Leia said. "That skip is coming in fast."

"Right," Han said, clenching his jaw as he flicked switches. "I'm warming up the weapons systems and the engines. I don't care what's waiting for us out there, I'm making a break for it."

"Han, wait—" Leia started.

She stopped in midsentence. The ground ahead of them erupted. At first she thought that one of the Yuuzhan Vong missiles had hit them, but it wasn't an explosion. The ground opened up like a giant, fanged maw, spreading wide to swallow the *Falcon* whole. Leia had time only to gasp in horror at what looked like a thousand yellow eyes gleaming at her from the blackness within. Then the mouth came down upon them, and they were engulfed.

Tahiri struggled to think through a haze of tears. The voice of the shadow, the thing that had come to her, made her mind quake with fear. She didn't know what it was, or what it wanted. It was simply implacable, unstoppable.

And Riina wanted her to attack it . . .

What am I doing? she asked herself. All she felt was blackness—an oppressed, choking blackness that constantly threatened to close around her and devour her whole.

Whatever it is, Riina said, *it has to be better than fighting yourself.*

You're not me!

And you're not me; but apart, we're not anyone at all.

No! The exclamation came as much from grief as it did anger. The emotion was a reaction to Riina's words, but she directed the word at the shadow-creature. She wanted to destroy it, utterly—along with any unwanted truths it represented to her.

I don't— She stopped, afraid that to utter the words meant admitting defeat. The shadow-creature fell back a few steps, waiting for a renewed assault. *I don't want to lose who I am.*

Riina's expression changed to one of anger—an anger

that Tahiri felt course through her own body. *Neither do I!*

The Yuuzhan Vong girl lunged at the shadow. Perhaps something flinched, but Tahiri couldn't be sure. Was there really something out there, or was she just dreaming it?

Anakin would have known . . .

The thought of her friend—the one she loved—brought with it renewed grief, but not from within. This grief emanated from the darkness around her. She dropped her head, to hide from Riina the moisture gathering in her eyes. Nothing seemed to erase the pain that his death had brought her. No amount of tears could wash away the thought that there must have been something she could have done to save him. All the determination in the world couldn't stop her wishing that he could have lived, and that they were still together now, with every possible future ahead of them.

Even with the reptile god slain by her acceptance of her guilt, the grief never went away. It had returned as this shadow-creature. Clearly, it wasn't about to let her go. Unless . . .

A cool breeze blew in from the dark, touching the moisture on her cheeks.

I'm scared, she admitted quietly. *This world scares me.*

This world is all I've known since Yavin Four, Riina said.

Tahiri looked at her, then, understanding the simple truth of her situation for the first time. *This isn't a dream, is it?*

I'm as real as the shadow-creature we're fighting.

But Anakin killed you! You were dead!

Anakin thought he killed me, Riina said. *But he hadn't. He just forced me down deep into your unconscious. In many ways I suppose I was dead. I had no body, no senses, nothing to call my own. There was just me, trapped in this darkness. It was like a nightmare from which there felt like no escape. At times I thought I might go mad. In the end, though, I began to surface, and with me came my suffering and torment—the torment that has been affecting you all this time.*

Tahiri trembled at the notion. She knew it was the truth; she'd always known it. She just hadn't wanted to *accept* it.

It took me months to piece it all together, Riina went on. *And as I recovered, you weakened. It soon became clear to me that I didn't have to stay in this nightmare world. So I started to fight. Sometimes I even won. You had blackouts, and it was during these times that I was able to emerge. But my purchase on reality was feeble, and you kept pushing me back here. There were many times that I thought I'd be here forever—or worse, disappear altogether!*

I wish you had, Tahiri said. She couldn't help the bitterness.

Even then I knew I couldn't, Riina said. *Instead I decided to fight back all the more. I came after you, wanting to chase you down into the shadows of this world—to make you live here instead of me. I wanted you to experience this living death so that it would be you who'd wish to disappear. But then something happened: your guilt came after both of us! It was then that I realized that the two of us were inseparable. My torment was your torment; your guilt was my guilt. And impossible as it seems, Tahiri, we're stuck with each other. We either live together, or we die together. There is no in between.*

No! There has to be another way!

There isn't. Riina's voice was firm and inflexible. *Your hand is proof of that. Cut me and you bleed; kill me, and you die.*

Tahiri glanced at the wound Riina had inflicted on herself, which had affected her, too, as though by magic. Blood steadily seeped through the cauterized gash: the truth continued to trickle from it. Although Riina's words felt as heavy upon her shoulders as a thousand tombstones, she knew that the Yuuzhan Vong girl spoke no lies. There was no point denying it anymore. Her mind was inextricably linked to Riina's, tangled together like the roots of trees—and they had been ever since Yavin 4. There was no way to cut out one without injuring the other. They were conjoined twins, connected at a place where no surgeon's scalpel could ever reach: their minds.

So what are we? she asked. *Yuuzhan Vong? Jedi?*

We're both, Riina said. *And we are neither. We need to accept this and embrace this hybrid creature we have become. We need to merge, Tahiri, and become one.*

But who will I be?

You'll be someone new, Riina said. *You'll be someone* strong.

Tahiri couldn't talk any longer. Her tears choked her thoughts, blurred her vision again. She stared into the shadows around them, seeking out the guilt-creature hiding there. Was this how she was to "embrace" Riina? By killing this creature? Would they then, together, awaken from this terrible nightmare? It felt right on some level, and yet on another it seemed . . . *dark.* It felt *wrong.* And yet there seemed no other way!

A cry sounded out from the darkness. The shadow-creature, her guilt, was calling out to her again. She couldn't understand the words, but the sentiment was there in her tone.

My guilt calls out to me, she said.

You have nothing to feel guilty for! Riina insisted.

My love is dead, and I am alive. And I carry with me the kiss he wanted me to share with him. I told him to collect it later, but there was no later. Was there?

Do you think that's what you're accused of? They are

*not the words of your guilt, Tahiri; those are your own
words!*

How do you know what I'm feeling?

*How do I know? Haven't you been listening to what
I've been saying? We are one and the same mind!*

Tahiri recoiled in revulsion at the idea, although she
knew it to be the truth. She was just still railing against it.
Her thoughts had been open to her alien twin all along.

You've been punishing yourself, punishing us, Riina
said, *and it has nothing to do with Anakin's death or
holding back on a kiss.*

Then what is it?

*You feel guilt for having gotten on with your life. It's
not that you are alive; it's that you've learned to live
without Anakin. It's that you have healed, and you don't
think you should have by now.*

Tahiri wanted to refute it, but she couldn't. The truth
burned her in ways she couldn't ignore.

*You have to let go, Tahiri. There is no shame in that.
The time has come to stop grieving. You have already
stopped; you just don't know it yet. That's all.*

Bitterness clouded Tahiri's vision. She hated Riina for
speaking words that revealed the truth of her feelings.
Angrily she hurled her lightsaber into the dark. It spun
wildly through the air, lighting up the shadows as it
went, illuminating the rocks and crags of the worldship
they stood on. And as it cut through the darkness, she
could feel her grief ease and part; she could feel a sense of
awakening.

I know what to do now, she told Riina. Even as she
spoke the words, she quailed, thinking of everything she
might be leaving behind. The Solo family, her duty as a
Jedi, her memories—

But, she suddenly asked herself, how much of it was
hers at all? Anakin's family wasn't hers. The Jedi Knights

could carry on well enough without her. And her memories only served to bring her pain. As long as she didn't fall to the dark side, she could turn her back on it all with a clear conscience . . .

The time for thinking was over. Slowly, with a feeling like falling, she reached out, and her lightsaber flew back into her hand.

At the same time, the shadows seemed to part. She saw the thing that had come for her and Riina with startling clarity. It wasn't a god from the bowels of an alien mind; it wasn't the dark side; it wasn't her guilt, or her despair.

It was Jaina.

Tahiri turned to face her mirror image one last time.

I know what you're thinking, Riina said. *You mustn't listen to what she's saying. She's telling you lies, making things worse. She doesn't want to help. She only wants to keep you caged, with me.* Riina stepped closer, her injured hand outstretched. *Join me now; together we will do what we need to do to be free.*

Yes, Tahiri said slowly. *I think I understand now.*

So let's not think. Let's just do it.

Shakily, Tahiri reached out and took Riina's hand. Together they faced the darkness.

"If we don't start getting some answers soon," Mara said hotly, "I'm going to start giving you people reasons to be afraid of the Jedi."

Luke attempted to placate his wife by putting his hands on her shoulders beneath her red cascade of hair. But she was too angry to see reason right now, and ignored his efforts.

"I'm telling you the truth," returned the Ferroan woman called Darak. "We don't know who is responsible for this attack!"

"*Somebody* must know!" Mara argued. "Dissident

groups like this don't just pop up overnight. They take time to form."

"The idea of a dissident group is preposterous," Rowel said. "There hasn't been any unrest on Zonama for decades!"

"Well, there is now! I'm telling you: that attack was well planned and organized. Look," she said, "I'm not trying to be critical of you or your way of life here. I just want to know what's happened to our friends. The fact that you don't seem to care annoys me."

"But we *do* care," Rowel said. "We care that strangers are wandering loose on our planet doing untold damage. We care—"

Luke didn't give him chance to finish; he was only going to anger Mara further. "Perhaps Sekot could help us," he said. "Is it possible to ask it if it knows of their whereabouts?"

The Ferroans exchanged glances. "Sekot has been regenerating after the attack of the Far Outsiders," Darak said. "Its attention has been elsewhere, so it is unlikely to know the whereabouts of your friends."

"We could at least ask," Mara pressed. "What about the Magister? She could ask for us."

"She is resting."

"Well, we wouldn't want to put her out, would we?" Mara said dryly.

"Please wake her for us," Luke said, his calm tone a counterpoint to Mara's growing irritability. "After all, I'm sure she would want to be informed about a development as important as this, don't you?"

The Ferroans exchanged another glance, then Darak hurried off to do as the Jedi asked.

Luke felt little satisfaction at having accomplished that much. It was only the first of many hurdles. The rain was still falling, dripping down from the trees in a steady, fat-dropped stream. Somewhere deep in the tampasi, Jacen, Saba, and Danni remained hidden from his senses. If they didn't return of their own accord, he would be hard-pressed to find them without Sekot or the Magister's help.

"You are mistaken to believe that Sekot is aware of all things taking place on its surface," Rowel said. "It is no more capable of this than you would be of tracking every cell in your body."

"It seemed to find us easily enough when we arrived," Mara said.

"Out in space it is different. A grain of sand is immediately noticeable if it gets in your eye, but that same grain of sand would be almost impossible to find on a beach." The Ferroan looked uncomfortable. "We have notified surrounding communities to be on the lookout for anyone moving through the tampasi. Darak will also try to coax the airships into flying in this weather. Perhaps they can discern something from above that we are missing on the ground."

"That's a good start," Luke said. "Thank you."

"Please don't believe that this kind of behavior is normal for my people. We *are* peaceful. This sort of thing simply doesn't happen here."

"Fear of that which is new or different can make people act irrationally," Mara said, putting on a conciliatory tone. "But all that concerns us now is finding our friends."

"I can assure you that they *will* be found. We will make every possible effort."

A sudden feeling came through the Force. Luke closed his eyes in order to focus on it. It was coming from some distance away, but the intense life energies of the tampasi made it impossible to tell which direction it came from.

Mara touched his arm. "You feel it, too?"

He opened his eyes, nodding. "It's Jacen. I think he's safe for the moment. I sensed no immediate danger."

"Are they on their way back?" Hegerty asked.

"I'm not sure," Luke said. "I don't think so."

"What about the others?" Hegerty pressed. "Are they all right?"

"I can't tell," Luke said, reaching into the Force in an attempt to understand the message that Jacen was trying to send. "But I think they're all okay, for the moment."

"We should still try to find them, though," Mara said.

Luke nodded. "Yes."

Rowel opened his mouth to say something but was cut off by the sudden return of Darak. Her expression was one of profound alarm.

"She's gone!" she exclaimed.

"Who?" Mara said. "Who's gone?"

"The Magister!" The panic in her voice gave her an air of vulnerability Luke hadn't seen before. "She's been taken from her rooms!"

"What do you mean 'taken'?" Rowel asked, aghast. "Why would anybody do that?"

"I think I know," Luke said. "The kidnap of Danni was just a distraction. She wasn't who the kidnappers were after. It was Jabitha. While you were busy here trying to sort things out, they moved in on her."

The alarm in Darak's and Rowel's eyes increased tenfold at the suggestion.

"First Danni," Mara said, "then Jacen and Saba, and now the Magister. Could anyone else possibly go missing before tonight is over?"

Jag reached Tahiri's room in record time. There he found *Pride of Selonia*'s chief medic, Dantos Vigos, and Selwin Markota, Captain Mayn's second in command. Both looked up, startled, as he skidded through the doorway to a halt.

On the bed beside Tahiri was Jaina, her outstretched

form dressed in the clothes she usually wore about the ship. Her eyes were shut, her face expressionless, and her breathing was fast and shallow.

"What happened?" he asked, wrenching off his flight helmet. He was unable to take her eyes from her face.

"Relax, Jag," Markota said. He put a hand on his shoulder, but Jag shrugged it off.

"I'll relax when I know what's going on."

"That's the problem," Vigos said. "We don't *know* what's going on. We found Jaina unconscious shortly after arriving around Esfandia. No one noticed before then because of all the confusion and the fighting. She was slumped beside Tahiri, having collapsed onto the bed. Their hands were locked together. We've scanned them both and found no signs of physical abnormalities, but their minds are furiously active."

Jag faced the medic with a frown. "How do you account for this?"

Vigos shrugged. "I don't."

"But you must have an idea," Jag said. "You must have a theory, at least!"

Vigos sighed wearily. "Okay, but it's only a theory based on what I've been told of Tahiri's background and recent behavior. In my opinion, Tahiri has retreated into herself. She has a split personality that is fighting for dominance over the body. I think Tahiri has deliberately internalized that conflict—she's keeping it in her head so that neither personality has access to the outside world."

"I can understand that," Jag said. "But what does this have to do with Jaina?"

"I think they've melded," Vigos said. "I'm not a Jedi, but I suspect that Jaina may have attempted this in an effort to assist Tahiri. She's helping Tahiri survive."

Jag studied Jaina's face. Despite the appearance of being asleep, she looked exhausted.

"So why won't she respond?" he asked. "If she's in

there voluntarily, why doesn't she just wake up and tell us what's going on?"

"It's impossible for me to say for sure," Vigos admitted. "I'm sorry."

A bizarre image came to Jag then—one he couldn't quite get his head around. He pictured Tahiri's mind as some sort of animal trap, snaring anyone who ventured within it. Jedi after Jedi could throw themselves in and be lost forever. But how could this possibly serve Riina?

The three men stared at the two unconscious women for a long, frustrated moment. Jag didn't want to let the matter lie there, but he wasn't sure what he could do about it. Had he been Force-sensitive, he wouldn't have hesitated to try to join the meld. The woman he—

His mind retreated from the admission, then grasped it and kept going. Yes, the woman he loved was in danger. There had to be *something* he could do.

"Maybe you're right," he said. "Maybe you have done everything you can to help her. But *I* can still try."

Vigos glanced uncertainly at Markota, then back to Jag. "What did you have in mind?"

"I'll talk to her," he said. "If she is in there, she'll be able to hear me."

"Colonel, we've tried—"

"Just leave me alone with her, okay?" Jag interrupted.

Markota hesitated, then nodded to the medic. "We've got nothing to lose."

Vigos acquiesced. "Okay. But call if there's any change in her condition."

"I will," Jag promised.

When they were gone and the door had shut behind them, Jag put his flight helmet down on the end of the bed and sat beside Jaina. He took her free hand in both of his. It was limp and lifeless, and cool to the touch. Despite his determination to want to help her, now that he was alone he had to admit that he really didn't know if there was anything useful he *could* do. There was no enemy he could line up in a targeting reticle and fire upon; there was just Jaina, locked in the mind of a very sick young woman who also needed help.

"I'm here," he whispered close in to her ear. "And I'm not going anywhere, Jaina. Not until you wake up. You know what that means, don't you? It means that Twin Suns Squadron is unattended. And we can't have that, can we?"

He stared at her face in silence. He hadn't really expected his words to have an immediate impact upon her condition, but he couldn't help hoping they would—that just hearing his voice would be enough to make her come back. But when he searched her expression for any sign of recognition, he found none. She remained still, emotionless, sleeping . . .

He squeezed her hand between his. Although he knew the room was probably being monitored, he didn't care who saw him, who heard him, or who might disapprove of his sentiments. All he cared about right now was Jaina. And from the way his heart ached, that's all he felt he could ever care about.

"I love you, Jaina," he said. The words came easily for him. "Please come back to me."

Saba kept all her senses alert as she matched her pace to that of the Ferroan kidnappers. The path they'd been following had run out half an hour earlier, and they were now moving through unbeaten wilds of the tampasi. Despite the lack of any obvious trail, though, the Ferroans seemed to know where they were going. They moved as one with silent determination through the dense undergrowth. Every now and then they gave directional orders to her or Jacen, but never allowed themselves to enter any conversation. Nor were they prepared to come within a meter of her—although Saba had no doubts that this would change once they reached the camp where Senshi and the other conspirators were meant to be located. Security of numbers would inevitably make them feel less intimidated by the Jedi Knights.

The farther they traveled, the more uneasy Saba became—mainly because of Danni's condition. She knew that Jacen would never knowingly put Danni's life in jeopardy, and the fact that the young scientist remained unconscious was obviously weighing heavily on his mind, but Saba still felt compelled to take the girl and try to find a way back to the others in the hope of getting her some medical attention. The only thing that stayed her urges was her trust in Jacen's judgment. He saw things differently from her, on a deeper, more fundamental level, and for that reason she was prepared to bow to his command.

They came to a bridge formed from a massive tree trunk that stretched across a swollen river. Three of the Ferroans crossed first, then waved for Saba and Jacen to follow. Once they were on the other side, the remaining four Ferroans crossed also, then the trek continued through a dense thicket of wild, red-leaved bushes. Sharp thorns slashed at Saba's tough green skin. She did her best to avoid the worst of it, and to keep Danni from being scratched, subtly using the Force to push the thicket branches aside.

Finally they came to a cliff face that was hidden from view by a stand of enormous boras. At the base of the cliff was an overhang five meters high and stretching a dozen meters into the rock. Jacen and Saba were directed under its shelter, where a larger group of Ferroans waited.

They gathered around the new arrivals as they entered the shaded, sandy area, parting only to admit a very old Ferroan male to the front. His face was as heavily lined as Jabitha's, but his rich, deep black hair was short to the scalp. The pale blueness of his skin made him look as though he were composed entirely of ice, and his gold-and-black eyes regarded the new arrivals with ill-disguised contempt.

His gaze flickered across Saba, Jacen, and the comatose Danni. "I ask for one of the visitors as a hostage, and you bring me the entire group. What is the meaning of this?"

A look of confusion passed over Tourou's face. "Three seemed better than one, Senshi . . ." The residue of the implanted suggestion from Jacen had faded, and the kidnapper's sentence trailed off uncertainly.

"You fool," the old man said. "The outsiders have ways about them—ways to make their words seem reasonable."

"It's true that I influenced their decision to bring us here," Jacen said, "but I only did so because I wanted to speak with you. It's important that you see reason. We didn't come to your planet to cause trouble; we came because—"

Senshi's laugh cut him short. "Don't try to win *me* with your words, Jedi! I respond to actions, not empty words or promises. The recent actions against our world speak volumes!"

"Those attacks came from the ones you refer to as Far Outsiders," Jacen said. "They had nothing to do with us."

"You are all outsiders in our eyes," he argued. "The actions of one reflect intentions of the other."

"And what about *your* actionz?" Saba asked. "What does kidnapping say about you?"

Before Senshi could reply, a peal of thunder rumbled through the tampasi, and rain began to crash down with renewed strength outside the overhang. As the thunder died in the distance, Senshi looked triumphantly at his hostages and ignored Saba's question completely.

At that moment, another group of Ferroans stumbled in from the rain, bearing another body on a stretcher, covered from head to foot with a tarpaulin. Her first thought was that the kidnappers had returned for Soron Hegerty and somehow snatched the elderly woman from the care of Master Skywalker and Mara. But when the new arrivals set down the stretcher and pulled back the tarp, Saba's concern quickly changed to puzzlement. It wasn't Hegerty at all; it was the Magister.

Senshi stared down at the unconscious figure, smiling thinly. "Now they won't be able to ignore us."

There was a murmur from the Ferroans standing around him.

Jacen stepped forward. "Why would you do this? Why take the Magister?"

"Because she has forgotten," he sneered. "She has forgotten the pain and suffering we endured the last time strangers came here after years of searching: the fires and the groundquakes; the terrible losses as whole villages fell; the hurricanes that tore entire boras out by their roots; the smoke that covered the sky. She forgets that we all lost loved ones, and that we stand to lose more if we allow her to throw away everything we've worked for. We didn't come here to rest and rebuild and then just throw everything away on a whim! We came here for *sanctuary*."

"You remember the time before the Crossings?" Jacen asked.

"As clearly as if it were yesterday," Senshi said, his expression haunted. "I lost my children, my partner, my parents, and my brother and sister. And I lost too many friends to even count! I was alone, wishing that I had died with them. But I was spared; I lived on. I endured with Sekot as we searched for sanctuary, and I rejoiced when we finally found the peace we had so long yearned for. And now I feel misgivings at the return of the Far Outsiders—as well as the Jedi." He indicated the storm raging anew outside the overhang. "We have seen this combination before; we know what it means. I will not let the Magister plunge us into another cycle of death and destruction."

"Sekot welcomed us here," Jacen protested.

"Did it? I have only the Magister's word on that."

"Why would she lie?"

"Because by forgetting, she has become confused. And that confusion weakens her, putting us all at risk. I for one do not want to become cannon fodder in someone else's war."

Saba could sympathize with the man. She felt his pain as keenly as she felt her own. Had she been faced with the possibility of losing her loved ones and her home-world over again, she, too, would probably take drastic steps to prevent it. But she couldn't imagine the Magister ignoring either the will of her people—if Senshi's feelings were widespread—or the will of Sekot. That would run counter to her purpose. It was unlikely that Sekot would tolerate such behavior in the person it had chosen to act as mediator between itself and its citizens.

"So what happens now?" Jacen asked. "What do you hope to achieve by all this?"

"We have achieved as much as we dared dream," Senshi replied. "We've shown that we cannot be easily ignored. When the Magister wakes, she will have no choice but to listen to us. And if that fails, if she still turns her back on us, we still have you to bargain with. Either way, disaster *will* be averted."

"But by turning your backs on *us*," Jacen said, "you risk a much greater disaster."

"Such as?"

"Such as the domination of the galaxy by a power more destructive than you could possibly imagine. Once that power has consolidated its forces on the ruins of our worlds, it will come for you. The Far Outsiders may have been repelled once, but they won't be so easily repelled when this system is filled with their warships. They will seed every planet in the system with biological factories in order to replace every ship you destroy. They'll place interdictors across the entrances to this hyperspace bubble to make sure you can't escape. And what happens then, Senshi? Who will you call upon for help when everyone else in the galaxy is gone?"

The young human spoke with the confidence of one in possession of a cold, hard truth, and Saba could see through Senshi's glare that what Jacen was saying was having an impact—even if he didn't want to admit it.

"You will never convince me that we need your help."

"Thankfully it's not you we need to convince," Jacen replied. "It's Sekot. And if you truly have the best interests of the planet at heart, then you'll abide by its decision. Whether it listens to me through you or the Magister, it *will* hear my words—and then it can decide for itself."

A low rumble rolled in across the tampasi at the conclusion of Jacen's challenge. Saba felt an involuntary muscular contraction ripple down her spine. The Ferroans were silent, transfixed by the confrontation between Senshi and Jacen. There was fear in their eyes, as well as uncertainty.

"It's been a long day," Senshi said after a few moments. "We are all tired. Unless the Magister wakes before, we will rest until dawn. By the light of day, things may be clearer."

"We will stay until then," Jacen said. His tone was soft, but there was no escaping the antagonism of his words.

"You'll stay until I decide you can leave," he returned coldly.

"This one iz prepared to argue the point," Saba said, matching his frosty tone.

The Ferroan leader shot her a baleful glare, but didn't challenge her. He turned his back on them and issued orders to the rest of the kidnappers. The group slowly dissolved into clumps of people unfolding bedrolls and breaking out supplies. Tourou guided Saba and Jacen to a niche at the rear of the overhang, where they lay Danni's stretcher down and covered her with blankets. There, surrounded by nervous Ferroans, they made themselves comfortable for what little remained of the night. Saba had no intentions of sleeping, and neither, clearly, did Jacen. He sat up, his face glowing in infrared as he stared past the Ferroan guard to where Senshi stood talking to a couple of his people.

"What now?" Saba asked, interrupting his thoughts.

He faced her in the dark. "Now we wait."

"Do you have a plan?"

"None at the moment, except to demonstrate to Senshi that we don't mean them any harm—no matter how much they try to provoke us."

"We don't have to cause them harm," Saba said. "This one could carry Danni while you free the Magister. Together—"

"Too difficult," Jacen responded. "There are too many of them. Someone's bound to get hurt. We can afford to be patient a little longer."

Saba wasn't so sure.

"Danni haz been unconscious a long time, Jacen," she reminded him. "She will need medical attention soon."

Jacen looked down at the unconscious scientist. One hand reached out to brush damp strands of hair from her face. "She'll be all right," he said. The Force stirred at his touch, to help promote healing. "I'm sure she will."

But he couldn't look at Saba as he said it, and he didn't sound convinced.

* * *

Tahiri trembled as she felt the shadow of Jaina, lost in the prison of her mind.

Let's kill her! Riina said, her voice full of eagerness. *She's vulnerable in here, and we'll take her by surprise.*

No, Tahiri said simply. *No, we mustn't. I mustn't. To do so would not relieve me of my grief; it would compound it. To kill her would send me to the dark side. And that's what you'd like, isn't it, Riina? That's why you clouded my sight, so I couldn't see!*

The Yuuzhan Vong girl seemed infinitely smaller than she had a moment earlier.

You spoke the truth when you said we could never be separated, but you feel that if I embrace the dark side then I will become a prisoner of these shadow lands, allowing you to become the dominant personality.

Riina said nothing in return.

Tahiri shook her head. *I would sooner we both stay here forever than unleash you upon my world!*

Riina snarled and tried to pull away, but Tahiri held tight. Their fingers were slick with blood, but her will was strong.

It's time, she said. *I'm tired of being lost.*

The ragged edges of their wound sought each other and sealed as though it had never existed. Tahiri gasped at the unsettling sensation, and heard Riina do the same. She watched with alarm as their entwined fingers melted into each other, as though their skin had wrapped around both hands, binding them together. Tahiri met Riina's eyes and recognized the horror she saw there. Then the two of them stared as the lumpy knot of flesh that was their combined hands began to spread along their arms. Tahiri could see the bones moving beneath, testing their new environment. Then the knot began to move up their forearms, drawing them closer together.

Riina continued to try to fight it, but Tahiri refused to

relent—even though she shared the Yuuzhan Vong girl's fear and revulsion for what was happening to them.

There's still time to change your mind, Riina cried as she struggled. *We don't have to do this!*

You're wrong, Tahiri said. *We do have to do this. It's the only way.*

Despite her determination, though, the words didn't ease the dread tightening in her chest. While she felt sure that this was what needed to be done, she really didn't know what the result was going to be.

The knot reached their elbows, and Tahiri felt her hand sliding under the skin to Riina's shoulder. It felt as though an outside force were at work, pulling the mirror image of herself into a tight embrace.

Tahiri met Riina's wide-eyed stare again.

We must embrace, she told her Yuuzhan Vong counterpart. *Our cultures, our beliefs, our knowledge.*

Some of the fear ebbed from Riina's gaze, then. *We must embrace,* she concurred. *Our emotions, our lives, our selves.*

Tahiri took a deep breath as the knot of skin reached their heads and slowly pulled them together so that their noses were almost touching.

The good and the bad, Riina said, her lips brushing lightly against Tahiri's own.

The light and the dark, Tahiri said. *We must embrace . . .*

"It's a trap!" Droma's cry of alarm was echoed by C-3PO, who threw himself backward as the floor tipped beneath them and *Millennium Falcon* was sucked down into the gaping maw.

Leia hung on desperately while Han struggled to reach the controls in front of him. From his annoyed expression, she knew that he was about to blast their way out of danger—and he wasn't about to consult with the aliens before doing so, either.

But there was something about the unfolding space ahead of them that caught Leia's eye. Still gripping her seat, she leaned forward in the hope of getting a better look.

"I think I know what it is!" she said.

"I don't *care* what it is! Anything intending to eat us is trouble!"

"That's not what it's doing. Look!"

All eyes in the cockpit turned to the display just as the maw fell shut around them. The light-enhancing algorithms adjusted to this new level of darkness, searching out infrared and other frequencies for information on their new environment. The *Falcon* seemed to be surrounded by numerous vertical columns, like teeth in an enormous mouth.

But if it was a mouth, it wasn't eating them. There was no rending, no crushing, nothing at all to indicate that they were about to be ingested into the belly of some giant subterranean beast.

"See those columns?" Leia said, pointing at the display. "They're legs. And as for the eyes . . ." She watched carefully as the sensors scanned the ceiling.

Han chuckled before she could finish what she'd been about to say. "Portholes, right?"

"The relay base?" Droma sounded as though he could hardly believe his eyes—or his luck.

"It was here all along," Han said, cutting power to the repulsors and letting the *Falcon* settle to the bottom.

"Perhaps not." Leia watched as a slender wire snaked out of the gloom and attached itself to the hull of the battered freighter. "Don't go giving your Solo luck any medals just yet."

"This is Commander Ashpidar of Esfandia Long-Range Communications Base," came an emotionless, female voice from the comm. Leia identified its speaker as a Gotal, which seemed appropriate. The bi-horned, energy-sensitive beings would perfectly suit a gloomy place like Esfandia. "I'm sorry we took so long getting here. Word travels slowly among the Cold Ones."

"You know who we are?" Leia asked, making sure to reply the same way Ashpidar's communications arrived—along the wire. The Yuuzhan Vong search parties were too close to risk any sort of broadcast.

"We know you came to help us, and that's all that matters. We were sheltering in some nesting plains several dozen kilometers from here when word arrived. The tunnels connecting the plains are cramped but easy enough to negotiate. We came as soon as we could."

"How many are there under your command?"

"Fifteen," Ashpidar replied. "We lost two when the bombardment began. They were servicing one of the detectors when the Yuuzhan Vong destroyed it. The rest of us are in here, though—safe for the moment."

Leia hoped that remained the situation. Taking in the *Falcon* had been a calculated risk with the Yuuzhan Vong searching so fervently above. She would hate to be responsible for any more lives lost.

She quickly identified herself, Han, and Droma, and put a name to the ship. Then she explained what they were doing there, and who they'd brought with them to defend the base.

"Imperials?" the Gotal said, surprised. "They're the last people I expected to see you working with."

"Times change," Han said. "But listen, we're going to need to work out what we're going to do next."

"I will organize a docking umbilical to enable us to meet and discuss this in person."

"That's a good idea," Leia said. "We'll have to find a way to keep you safe until the Yuuzhan Vong leave."

"We're safe enough right where we are," Ashpidar

said tonelessly. "Unless we break comm silence or expose ourselves, we could hide here indefinitely."

"Assuming their tactics don't change, of course."

"Speaking of which," Droma said, waving for silence. "Listen."

Leia and Han did so, but the only sound to be heard was that of the air scrubbers recycling air through the cockpit.

"I don't hear anything," Han said.

The Ryn nodded, his tail sweeping the floor behind him. "The bombardment has stopped. And that can only mean one thing."

"They've given up?" Han said.

Droma frowned. "Actually, I was thinking more along the lines that they're coming down for a closer look."

Leia's stomach sank. She liked the sound of her husband's suggestion better, but she knew Droma was right.

"Commander, you'd better get that umbilical across fast," she said. "I think we're going to be having company real soon."

Luke and Mara stayed up with the Ferroans as they attempted to locate the kidnappers. Airships came and went throughout the night, moving across the stormy sky like ghostly clouds. A vast root system covered the entire planet, Luke learned, linking boras to boras, tampasi to tampasi in a vast organic network. Communications traveled along the network with representatives of far-flung sections of the globe getting involved in the discussion of the abduction. Some had suggestions to make; others just called to express their fear and uncertainty at the thought that the Magister might be in any danger.

Darak and Rowel assured them all that everything would work out in the end. Their voices were calm, but Luke knew that they were more worried than they were prepared to admit.

That worry only increased as hints began to emerge from the boras network, reports of missing people and notes offering the first hints into the minds of the kidnappers. A sketch of a conspiracy formed, one that had acted exceedingly quickly to take advantage of the Jedi Knights' arrival. Almost too quickly, Luke thought . . .

"Any idea what this Senshi might want?" Mara asked.

Rowel shook his head. "None, I'm afraid."

"I know of Senshi," Darak said. "He comes from one of the settlements farther north. He has a plantation up there where he grows rogir-bolns—the white fruit whose pulp you were served earlier. He's known for his talks on the Crossings and what it was like. He's also very vocal about his ideal of a perfect and pure Zonama—which involves the exclusion of *any* outsiders."

"Does he have any history of active dissent?" Luke asked.

"Not that I'm aware of," Darak said. "But he does have a lot of supporters. He'd certainly have the resources and contacts to put such a plan into motion."

"Is it possible he's taking the hostages to his plantation?" Mara asked.

"No." Darak was firm on this. "The plantation is in the opposite direction from the one we know they took. We have people waiting there, in case they've doubled back, but I don't expect them to find anything."

Luke sighed tiredly. The occasional wave of reassurance came from Jacen, but his nephew's presence in the Force was still weak and indistinct. Nevertheless, that he was getting anything at all was a good sign, and for that he was thankful.

After a seemingly endless night, a greenish dawn finally began to filter through the treetops. The rain eased slightly, and some of the forest's fauna emerged from hiding. Gleaming birds swooped through the long branches, while lithe, long-limbed climbers emerged from shelters in the nooks of tree trunks to collect and munch on fronds and flowers. Sinuous tentacles swayed around the bases of the massive boras, almost as though licking at the mobile fungi that moved around the trunks in search of sunlight.

Everywhere Luke looked, he saw life stirring. Resources moved up the food chain as one creature ate another, then back down via waste and decay. There was a dynamic joyousness to the scene that put some of his concerns in perspective. No matter what happened to Jacen, Saba, and Danni, or even Jabitha, life here would continue to go on, much as it had before.

Captain Yage called from the *Widowmaker* as Zonama's terminator rolled westward around the planet, bringing dawn wherever it touched.

"Everything's quiet up here," she said. "I'm maintaining the orbit we've been given, not deviating a centimeter. I've sent probes across the system, but there's no sign of the Yuuzhan Vong."

"Any word from Mon Calamari?"

"Not a peep. Either they're ignoring our hails or someone's cut communications between here and there."

"I'll give you one guess who that someone might be," Mara said.

"Have the Chiss reported any concerted troop movements on the border of the Unknown Regions?" Luke asked.

"Not on their side," she said. "But if someone's taken out the relay bases between here and home, they wouldn't need to come that far."

"Well, here's hoping someone else is doing something about it," Mara said. "I'd hate us to have good news and no one to tell it to."

Luke clicked his comlink and called Tekli. The Jedi healer was awake and had little to report. *Jade Shadow* was still held fast by the planet's vegetation, but nothing had made a move on her so far, which Luke was thankful to hear. It seemed that the policy of nonaggression was having exactly the response that he and Jacen had hoped for. Sekot clearly wasn't about to do anything unless they attacked first . . .

As the light of day strengthened, it became apparent that the kidnappers weren't about to be found in a hurry. Even with the storm easing, they were still no closer to finding Jabitha or Jacen, Saba, and Danni.

After nibbling at slices of fruit that had been served in bowls for breakfast, Hegerty stood up to stretch. The doctor looked weary and haggard after the long and troubled night. Luke had suggested she try to get some rest on a couple of occasions, but she had said there was no way she could sleep—not with the others still missing and the kidnappers still at large. The doctor was no fighter, and the attempt on her life the night before had left her understandably rattled.

"Are you okay, Soron?"

The doctor nodded. "Just thinking."

"What about?"

She stepped back up to the group around the fire. "Well, Senshi has to have kidnapped the Magister for a reason, right?"

"Right."

"Well, it seems to me that, if it wasn't to harm her or ask for a ransom, then it could have only been for one reason."

"Which is?"

"He wants to talk to her." She nodded thoughtfully for a moment. "Maybe she didn't want to give Senshi the implied approval that would bring before now. Maybe she did listen, but ignored him. But since all of our attempts to locate his group have so far failed, she may now have no other choice."

"You sound like that would be a bad thing," Luke said.

"That depends entirely on what he's got to say, I guess." Hegerty rubbed the bump on her head left by the attempted kidnapping. "And on how convincing he can be . . ."

Pellaeon stood on the bridge of *Right to Rule*, savoring the silence but in no way relaxed by it. The withdrawal of the Yuuzhan Vong to a geosynchronous orbit high above the western hemisphere of Esfandia was fortunately timed, allowing exhausted Imperial pilots to return to their base ships and restock. But it was only a temporary reprieve, prompted by Jag Fel's superb disruption of the northern flank. Commander Vorrik still had the superior force and could wield it whenever he wished. Once he had regrouped, Pellaeon had no doubt that he would do just that. For now, though, a tense but stable stalemate persisted.

The surface of Esfandia was safe from heavy bombardment, at least. With the chaos of battle behind them, it was much easier for both sides to detect and intercept anyone trying to reach the surface. That meant, effectively, that it was off limits to both sides, and that whoever was currently down there was safe for the time being. And stuck there.

"Excuse me, sir," said Pellaeon's aide, standing patiently to attention behind him. "I have the information you requested."

He didn't know how long she'd been there. It could have been minutes; he'd been so caught up in his thoughts. "Go on," he said without turning.

"Close analysis of telemetry reveals at least two surface landings during the battle," she said. "One was almost certainly *Millennium Falcon*."

"I should have known that's where they'd go. Right

into the thick of it, as usual." He nodded, hiding his relief at the news. "And the other?"

"A yorik-trema landing craft. The Seventy-eighth destroyed two other such craft also attempting to land, but lost this one during the fighting. It was assumed to have burned up on entry. We now suspect otherwise."

He faced the aide. "Do we know where it put down?"

"We have an approximate region, one hundred kilometers across. But it is possible that it has since moved under the cover of the atmosphere."

"So we've lost it?"

"Yes, sir."

"And *Millennium Falcon*?"

"The same. We weren't actively looking for either, sir, otherwise—"

"I suggest we start looking for them immediately."

"Yes, sir."

"What about that concentrated bombardment we saw? Could that be related?"

"That is possible, sir. It's equally possible that the Yuuzhan Vong detected some sign of the relay base in the region."

He nodded thoughtfully. "I guess the main thing is that we've stopped them firing on it."

"Yes, sir."

"Good work." He looked the aide over briefly, and saw deep lines of exhaustion on the woman's face. "And now I'd like you to excuse yourself from the bridge and get some rest."

"Sir?"

"I'll summon you when things heat up again. Of that I can assure you."

"But—"

"That's an order. I need my crew fit and alert, first and foremost. That applies to everyone. See to it that *all* crew are rotated so that they receive both rest and nourishment. It might be some time before we have another breather like this."

She saluted, but the formality didn't hide the gratitude in her eyes.

When she was gone, he turned his attention to the officer nearest to him.

"Get me Captain Mayn of *Pride of Selonia*," he ordered.

"Right away, sir."

Seconds later, her hologram was visible before him.

"Grand Admiral, how may I help?"

"We've noted the presence of the *Millennium Falcon* on the surface of Esfandia. What is the nature of her mission there?"

The woman hesitated, as though warring with herself whether or not to answer his question.

He sighed tiredly. He didn't have time for suspicions. "Captain, may I remind you that we are on the same side?"

Military training took over, then, and she visibly stiffened at his tone. "They are attempting to assist the crew of the relay base. An opportunity arose for them to break the blockade, and they took it."

"Have you heard from them since?"

"There was a garbled transmission from the region most recently targeted by the Yuuzhan Vong, but it was jammed. We suspect it was from the *Millennium Falcon*, advising us of their intentions, but the content of the message, and its source, is unknown."

He nodded, wondering again just how far he should trust the Galactic Alliance officers he had been pressed into dealing with. If there was something else going on, something Leia Organa Solo wanted kept secret even though it might jeopardize the lives of his officers and crews, would this Captain Mayn tell him? Her initial reluctance in answering his question made him doubtful.

"Commander Vorrik has sent a landing party after them," he said. "We believe they're both looking for the same thing, possibly in the area most recently under fire. Do you have any plans for a recovery operation?"

"None at the moment," she admitted. "But no doubt we'll put something into effect once—" She hesitated minutely, then concluded, "Once the situation here is stabilized."

"Is it possible to advise me in advance of any such operation being put into effect?"

"We will advise you of our intentions," she said evenly.

He wondered if she shared his suspicions. Did she question whether he could be trusted? Was she afraid that he would attempt to stop them from saving the Solos?

"Excellent," he said. "We might even offer our assistance in that venture, should the opportunity arise."

Mayn nodded, and the hologram faded out. He longed to rest his feet, to take the strain of standing off his healing back muscles, but he had one more job to do before he could think of retiring.

"See if you can raise Commander Vorrik," he said. A muted rustling swept through the bridge at the request, and the comm officer bent seriously to the task. They hadn't directly communicated with the enemy since chasing them from Imperial Space, and each time they had it turned out to be quite a show.

Pellaeon forced himself to relax, affecting a look of casual amusement. He didn't know how well the Yuuzhan Vong had learned to appreciate human expressions, but he wasn't going to miss an opportunity to unsettle his opponent.

A snarling, scarred visage appeared on the bridge's main screen. Visual communications with the Yuuzhan Vong were primitive, reflecting the fundamentally different technologies applied by each culture, but there was no mistaking that face. Vorrik had had his skin peeled back from his cheeks, exposing ribbed muscle tissue and pulsating veins. His scalp had been similarly flayed, leaving thin, jagged strips of hair where the scalping hadn't been completed. Tattoos blackened what skin was left, lending the commander a truly horrific appearance.

"I foul my senses every second I endure your likeness, infidel," came the ragged, hate-filled voice. "Be quick, so I can erase your sight from my eyes."

"This is just a social call," Pellaeon said, smiling in response to the commander's insults. "I was wondering how *Kur-hashan* was faring?"

"You dare mock me with your trivial—"

"Mock the great commander? I wouldn't dare." Pellaeon couldn't hide his amusement. "I leave that to your superiors, who send you off on a fool's errand while they bask in the glory of the Core."

The roar of rage he received in response was gratifying. Vorrik was easily rattled. He was about to launch another string of invective at the Grand Admiral when Pellaeon spoke over the top of him.

"I thought it was time to discuss the situation," he said, loudly enough to be heard. "We have something of a standoff in place at the moment, Vorrik. I trust some thoughts on how to break it would have crossed that flat-browed mind of yours?"

Vorrik looked like his flayed head was about to explode. "It will break when we crush your puny fleet!" he roared. "When we squash you like bugs beneath our feet! Then I will break *you* personally—bone by bone, nerve by nerve, until you are nothing but slime."

"Am I to take it, then, that negotiating a withdrawal is not an option?"

"Withdrawing is not the Yuuzhan Vong way."

"That's odd, because I seem to recall you withdrawing at Borosk." Pellaeon paused long enough to allow the commander to think of a response, but not enough time to actually utter it. "And here I was thinking that we were finally managing to breed some sense into your barbaric species. Now I see we still have some way to go."

The black blood drained from Vorrik's face, leaving him gray with rage. With a snarl, he struck the oggzil villip transmitting his side of the conversation. There was a blue flash, an organic squelching sound, and then nothing.

Pellaeon turned away from the projector, eminently satisfied. Vorrik would be too enraged to think clearly for some time now. His tactics would be clouded and more ineffective than they would otherwise have been—and that could only be a good thing. Pellaeon had to survive until Vorrik was reminded that his orders almost certainly didn't include wasting his time on some out-of-the-way worldlet while more pressing battles called for him elsewhere.

Pellaeon's smile gave way to a look of exhaustion as he finally stood down for the shortest possible rest period he would allow himself. Given that the Imperial and Galactic Alliance forces were in a position that was untenable in the long haul, he hoped that Vorrik's superiors wouldn't take too long.

Jacen lifted himself out of a recuperative trance at the same time that Saba beside him stirred. He'd been lending his strength to Danni, who was still out cold, while Saba had been exploring the life fields of the planet in an attempt to ascertain exactly where they were concentrated. The question of whether Sekot existed uniformly through the planet's biosphere or focused in particular areas was still very much open. If Sekot's mind *was* focused nearby, there was a chance they could contact it and, through it, talk to the others.

What had roused them from their meditations was the sound of the Magister's voice resounding through the cave.

"Tell Senshi I wish to speak with him," she said evenly. Her supine body was still bound and blindfolded, yet she commanded authority.

One of the Ferroans who had been assigned to watch over the prisoners hurried off to find Senshi. The remaining four guards stepped away from Jabitha, as if the Magister might somehow attack them even in her trussed state.

Senshi soon came and crouched down beside the Magister's body. "You've been listening in on us, I see," he said. There was amusement in his voice.

"You must have known I would," she replied. "In fact, you probably wanted me to. Otherwise you would have blocked my ears as you had covered my eyes."

He reached down at this and removed the blindfold. Even from where Jacen was sitting, they could see the dawn's greenish hue reflected from the woman's black irises as she blinked in the sudden light.

"Sit her up," Senshi said, and two Ferroans hoisted her up so she was resting with her back against the rocky wall of the cave.

"I suppose untying me is out of the question."

Senshi ignored the request. "You brought outsiders here," he said instead, glancing at the Jedi. "That was a mistake."

"I do only what is best for our planet."

He shook his head in disagreement. "You've put us all in danger, Jabitha."

"If I have, then it's at Sekot's behest. It recognizes the Jedi; it is curious about their kind."

"We recognize them, too," he said. "But that doesn't automatically make them our friends. You recognize the Far Outsiders. Would you invite them here, too?"

"You know as well as I do that the Far Outsiders would not be not welcome here. They don't participate in the endless flow of life as Jedi do."

"That fish swim in the same direction along a stream doesn't make them the same species," he argued. "Nor does it mean they'll get along together."

"The Jedi have done us no harm, Senshi. I don't understand why you've gone to such lengths to protest actions that have been sanctioned—"

"Please do not continue to suggest that Sekot has willed this," the elderly Ferroan interrupted sharply. "Sekot is not happy, Jabitha."

"How could you possibly know this? I am the Magister; *I* am the interface. If anyone can claim to know Sekot's thoughts, it would be me."

"If you do, you are not sharing them all with us." He stood, his outstretched arms attempting to indicate everything around them—in the cave and beyond. "The mind of a living world is vaster in scope and depth than any of us could hope to comprehend. We could live a hundred lifetimes and not grasp more than a fraction of its thoughts on any single matter."

"It makes its will known to me," Jabitha said defiantly, "and I pass it on to you. This method has served us well for decades. Why do you question it now? How have I changed to suddenly become untrustworthy?"

"*You* haven't changed, Jabitha. The times have. And we must change with them."

"I agree," Jacen said, gently easing into the debate. When both Senshi and Jabitha faced him, he continued: "That's exactly why we're here. We want Sekot to leave its place of sanctuary, to abandon the security it's found in Klasse Ephemora system and rejoin the rest of the galaxy—a galaxy that is at war with the Far Outsiders. It is a war we might not win. If you join us, you'll be risking your lives. But if you *don't* join us, and we lose without you, there'll no longer be anything to stand between you and the Far Outsiders. This is the unpleasant message we bring to both Sekot and your people. If you wish to live in this galaxy, then you must address the issue of the Far Outsiders once and for all. Now."

"And what's in it for you?" the rebel Ferroan asked. "Why do you want us so urgently? What does one more world matter in this war of yours?"

"This iz not just another world," Saba hissed. "There are no worlds az marvelous as Zonama Sekot anywhere in the known galaxy."

The skepticism emanating from Senshi was so intense it was almost tangible. "And you've agreed to this?" he asked Jabitha. "You've set us on this path to destruction?"

"I've done no such thing!" she snapped back. "I, too, have seen the horrors of war; I, too, know what the Crossings cost us. I want this as little as you do, Senshi—but I will not send these people away or treat them as though they're criminals simply because they come to us for help! They deserve better than that."

"Why? Because they're Jedi?"

"Because they do not mean us harm."

"Is that your opinion or Sekot's?"

"Sekot's." Here Jabitha faltered, her jaw tightening. "I have counseled caution, just as you do. We cannot accept the word of strangers without question. But at the same time we must not make new enemies. If the Jedi are right about the Far Outsiders, we might need them as much as they need us."

"And is that Sekot's thought or yours?"

"That is mine," she admitted.

Senshi's expression was scornful. "You are gambling on *your* feelings when all our lives, as well as the life of Sekot itself, are at stake." He shook his head firmly. "I can't allow you to do this, Jabitha."

The Magister's expression hardened. "And what will you do if I refuse to stand down? Kill me? Kill the Jedi?"

"That iz not an option," Saba hissed, standing.

Senshi glanced at the Barabel. There was a flicker of nervousness behind his eyes as they danced back to Jabitha. "I talk to you knowing that your eyes and ears are the eyes and ears of Sekot. It will hear me and make its own decision. It will know the *truth*."

"You have told it nothing it hasn't already heard, Senshi."

"You're wrong," he said. "I've told it that we are prepared to do whatever it takes to protect our peace. It has never heard our defiance before. Soon, though, it will see just how far we are prepared to go." He turned aside to issue orders to one of his co-conspirators. "We're moving out in five minutes. Blindfold the Magister. I don't want her to see where we're going."

"What about the Jedi?" Jabitha asked.

Senshi met Jacen's stare. The nervousness and uncertainty were still there, even though he was desperately trying not to show it in his expression. He knew that there was no way he could keep them if they didn't want to stay.

"If they wish to come with us, then let them," he said. "After all, the more witnesses we have, the better. But they can leave if they wish to. Even if they return straight to the settlement, they won't get back in time to bring help, and we have no need for additional prisoners."

"Trust me," Saba said. With hands outstretched and a simple tug of the Force, the two lightsaber pommels flew from the belt of the Ferroan looking after them back into her hands. She handed Jacen his. "We were never your prisonerz."

The Ferroan guard became agitated by the display of power from the Jedi, but Senshi remained impassive.

"If you try to interfere in any way," he said, "then we

will fight back. We might not be able to defeat warriors such as yourselves, but we *will* fight back." He turned to address the Ferroan guards. "Blindfold her—now."

Senshi turned and moved away, dismissing them. Jacen and Saba exchanged concerned looks, then faced Jabitha. She, too, had worry in her eyes.

"Don't worry, Magister," Jacen said. "We're not about to leave you."

"No harm will befall you in this one'z care," Saba added.

Jacen nodded as reassuringly as he could, but doubt was beginning to flower at the back of his mind. Looking down at Danni's comatose figure, he couldn't help wonder what he and his friends were getting into.

Jag felt Jaina's hand move within his. He jerked out of an exhausted half sleep and leaned over her. Her eyelids were half opened, and the fingers of her hand clutched his.

"Jaina? Can you hear me?"

"Jag?" Her voice was ragged.

She started to say something else, but was interrupted by a low moan from the bed next to hers. Jag's relief was muted by the realization that Tahiri was waking, too. He reached across Jaina to call *Selonia*'s chief medic.

"Vigos, I think you'd better get down here!"

The medic didn't ask for explanations, or waste time replying. With a click to indicate that he'd heard the message, the line went dead.

"Don't . . ." Jaina swallowed. Her lips were dry and cracked.

He handed her a cup of water with a straw feeder and let her drink, all the while uneasily watching the blond girl stirring on the bed beside her. Green irises appeared through fluttering eyelids. Who was waking up? Tahiri or Riina?

Jaina must have seen the apprehension in his stare. "It's going to be all right," she croaked. "I think."

Before he could ask her what she meant by this, Dantos Vigos and a full medical team burst into the room. Tahiri moaned again, and suddenly jackknifed on the bed, limbs flailing. Whatever she was trying to do, her muscles weren't responding properly. Vigos and his team surrounded her instantly, gently restraining her while taking readings. Two of the medics came to check on Jaina's vital signs. She assured them that she was fine, but they checked just the same.

Jag believed her. Jaina's eyes were red and her skin was pale; she looked as though she'd been run through an ice harvester.

"I heard you," she whispered.

He frowned at this. "What do you mean?"

"In my dream, I heard your voice. I heard what you said."

Her smile filled him with incredible warmth, and he realized that the sentiments he'd expressed to her earlier were being reciprocated. She didn't have to say anything; he just knew from that smile that she loved him, too.

"Tahiri?" Vigos spoke close to the girl's face, gently prizing open her eyes with his fingers to flash a light in to check her pupil reactions. "Can you hear me, Tahiri?"

"My name—" The girl's dry lips cracked open and emitted a voice like a desert wind. She swallowed and tried again. "What's my name?"

Jag's stomach went cold.

"Ish'ka!"

He stood and put himself between Jaina and Tahiri— the *thing* in Tahiri's body! "Call Captain Mayn," he instructed Vigos. "Tell her—"

A hand gripped his forearm, and he looked down in surprise to find Jaina restraining him.

"Wait," she said. "Let's hear her out."

"If she doesn't know who she is, then how do we know she's Tahiri? I'm not giving Riina the chance to get better so she can stab us all in the backs with Tahiri's lightsaber!"

"I am—" Coughs racked Tahiri's body as whatever inhabited it struggled to speak. "I am not—"

"I saw them, Jag." The strength returning to Jaina's voice held him still despite all the sirens sounding in his mind. "I won't pretend that I saw or understood everything, but I saw them together, in Tahiri's mind. Riina was there, fighting her. It was like a dream. They were fighting, then hunting something—me, I think—then it looked like Riina was trying to convince Tahiri to turn on me." She hesitated slightly. "Perhaps even to kill me. But it didn't happen. Tahiri found another way. She—"

Jaina hesitated again, as though searching for words.

"Tell me, Jaina," Jag urged her. "Tell me why I shouldn't sound the alarm and have her restrained."

"Not *just* Tahiri," the girl beside them croaked, her voice slowly firming. "I'm not *just* Riina, either. I'm someone new." The girl's eyes bored into his with startling clarity. "I've changed, but my face has not."

"Changed?" Jag heard Vigos's voice as though from a great distance.

"She's neither one nor the other," Jaina said. "But both of them. Tahiri could no more get rid of Riina than the Yuuzhan Vong makers could get rid of her. They had to join together. It was that or go crazy."

The idea intrigued Jag. How did two completely different minds join? And would Tahiri be anything like she had been before? What if her Yuuzhan Vong half led her astray? A thousand questions rushed his thoughts, none of them, he was sure, easily answered.

"For the first time in years, I feel ... whole," the girl said. "And that has to be right, surely?" She looked at Jaina. "I remember you being there, trying to help me. You didn't do anything; you were just there. Even when part of me wanted to attack you, you didn't fight back. That convinced me that fighting was wrong. Your example helped heal my wounded mind. We would have destroyed each other had it not been for you."

The girl's hands moved weakly, made a strange gesture in front of her face. Then she reached out to take Jaina's hand.

"That's known as *us-hrok*," she said. "It indicates my indebtedness and loyalty to you for your help. I offer it to you not as a Yuuzhan Vong, nor as a human who knows a few foreign traditions. This is from *me*." The girl's certainty seemed to falter for a second, then her determination firmed. "I will be grateful to you forever, Jaina Solo, sister of the one I loved. I will always consider you family, and will protect you with my life. I vow this on my honor, with all my strength."

Jaina glanced briefly at Jag, flustered. "Thank you."

Jag, too, was thrown by the girl's newfound confidence. Where before there had been uncertainty and doubt, now he saw strength and surety.

"This is going to take some getting used to," he said.

Tahiri nodded weakly. "For all of us," she said.

"Well, you're going to be okay." Vigos stepped between them. "Your respiration is even and your pulse strong. You haven't been out long enough for serious muscle deterioration to begin. You should be on your feet in no time."

Tahiri tried to reply, but choked on her dry throat.

"Mom will be pleased to hear that," Jaina said, filling the silence. "Where is she, by the way?"

Vigos glanced at Jag, who said simply, "On the *Falcon*."

There was no keeping anything from her. "What's happened, Jag?"

"A lot, to be honest. I wouldn't really know where to start."

"Just tell me what's going on," she said, sitting up in the bed, concerned.

"We're in orbit around Esfandia. The Yuuzhan Vong are here, and so is Pellaeon." He debated whether to tell her about the little surprise the Grand Admiral had ordered, but decided to save that for later. "The relay base itself has gone into hiding, and your parents went to look for it. They're trapped somewhere on the surface right now. We can't get in to them, and they don't seem able to get out, either."

She raised her eyebrows and shook her head, dumbfounded. "I must have been out for some time."

"Don't worry," rasped a dry throat from the other bed. Tahiri's eyes were fixed on Jaina. "The one thing a warrior never does is abandon her family. We'll find them and bring them back, I promise."

"Rest first, then fight," Jaina said, smiling at the young girl. "And I'm sure we can fit a 'fresher in there somewhere, too. I barely feel human at the moment. I dread to think how *you* feel."

"Like a vua'sa's armpit." Tahiri laughed and Jag felt some of the residual tension ease from his posture. He didn't need to understand the reference to get the joke.

Jaina looked up at him then, and her eyes were shining. That convinced him that it was all going to be okay. Jaina had expressed no reservations about Tahiri's "new" character, or held any concerns for the girl's recovery. She was absolutely confident that what had happened was to the young Jedi Knight's benefit. That spoke volumes in her favor. On the strength of that, and as long as Tahiri stayed fighting on the right side, he would gladly call her a friend.

Nom Anor's eyes snapped open in the darkness. Instantly awake, but disoriented, he tried to work out what it was that had awoken him. Had he been dreaming? Had he forgotten to do something? It took him a good ten seconds to realize that the answer lay all around him. When he had reclined on the cot to rest his eyes, he had left a single yellow lichen torch glowing over his desk. Now the room was dark.

He lay silently in the darkness, listening. A soft movement came from the middle of the room, and he tensed, wondering what he should do. He could yell for the guards outside the door, but the chances were that if intruders had made it into his quarters, they'd already taken care of the guards anyway. He could reach for his coufee where it lay beside his cot, but he would have to expose his throat to do so. He could launch himself at where he thought his attacker was standing, judging by the sounds he'd heard, but it would be too easy to miscalculate and miss, or accidentally throw himself into the path of a ready weapon. Numerous possibilities tumbled through his mind, but each was quickly dismissed.

His plaeryin bol tensed automatically, reacting to the stress hormones that had begun to surge through his blood. If he could get in just one good shot at his attacker—

"Now!"

The word spat out of the darkness, and in an instant Nom Anor was rushed from two sides at once. He felt hands clutching at him, trying to pin him down. He fought them off as best he could, but it was difficult, surprised as he was by both the attack and the number of people involved.

He faced the assailant to his left in the hope of getting a better look. It was impossible. All he saw were shadows within shadows. He could make out an outline of the figure, however, and that was enough for now. Relaxing as though in defeat, he focused on the individual and

fired his plaeryin bol directly into the attacker's face. He
fell back with a cry. With his arm now free, Nom Anor
swung his clenched fist at the one restraining his other
arm and struck him firmly on the side of the face.

There was a grunt of pain, but this attacker continued
to hang on.

"Hold him!" someone cried, and suddenly more figures emerged from the shadows.

Hands clutched at his skull and something pressed
tight against the eye socket containing the plaeryin bol. It
spasmed but was unable to fire.

How many are there? he thought desperately, kicking
out at the new attackers trying to restrain both his legs
and arms. It was hopeless. Soon two of them had managed to pin down his shoulders, while his legs were being
crushed beneath the large torso of a third. In the end he
let the fight genuinely leave him and his body sag back
onto his cot. There were simply too many of them. Better
to conserve his strength than waste it on a pointless
struggle.

He took deep and steady breaths in order to relax and
focus. Battles were rarely won with blind rage, he reminded himself. He needed to know his enemy before he
could beat them, and here in the shadows he knew nothing about them whatsoever.

A lambent flared from the doorway, casting a dim light
across the faces of those holding him down. He didn't
recognize the two pinning his shoulders, although that
hardly surprised him. They might have been members of
his own group, but he rarely paid attention to any but
those important to his plans. Whoever they were, they
were just the lackeys of whoever was the mastermind behind the attack. A traitor, presumably.

The figure holding the lambent was another story altogether. Shoon-mi stepped forward with a coufee in his

other hand. The light gleaming off it matched the light in his eyes: cold, hard, and deadly.

Nom Anor frowned, feeling both confused and, strangely, delighted at the impudence of his religious adviser. This was not what he had expected at all.

"Shoon-mi?" he said, feigning debilitating surprise.

The Shamed One stared down disdainfully at Nom Anor, the blue sacks beneath his eyes pulsing with repressed delight. He shook his head slowly, as if in disapproval of his master.

"You see?" he said to his lackeys. "He is no *god!*"

"Nor have I ever professed to be, you fool!" Nom Anor responded. "Haven't you listened to anything I've taught you—"

"But you *could* have been."

A sense of the absurd rolled over Nom Anor as he lay there, pressed flat to the bed. He was unable to resist a bark of laughter. "You are either far more intelligent than I gave you credit for, Shoon-mi, or more stupid than I could have ever imagined."

The Shamed One uttered a vitriolic hiss and struck Nom Anor across the face with the back of the hand holding the coufee. Then, flipping his hand over, he pressed the blade firmly against the ex-executor's throat. "You dare call *me* stupid when I am the one holding your life in my hands?"

"Holding the power of life or death over another doesn't automatically give you intelligence, Shoon-mi," Nom Anor retorted. "You have me at a disadvantage at the moment, that's all."

"At the *moment?*" Shoon-mi laughed. "You believe you can escape your end here, *Master?*"

There was only a hair's breadth of skin between Nom Anor's artery and the coufee. A simple push was all that separated him from death. Nevertheless, he didn't allow alarm to show on his face.

"The question is not whether I will escape my death," he said slowly, carefully, "but rather how *you* will escape yours."

Shoon-mi glared down at Nom Anor. "You threaten me even when you stand on oblivion's precipice?"

There was a manic look in Shoon-mi's eye—a desperate need to prove himself against the one who'd had him at such a disadvantage for so long.

"I'm in no position to threaten you, Shoon-mi," he said. "I'm merely wondering how you ever expect to get away with this. The faithful will rise against you when they find out. You know that, don't you? Without me, there will be nothing to hold them together."

"That would only be a problem if they knew you were dead."

"Ah." Nom Anor would have nodded, but with the coufee against his throat, it wasn't advisable. "The Prophet will not be dead, although I might be. You're planning on becoming me, is that it? Using the masquer, you intend to use my public face to hide your own and take control of the heresy."

Shoon-mi allowed himself a slight smile, then. "Yes, I do."

"And you'll explain your own disappearance by mutilating my body and saying it's yours. Then you'll announce that you narrowly averted assassination by killing the one who was supposed to be your most loyal supporter."

"It seems a practical plan," Shoon-mi said. "I shall hide the truth behind the truth—a practice I have learned from you, Master."

Now Anor allowed himself a faint smile; even now, Shoon-mi still didn't know the entire truth of Nom Anor's identity.

"And what of these you have turned against me? What have you promised them, Shoon-mi?"

The Shamed One hesitated, glancing at those holding Nom Anor down. That brief hesitation was all Nom Anor needed to know what lay in store for them: they would be killed at the first opportunity because they knew too much about Shoon-mi and his ambitions.

"They will stand beside me as we attain our freedom," the Shamed One said. "They will be the personal bodyguards of the Prophet."

"Indeed. And they expect you to show them the same sort of loyalty as you've shown me this night, Shoon-mi?"

"I would have remained loyal to you until the end," the Shamed One said earnestly. "For a while I even believed in you. But now . . ." He shook his head. "This movement needs clarity of vision; this movement needs a *true* leader."

"But you're forgetting one thing," Nom Anor said.

"I'm forgetting *nothing*," Shoon-mi hissed.

"No, you are," Nom Anor insisted. He knew he had to keep Shoon-mi talking, keep playing for time. Every second he stayed alive was a second longer that a chance to reverse his situation might present itself. And the best way to do this was to play upon the Shamed One's insecurities and uncertainties. "In fact, I can't believe you're so naive as to have missed it."

"If you think for a second that that I won't kill you—" Shoon-mi started, and the coufee pressed harder into Nom Anor's throat.

"I have no doubts that you would kill me, Shoon-mi," Nom Anor gasped placatingly—although there was a look in Shoon-mi's face that made Nom Anor wonder if the Shamed One really *could* kill him. He was certainly taking a long time about it. "My life is most definitely in your hands; I don't deny this. But why are you *really* betraying me? Because I ordered you around? Because I kept you in the dark about certain things?"

Shoon-mi pulled back slightly. Nom Anor took the opportunity to catch his breath.

"Tell me, please, so that I may at least understand why I am to die at your hand."

"Because you offer your followers no better than what they had under Shimrra!" There was such vitriol in the Shamed One's tone that it startled even those holding Nom Anor down. "People came to us, and you used them as though they were *nothing* to you. You sacrificed them without even the decency of learning their names, while yours was on their tongues constantly. They *believed* in you; they believed in the *Jeedai*!" Shoon-mi shook his head. "The *Jeedai* would never have done what you did, Amorrn. All of this has been for nothing but your own glory. You have not spread the word of the *Jeedai* for the sake of the Shamed Ones; you have used it for your own benefit!"

"As you do now for yours, Shoon-mi?"

The blade was once more against his throat, this time hard enough to break the skin. Nom Anor felt blood seep around the edges of the coufee and trickle down his neck.

"I should—"

"Yes, you should," Nom Anor interrupted. "Kill me! Come on, Shoon-mi! I'm sure you have more pressing things to do than stand around here talking to me. You need to start planning your freedom, remember?"

"You mock me even with death's breath upon you?"

Nom Anor allowed himself a wide smile. His display of fearlessness had clearly rattled Shoon-mi.

"You know, perhaps I was wrong about you, Shoon-mi. Perhaps I was wrong when I said you'd forgotten something. Perhaps you never really knew it at all."

"Knew *what*?" It was clear that, despite the obvious advantage, Shoon-mi wasn't as self-assured as he was prepared to admit.

Nom Anor smiled. "That it's not going to work."

"Nonsense. You're as good as dead—"

"Not me, you idiot: Shimrra. You're never going to convince him to give your freedom and honor back. Why would he listen to you? Why would he care the slightest atom about what you want? You can't see what's going on under your misshapen nose, let alone in the court of a ruler a million times more powerful than the Prophet will ever be—irrespective of who wears the mask. Whatever power you gain tonight will vanish upon your death, and the death of everyone tainted by your foul stench. Your life was forfeit from the moment you entered this room. My only sadness is that I won't be there to see it happen."

Instead of showing doubt, the Shamed One smiled back. "Don't think you can trick me, Amorrn. I know you're only trying to—"

Something jolted Shoon-mi from behind, causing him to fall forward and lose his grip on the coufee. Nom Anor twisted to avoid the razor-sharp edge as Shoon-mi fell across him, dropping the lambent and turning the world to darkness.

Sudden commotion in the blackened room renewed Nom Anor's desperation to survive. He struggled wildly, ineffectually, under the heavy weight of Shoon-mi's body. Voices in the dark, the sound of painful grunts, the slashing of blades, the soft, wet sound of tearing fabric and flesh, the clash of weapons—all filled the air in a grisly cacophony. The hands that had been holding his shoulders down and his plaeryin bol closed had gone, but he was still pinned beneath Shoon-mi, who was breathing heavily, painfully. An agonized cry came from someone nearby, followed by the sound of a body crumpling to the floor.

Nom Anor finally rolled from under Shoon-mi's limp body, removing the coufee from the Shamed One's hand as he did. Shoon-mi hit the ground with a grunt and whimper, but didn't make any attempt to move or defend himself. Then Nom Anor collected the lambent and cast the light in the direction of the fighting. The sudden light upon the two combating warriors was enough to startle one into turning marginally. It was all Kunra needed to gain the advantage and dispose of his opponent. Crouching low, he swung his long blade and buried it deep in the other warrior's side. The eyes of the Shamed One died as they stared at Nom Anor, then the body sagged to the ground with the others, cut virtually into two halves.

Kunra straightened, wiping the flat of his blade clean on his robes.

"You all right?" he asked.

Nom Anor nodded, glancing around at the bodies lying about his chamber. "I will be now."

"Sorry it took me so long," the ex-warrior said. "Three of them jumped me in my room. I figured when they didn't kill me right away that it wasn't me they were after. They just wanted to keep me out of the way until Shoon-mi had finished with you. I guess they thought I might decide to join up with them once he'd taken over role of leader."

Nom Anor put a hand on Kunra's shoulder. "Either way, that was astoundingly good timing."

"Not really. I stood outside for a while, listening." Kunra's flat, gray eyes looked away.

Nom Anor studied the ex-warrior. "Of course you did. You thought about letting Shoon-mi kill me. Then you could have killed him at a later date and taken over as Prophet yourself, right?"

"Perhaps." Kunra placed his weapon beneath his robes. There was no sign of an apology, but Nom Anor didn't want one. He didn't mind treacherous thoughts, as long as the end result was loyalty.

"You would have made a better Prophet than Shoon-mi could have ever hoped to." Nom Anor looked down at the Shamed One on the floor, moaning piteously with the handle of a coufee protruding from his back. The blade had severed his spinal column, rendering his limbs useless.

"What you said to him just then," Kunra started, then stopped, unsure of either himself or the question he was about to ask.

Nom Anor faced him. "What about?"

"You told him the plan to reclaim our honor couldn't work," he said. "That the Supreme Overlord would never listen to us."

"I was merely bluffing."

Kunra shook his head. "No, I could tell from your voice that you meant it."

Nom Anor nodded, understanding Kunra's doubt. *Was* their quest a hopeless one? There were very real uncertainties in his mind—particularly after seeing Shimrra in all his splendor in the palace again.

"Who knows, Kunra? Shimrra is powerful; there's no questioning that. But maybe we can convince him. If I had a thousand more warriors as loyal as you by my side, I would have no doubts whatsoever."

Nom Anor glanced down again at Shoon-mi. With his foot he rolled the Shamed One over, pushing the coufee in Shoon-mi's back even deeper. Shoon-mi cried out in discomfort, his pathetic features staring up pitiably at Nom Anor.

"Forgive me, Master," he whimpered. "I was a misguided fool! You truly are one of the gods!"

"No, Shoon-mi," he said. "You were right the first time. I'm not one of the gods. I spurn them as readily as I spurn you. I prefer the company of the living."

With that he reached down and took the Shamed One's

throat in his hands and crushed the remaining life out of him. The terror of death in Shoon-mi's eyes lasted no more than thirty seconds before being replaced by an almost serene emptiness.

Standing upright, Nom Anor faced Kunra.

"Get rid of the bodies," he said dispassionately. "I don't want anyone knowing about this. The last thing I need is for others to get the idea into their heads that the Prophet is vulnerable."

"I understand," Kunra said, and immediately began to drag the corpses to the door.

Nom Anor reached up to touch the seeping wound at his throat that Shoon-mi had inflicted. "I need to see to this," he said. Before he left the room, he faced Kunra one last time. "You did well this night, Kunra. I won't forget it."

Kunra nodded solemnly, then continued with his grisly work.

Luke listened to the news from the boras network with a feeling of foreboding.

"Senshi's made no attempt to talk to anyone," he said when the latest reports came to an end. "But he's up to something."

"I agree," Mara said. "Did he give you any idea what that might be?"

"Something dramatic, decisive, attention getting." Luke steepled his fingers under his chin and tried to think. They were seated on the upper floor of one of the mushroom-shaped habitats. Large pores in the ceiling and walls admitted air and light into the domed space. Bowls of aromatic tea had been served on a table around which they had gathered to consider their next move.

"It would help if we knew where they were going, at least," Mara said, scowling into her bowl. Both she and

Luke had tried to sense Jacen through the Force, but they had given up after an hour; the eddying life fields of the planet simply proved too difficult to penetrate. It was now afternoon, and Luke had yet to ascertain whether such interference was normal, or somehow manufactured artificially.

"We are narrowing down the possibilities," Darak said from the edge of the habitat. She had taken to pacing nervously, worrying at her hands as she pondered the Magister's fate. "It's not easy; the tampasi is very dense in that region, and the trail isn't marked, but I believe I can guess at his destination."

Mara looked up hopefully. "Where?"

"To the northeast of here lies a stand of rogue boras. Sekot permits their existence in order to encourage genetic diversity."

"Rogue?" Mara frowned. "How?"

"Boras can be very dangerous and territorial when allowed to grow wild," Darak explained. "They are as strictly contained as they can be."

Hegerty's expression was one of incomprehension. "Wild *trees*?"

"Boras are more than mere trees." There was rebuke in Rowel's words. "Boras seeds are mobile. They migrate to a nursery every summer, where lightning called down by the boras launches them on the next stage of their life cycle. There are many different types of boras, and correspondingly many different ways that mutants can be harmful."

"Particularly during a thunderstorm," Darak added.

"So why would Senshi be taking them there, then?" Mara asked.

"Maybe he's unaware that the mutant stand is in his path," Hegerty suggested.

"It's not important why," Luke said. He fixed Darak with a sober gaze. This was the best lead they had had in hours. "Is it possible to cut them off before they reach it?"

Darak shook her head. "Even our fastest runners couldn't get there in time. They'll be there within two hours."

"What about airships?" Luke pressed.

"The boras will prevent them from landing."

"*Jade Shadow* could do it," Mara said. "I can summon her here with the slave circuit. If you'll release her from the landing field, we could be there in less than an hour."

"We can try to ask Sekot," Rowel said, "but it will be difficult without the Magister."

"Try anyway," Luke said. The Ferroan bowed and left the habitat.

Luke's comlink buzzed, and he answered it. The voice at the other end belonged to Captain Yage.

"Master Skywalker, telemetry is picking up gravitation readings on the third moon of Mobus."

"Source?"

"Unknown. But M-Three is little more than a rock. There can't be anything big enough down there to generate gravity waves."

"It could be a damaged coralskipper," Luke said.

"Or one that's working just fine," Mara added.

"That was my thought," Yage said. "We'd like to send a couple of TIEs to investigate."

A glance at Darak confirmed to Luke that their hosts would be less than happy at the thought of Imperial fighters swarming over the small moon. "I'll get back to you on that, Arien," he said, and clicked off the comlink.

Before he could speak, Darak was shaking her head. "We will not permit what you are about to ask."

Luke sighed, fighting to keep his tone even and reasonable when he spoke. "Please understand that we wish you no harm. We have done nothing so far to hurt you or your world. In fact, we may have found a security breach that you missed. All it would take is one ship to escape from here, and your Sanctuary will be shattered. Instead of being afraid of us, you should be letting us help you."

"Perhaps." Darak still wasn't convinced, but at least she was listening. "We shall check our own observations. If there really are gravity waves coming from that moon, we will detect them and take action for ourselves."

Luke nodded. "That sounds reasonable."

"But don't take too long," Mara said as the Ferroan woman exited the room. "I don't like being stuck here while who knows what might be warming up their drives over our heads."

"Sekot will protect you," Rowel assured, returning to take Darak's place.

"And who'll protect Sekot?" Mara's words were steeped in annoyance and frustration, although beneath them Luke sensed a genuine sympathy for the Ferroans. "You've been out here too long. You've forgotten how big the galaxy is. Maybe Sekot has forgotten, too. I admire your faith in this planet you live on, but I'd hate you to get a rude reminder of how things really are."

"You know little about Sekot," the Ferroan said. "Your information is decades old, scavenged from rumors and legends. You have no concept of what Sekot is capable of."

"Which is why we're here," Luke said. "We *want* to know, because Sekot is at the core of our solution. With that knowledge, perhaps we can find peace in a way that won't involve the death of trillions."

"We're going in circles," Hegerty said. "And until Sekot decides to trust us, we're just going to keep on going that way."

"Sekot has no *reason* to trust you," Rowel stated flatly.

"Then we'll just have to give it one," Mara said.

Luke nodded in agreement, thinking: *But* what? *What would Obi-Wan do in my place?*

The thought that Obi-Wan and his father had been here, long ago, still nagged at the back of his mind. If there were any way to summon the spirit of his lost teacher, he would have done so immediately.

What happened to you when you were here, Ben? Does it have any bearing on what's happening to us now? And what of my father? Was his fate bound in any way to what happened to him here?

His thoughts, of course, received no answer, so he released them with a sigh. He returned to the discussion with the others, empathizing fully with Mara's growing frustration . . .

The corridors of the Esfandia Long-Range Communications Base were narrow but surprisingly tall. Obviously, Leia thought, it had been designed that way with its Gotal commander in mind, whose twin energy-sensing horns stretched a meter above Leia's head. On the *Millennium Falcon*, Ashpidar would have had to crouch at all times; here the commander had to duck only occasionally on her tour of the base.

The heights of the rest of the crew, however, were on the whole decidedly below average. Three slight Sullustans made up the core engineering and technical expertise on the base, while five stocky Ugnaughts were there for grunt work. There was a Noghri security chief called Eniknar who came up to Leia's shoulder; his assistants were two squat Klatooinians. Two human communications specialists and a Twi'lek science officer defended the average.

The tour, given by the commander and her security chief, shouldn't have taken long, but Ashpidar insisted on introducing Leia and Droma to everyone they met. Her Noghri bodyguards hovered close behind at all times. They were quiet and unobtrusive, but Leia could always sense them there.

Droma had chosen to accompany her to the base because he'd said he needed to get out of the *Falcon* for a while. After what they'd just been through, he was feeling a little claustrophobic. Han had opted to stay back with his ship, because he felt that someone needed to keep an eye on her. Besides which, he said it would give him the chance to do diagnostic checks on the engine and shield generators.

"This is our extravehicular bay." Ashpidar opened an internal air lock to reveal five speeder bikes. Next to them stood a cupboard containing enviro-suits suitable for the dense, frigid atmosphere outside. "Although the base itself is mobile, there are times when we must travel individually to the sensor stations to perform minor repairs. The sensors are temperamental devices, requiring frequent maintenance."

Leia nodded. Half a plan was forming in her mind; if the other half fell into place, the speeder bikes would be essential.

Outside the base, silence still reigned. While the pounding stopped, the Brrbrlpp were safe. She was grateful for that, at least; it gave her time to think.

"Sensing transmissions from the Unknown Regions is just half the story, surely," Droma said. "You'd have to broadcast them again, into the rest of the galaxy. Where do you do that?"

"The sensors accomplish that task, also," Ashpidar droned. Her flat, monotone voice made it hard to feign interest. "Every signal detected by more than one sensor is error-checked and boosted toward the Core by at least half of the remaining sensors. Juggling the reception-

and-transmission load is one reason why the system is so delicate, and why we try to maintain a healthy margin for error. I endeavor to operate on a fifty percent surplus capacity."

"How many sensors have you lost due to the Yuuzhan Vong?" Leia asked.

"Thirteen out of forty."

"Could you function normally with that?"

"As long as there are no further bombardments, then yes, we could operate for a time. But we would require additional resources to bring up that safety margin."

"I'll do everything I can to make sure you have them," Leia said. *And quickly,* she added to herself. Who knew what messages Luke might be trying to send her from the Unknown Regions?

When the tour was complete, Ashpidar took them to her cabin, which doubled as an office. She took a seat on one side of her expansive desk, while Leia, Droma, and the security chief sat on the other. Leia's bodyguards stood just outside the door.

"This is a secure environment," Eniknar assured her in his sibilant voice. The Noghri was whip-slender and corded, his reptilian face a picture of intensity. "What you're about to see has not been revealed to the rest of the crew."

Ashpidar opened a safe on the wall opposite them and revealed a leathery ball with a supple, ridged surface. A vein pulsed at its base, indicating that it was a living thing. A wiry husk surrounded the creature, culminating in a long, tapering tail.

"A villip," Leia said. "Is that how the Yuuzhan Vong knew you were here?"

Ashpidar agreed. "They were summoned here. Exactly when or why we have no way of knowing. There must have been another on Generis, too."

"This one was found two days ago in a maintenance recess deep in the belly of the base," Eniknar said. "Anyone could have hidden it there. The person who owns it must know by now that it's been discovered, but they have not revealed themselves. Therefore, unfortunately, our betrayer still walks among us."

"We'd just begun conducting low-key security sweeps when the Yuuzhan Vong arrived," Ashpidar said. "Obviously survival takes preference in the short term. Until we can locate the traitor, I've kept the villip here, where no one can access it but me." So saying, she closed the safe and locked it. "All other forms of communications are sealed tight. Nothing and no one gets out of this base without my authorization."

Leia indicated her approval. "We can show you how to sweep for Yuuzhan Vong in disguise. We have mouse droids designed to do so discreetly. You don't have to be a Jedi to do that."

The expressionless Gotal inclined her head. "My thanks."

"All we need to do," Leia said, "is ride out the crisis. Once the Yuuzhan Vong have been knocked out of orbit, you'll be able to emerge and conduct a proper inquiry."

"That is my hope. I do fear, however, that—" Ashpidar's desk comlink bleeped, interrupting her. "Yes?"

"A message from the *Millennium Falcon*," reported one of the commander's communications officers. "Coded telemetry data has arrived from orbit."

"Patch it through, Ridil." A holodisplay came to life on Ashpidar's desk. It showed the disposition of the Yuuzhan Vong and Imperial forces over opposite hemispheres, keeping each other at bay. Flashpoints came and went as either side probed the defenses of the other or attempted to drop forces down into the atmosphere. No one was getting through. As Leia watched, the image zoomed in to the surface to show entry points for a small

Yuuzhan Vong force that had managed to make it down to the atmosphere while the battle had been raging.

"We've got company," Droma said.

"So it would seem," the security chief said.

"If they're combing the area," Leia said, "then it will only be a matter of time before they find us." A distant pressure slipped into Leia's mind. Relief rushed through her as Jaina's mental presence made itself felt. It wasn't some strange psychic attack, but a long-distance version of a Jedi mind-meld. The link was tremulous, severely attenuated. It was obviously taking a great deal of effort to keep open, and it soon ebbed and faded altogether.

"Princess?" Leia broke from her thoughts now to face Ashpidar, who was looking at her with some concern. "Are you all right?"

"I'm sorry," Leia said, standing. "As long as no stray emissions alert the Yuuzhan Vong to our presence here, we should be safe for the moment. The traitor *inside* the base is what we need to be focusing upon. Come with me to the *Falcon* and I'll equip you with mouse droids. While you're addressing that problem, we'll work on the other."

Ashpidar stood and bowed her high, horned head. "I am grateful for your assistance."

Eniknar escorted them back to the *Falcon*. No one spoke for the duration of the short trip, but once they were safely back on board the freighter and the security chief had gone, Droma immediately turned to Leia and shook his head.

"I don't like him," he said.

"Who? Eniknar?"

"Yeah, Eniknar," Droma said. "Did you see his expression when that telemetry came through?"

Leia nodded. "There was something not quite right about him." She turned to her Noghri bodyguards. "Did you recognize Eniknar's clan-scent?"

"We do not know him," Meewalh said.

"He has distanced himself from Honoghr," Cakhmain agreed.

"Or was never part of it," Droma said. "Let's set those droids on him and see what happens."

"They'll only detect a Yuuzhan Vong hiding under a masquer," Leia said, "and I would have noticed that already. If he is a traitor, then we're going to have to force him to reveal himself."

Droma's eyes studied her closely. "You have a plan?"

"Maybe," she said thoughtfully. "But I have someone to talk to first."

Captain Mayn brought Grand Admiral Pellaeon up to date via the comm unit. Jaina was still with Tahiri, Jag by her side, listening in via the comm unit in the *Selonia*'s medical wards. Pellaeon came through loud and clear from *Right to Rule*. Jaina's mother had managed to open contact with those in orbit via a transmission from a modified research droid. The droid, little more than a repulsor unit with a subspace transmitter strapped to its back, had been quickly redesigned to receive the same radio frequencies employed by the planet's native life forms. In order to further avoid giving away the relay base's location, the *Falcon* had communicated with it only by brief laser pulses on that frequency. Even so, the transmission from the droid relay had barely lasted long enough to bring all parties up to date. Within moments, a Yuuzhan Vong volley had cut the conversation dramatically short.

"So the *Falcon* and the relay base are effectively trapped," Pellaeon said once Captain Mayn had finished.

"That's correct, sir."

"And there's been no sign of those ground troops yet?"

"None, sir."

"That won't last long. Commander Vorrik is impatient. He won't allow them to sit on their hands down there; he'll want results, and he'll want them fast."

"Their first task," Tahiri said in low, confident tones, "will be to search the bombardment sites for signs of wreckage. When they've been cleared, the spaces between will be examined. They'll begin at the center of the bombed region and work outward. Although they have effectively missed, they will assume that their information was correct and that the relay base is most likely near the middle."

"And where is it, exactly?" Pellaeon asked.

"Near the edge," Captain Mayn said. "The bombed region centers on the approximate location of the *Falcon*'s last transmission. They won't know that it's moved."

"So we have them at a slight disadvantage," Pellaeon said.

"All we need is a window of opportunity in which to act," Jaina said. "Our first priority is to get someone down there to help them. At the moment, Vorrik is hanging in there because he feels confident of finding the base. If he has priorities elsewhere, then his time isn't unlimited. Make it harder for him to find the base and he might just decide that it's not worth it."

"It would give me immense pleasure to force that battle-clouded fool to retreat from a fight." There seemed to be a hint of a smile in the admiral's voice.

"What about the traitor on the ground?" Jag asked. "How are we going to coordinate any sort of action knowing it could be undermined at any time?"

"That's a risk Mom is prepared to take," Jaina said. "She thinks they've already identified the traitor."

"The mouse droids?" Jag asked.

Jaina shook her head. "They didn't pick anything up. But she's keeping an eye on him, in case he tries anything."

"We can do little about the traitor down there," Pellaeon said. "Our issue is to focus on how to get a team onto the surface. Vorrik has Esfandia effectively closed off. Neither of us can get down there."

"I think I might be able to help," Tahiri said. "All I need is access to a Yuuzhan Vong hulk. I'm sure there must be at least one floating around out there left over from the battle."

"Actually, we have the orbits of six charted," Pellaeon said. "But I doubt you'll get away with taking one of them down to the surface. After Colonel Fel's performance, they won't fall for that trick in a hurry again."

"That's not what I intend. There might be a living villip choir on one of them. Give me that, and I'll give you the window you require."

The blond girl's expression was fiercely determined, almost stern; she was a far cry from the confused, broken girl who had come to Mon Calamari for help prior to setting out on the mission.

"And how will you do that, exactly?" Pellaeon asked.

"I will tell Vorrik that I intend to lead the *Falcon* and the relay base into a trap," she said. "I'll tell him that I plan to betray Princess Leia and Captain Solo in the bargain."

Pellaeon seemed uncertain. "He'll suspect a double cross."

"Perhaps," Tahiri said easily. "But he won't be able to afford *not* to take advantage of the offer. A quick and easy victory will enable him to move elsewhere without disgrace."

The Grand Admiral still didn't seem convinced, and Jaina could understand why. What if Tahiri really *did* betray Han and Leia, not Vorrik at all? What if she was planning a triple cross with Pellaeon himself on the receiving end?

"I trust her," Jaina said. At some point she knew that

they were going to have to let Tahiri prove herself worthy, and now seemed as good a time as any—especially since the combined knowledge of Tahiri and Riina might be the only thing capable of getting them out of the mess they had found themselves in. Besides which, her gut instincts told her that Tahiri was whole and strong. "I trust her with my life."

Her bold declaration had the required effect.

"Very well," Pellaeon said after a moment's thought, seemingly satisfied.

Beside her, Jaina also noticed the tense set to Jag's shoulder ease noticeably. She even felt a slight lessening of intensity from Tahiri.

"I'll leave you to organize the details with the *Falcon* and the relay base, once they open communications again," Pellaeon went on. "I ask only that you advise me of the outcome. I'll maintain the situation up here as long as I can. If you need assistance, you have but to ask."

The admiral's small speech was stiff, almost formal. Jaina suspected she knew why, and it surprised her.

"Of course we'll need your assistance, Admiral," she said. "We're not going to get through this blockade on our own. You loaned Captain Mayn a TIE squadron during the initial advance. I'd like to requisition another one to Twin Suns Squadron for the time being. Would this be acceptable?"

"Jaina Solo," he said with some amusement, "you're as much a politician as your mother."

"I'll take that as a compliment."

"As it was intended."

When the line to the Grand Admiral closed, Jag faced Jaina with a frown.

"What was that all about?" he asked.

It was Tahiri who answered him.

"Trust," she said. "If we don't use the Imperials, they'll feel as though they're being left out, and then they'll wonder why. If we're not actively keeping secrets from them, then we should let them participate in everything we do. I suspect that this is why peace accords with the Empire have failed in the past. A lack of fighting isn't peace; it's just a temporary cessation of war."

Jaina nodded. "If we're going to work together, the Empire and the Galactic Alliance have to not just communicate with each other, but *use* each other, also. Talking isn't enough. Until we fight together, risk our lives alongside one another, we will always be apart."

"I'll give the squadrons some work to do until you're ready to commandeer what you need," Captain Mayn interjected into the conversation. "As the ranking Jedi here, I'll take your instructions on what you require the *Selonia* to do in support of your mission."

It hit Jaina, then, that she was effectively in charge. Yes, she was relaying her orders, but the finer points would be under her command. Even the Grand Admiral of the Imperial Fleet was prepared to take her recommendations. It was strange, but she didn't feel discomforted by the authority she suddenly found herself carrying.

"Tahiri and I will confer," she said. "I'll issue instructions within the hour. Keep everyone on red alert. If our situation changes, we'll need to act immediately."

"Understood," Mayn said. She signed off.

"Well," Jag said, nodding as if impressed. "Check out Chief Jaina."

"You should watch yourself," she said. "I could have you up for insubordination with talk like that."

"Is that so? You may be able to throw your weight around here, Colonel Solo, but when next we meet on the sparring mats it will be a different story altogether, I assure you."

"Funny, but if I recall, it was *me* who had the upper hand last time we clashed, back on Mon Cal."

Tahiri's laugh surprised them both. Together they turned to face her.

"What's so amusing?" Jaina asked.

"You two," Tahiri said. There was a smile on her face the likes of which Jaina hadn't seen in a long time. She'd smiled before, but not like this—not so *completely*. "If Anakin were here, I'm sure he would have told the two of you to get a room or something."

Jaina returned the smile, certain that both of them felt the same pang of grief below the happy memory—and certain, too, now, that Tahiri was going to be all right.

Saba felt as though she were drowning in fragrance. The kidnappers, many of them riding giant, three-legged creatures they called carapods, followed Senshi down a steep, wriggling path into a deep valley, the sides of which hung with thick vines that cascaded down the slopes like a green, still-life waterfall. As they descended, the air grew thicker and hotter, and was heavily laden with pollens and moisture. It made Saba's head spin; her pulse raced and her skin itched as her body worked to combat the extra heat.

The steady rainfall wasn't helping, either. The air was so humid that evaporation was almost impossible. She felt as if she were surrounded by a boiling fog, a swirling glow in infrared that turned the green of leaves and moss to crimson.

"How much farther?" Jacen asked the Ferroan ahead of them, a muscular woman with her hair folded back in a fat bun.

"Not far," the woman said without looking back.

Saba could feel the young Jedi's irritation. He was concerned about Danni, who was strapped to the carapod behind them—just as Jabitha was to another beast ahead of them. She still hadn't woken from the blow that had knocked her unconscious. That worried Saba, too. Neither of them was a healer, and they had exhausted their ability to help her very early on. Danni didn't seem to be worsening, but neither was she improving. If she remained as she was for much longer, getting her to Tekli would become a priority.

Saba then fixed her thoughts on their destination. She sensed a knot of darkness ahead, deep in the valley; a break in the flow of life sweeping through Zonama. When she probed at it and tried to picture it in her mind, the image that came was of a whirlpool storm in the atmosphere of a gas giant. Normal flows continued around it more or less undisturbed, bending only slightly to make way for its presence, but anything that came too close was sucked in and devoured.

Senshi was leading them down into that heart of darkness. It called Saba through the fog, whispering directly into her mind. But the darkness wasn't deliberately calling her, she knew; it was just triggering the darkness that was already *in* her—the doubts of her self-worth, and the residual guilt for the loss of her homeworld . . .

No! she told herself firmly, pushing the emotions from her mind. She wasn't about to allow this darkness to take hold of her thoughts. It was not real; she had to stay focused!

Thankfully, the dark allure receded slightly in response to her determination, and she continued resolutely to follow Senshi on their downward trek.

Everything was ready. A shuttle supplied by the Imperials had stocked the gutted yorik-stronha picket ship analog that had once been called *Hrosha-Gul*—a name that meant "price of pain," Tahiri knew. Jaina had immediately rechristened it *Collaborator* upon assuming control.

Tahiri stood amid the wreckage that had once been the

bridge and pondered what that name indicated for her future. Things seemed to be going well in her mind, but she was ever vigilant for signs of disturbance. While the part that had once been Riina had reservations about attacking the Yuuzhan Vong, there was no resistance to the plan Jaina had devised.

The part that had once been . . . The words seemed strange, irrelevant. She was thinking with one mind now, not two. Her thoughts were her own, and the time when her body had carried both Tahiri and Riina was little more than a bad dream—an increasingly distant one at that. The knowledge they shared didn't come in words, as though from separate minds. It felt more as one would converse with a conscience, a part of oneself. It felt *right*.

The Yuuzhan Vong did this to me, she told herself. *Whether I was Tahiri or Riina, they abused my mind and left me to suffer. And then they took Anakin away from me. For that, if nothing else, I will fight them.*

Earlier, she had located the lingering remnants of a villip choir. Setting up a primitive nutrient feed, she had coaxed it back into a semblance of functionality. She didn't know how well it would work, but it would definitely transmit, and possibly receive, too. The latter depended on how fundamentally the coral hull of the picket ship had been damaged. The equivalent of an antenna threaded through the yorik coral in the form of spiraling fibers, attuned to the subtle vibrations of the Yuuzhan Vong communications system.

Tahiri took a deep breath and activated the choir. She could feel the stares of the others in the mission, staying silent and watchful out of range of the villips. For the moment, everything depended on her performance.

The villips folded themselves inside out and the two surviving beacons quivered to life.

"I, Riina of Domain Kwaad, seek to humble myself

before Commander B'shith Vorrik," she said, loudly and clearly in the Yuuzhan Vong language.

The villips fluttered like aquatic creatures feeding in an inrushing tide. Strange patterns fluttered across the choir's field of view, tantalizing but never quite taking coherent form. A liquid, static-filled voice tried to speak to her but emerged as nothing but grating vowels.

She tried again. "Riina of Domain Kwaad calls from the valiant husk of *Hrosha-Gul*. I abase my unworthy self in hope of an audience. My service to Yun-Yuuzhan's glorious cause has not yet ended."

More grating sounds, then suddenly a harsh, guttural voice coalesced out of the noise.

"The commander does not waste time with failed domains."

"Domain Kwaad did not fail. I am Riina, a warrior, shaped to obey. Hear me out if you wish your enemies delivered."

"Your words are lies, and your lies are empty."

"My only lies are to our mutual enemies. It is they I send to their deaths."

There was a slight delay. Then, after a pause sufficient to be insulting, a new voice growled at her:

"Speak, feeble one."

"Do I have the honor of the commander's attention?"

"No. You are unworthy to inhabit the same universe as him. Speak!"

"I bring intelligence of the enemy's movements," she said. "The infidels have taken me into their trust. I will betray their conspiracy in order to further Commander Vorrik's glory."

"And who are you to promise such things?"

"I am Riina of Domain Kwaad. I am the one-who-was-shaped."

Another pause. "I have heard of this heresy. You are a *Jeedai* abomination."

"I am the pride of Yun-Harla. The shapers made me to obey. I abase myself now in the hope that you will allow me to perform my sacred duty, so that I might return to the fold of the mighty Yuuzhan Vong."

Yet another pause, this one longer than the previous. She suspected she was being transferred to someone still higher along the hierarchal chain. Sure enough, when the quiet was finally broken, the voice belonged to another warrior.

"Your claims offend my ears. You have the time it would take for me to drain the blood from a heretic to convince me not to blow your worthless life out of the skies!"

And so it went. The process was laborious, but necessary. Every Yuuzhan Vong leader relied on this process of trial by underling to ensure that anything reaching him was worth listening to. If it wasn't, every one of those underlings in the chain would pay dearly, and they knew it. But with every underling she convinced, Tahiri became increasingly certain that she would soon be talking to the commander himself, and that she would be able to convince him as she had his underlings.

Finally, the roughest, foulest voice of all spoke to her from the damaged villip choir. It *had* to be the commander. His insults echoed those she had already received in regard to content, but the tone was infinitely more malicious.

"Your visage offends my eyes," he said slowly, precisely, venom dripping from every syllable. "Your very existence is an affront to the proper order of the universe. You will offer yourself as sacrifice to Yun-Yammka at the first opportunity to ensure that no others attempt what the Kwaad heretics attempted."

Tahiri lowered her eyes. She had expected something like this. "Lord Commander, I shall obey. The Slayer may take me through your very hands, if you wish. Once

I have delivered victory over the infidels to you, I will have no further reason to live."

This seemed to please him, marginally. "Speak, then, of how this *victory* may be accomplished."

"I have convinced the Jedi that I can be trusted, and that I will provide safe passage onto the surface of the planet Esfandia. In exchange for their trust, and for your assistance in expediting our safe journey, I will betray them at the first opportunity and reveal to you the location of the communications base you seek."

"How do I know that you can be trusted? You speak as a Yuuzhan Vong, but your appearance is that of an infidel!"

"You can see me that well, Great Commander?"

"The image is poor, but clear enough to cause me revulsion."

"As it should, Commander. Were I not to be sacrificed, I would beg the shapers to give me a body more suitable of service to Yun-Yammka." She took a deep breath and concentrated. "As it is, I wish only to prove my dedication to the gods. I am a faithful servant of Yun-Harla. The Cloaked Goddess protects me among the infidels. She keeps my true face hidden. But it is there, beneath this foul visage. I ask her for a sign that will prove my loyalty to you. I beseech the Trickster for one last chance to cleanse myself of the stain of abomination!"

Tahiri tipped her head back. The old scars on her forehead burned as she sent the Force through them. Inflicted by the Shaper Mezhan Kwaad during the implantation of Riina, Tahiri had kept the scars as a memento of her trials. They had come to symbolize everything from her loss of self on Yavin 4 to the death of Anakin. They were to play a much more important role now.

Under her will, the deep wounds opened afresh. Blood trickled down her temples and face as her skin parted and peeled back. She was careful not to show any emotion but joy, keeping her mind focused on the Force rather than the pain. The villip would be showing Commander Vorrik everything. The slightest flicker of humanity, and he would know that she was lying.

Eventually Vorrik spoke. "Enough," he said. "You will be given the chance you request."

Tahiri tipped her face forward. Blood dripped from her chin to her chest, but she ignored it. "I am not worthy, commander."

"Today, abomination, Yun-Harla favors you. That is enough for me. The yorik-stronha you have commandeered will be allowed to enter the planet's atmosphere. Any other craft attempting to escort you, however, will be destroyed."

"Yes, Great One. This vessel will appear to descend under an uncontrolled burn. The Imperial infidels will ignore it, as they would ignore any other piece of space junk. I ask only that you ignore it, too."

"It shall be done. We shall await your signal. Do not fail me, Riina of Domain Kwaad, or this will be merely the beginning of your torment."

Tahiri bowed. "I won't, Commander."

Tahiri straightened and stroked the villip choir's control nodule. The ball-shaped organisms inverted with a sigh, as though they knew that their usefulness had been exceeded, and that they could now die in peace. As soon as she was sure the choir had ceased transmitting, Tahiri let herself relax.

"Hu-carjen tok!" she cried out as the pain of her reopened wounds rushed in.

Jaina ran out of hiding to soothe her. "You didn't need to do that," she said. "Are you all right?"

Tahiri nodded, but didn't argue about need. There had been little choice. She wasn't little Tahiri any more; she was someone new—and this someone didn't balk at what had to be done.

Jag was looking at her in a way he had never done before—almost as if he was reevaluating his opinion of her.

"We'll start the burn in five minutes," Jaina went on, applying synthflesh to the wounds on Tahiri's forehead. "That'll give you an hour to go into a healing trance. And I'm ordering you to do just that, okay? I need as many hands on deck as possible."

Tahiri nodded. She was a warrior and a Jedi, and both sides of her knew to follow orders when they made sense. After receiving a spray hypo of painkiller, she took a crash couch at the rear of the hollowed-out space and closed her eyes.

The *Millennium Falcon* seemed empty without Droma and Han. Leia had little do but wait as the plan was put into effect. The mission to the communications transponder had left two hours earlier. Leia had been there as Han had suited up and tested the controls of his speeder bike.

"Sure you don't want to come?" he'd asked her, his voice muffled behind the transparent visor of his flexible enviro-suit. He'd smiled wryly and added, "Could be romantic, the two of us slipping away from the others to do a bit of sight-seeing."

She'd laughed at this. "Sight-seeing on a planet with an atmosphere of methane and hydrogen? I think I'll pass, thanks all the same."

The suits were designed to keep the deep cold of Esfandia at bay as well as provide the right atmospheric mix for several species. They could accommodate many different body types, which was fortunate given the people on the mission. As well as Han, there was another human communications technician, the Noghri security head, Eniknar—"Where I can keep an eye on him," as Han had put it—a hefty Klatooinian security guard, and

Droma, whose tail was snugly tucked away down one leg of the suit.

"Besides," she'd said as she watched the motley bunch ready themselves for the mission, "somebody needs to stay behind to mind the ship."

He couldn't argue that point. As much as he would have loved for Leia to be with him, he was practical enough to know the importance of keeping an eye on his freighter.

She had kissed his visor and wished him luck. Once outside the base and beyond the confines of the nesting plain tunnels, the five speeder bikes were under strict comm silence. The slightest transmission would alert the Yuuzhan Vong ground teams to their whereabouts. If they maintained the ban on emissions and kept low to the surface, it was unlikely they would be discovered— unless, of course, they were unlucky enough to run into one of those ground teams along the way.

Commander Ashpidar had offered Leia a refreshment in her office, and she had accepted. They had talked for perhaps half an hour about anything other than their situation, and she couldn't help wonder if the mood-sensitive Gotal was trying to distract Leia from her concerns. Ashpidar talked about life on Antar 4, where she'd met a commercial interpreter and planned to raise a family. Her mate had died in a mining accident, however, and Ashpidar, stricken with grief, had left her home to explore the larger galaxy. That was twenty standard years ago, she said, and she'd never looked back.

"Tell me about the Cold Ones," Leia said, using the commander's own term for the species of intelligent life indigenous to Esfandia—a term considerably easier to pronounce than *Brrbrlpp*. "When were they taught to speak trinary? And by whom?"

"That was the previous base commander," Ashpidar replied. "Before my time. Communications traffic was less, then, and the full-time crew correspondingly smaller. Commander Si was an exiled Gran, and lonely with it. In his off-duty hours he studied the Cold Ones and deciphered their calls, noting what no one else had: despite the lack of physical evidence such as tools, it was clear that the creatures had a culture. As proof of this, he taught them to speak trinary, which is much easier to understand than their native tongue. They communicate exclusively with us in that language now, keeping us informed of their movements so we're aware at all times of their whereabouts."

Leia nodded solemnly. "That way you avoid accidental deaths like the ones we were responsible for."

"Exactly."

"Do they communicate with you often?"

Ashpidar came as close to smiling as Leia had seen, but her tone remained dull and lifeless. "The Cold Ones love to talk. Their calls can travel great distances. Sometimes the whole planet seems alive with their chatter."

"Are there many of them?" Leia asked.

"They're not a bountiful species, and never have been. We estimate their numbers to be in the thousands."

"That's not a lot."

"No, but then Esfandia isn't the sort of world that can support a large and varied ecosystem. As the core temperature winds down, the available niches are contracting. The fact that there are no tides or seasons tends to mean that the same species have propagated across the entire planet. What Esfandia has at the moment is a sort of equilibrium. Relatively speaking, the Cold Ones are like rancors, at the top of the food chain, eating anything they can get their mouths around farther down. They tend vast gardens that stretch for kilometers, and herd flocks of flying insects that they trade for trace minerals filtered from the air. It's a complex system that's very gradually devolving, but it serves them well for the moment."

"And now the Yuuzhan Vong have come along and disrupted everything."

Ashpidar nodded her great horned head. "Explosions and vehicular wakes have a profound effect on the biosphere. That's why this base's design was structured on that of an All Terrain Armored Transport. In time, perhaps, the energy input to the system will actually increase growth in some areas, but initially it causes nothing but widespread destruction. I have suggested that the Cold Ones take shelter in the nesting plains until the crisis is over, but they are a curious species. Many of them, particularly the younger ones, would happily risk death for just a little excitement in their lives."

Later, back in the *Falcon*, it was these words that Leia found herself pondering. Some things, it seemed, were universal. Her own children were no different from those of the Cold Ones—and they were no different from how she had been at their age, either. What was it about youth, she wondered, that sent them on such extreme quests for selfhood and experience? What was the point of finding out who you were if it meant dying in the process?

"I must be getting old, Threepio," she said to the golden droid.

"We all are, Mistress," he chirped mournfully in reply.

The atmosphere was gloomy and close when they reached the floor of the valley. Jacen looked warily around him, sensing hostility but not able to identify its source. Hanging vines and ropelike roots, sliding in and out of cracks in the rock like snakes, hid the steep V of the valley below. High above, the dense canopy formed a distant ceiling from which rain fell steadily. He felt as though they'd entered a vast underground chamber.

Their destination wasn't far away. A narrow river

flowing noisily along the bottom of the valley had been blocked by a rockfall, forming a dam around which a stand of boras grew. These trees clawed their way through the stone walls and floor of the valley, their trunks coiling around each other, knotted in a dense and sinister-looking mat. Jacen sensed a furious struggle caught in the posture of the trees, as though the boras had been frozen in the act of trying to devour one another. The strangely motile limbs of the giant trees swayed and snapped between the trunks, unnervingly like the tentacles of a sarlacc, seeking prey.

"We're going in there?" he asked the Ferroan ahead of them.

"Yes," she replied, as curtly as she had to every other question he'd asked.

"Mind telling me why?"

"You'll find out soon enough," she said.

The carapod bearing Danni plodded along behind them. Jacen felt a strange excitement brewing in the creature's mind—as though it recognized this place—but he could get nothing more from it than that. Its hide was as thick as a bantha's, and oddly rich in metals, glinting occasionally in the poor light.

At the edge of the stand of boras, Senshi stopped the party. The Ferroans riding carapods quickly dismounted. Danni's and Jabitha's stretchers were unloaded.

"We walk the rest of the way," Senshi said.

"Wait a minute." Jacen shouldered his way through the knot of kidnappers to the Ferroan leader. "I don't like the look of that place."

Senshi shrugged. "That's not my concern. You chose to accompany us, and this is where we are going. You can either come with us or leave. The choice remains yours."

"There iz a third choice," Saba hissed menacingly.

Jacen put a hand on her arm to stay any hostile ac-

tions. He could feel her muscles vibrating like overtight-
ened wires beneath her scales. "We'll come with you,"
he said. "But if you make any attempt to harm—"

"What?" Senshi interjected sharply. "What will you
do, Jedi? All I hear are empty words. Make good with
your threats or stay out of my way!"

Without another word, the kidnappers continued into
the stand of boras. Their silent compliance unnerved him
as much as their destination. Senshi seemed to have them
all hypnotized.

They circled the muddy lake and came to the natural
dam that was its genesis. It rose like a scar across the bottom of the valley, ten meters high, blocking off the river.
Waterfalls trickled down the far side of the dam, creating
a series of smaller rivers that joined up farther down the
valley. The stand of boras was densest there, towering
above them. Their trunks merged and joined in one particular space, isolating a blackened pit with a stone floor.
Charred tentacles rose from its edges like frozen smoke.

Jacen looked nervously around him as the party continued their descent. He and Saba kept to the rear, stepping carefully from root to root down the steep slope.
The air around them smelled of damp charcoal, as though
countless fires had been kindled and quashed here over
the years.

At the bottom of the pit, the kidnappers came to a halt
again. Senshi ordered the stretcher bearing the Magister to be placed on the buckled stone floor, Danni's beside her.

"This one iz concerned," Saba muttered to Jacen, her
eyes searching the gloom. "The life energies here are . . .
tangled. We are all in danger."

Jacen wasn't about to argue with that; he had exactly the same reservations. He confronted Senshi with
his concerns. "What is this place, Senshi? Why are we
here?"

"Boras have a complex life cycle," the head kidnapper said. "They are a magnificent species in all respects. Their seeds are more like animals than plants. They channel lightning to fuel complex organic processes, deep within their trunks. Their roots link and merge in a communications network that spans the globe. We cohabit the surface of Sekot, the boras and us, and we respect each other's differences."

The ground seemed to tremble beneath their feet. "Just like all organic systems," Senshi went on, "there can be injuries, diseases, cancers. This is one such place, where the natural patterns of Sekot have been stunted, twisted. There are malignant boras, just as there can be malignant people. On the whole, such boras are perfectly safe—unless you disturb their seeding grounds, of course, in which case you are in great danger."

Jacen felt compelled to ask, even though part of him already knew the answer: "Where are they, these seeding grounds?"

A sudden swirling of antipathy swept around them, radiating from the boras.

Senshi smiled. "We're standing on them."

Saba had had enough. She snatched her lightsaber from her side and ignited it with a touch of its activation stud. Everyone around the pit turned to her, their faces painted by the bright red glow from her blade.

The action seemed to whip the malignant boras to a new level of excitement. Saba felt subsonic rumblings pass through her claws to the pads of her feet as the tentacles of the trees flailed over their heads, snapping and crackling like an angry brushfire.

"Saba, wait!" Jacen called out.

"We cannot stay here." She kept her stare fixed on Senshi as she spoke. "It'z not safe. And Danni needz attention! This one iz telling you to take us out of here *now*."

She flexed her muscles to add her considerable Barabel weight to the request.

"No," Senshi returned, unmoved by either her words or her posturing.

"It's okay, Saba," Jacen said, stepping up to her and motioning for her to lower her weapon.

She stared at him, confused. Couldn't he see the danger they were in? Couldn't he sense through the Force that something wasn't right here?

"Please," he urged. "Trust me."

Despite her reservations, she deactivated her lightsaber and lowered it as he requested. He nodded his appreciation, then faced Senshi.

"Please, before someone gets hurt, can't you explain to us what is going on? What is it you hope to achieve by bringing us here?"

"That all depends on what you intend to do about it."

"What does that mean?" Jacen said in obvious exasperation. "I don't understand."

"You will, soon enough."

"Great is the Potentium . . ." A low chant came from the combined voices of those around them. "Great is the life of Sekot."

Saba felt the energies of the boras gathering together. The trunks shuddered and stretched, as though reaching for the sky. She felt a gathering potential in the air, building with every second. Whatever was going to happen, it was coming fast.

"All serve and are served," the crowd chanted. "All join the Potentium!"

Jabitha moaned. Before Saba had chance to react, Senshi was on the ground beside the Magister, one hand across her throat and the other pressing one of the organic lightning rods against her temple.

"Move and I'll kill her," he said to the stunned Jedi Knights.

Saba froze, her thumb hesitating over her lightsaber's activation stud.

"This isn't what I expected," the Magister said, her eyes flickering open to look at those gathered around her.

"That was the idea," Senshi hissed, dragging her and the stretcher closer to the edge of the pit. "Now what, Jedi?" he asked Jacen. "Now what?"

"Now we'll see," Mara whispered as Darak hurried back into the habitat—armed, Luke hoped, with the results of the analysis of the anomalous gravity readings from Mobus's third moon.

Darak whispered to Rowel in a language that Luke couldn't understand. Then, as one, both the Ferroans turned to face him.

"Our sensors detect no gravitic anomaly," Rowel said.

"*What?*" Mara said. "You're saying you detect *nothing*?"

Rowel nodded. "Your comrades must have been mistaken with their readings."

"Either that," Darak put in, "or you have been attempting to mislead us."

"Or *you* could be wrong," Mara said angrily.

"We have studied this system for decades," Rowel said, rearing back defensively. "We know its moons intimately. We are not wrong."

"Perhaps you are being lied to," Luke said, trying to ease the growing tensions. "Tell me, who did your information come from?"

"From Sekot, of course, via the boras network," Rowel replied in a tone that suggested Luke had to be a fool for even asking. "Everything on Zonama begins and ends with Sekot."

Luke nodded his understanding, raising the comlink

to his lips. "Captain Yage, I want you to send a flight of TIEs to investigate that anomaly."

"I have a flight on standby now, sir," Yage responded immediately, clearly picking up on the more formal tone in Luke's voice. "They'll break formation in ten seconds."

"What—?" Darak stepped forward, her face pinched in alarm.

Luke ignored her, speaking to Yage again via his comlink. "Good work, Captain. You may authorize them to use destructive force if necessary."

"You can't do this!" Darak protested heatedly. "You don't have the authorization to maneuver in our vicinity— let alone take aggressive measures!"

"If you aren't prepared to do what needs to be done," Luke said smoothly, "then I will do it for you."

"This is unacceptable!" Rowel exclaimed. "Recall those fighters immediately or—"

Mara rose to her feet and placed both hands defiantly on her hips. "Or what, exactly?"

"You don't intimidate me," Rowel said—although the tremor in his voice belied his words. "Nor do you intimidate Sekot! Remember, it is only by its goodwill that you are here at all. Push that goodwill too far, and your fate will be the same as that of the Far Outsiders!"

"You'd like that, wouldn't you?" Mara said. "Maybe that's *why* you're lying to us—to provoke us into getting on your precious planet's bad side!"

"That's preposterous! Why would we bother going to such lengths—"

"You tell me," Mara said, coming around the table to face Rowel.

He retreated a step, eyes widening. "Great is the Potentium," he whispered hastily, as though in prayer. "Great is the life of Sekot!"

Luke sent a mental prompt to Mara, and she backed

off. "We're not here to threaten you," he said to Darak. "We'd just like to help, that's all."

Rowel snorted. "Sekot is the only help we require."

"Really?" Luke said. "Suppose one of the Far Outsiders' ships managed to survive the attack we saw; what do you think would happen if the pilot of that ship slipped out of your bubble of safety and reported to his superiors about what he found here? The next thing you know, you'd have a fleet ten times bigger than the one you saw here yesterday bearing down upon you. Could Sekot defend you against that?"

"Easily," Darak said.

"And the fleet after that?"

"Of course!"

"And the one after *that*?" he pressed.

She hesitated this time, the notion of repetitive attacks clearly dawning behind her confident facade.

Before anyone could speak again, Luke's comlink bleeped. He answered the call. "Yes?"

"The fighters are approaching the moon," Captain Yage reported. "I'll patch a live telemetry feed through to *Jade Shadow*. Tekli can relay the information to you from there."

There was a delay of two seconds before the Chadra-Fan's voice came over the line.

"I'll do my best to describe what's going on," she said. "There are three TIEs closing in on the source of the gravity waves."

"I insist you turn them back," Rowel said.

With a look from Mara, the Ferroan fell silent and stormed from the room.

"The source is steady," Tekli continued. "It's a regular pulse coming from behind M-Three."

"Does it match any known dovin basal patterns?"

"No, it's not something we've seen before. It could be

a beacon, or a long-range carrier wave of some kind."
There was a slight pause. "The TIEs are conducting a preliminary survey of the moon now. It's old with a rugged, heavily cratered surface. Deep and cold—it's perfect for hiding in. There seems to be traces of several recent flybys."

"We occasionally mine this moon for selenium," Darak said when Mara faced her questioningly.

"Recently?" she asked.

"No, but—"

"They've found the source," Tekli said. "It's a deep pit on the far side. *Very* deep, in fact. One of them is going in to investigate."

"Tell them to be careful," Luke said.

"They're taking every precaution," Captain Yage assured him over the line. "They're following standard Imperial search procedures. Two remain back while one sweeps the location. If they see anything they'll pull back immediately to report. Depending on the data—"

Yage came to an abrupt halt.

Luke stiffened, feeling a premonition through the Force. "Captain Yage? Tekli? Report!"

"The emissions just spiked," Tekli said after a few seconds' silence. "There's definitely something in there. Whatever it is, it reacted when the TIE came closer to take a look. The TIE is moving in for a second pass. The gravity waves are all over the place and there are seismic vibrations—"

Again the transmission ceased in midsentence. The break was only for two seconds, but it felt longer to Luke. "It's out!" Tekli cried. "They flushed it out! It looks like a coralskipper, and it's making a break for it!"

Luke spoke rapidly into the comlink. "That ship cannot be allowed to leave the system! Captain Yage, you must deploy all available forces to intercept. Whatever is required, it *has* to be stopped!"

"There is no ship," Darak fumed as she hurriedly exited the room also. "This is just a ruse to allow you to mobilize your forces against us!"

"Check your sensors if you still don't believe us," Mara called after her. "You couldn't possibly be missing this."

"The *Widowmaker* has deployed all its TIEs and broken orbit itself," Tekli reported. "The skip is evading pursuit, using Mobus's gravity to whip itself out to the edge of the system. The three TIEs that found it are following as best they can."

"Is it going to get away?" Luke asked.

There was another pause. "It might."

Luke could hear Mara's teeth grinding in nervous tension. "If we had *Jade Shadow*, none of this would be a problem."

Darak returned with Rowel, with a small contingent of Ferroan guards in tow.

"Our sensors show nothing," Rowel said. "The system is empty! You have betrayed our trust—just as we knew you would!"

"Seize them!" Darak pointed and the guards moved in on Luke, Mara, and Dr. Hegerty.

In a flash, Mara was on her feet, lightsaber in hand. Luke joined her, his bright green blade in front of him and the doctor safely behind.

The guards hesitated, and in the brief silence before anyone spoke, Luke found himself wondering in dismay how the quest for Zonama Sekot could have come to this. Whatever Vergere had intended by sending them here, it now looked like it was going to come to naught.

"This isn't going to solve anything," Hegerty said. "There has to be an explanation for what's going on!"

"Name one that doesn't involve your duplicity," Darak sneered.

"Bioscreens," the elderly scientist suggested quickly.

"Something the Yuuzhan Vong have developed that interferes with your sensors, perhaps, but not ours. They could have been spying on you for ages without your knowing—until we came and flushed them out!"

"If there are any intruders in our system," Darak said, "then Sekot will be able to deal with them. We don't need your help."

"If we can't catch this thing," Mara said, "then how do you expect to?"

"Sekot has powers far beyond your own. If it so chose, it could reach across this system and snuff the life out of a single cell." Then, with a dark expression, she added, "It could sterilize your *Widowmaker* with little more than a thought."

Luke sensed his wife beside him tense at the threat. While he questioned Darak's statement, the thought of Yage and her crew being destroyed made him feel ill.

"If you insist there is something in our system evading our senses," Darak went on, "then Sekot can choose to destroy everything in that sector, just to be on the safe side."

Mara glanced at Luke. "That would certainly fix the problem. We should tell Yage to get those TIEs out of there and let Sekot do its stuff."

"I'm not saying it *will* do this," Darak said. "Sekot takes its own counsel. The decision does not lie with you or me."

Mara was watching Luke closely, waiting for his decision. But for the moment he had no words to offer, no orders to give. His mind was stuck on how Sekot could act across such a vast distance quickly enough to stop the fleeing coralskipper. Conventional weapons simply wouldn't work in this instance, he knew, and the Force, of course, wouldn't work against the Yuuzhan Vong. And even if it did . . .

Great is the Potentium, Rowel had said. *Great is the life of Sekot.*

The Potentium was an unusual view of the Force, and not one that Luke found he could easily relate to. Its teachings didn't acknowledge the existence of the dark side. Jabitha had indicated that she regarded the intention behind an action to be more important than how the act was executed: the same argument, in other words, that others had advocated in the early days of the war against the Yuuzhan Vong. The ends justified the means. But the dark side was ultimately corrupting, and would turn anyone who used it against the very ones they were trying to defend.

Anakin killed with the strength of his mind. Until that moment, we had not known that such things were possible . . .

"Sekot must not act," Luke said finally.

"What?" said Mara and Darak at the same time.

"Call it off," he insisted. "I don't care how you do it, but Sekot must not attack that coralskipper!"

Renewed suspicion filled Darak's eyes. "You would only say that if you'd been lying all along. There *is* no coralskipper, is there?"

Luke didn't have time to argue his case with the stubborn Ferroan. He closed his eyes, looking for inspiration and strength to do what his instinct told him he had to do.

Taking his comlink, he quickly contacted the *Widowmaker.* "Captain Yage, recall the TIEs and return to orbit. Under no circumstances are you to provoke Sekot."

There was uncertainty in the heartbeat of silence before Yage spoke. "Understood."

"The TIEs are turning back," Tekli confirmed a couple of seconds later. "The skip has a clear run for the edge of the system."

Mara was staring at her husband as though he'd lost his mind. "Luke, if that skip gets away—"

"I know, Mara," he said. "Trust me."

Better that the coralskipper escapes and tells the Yuuzhan Vong where Sekot is, he thought to himself, *than Sekot turns to the dark side.*

The thought of a living planet serving the forces of destruction and terror—the same planet that was the symbol of the Yuuzhan Vong occupation of the galaxy—was a disturbing one. All it would take was a single step in the wrong direction for Sekot to begin the long, inevitable fall. And that step could be something as simple as the destruction of that Yuuzhan Vong skip . . .

"The coralskipper," Tekli said over the comlink, breaking into his thoughts. "Something's happening to it!"

PART FOUR

REVELATION

Ngaaluh joined Nom Anor and Kunra deep beneath the quarters she had most recently been assigned. A double shift of guards outside the Prophet's personal chambers let her through after checking with their master. Her expression was wary, concerned.

"Master." She bowed her head in respect and nodded a more cursory acknowledgment of Kunra. "I came as quickly as I could. What is the emergency?"

"The emergency has passed, for now. I called you here to keep you informed." In an unhurried, matter-of-fact tone, Nom Anor explained to his chief spy in the court of Shimrra what had happened the previous night. As she learned of Shoon-mi's betrayal, her eyes widened. Even after years of training in the deceptive arts, she was unable to completely hide her shock.

"This is impossible," she said at one point, shaking her head as though refusing to hear. "I cannot accept that Shoon-mi would do this."

Nom Anor lowered the collar he had worn high all day, revealing the gash the traitor had put in his throat. "It happened," he said. His tone remained calm, belying the rage still burning in his gut and the dark suspicion that was rising to take its place. "The fool dared raise his hand against me, and has paid for it. But I wonder if this is not the end of it."

"I have asked around," Kunra said, his expression

grim. "Shoon-mi was not alone in his discontent. There is a feeling growing that we are not moving quickly or decisively enough."

"And I wonder at Shoon-mi's boldness," Nom Anor added. "He simply didn't have the brains to organize such a coup on his own. There has to be someone else behind it."

Ngaaluh glanced at Kunra, then back at her Prophet. Her eyes were full of confusion and uncertainty. "Who would that be, Master?"

"At this point," Nom Anor said, "your guess is as good as mine. But we will find them, and eliminate them."

"There are rivals," Kunra said. "There are at least two subordinate acolytes, Idrish and V'tel, who would take power for themselves, if they thought they could get away with it."

"I find it . . ." Ngaaluh struggled for the right words. ". . . appalling and inconceivable that someone in whom you have placed so much trust would consider turning on you."

"That they would consider it is what makes them such good emissaries." Nom Anor examined her alarm at the thought and found it sincere but puzzling. "Why does this surprise you? You are an expert at deception. You know that it is in everyone's nature to betray—if not Shimmra, then me, or both of us."

"But no—" She swallowed. "To attack *you* would undermine everything we have worked for. It is not something the *Jeedai* would sanction."

Ah. The words of a true fanatic to whom the movement was as pure and incorruptible as its ideals. To Nom Anor, a realist, the heresy was something quite different, and it behaved as such. To him it was a means of attaining power, and there was nothing stopping others within the movement from trying to use it toward exactly the same end.

"Not all are as dedicated as you, dear Ngaaluh," he said. "Not all see things so clearly."

"Perhaps the attack came from outside the movement," she said, her lips tightening into a thin, angry line, "from Shimrra."

"The Supreme Overlord *has* tried to infiltrate us in the past," Kunra conceded, "but he could never have gotten so close as to turn Shoon-mi without us knowing."

"And he hasn't the patience for such a plan," Nom Anor said. "He would have used Shoon-mi to lead his warriors into the heart of our hiding place, then destroyed us in one sweep. No." He shook his head decisively. "Had Shimrra been behind it, we would be rotting in the yargh'un pit right now with the other heretics."

"If word spreads of this attack on you," she said, exhibiting more of her usual spirit, "that might make a suitable cover story. It will provide a more palatable explanation than that one of your closest turned against you."

"Word will not spread," Kunra said grimly. "I have made certain of that."

"And what good would such a tale do anyway?" Nom Anor asked. "It would fill our masses with anger and the need for revenge. They would demand that we attack Shimrra directly, to make it known that we cannot be intimidated. We cannot do that. It would be death for us all to make a move on the Supreme Overlord before we are ready."

"If we were ready soon—"

"We won't be, Ngaaluh. Our undertaking is massive and the risk great. Small acts of terrorism are one thing; we can afford to lose a cell or two if the perpetrators are discovered. But to throw everything into an ill-prepared confrontation with Shimrra?" He shook his head. "It would be less a case of doing than dying."

She nodded slowly, as though faintly disappointed.

What *was* it with fanatics? Nom Anor asked himself. Why were they ever willing to throw their lives away on doomed quests? This was one instance when the Jedi were setting a very bad example. After Ganner and Anakin Solo, pointless death seemed to have garnered a powerful glamour.

But not for Nom Anor, he swore. If he was going to fall, it wasn't to be with some scruffy rabble on a misguided quest that had no hope of succeeding.

She seemed to accept it at last. Ngaaluh's head hung down onto her chest as she said, "You are right, of course, Master."

"I am," he reassured her with more than a hint of command in his voice. "We are striving on numerous fronts. Our numbers grow every day. Shimrra is aware of us and our efforts. It's only a matter of time before he accepts the inevitable."

"Yes, Master." Her head came up, and he saw in her eyes that she had swallowed his rhetoric completely. "He cannot ignore us forever."

"So we continue with our plans. We will spread the message ever more widely, and facilitate its spread by getting rid of those who oppose us. The campaign against Zareb goes as expected, I presume?"

"Those who will speak against him have successfully infiltrated his household," she said. "When the time is right, they will be captured and interrogated."

"The time is right," Nom Anor said. The time was *always* right to watch another rival fall. "Set the plan in motion tomorrow."

"I worry about this," Kunra said. "We are wasting resources, throwing novices in such numbers to their deaths."

Nom Anor nodded. This was the strongest argument against his plan of revenge, but it was easily countered.

"We will find more. The one thing we don't lack for at the moment, Kunra, is a willing congregation."

"They may become less willing if our targets remain lowly intendants and executors."

"Not so lowly," Nom Anor said with a scowl. He remembered his days as an executor with fondness after long months of squalor behind the mask of the Prophet.

"But it is hard to see their relevance in the larger scheme of things. Yes, they may create opportunities for those loyal to us to rise, but how long must the faithful wait before they are free?" Kunra's eyes narrowed, as though he were squinting into a bright light. "I repeat only that which I hear on the lips of malcontents. It is not my opinion."

"No, because you have no more wish to commit suicide than I." Nom Anor exhaled heavily. "We will deal with malcontents as they arise. Let *them* attack Shimrra if they want. They will do it without my support, or my resources."

"Perhaps one of them will get lucky," Ngaaluh said with a gleam in her eye.

It was time to stop the conversation in its tracks. Killing Shimrra, Nom Anor knew, would have disastrous consequences for the heretics. Chaos would reign for as long as it took a new Supreme Overlord to take power—and how much harder would it be to curry favor from Warmaster Nas Choka or High Prefect Drathul, both of whom were relatively unknown quantities? Nom Anor needed Shimrra exactly where he was. If Shimrra fell and the war effort failed, he doubted that Mara Jade Skywalker and the Galactic Alliance would show much mercy when they found out who was really behind the Jedi Heresy . . .

"You received a courier today," he said to the priestess. "I presume he carried word from Shimrra's court."

"Yes," she said, momentarily flustered by the change

in topic. "I have underlings bring me news on a regular basis. It does not do to keep out of touch for long. A misstep can be fatal."

That Nom Anor knew well. "Do any of the developments concern us? Has High Priest Jakan's spineray notion been approved?"

"It has been turned down, as expected." She thought for a moment. "There was one matter my underling reported. It may not be of direct concern, but it is still intriguing. Do you remember that mission to the Unknown Regions I mentioned before?"

"The commander who thought he had found Zonama Sekot? He went missing, if I recall, after making his claims."

"Yes. There is more to the story, now. It appears that this Ekh'm Val didn't just claim to have found the living planet. He claimed that he had brought a piece back from it."

"Really?" Nom Anor feigned interest. "Has this Commander Val been located yet?"

"No, Master."

"And what happened to that piece of Zonama Sekot?"

"It has disappeared, too."

He snorted. "Very convenient. What do you think, Kunra? Another boastful warrior with nothing to back up his claim?"

"There is corroborating evidence," Ngaaluh said before Kunra could answer. "A yorik-trema was impounded about the same time as Commander Val is supposed to have made his claims. Also, a vessel by the name of *Noble Sacrifice* entered orbit around Yuuzhan'tar immediately prior to then. It was destroyed on suspicion of harboring infidel spies. The landing field records indicate that the impounded yorik-trema came from *Noble Sacrifice*."

"I don't understand the mystery," Nom Anor said.

"Why can't this ship have been exactly what we're told it was?"

"It is not in Warmaster Nas Choka's nature to hide incursions of this kind. He would have reported it, used the fact that his warriors successfully stopped it to gain advancement in Shimrra's eyes. He wouldn't bury it like this."

"Are you certain it *has* been buried? Perhaps your informants conveniently ignore a proper handling of the affair for the sake of a good story."

Ngaaluh shook her head. "I checked. There is no mention of this Commander Val anywhere, in any of the official recordings."

"So he didn't exist at all."

"Yet I did find him."

That surprised him. "I thought you said he'd disappeared."

"Not for those who looked hard enough."

Nom Anor was intrigued now, whether he wanted to be or not. "Where is he, then? Have you spoken to him?"

"Sadly, no. He is in no condition to talk. Commander Val is dead. My underling found his body in the yargh'un pit. It had been stripped of all identifying features and tossed, lifeless, with the others Shimrra has shamed with a dishonorable death."

For a moment, Nom Anor was convinced. Something was afoot; someone had wanted Commander Val silenced, for some sinister reason, perhaps inimical to Shimrra . . .

Then his usual skepticism returned.

"How did you know it was him?" he challenged her. "You said the body had no identifying marks."

"The timing of the body's death coincided with Val's supposed disappearance," she responded. "Besides, how many perfectly fit warriors have you seen thrown into yargh'un pits? That honor is reserved for those of the lowest ranks, starving heretics convicted of the foulest crime of heresy."

"Treachery is not much higher. If Val had collaborated with the infidels, or allowed himself to be corrupted, his fate might have been the same. Your underling could have been mistaken—or simply added his own elaborations to the tale."

"It's possible," she conceded.

"I fear that you have been taken for a fool, Ngaaluh. You should know better."

"I will not argue that point with you, Master." The priestess bowed her head. "I am simply saying what I have heard."

"And my thanks for that. It is a diverting tale." Nom Anor glanced at Kunra, who seemed immoderately fascinated by the conversation. The Shamed warrior's critical faculties either had not kicked in, or lacked the capacity to separate likely falsehood from an unlikely truth.

"Look into the matter more closely when you return to Shimrra's court," he allowed her. "I'm always happy to be proven right. And if I'm wrong—well, perhaps there is something in it we can use."

"Yes, Master." She bowed again. "I will return in two days to present my evidence against Prefect Zareb."

"Excellent." Nom Anor experienced another pleasing rush at the thought of another old rival destroyed, the third in a row. "This plan is working perfectly well. As far as I am concerned, we are following the ideal course. And any who disagree with me can join Commander Val in the yargh'un pit."

"That can easily be arranged," Kunra said, "with Ngaaluh's help. Any rumbling in the ranks will soon be quelled."

"As my master wills it." The priestess bowed her head a third time, and begged permission to leave. She was tired and required time to prepare for the days ahead.

Nom Anor permitted her to go, explaining that his concern over Shoon-mi's betrayal had evaporated. What did he have to fear with contingencies such as this in place?

Pleased, she bade him a good rest himself, and left.

When Ngaaluh had gone, Nom Anor turned to Kunra. "Well?" was all he asked.

"I believe her," the ex-warrior said. "She is not the one who covets your throne."

A knot eased in him, but he did not allow himself to relax. "Ngaaluh is a master of deception. You could not tell that she was lying simply by looking at her. Her prattle about this mysterious Commander Val could be nothing more than a distraction, to draw attention away from herself."

Kunra shrugged. "That's possible," he said. "I am not as skilled as you in exposing lies."

Nom Anor narrowed his gaze. Was that sarcasm he heard in Kunra's voice? Perhaps they were in league together, he thought: the two closest to the Prophet plotting to unseat him and presenting a united front when the attempt failed.

Certainly Ngaaluh seemed keen to attack Shimrra—and she *had* received the mysterious courier that day . . .

"She remains useful," he said, coming to a similar conclusion about Kunra even as he spoke the words. "While she remains so, I can live with my doubt. And I can take precautions. It takes more than a coufee in the dark to kill me, now more than ever."

"That is eminently so."

Nom Anor ignored the smugness in Kunra's tone, just as he had ignored the sarcasm. "And our work continues. When is my first congregation here due?"

"Whenever you feel up to it."

"Why wouldn't I be up to it? Tell—" He hesitated, then quickly chose Shoon-mi's replacement. "Tell Chreev he's now the chief acolyte. He will make arrangements immediately in the morning. I see no reason to pause and give people reason to worry."

The former warrior smiled. "I agree. Now would be the wrong time to lose momentum."

That's enough, Nom Anor thought. *Saving my life doesn't automatically give you a premium on my ear.*

Nom Anor pointed at the door, but bit his tongue on harsh words. The time would come to teach his strong arm a lesson in humility. "Go. You have done enough for one day."

Kunra bowed with barely sufficient reverence, and left.

The ride down was bumpy. Jag's hands itched to take control of the ship and smooth out their descent, but he couldn't. Although both sides knew that *Collaborator* was a ruse, it was important that the pretense was maintained. The rechristened picket ship would, therefore, spiral unpowered down to the upper atmosphere, at which point atmospheric drag would begin to decelerate it. Only when they were safely out of sight would Tahiri bring the barely skyworthy craft to an inelegant landing. It certainly wasn't the way Jag preferred to fly, but it was important he didn't interfere.

That everything went without a hitch didn't surprise him, however. With the hopes of both sides riding on the mission, fighting had enjoyed a tense lull since the mission's launch. Only the occasional skirmish marred Esfandia's dark skies.

Something rattled violently from behind him. "Are you sure everything's securely stowed back there?" he called out to Arth Gxin, the Imperial sergeant who had volunteered for the mission.

"Positive," the sleek, black-haired man responded. Gxin looked more like an aristocrat than a dirt flier, but

Pellaeon had assured Jag that he was the best atmospheric pilot he had. "Something's probably just worked loose in the wreckage, that's all."

Jag nodded, satisfied by the explanation. It wasn't as if any of them could get up to look, anyway. They were firmly strapped in, and would remain that way until their flight path had leveled out.

They were a diverse group, and among them they represented just about everyone who had a stake in the outcome of the battle. Jag and Jocell stood for the Chiss; Gxin came from the Empire, as did the six military-issue speeder bikes they'd brought with them on the mission; the Galactic Alliance was represented by Jaina and Enton Adelmaa'j; and Tahiri carried the Yuuzhan Vong inside her now. They were a motley crew, it was true, but together Jag was sure they'd be able to teach the Yuuzhan Vong ground forces a thing or two about atmospheric combat.

His idle reveries were interrupted when something seemed to hit them, spinning the ship into a tumble. He looked over to Tahiri, who was studying the meager range of instruments before her with a look of fierce concentration.

"Almost there," she whispered. Her knuckles were white as they gripped the armrests of her crash couch. "Got it!"

Her hands came up to the controls, and Jag took that as his cue to join in. Together they wrestled the decidedly unstreamlined shape of the *Collaborator* under some semblance of control. Their altitude dropped alarmingly through the dense layers of Esfandia's atmosphere, and he imagined he could feel the air around them heating up. The coordinates marking the location of the relay base—as given to Jaina by her mother—vanished around the bulge of the planet, followed a second later by the rendezvous point. They had one more turn around the world before they had to put down.

Put down was, of course, a euphemism. The plan was to ditch the ship entirely, in order to confuse pursuit. *Collaborator*'s reentry path would stand out like a fire breather on an ice floe, and he had no doubts that the Yuuzhan Vong ground crew would immediately converge on its terminus. If all they found was a burning wreckage, then all the better.

Glad that the locals had been warned to keep well out of their way, Tahiri applied some final adjustments to *Collaborator*'s trim and announced that he was happy with the vector. Jaina unclipped her safety harness and she stood cautiously, fighting the constant bucking of the floor beneath her.

"All right, let's get those speeders warmed up."

The six of them headed back to where the vehicles rested in makeshift harnesses. Jag donned his armored enviro-suit's helmet and enabled his maser communications systems. He could communicate with anyone via the suit's speakers and mikes, if they were close enough; for long-distance communication, while comm silence was being maintained, a microwave laser network could keep everyone in line of sight in touch.

"Testing, testing."

"Loud and clear, Colonel Fel." Sergeant Gxin was already in the saddle, flicking switches. His enviro-suit was as black and shiny as his hair. "All systems green."

"Green for go," Jocell echoed, two speeders along.

Jag took the speeder between them and punched its repulsor engine into life. The air was rapidly filling with the high-pitched whining of machines eager for freedom. One by one, they all confirmed their status.

"Charges armed," Jaina said. "We are go in three, two, one."

Jag felt the explosion through his suit. It was immediately overwhelmed by the shock of the hull breaking apart. In no time at all the alien hulk had cracked open completely, as per the plan. They were sucked out, one by one, into a swirling hurricane. Jag fought the turbulence, feeling his speeder kick in as he approached the hard ground below. He didn't have time to note the locations of the others, but the maser system kept tabs on all of them, displaying their locations as red dots on his helmet's display.

A thundering boom signaled *Collaborator*'s ungentle crash landing on Esfandia, a safe distance away.

"Everyone okay?" Jaina's voice came clear and clipped over the maser intercom. The dots converged on hers as everyone confirmed that they'd exited the ship safely.

"We're a little off target," she said, taking the center position of a triangular aerial formation. Jag, from the rear starboard point, could see her checking map data and triangulating on navigation signals broadcast by Imperial ships high above. "Our heading is thirty degrees south, five kilometers. Sergeant Gxin, you lead the way."

The Imperial gunned his speeder bike in that direction, quickly accelerating to maximum velocity. The rest followed close behind. Jag checked his weapons as he flew, single-handedly steering his speeder over the undulating, rubble-strewn plains. As well as the fixed cannon on his speeder bike, he had a heavy blaster pistol holstered at his side, a belt of thermal detonators, and his charric slung across his back. Webbing held four 4HX4 land mines securely on either side of his saddle. Only when he felt sure that their rough landing hadn't damaged his mini arsenal did he take the time to actually look around.

As viewed through the light enhancers built into his helmet, the sky appeared burnt orange and muted. Heavy wind pulled at him, but it wasn't the usual sort of air he would find on a planet of this size; Esfandia's atmosphere, primarily methane and hydrogen, was normally associated with gas giants. Although Jag couldn't actually feel the cold, he was acutely aware of its presence just millimeters from his skin. If his enviro-suit were to fail, his blood would freeze in seconds. All in all, it wasn't the most hospitable environment he'd ever visited.

Gxin led them dodging and weaving through a forest of slender columns that resembled the trunks of petrified trees. What they were actually made of, though, Jag couldn't tell—nor did he have the time or the inclination to stop and find out. As far as he was concerned, the sooner he was off the planet the better.

A thin spire rose out of the gloom ahead. Twenty meters tall, its tapering, geometric lines distinguished it from the "tree trunks" in the area. This, Jag knew, was the transponder rendezvous point. They approached it cautiously, Gxin decelerating as they came around the transponder's wire-framed, expanding skirt. Jag kept his eyes peeled, conscious of the many hiding places in and around the main structure. Jaina had said something about a traitor among the expedition; if that person had managed to overpower Han and the others, he could well be waiting for them now, intending to pick them off one by one as they arrived.

A snarl of speeder engines from Jag's right brought him around in a tight turn. The triangular formation dissolved to present as dispersed a target as possible. Jag kept one finger on the trigger while ducking to target whoever was approaching out of the murk.

A buzz of static sounded in his earpieces as his comm located and locked on to a signal.

"—else could it be using these frequencies? You worry too much, Droma."

"That's what has kept me alive this long."

"And there I was thinking it was because of your good looks and charms."

"Dad?" Jaina's voice cut across the chatter. "Your signal is coming in loud and clear."

"As it should be. We're right on top of you." Five more speeder bikes appeared out of the gloom. The size of the riders varied greatly. "Welcome to Esfandia," her father said, pulling his speeder bike up to a halt next to Jaina's. "Glad you could make it, sweetheart."

"Likewise," Jaina replied. The relief at finding her father all right was obvious in her voice.

"What do you think of Esfandia so far?" he asked.

"Not the kind of place I'd spend a holiday."

"I wouldn't say that too loudly," Droma put in. "You might offend the locals."

As the wake of the speeder bikes settled, shadowy circular shapes drifted in from the gloom. Jag was startled until he realized that this was what Droma had meant by "the locals." The indigenous life-forms of Esfandia seemed to float like kites in the thick atmosphere; every now and again one would collapse in upon itself, as though clenching like a fist, and then suddenly shoot forward. He assumed they were sucking in the thick air and then blasting it out a rear vent in order to propel themselves along. It wasn't the most graceful means of propulsion he'd seen, but it seemed effective nonetheless.

"Don't they know it's dangerous being around us?" Jaina asked.

"We've tried telling them that," Droma said. "But they followed us anyway. They can put on quite a turn of speed when they want to."

"The Cold Ones may be curious," Han added, "but they're not stupid. Mark my words, they'll get out of the way when things really heat up."

"How close are we to being ready?" Jaina asked.

Han introduced the communications tech they'd brought along to reprogram the massive transponder. He explained that it would take the man about half an hour to bypass the automated systems and give the transmitter its new instructions.

Jaina nodded. "Get started immediately, then. We'll prepare the perimeter."

She dismounted her speeder bike to dole out the mines with the help of Adelmaa'j, her father and Droma, and a Klatooinian security guard from the relay base. Jag unloaded his mines, then swept the area with Jocell to make sure it was clear. This proved more difficult than he'd first thought. What with the dim light, the dense atmosphere, and the irregular terrain, there were a thousand ways they could miss someone sneaking up on them. The only good thing was that sound carried a long way here, allowing them a good lead time before an airborne strike arrived. But even that could work against them: the sound of *their* engines would be audible for a much wider range, increasing the chances that one of the Yuuzhan Vong ground teams would find them before they were ready.

Only once did the sensors on his suit detect anything remotely threatening. A hissing rumble, like a blast of white noise from a long way away, rose out of the background static. It didn't sound like a tsik vai, the Yuuzhan Vong equivalent of an airspeeder, but Jag called an alert just to be on the safe side. As his repulsor engines wound down, the approaching sound seemed almost deafening against the background moan of the wind. It doubled in volume before peaking, then slowly trailed away.

"Yorik-trema," Tahiri said. "One of the landing craft. This is a hostile environment, so its hold will be full of tsik seru rather than the usual ground troops."

"And they are?" Jag asked.

"Tsik vais equipped with plasma blasters, designed to move fast and make nuisances of themselves."

"Any other weapons?"

"Netting beetles, razorbugs, needle thorns—anything the pilots can carry."

"Great. Thanks for the tip."

Jaina's voice was taut as she made a stab at reassurance. "It's gone past us, and that's all that matters. We should be safe now."

Ten minutes later, the comm tech announced that the transponder was ready. Tahiri gave him the message, the last piece of the puzzle. It was shorter than Jag had expected, and utterly incomprehensible. The subtleties of the Yuuzhan Vong language, which sounded to his ears like nothing more than a series of guttural grunts and painful throat clearings, eluded him completely. He had to take on faith that it said what Jaina intended.

"One more mine to place," Han said, the sound of digging coming over the comm. There was a grunt, followed by, "Well done, Droma. You've just earned your passage on the *Falcon*."

"Passage nothing. Give me a good lawyer and I'll sue you for damages."

"Back on the speeders, people. This thing's set to go off in three standard minutes, once I give the word. You know what you have to do."

Jag circled the transponder for one final check, and made sure everyone's navigation systems were updated with the location of the mines. He didn't want anyone stumbling into one by mistake.

"We need to hurry. Vorrik won't wait forever," Tahiri said. "The longer my message takes, the more frustrated he will become."

"Then let's get under way. Start the timer ticking . . . *now*."

The eleven speeder bikes accelerated away from the transponder, scattering the Cold Ones in their wake. Jag had no qualms about that. Scaring the natives was the best thing to do given the circumstances. In a very short time, the area around the transponder was going to become very unsafe for everyone.

Sergeant Gxin led the retreat to safer ground. He'd scouted the area during the preparations and found two ideal locations for speeders to hide in waiting. One was an overhang hollowed out by winds. Jaina left Jag, her father and Droma, Jocell, and the comm tech there while she took the rest to the second location, a kilometer away.

When the sound of their engines faded, there was less than thirty seconds to go. Jag used the time to load his charric, fastening it to the saddle by his right thigh so that it was easily accessible should he need it.

Barely had he finished doing this when the giant transponder awoke with a blast of static to relay Tahiri's message to all the Yuuzhan Vong hanging in wait above Esfandia.

Pellaeon glanced up from the charts before him as an alarm sounded on the bridge of *Right to Rule*.

"Report."

"Audio signal from the ground, sir."

"Let's hear it."

The voice of the young female Jedi filled the bridge, spitting and snarling in the Yuuzhan Vong language. The electromagnetic radiation carrying the message radiated from a point on Esfandia's surface and out into space. No one with ears could miss it for millions of kilometers—which was the idea, of course. Pellaeon had no idea what the message contained. He had to trust Jaina Solo's assertion that Tahiri was saying what she was supposed to. If she did, then the effect would be instantaneous.

Ten seconds passed. Twenty. Every sensor at *Right to Rule*'s disposal was focused on the source of the signal. It was hard to see anything through the thick smog Esfandia called an atmosphere. Through a confusion of random heat impressions and radar images, he tried to detect any sort of coherent reading. Was that a speeder bike wake? Did a Yuuzhan Vong lander cast that sort of shadow?

When it came, there was no mistaking it.

Bright orange heat blossomed on the infrared scan. It flowered to white intensity, then faded to a red background.

"We have a detonation," his aide called.

"I'm picking up flashes," a telemetry officer said. "High-energy weapons fire."

"Where?"

"Multiple sources, all around the target."

Pellaeon's aide looked up at him. "It's started, sir."

"This isn't right," the Magister said.

"Quiet!" Senshi pushed the lightning rod harder into Jabitha's temple, provoking a wince of discomfort. "I want to hear what the Jedi have to say."

Jacen took a deep breath. He could sense everything focused on him: the Ferroans surrounding them, the boras whipping angrily overhead, Saba watching tense and puzzled beside him, Senshi, the Magister—perhaps even Sekot itself. What he did next would be critical.

His options were limited. He and Saba could easily use the Force to take out the Ferroan kidnappers, but that would leave Danni and Jabitha at Senshi's mercy. He could knock Senshi's weapon aside, removing Jabitha from the immediate threat, but could he be quick enough to stop the other Ferroans from firing their weapons? Using his lightsaber was a possibility, but the question was, what would he do with it? How would that help Danni? No, there had to be a solution that didn't involve aggression . . .

The sharp-tipped end of a boras tentacle thudded heavily into the dirt beside him, then snapped back up into the air ready for another strike. That was all the incentive he needed. As Saba staggered back, flailing at a tentacle that had lashed down at her, Jacen straightened his posture and closed his eyes. Ignoring the rain on his face, shutting out the booming of thunder from the sky and the strange cries of the boras, he extended himself into the warmth of the Force, and went searching . . .

Up . . .

Past the Ferroans.

Higher . . .

Between the cracking tentacles and into the branches, where drenched birds and other animals huddled for shelter.

Higher still . . .

To the tops of the trees, where static electricity sizzled from the storm and wind whipped leaves in furious waves.

What he was looking for wasn't there, though. He was thinking too much in human terms. He chided himself for taking anything for granted on a world like this and sent himself hurtling down the side of the nearest boras—along thickening branches as the trunk opened up to embrace the soil, and then into it, into darkness where strange small minds lurked, living among the knotted roots and dining on the remains of the surface world.

And it was there that he found what he was looking for: a knot of intense anger that was the heart of the malignant stand of boras. It wanted to kill those who had invaded its most sacred place; it wanted to crush them into fertilizer, grind their bones into the dirt, and seed their graves with scavengers to erase every last memory of their presence.

As tentacles rained down on the seeding ground, Jacen's mind slid into the convoluted spaces of the outraged plant.

Violated! the primitive mind shrieked. *Protect!*

We're not harming you, Jacen assured. *We'll be gone soon.*

Even as he said it, though, he could sense that advanced concepts like future benefits would be beyond the creature's simple understanding.

Bones make us strong!

You are strong enough, Jacen told it, trying to ease the anger of the plant-mind with suggestive thoughts.

Stronger!

Jacen plunged deeper into the boras's mind and found a furious tangle. Pressure mounted around the tangle, forging a buildup of primitive frustration and rage. He tugged gently at it.

Isolation leads to stagnation, he whispered.

He teased the inflamed threads in new directions.

Stagnation leads to corruption.

The tangle slipped apart under his mental touch, prompting a surge of pent-up energies in all directions.

Corruption leads to death.

The mind of the boras exploded in a shower of bright sparks. Somewhere, seemingly far away, Saba Sebatyne roared.

Jacen's eyes snapped open. Saba was standing over him and Danni, shielding them with her lightsaber. Above and around them was a tightly knit cage of angry boras tentacles, poised ready to attack.

Then, with a smooth, hissing sound, the tentacles retracted, sliding smoothly back up into the canopy, their pointed tips curling in on themselves so that they were no longer a threat. The mind of the boras had retreated into itself, to lick its wounds and examine its sudden relief.

But Saba wasn't about to lower her lightsaber; the hunter in her simply wouldn't allow it. The look in her slitted eyes suggested she wasn't about to be lulled into a false sense of security.

"It's okay, Saba," he said, placing a hand on her shoulder. He felt her ropy, reptilian muscles relax under her thick skin. "It's over."

"And yet," said a voice from behind him, "in a very real sense, it's only just beginning."

Jacen turned, unable to credit his ears. The sight before him caused his heart to race and his mind to reel.

"But you're . . . *dead*!"

Vergere didn't reply. She just stood in front of Jacen, smiling faintly as though waiting for him to understand.

Jaina tensed as the yorik-trema rose around her. The electronic hollering of Tahiri's message was loud in her ears, blasting out of the transponder at close range. Her address to the commander was brief, its message simple and brutal.

"The cowering infidels await your vengeance, Great Commander. I give them to you as tribute. Crush them beneath your heel as you would a diseased dweebit!"

The yorik-trema was so close that Jaina was amazed she couldn't see it through her enviro-suit visor. The sound of it made her teeth vibrate.

Then there was a bright flash and a sound like a peal of thunder. A powerful shock wave rolled over her and the others where they'd taken shelter in a small cave tunneling through a rocky spar. The yorik-trema, or one of its tsik seru fliers, must have run into a mine protecting the periphery of the transponder. The detonation acted as a signal to her speeder bikes. With a snarl of engines, they burst out of their hiding place and split up into groups of two, weapons armed and ready.

Jaina paired herself with Eniknar, the skinny Noghri her mother suspected was a traitor. He flew confidently and economically into battle, crouched low over his saddle to her right. The Klatooinian security guard and Enton Adelmaa'j peeled off to approach the Yuuzhan Vong from the far side. Gxin and Tahiri sped off together. Jaina expected them to separate before long, but didn't mind. Together or apart, they would be capable of a great deal of damage.

Infrared blossomed ahead of her. She hunkered down and armed her blaster cannon when something large and dark loomed out of the smog. She raked it with fire before swooping up and over it and coming around for a closer look.

The yorik-trema had caught the mine on its underbelly, crippling it. Bodies spilled from a wide crack in its fuselage. Reptoid ground troops swarmed from a rear hatch, too confused to return her fire. She sent a dozen rounds into the breach and was gratified when something exploded with a solid *crump* from within.

"Fliers approaching," crackled Eniknar's voice over the maser comm.

Jaina took a second to check her tactical display. There were no blips on the display, so clearly the fliers weren't friendly. She took another pass around the downed yorik-trema and joined the security chief in meeting the fliers head-on. A formation of seven tsik seru peeled apart in disarray as blasterfire cut hot lines between them. Jaina braked back in a tight turn, then came around again to play havoc with their rear vents. Any hope of maintaining order to the fight dissolved at that point. With visibility low, her sensors restricted to nonemitting radiation, and dozens of targets appearing and disappearing all around her, the skirmish dissolved into a furious free-for-all. Her blaster pounded beneath her, knocking chunks from alien coral and tearing reptoid troops limb from limb. Eniknar was nowhere in sight, but she didn't have time to dwell upon that.

"Watch your rear, Jaina." Jag's voice came out of the fierce clamor of battle, startlingly clear over the comm. She looked over her shoulder and saw two tsik seru jockeying for attack position. She crouched low over her saddle to present a smaller target and led the two alien fliers on a harried chase. She dodged plasma fire and a rain of netting beetles while swinging wildly around the treelike ground features. Her face was locked in a grim smile as she rounded a steep rock shelf and gunned her speeder in a tight port turn, too fast for the fliers behind her to see or imitate. By the time they came wide around the same corner, she was pushing her speeder to its maximum acceleration in order to get as far away from the area as quickly as possible.

The explosion as the two fliers hit the mine picked her up and threw her forward on a blast of hot air. The world exploded with stars as her speeder clipped a rock formation and sent her flying.

Tahiri felt the growling power of the machine beneath her as it swept through the air toward the Yuuzhan Vong warriors. The Yuuzhan Vong part of her instinctively mistrusted something that wasn't alive, and the Jedi in her could sympathize somewhat, too. The living Force that flowed through every biological thing was more potent and persuasive than any machine.

Sergeant Gxin shadowed her to where the yorik-trema had spilled its contents onto the deep cold soil of Esfandia, then peeled away to seek other, less obvious targets. Jaina had beaten them there and was already peppering the downed craft's dying hull with fire. Tahiri didn't see the need to duplicate her efforts, so instead followed Gxin's example and went in search of more worthy prey. There was at least one other yorik-trema out there, and an unknown number of tsik seru, all converging on the signal she'd sent to Commander Vorrik . . .

Barely had she finished thinking this when three tsik seru swooped at her out of the gloom, disrupting her thoughts. Her new, joined self fought smoothly, instinctively. There was not the slightest awkwardness or hesitation in her actions. The Yuuzhan Vong part of her meshed with the Jedi Knight to create something truly deadly, something neither side had seen before—and she used that advantage to the fullest.

Plasma fire couldn't be deflected by a lightsaber, but the nozzles that spewed it forth—deep pits just above and forward of the tsik seru intake vents—could be closed by the Force. She applied a Force-push at exactly the right moment, tweaking the alien sphincter muscles just as they clenched to fire, causing the plasma cannon to jam. The resulting explosion—a messy burst that tore a huge hole in the tsik seru's triangular flank—sent it spinning out of control into a cliff face. The Yuuzhan Vong pilot was thrown free and landed with a bone-snapping crunch.

Satisfied with the result, Tahiri repeated the tactic on the remaining two fliers while dodging their attempts to cut her down. As the third tumbled like a broken-winged bird into the ground, a speeder bike buzzed across her path, wobbling precariously. Through the enviro-suit helmet, she recognized Droma.

"Having trouble?" she asked.

"Took a hit to a steering vane," the Ryn replied.

"Will you be okay?"

"As long as no one gets in my way."

A sharp twinge through the Force distracted her. She cast her mind out, seeking the source of the troubling sensation. Within a moment she had isolated it.

"Jaina's down," she said.

"Whereabouts?" Droma asked, tugging at the resisting controls of his speeder to bring it around.

She didn't wait to answer him. She just headed off in the direction she felt Jaina to be.

"The coralskipper," Tekli said, "it's changing!"

"I don't understand," Mara said. "Changing how?"

"It's changing shape, and its gravitic emissions are

adopting a different profile." The voice of the Chadra-Fan was unable to hide her exasperation with what she was seeing. "It's much faster—and turning!"

"It's coming back at us," came the calmer voice of Captain Yage over the comlink. "Whatever it is, we're ready for it."

"You're so *not* ready," came a voice off to Luke's right, "it's almost funny."

Luke turned at the new voice and found himself staring at a young boy standing in the entrance to the habitat's upper floor. He was about twelve years of age with blue eyes. His face was round under sandy, short hair, and his expression was one of amusement.

"What is the meaning of this?" Rowel asked, scowling. "Who are you?"

The Ferroan glanced accusingly at Luke, as if the boy's presence were somehow his doing. Which only went to show, Luke thought, just how little the Ferroans really knew about the planet they lived on.

He closed the distance between himself and the boy with a handful of cautious steps. The blue orbs of the boy stared back at him, full of confidence and power. They stripped every other concern from him, made him feel like he was falling. The mind behind those eyes shimmered in the Force, bright and potent as Jabitha's had been when she had met them on the landing field.

There was only one person it could be behind those eyes—and it wasn't really a person at all.

"Is that—?" Mara started, but was clearly unsure how to finish the sentence.

Luke crouched down before the boy, staring in wonderment at the ghostly image of Anakin Skywalker. "My father?" he finished for her. He shook his head. "No, it's not. It's Sekot."

The boy smiled broadly now, his eyes shining in a manner that suggested pride. "You are wise, Luke Skywalker," he said. "Your father would have been proud of the man you have become."

"Sekot?" This came from Rowel behind Luke. He emitted a choking noise, embarrassed by his initial response to the boy's presence. "Forgive me, please."

Neither Luke nor the image of the boy broke their stare to address the Ferroan. His awkwardness seemed irrelevant. *Everything* seemed irrelevant.

"Why have you taken this form?" Luke asked.

The boy shrugged, the amusement behind his eyes suddenly undercut with sadness. "Everyone with power faces a choice. It's a difficult choice, and the choice is different for everyone. Only time reveals which choice is correct."

The boy's face assumed an expression of deep sympathy as he cupped Luke's cheek gently in one small hand.

"This is how your father appeared to me many years ago," Sekot said. "He and I faced the same choice. We are both still waiting to find out whether we chose correctly."

Luke sensed Mara behind him radiating her love and sympathy out to him. He was transfixed by the boy's blue eyes. *The same color as mine,* he thought. No, not just the same color; they *were* the same . . .

"*That's* what Darth Vader looked like?" Hegerty's was voice thick with amazement.

"He was a boy once," Mara said softly.

"Master Skywalker," came Captain Yage's voice over the comlink, interrupting the surreal reunion. "The unidentified vessel is still approaching Zonama Sekot, and is refusing to respond to our hails. We're on full alert and ready to intercept. You just have to give the order."

Luke stood, pulling himself away from the vision of his father to address the captain of the *Widowmaker*. "Stand down, Arien," he said. He was acutely conscious of everything around him: the humid air; the scent of water-logged undergrowth; the breathless ring of Ferroans waiting to see what happened next. "That ship isn't about to attack us."

The image of his father moved to the center of the room. Luke faced him, feeling the pressure of the planet's attention upon him. He shook his head, wondering why he hadn't realized sooner what was going on.

"So, tell me," he said. "Have we performed to your satisfaction?"

Sekot looked at him with the wisdom of ages from the eyes of innocence. "If I were to say that you hadn't, what would you do then?"

Luke shrugged. "That would depend on the choices I had available to me."

"You don't have any." The innocent face broke into a smile. "That's what's so wizard about it."

"Then your question is meaningless," Luke said.

"Perhaps," Sekot said. "But the exercise wasn't. Since your arrival I have learned more about why you are here than you probably ever intended to tell me. Maybe even more than you know yourself."

"Then you know we came in search of an answer."

"I do. But I have no easy answer to offer you."

"Any answer at this point would be appreciated," Mara said.

The image of the boy looked in silence at all of those standing around expectantly, then finally nodded. "Very well," he said, gesturing for them all to be seated.

Luke did so gratefully. Ever since laying eyes upon the boy he had felt the tug of emotions that he hadn't accessed in a long time—emotions that were leaving him weak at the knees, even though he knew it wasn't his father before him.

When everyone was seated, Sekot began to speak.

* * *

Jag ducked as a tsik seru skimmed narrowly over his head, the tug of its dovin basal lifting him slightly from his seat. He dropped the power on his speeder as a large stone formation loomed out of the haze ahead, swinging around to give chase to the Yuuzhan Vong that had just buzzed him, only to find the tsik seru already coming back for another pass. Its pilot's face was all snarl and scars, partly obscured by a fleshy gnullith. Not obscured enough as far as Jag was concerned, though. He strafed laserfire in the small craft's path, making the Yuuzhan Vong pilot bank sharply as he fired a cloud of netting beetles in retaliation. The tsik seru had almost matched speed and vector with Jag's flier when something caught the pilot's attention and he swept away, disappearing into the murky atmosphere.

Left in the turbulent wake, Jag wondered what had torn the Yuuzhan Vong from his prey. Something important must have come up.

Jag came around and set off after the flier. What his speeder lacked in full-body coverage, it certainly made up for in velocity. He caught up with the tsik seru just as it crested a sharp rise and dipped down the far side. He saw its plasma launchers flex in readiness, then suddenly explode in a ball of green flame. With a pained shriek, the living craft curved away and crashed into one of the stony "stalagmites" that littered the planet's surface. With a loud *whump*, it exploded into a million red-hot fragments.

Only then did Jag realize what lay below.

Huddled against a boulder were three small, humanoid figures. They stood with their backs to the boulder, two of them firing repeating blasters or using lightsabers to keep two more tsik seru and a swarm of reptoids at bay. The third slumped against the stone and appeared to be having difficulty remaining upright.

Jag stitched a line of fire across the contracting line of alien foot soldiers. At least a dozen went down screaming.

"Jag, back here!"

The comm message was from Tahiri. She was warding off four reptoids, two of them armed with coufees. The other two were throwing thud bugs whenever they saw an opening. Jag swept in low across the fight and dropped a thermal mine in the middle of the reptoids, shooting at the two with coufees on his way out.

When the thermal mine went off, bits of reptoids were sent flying every which way. Something thumped against the side of his helmet, and he ducked in case more pieces were following. Guiding his bucking speeder around in a circle, he came back to check on Tahiri and the others.

"What happened?" he asked.

"Jaina took a fall," Tahiri explained, getting up from where she'd dropped. She lent Jaina a hand as she climbed to her feet.

Jag brought his speeder to a halt and jumped off to see if he could help. When Jaina spoke, her voice was thick and groggy. She was blinking her eyes too rapidly, as though trying to focus.

"My feet are cold."

"Her suit is failing," Tahiri said. "We have to get her out of here."

Jag tried to get her attention. "Jaina? Can you hear me?"

"Jag?" Her gaze caught him and held on. She nodded in a delayed response to his question. "I'll be all right. Just give me a second."

"I hate to be the bearer of bad tidings," Droma said, pointing over Jag's shoulder, "but . . ."

Jag turned and saw the reptoids getting up and regrouping.

He went back to his speeder and collected his charric blaster.

"We don't have much time," he said. "Where's Jaina's speeder?"

"Over there," Tahiri said.

Jag looked and saw the tangled wreck.

"Okay, then, she can take mine and head back to the relay base," he said. "It's the only shelter we've got down here. I'll hitch a lift with Droma."

"No, I'll take her," Droma said. "She shouldn't fly alone. And besides which, I know the way."

Reluctant though he was to lose another fighter, Jag nodded in agreement. It made sense to have someone with her, to help her if she blacked out or got lost.

"Get going," he said. "We'll cover your backs."

Droma helped Jaina to Jag's speeder. She protested vaguely, but was unable to put up much of a fight. When she was safely on the saddle, the nimble Ryn climbed up in front of her and activated the engine.

"Keep an eye on Eniknar," he said.

"We will," Tahiri said.

With a brisk wave, Droma sped off into the gloom.

"So where are *our* speeders?" Jag said, firing his blaster at a knot of reptoids who looked about ready to charge.

Tahiri pointed at a crater behind the line of reptoids. "A tsik seru took them out before I could take *it* out. We tried calling for help, but our line of sight is shot down here. We were lucky you came along."

He felt strangely like laughing, but doubted the approaching line of snarling reptoids would see the joke. "You're back where you started!"

"Not at all." Tahiri's grin was fleeting and joyful. "Now Jaina's safe, I don't have to watch my back." She tensed. "Try and keep up, Colonel. We're getting out of here."

With a powerful, Force-augmented spring, she somersaulted up onto the boulder they'd been sheltering in front of and began blasting the reptoids from above.

* * *

Leia paced nervously across the *Falcon*'s passenger bay, wishing there were something she could do. She'd felt the shock of Jaina's sudden plunge into unconsciousness, and had endured an anxious ten minutes until she felt her daughter recover. The relief had been enormous, but did little to assuage the underlying frustration. Somewhere out there a desperate fight was going on, and she was too far away to be of any use.

A bleeping from the cockpit came as a thankful distraction to her thoughts. She ran to find out what the instruments were reporting, and found new telemetry scrolling down the screens, courtesy of Pellaeon. The surface scans showed furious activity around the transponder site. At least five mines had blown, turning the normally frigid cloud patterns into relatively hot hurricanes. She only hoped the Cold Ones were keeping well away, as instructed.

In orbit, things were beginning to change. Responding to the lack of rapid progress on the ground, Vorrik was moving ships into strike range for a bombing run. Pellaeon had responded to the threat by boosting his presence along that orbit. Leia had witnessed enough muscle flexing in the past to know that the situation was at flashpoint. Unless the ground troops delivered—or appeared to deliver, anyway—a decisive victory to the Yuuzhan Vong, things in orbit would soon get very ugly once again.

At least the relay base was safe, though. That was a small comfort in the middle of such chaos and confusion. And she supposed she shouldn't complain too much. She'd been hiding only a matter of hours, whereas Ashpidar and her crew had been evading the Yuuzhan Vong for days.

Thinking of the base commander, she clicked open the comm to Ashpidar's office.

"Commander Ashpidar?" she said. "If you're interested, I have new telemetry from Pellaeon."

There was no response.

"Sekot!"

Jabitha's startled cry brought Jacen out of his stunned daze. He was gaping at the image of Vergere where she stood opposite Senshi, her diminutive figure commanding everyone's attention. She was dressed in a brown robe, and her large, almost hypnotic eyes were fixed on him. The fringe of feathers and whiskers around her face were, despite the rain, completely dry.

"You're not Vergere, are you?" After so long, there was no way his teacher could have returned from the dead—and he could tell from the image's presence in the Force that this was something much more than just a projection or an echo of someone who had once lived.

"I come to you in this guise as someone we have both known," the image said. "Someone who was close to you, someone you found trustworthy."

"Sekot does this," Jabitha explained. "It appears as my father sometimes, or as your grandfather. Sometimes it appears as me, and that is the most disconcerting of all."

Jacen remembered something the real Vergere had told him. She had been present at the birth of the living planet's consciousness, when Sekot had assumed the personality of its dead Magister and communicated with her and the Yuuzhan Vong. He had known about this all along and not realized . . .

"Why now?" Saba asked, her voice a growl of puzzlement. "Why not before?"

"It *did* before," Jacen said, "when we arrived. That wasn't the Magister Uncle Luke and Aunt Mara spoke to. It was Sekot in Jabitha's form."

"That still does not tell uz why."

Jacen looked around: at Saba staring uncertainly back at him, at Danni still unconscious on the stretcher, at Senshi with his weapon pressed against Jabitha's head . . . The image of Vergere watched him closely, waiting for him to answer the question for himself.

"You're testing us, aren't you?" he said.

Sekot shook its fringed head, smiling. "I'm testing *you*, Jacen Solo."

"And did I pass?"

Instead of answering his question, Sekot faced Senshi. The elderly Ferroan immediately removed the lightning rod from Jabitha's temple and climbed to his feet. The Magister sat up, rubbing at her neck where the kidnapper had been holding her. Sekot then glanced over the Danni on the other stretcher, and the young scientist stirred with a soft moan. Jacen went over to her, kneeling beside her in the mud.

"Danni?" He could barely contain his relief.

Danni opened her eyes slowly, blinking into the light rain falling across her face. She propped herself up onto her elbows, looking up at Jacen with confusion etched across her brow.

"Where am I?" Her eyes widened as she looked around. "The last thing I remember is the roof coming down—"

"It's all right, Danni," Jacen reassured her. "You're safe now."

Her gaze fell upon the Ferroans standing around her, some with their weapons held loosely at their sides.

"This would be the Solo definition of 'safe,' I'm taking it?"

"You will not be harmed," Vergere said, stepping up alongside Jacen.

Danni's eyes widened in surprise even more at the sight of Vergere. "But—I thought—"

"It's not Vergere," Jacen said.

"It iz Sekot." Saba finally extinguished her lightsaber. Jacen couldn't tell if she'd decided that Sekot meant no harm, or that there was nothing she could do about it even if Sekot did.

Danni turned back to Jacen, shaking her head as though the questions it carried were too heavy. "I don't understand."

"I think I'm beginning to," he said. "This whole thing was a setup designed to see how I react under threat. Do I fight or flee? Do I defend my loved ones, or do I use them as shields?"

"Or do you attempt to take the middle ground," Sekot said, "and allow both sides to win?"

"I'm sorry," Jabitha said. "I knew Sekot was going to test you, but I didn't know how. I convinced it that it should, rather than trust you implicitly. I had no idea that your lives were going to be put in any danger."

"You have nothing to apologize for," Jacen said, standing again to face Vergere's image. "It was Sekot who kept Danni unconscious, and who used Senshi to execute the kidnapping. Just as it used the boras here to threaten us."

"Actually, the boras were acting of their own will. They could not be controlled—only provoked or soothed. You had to solve that problem on your own. But the rest is true, yes. Does that fact make you angry?"

Vergere was the perfect form for Sekot to take, Jacen thought. This was exactly the sort of mind-expanding trick she might have played on him during his brief apprenticeship to her.

"No," he said. "I just want to know why."

"I had to know what manner of warrior I was dealing with before responding to your request."

"I'm uncomfortable with the term *warrior*," he said. "A Jedi stands for peace, not war."

"You do not believe in fighting for peace, for freedom?" Sekot spoke in a way that made Jacen feel he was being mocked.

"I believe that there should be a way of achieving peace other than fighting," he said.

"Have you found it, Jacen Solo?"

He looked down to the ground, reluctant to admit his failure to his former teacher—even though he knew in himself that it wasn't really her. "No," he admitted quietly. "No, I haven't."

"But that doesn't stop you looking."

He lifted his gaze again to meet Sekot's. "As the real Vergere once told me, I have chosen my destiny. Now I just have to deal with the consequences."

"As must we all," Sekot said. "As have those who came before us. We inhabit the galaxy that arose as a result of their decisions, just as our descendants will inherit the galaxy that will arise from our own. It is the responsibility of every generation to choose well."

"And what is your decision, Sekot? What sort of galaxy will you leave for future generations?"

Sekot smiled. "Let me tell you a little about myself, Jacen Solo."

"No word from the ground as yet, sir."

"What about those bombers?"

"Orbital insertion for surface run confirmed."

Pellaeon acknowledged the report with a nod. "Hit them hard."

His aide turned away to issue the orders. *Relentless* immediately fired its main engines and descended to a lower orbit. TIE fighters poured from its launching bays by the hundreds. Every turbolaser and heavy laser cannon targeted the bombers preparing to demolish the transponder on the surface of Esfandia.

Pellaeon didn't doubt that Vorrik would respond immediately, thereby ensuring an escalation in the battle, but that was unavoidable. As pointless as it was to defend a decoy, he had to make it look as though the effort was *worth* defending, at least, and therefore confirm it as a legitimate target. With any luck, Vorrik would spend entirely too much effort trying to get more firepower on the ground while Pellaeon picked at the commander's forces from above.

Fire flashed on all screens as Imperial fighters engaged the Yuuzhan Vong. As though that were the spark that lit the fire, conflagrations broke out within minutes in a dozen other locations. The massive warship *Kur-hashan* came about in a ripple of gravitic disturbances, every dovin basal on its hull and in its engine housings wielding arcane energies in order to prepare it for battle.

"All ships," Pellaeon ordered, "engage at will!"

The first truly conscious thought Jaina had was that she couldn't feel her left foot—and the sensation was slowly creeping up her legs. The second thought was that she was moving—and fast!

Opening her eyes, she realized with a start that she was actually flying.

"What—?" she called out, clutching the padded seat beneath her.

"Hang on, Jaina," said the figure sitting in front of her on the cramped speeder bike saddle. "Don't rock the boat."

"Droma?"

"How are you feeling?" he asked.

Jaina looked around to see if there were any tsik seru nearby. There weren't. "Like an idiot. I was downed before the fight even started!"

"Don't beat yourself up about it. This kind of thing

can happen to the best of us, I'm afraid." The Ryn's fluting voice was full of sympathy and understanding. "I'm taking you back to the *Falcon*. Your suit is leaking."

"I know. I can feel it."

He leaned the speeder over as he skirted a copse of towering rock formations, and she leaned with him, trying to patch together the scattered memories of how she'd come to be here. She vaguely recalled Jag being with her at some point, and Tahiri, but it was mostly a blur.

"Everything's going according to plan," he said, straightening the vessel. "You don't have to worry about a thing."

Jaina peered over his shoulder, just in time to see something dark and spiky loom out of atmospheric haze, coming right for them.

"Duck!" she called.

She grabbed the shoulders of the spindly alien and pushed him flat across the speeder. She scrunched down next to him, praying there wasn't anything else directly in their path. A loud, rasping hum rose up around them, momentarily deafening her, and something fleetingly snatched at her back.

Then the encrusted belly of the yorik-trema they'd grazed was past, and Droma attempted to bring the speeder back under control. It wobbled uneasily for a few seconds, then steadied.

"Do you think they saw us?" she asked, looking back over her shoulder as the alien lander faded back into the haze.

"I'm not sure," the Ryn said.

"Either way, we can't afford to take the chance that they might follow us back to the base," Jaina said. "Hang a right here."

Droma did as he was told. "You're thinking we should loop around and distract them, aren't you?" he said. "Or warn the others, right?"

"You have a problem with that?"

Droma's helmet moved back and forth as he shook his head. "No, but I do have a problem with you getting frostbite."

"I'm not so keen on losing any toes, either—but that's a chance we're going to have to take."

"It's too risky," Droma said. "Besides, I doubt those Vong would be interested in us. We're the ones fleeing the fight scene, after all."

Jaina glanced back over her shoulder. "You might want to tell *them* that, then."

Droma snapped his head back for a split-second look; then with a curse that would have made her father blush, he returned his attention forward. Jaina felt the engine surge beneath them as he pushed the speeder it to its max in an effort to outrun the pair of tsik seru that had locked on to their tail.

Jaina felt the pockets of her suit. Thankfully the cold hadn't affected her fingers yet, but it was still hard to feel through so many layers of insulation. She had her lightsaber, a repeating blaster, and two thermal detonators. She quickly withdrew one of the latter and activated it.

"Take a turn when I tell you," she said, arming one of the detonators.

"Which way?" Droma called.

"*Any* way!" she said, lobbing the device into their wake. "Now!"

The detonator exploded with a flash of heat and light, almost blinding her through her visor's light-enhancing systems. She couldn't tell exactly which heading Droma had chosen until her eyesight returned, then saw that he'd slipped them into a narrow crevasse that dipped below the surface of the plain they'd been traveling across.

"Did you get them?" Droma asked, his voice thin with the strain of following the crevasse's bends.

"One of them, I think," she said as a shadow fell across

them. One had survived, and it was now above them, attempting to match their speed.

A clutch of netting beetles ejected from a hatch at them, and Droma braked heavily. They decelerated quickly enough to miss the bugs themselves, but there was no chance of avoiding the sticky threads the creatures left in their wake. Two attached themselves to Droma's back, and one fell across her visor. On the ends of each fiber, grub-like finger-length insects began to reel themselves in.

Jaina tried to tug the threads from Droma's back while he navigated the narrow crevasse, but the threads were strong and refused to break. Reaching into her side pocket, she produced her lightsaber and activated the blade. If she didn't get the threads off in time, those bugs would soon wrap themselves around the two of them and bind them up for easy capture.

The threads snapped under the bright fire of her lightsaber, and two bugs dropped away from Droma's back. She followed the thread stuck to her visor and found the bug that was its source barely a meter away from her head, whipping along behind her. She snatched her hand away and sliced the thread in two.

Three down, she thought, but there was no time for self-congratulations just yet. She didn't know how many more there were. Her visibility at close quarters was poor through the visor, and her gloves weren't sensitive enough to find them by touch. It would take just one to foul up the speeder's steering vanes, or close Droma's fingers together at the wrong moment.

"We have to set down," she said. "It's the only way to make sure we're clean."

"But the flier—" Droma pointed up at the tsik seru shadowing them high above.

His argument stopped in midsentence, however, when he saw another of the netting beetles dangling from her hand, steadily wriggling its way closer to his suit.

He quickly put them down in a sliding skid across a surface thick with carbon dioxide snow. Jaina tried hard not to think of what standing on such a material was going to do to her toes. There were more important things to worry about for the moment.

She jumped off the speeder, with Droma close behind, frantically brushing himself down in a vain attempt to lose the beetles. When Jaina raised her lightsaber and approached him, he took a step back.

"Hey, wait a second! If that thing nicks my suit I'll—"

He shut up when she started to dart and weave her lightsaber, removing the bugs with easy, deft strokes. Then she turned the weapon on herself.

"On your thigh," Droma was saying. "And one on your shoulder!"

Something sizzled as she swung her lightsaber blindly behind her head.

"Okay, you're clear," he announced with relief. "Now let's—"

Before he could finish what he was saying, more threads fell around them. The shadow of the tsik seru, which had swung briefly out of sight, had returned, and a rain of bugs descended out of the flier's belly. Jaina didn't think; she just did what she had to do. Her blade seemed to sing in the murky air as she swung it with controlled, precise swipes that prevented a single one of the beetles from reaching her or Droma.

"Nicely done," Droma breathed in disbelief. "But I fear it's only a temporary reprieve."

The tsik seru was backing up and tipping forward.

"It's going to fire at us," Jaina said, already tensing to run.

"Do that thing!" Droma shouted, waving his hands. "That thing Tahiri did!"

"What *thing*?"

"She closed the throats of the plasma launchers!"

"*What?*"

"I saw her do it when you were passed out. It works, believe me!"

Time seemed to slow as she worked her way though what he was telling her. Plasma launchers . . . Tahiri . . . closing the throat . . .

Her body was one step ahead of her. At the very instant she realized—or so it seemed—her hand was already heading upward to point at the tsik seru's wings. The hand clenched into a fist just as it was about to fire, belching out its high-pressure plasma, full of potency and bile.

It hit the obstruction of her will and blew one side of the flier to smithereens. The second side detonated an instant later, showering them with glowing debris. Gas hissed from the ultracold snow beneath their feet. They ducked instinctively, throwing their arms up for protection. Peering through them, Jaina saw the remains of the tsik seru falling into the crevasse, tumbling in a spitting fireball right toward them. She grabbed Droma and dragged him out of the way just in time. Steam exploded around them as its fiery corpse finally came to rest.

Droma picked himself up, staring in amazement at the ruined flier. "Now that," he said, "was *too* close!"

"Just be grateful it didn't come down on the speeder," she said, tugging the dead weight of the vehicle away from the flames. The growing numbness in her left foot was making walking awkward.

"Believe me, I'm grateful," Droma said, lending her a hand. "More grateful than—"

A roar over their suits' external receivers cut him off. Something stumbled out of the flames and steam—something humanoid, blackened, and snarling. Jaina adopted a defensive stance as she grabbed her lightsaber, but her frozen foot betrayed her balance and she slipped over onto her side. Droma tried to put himself between her and the creature, but was smacked away by a smoldering limb. The creature loomed over him, its blackened face splitting where a mouth might have once been.

"Jeedai!"

The breath issued from the Yuuzhan Vong pilot in a furious rush. The only thing keeping him alive in Esfandia's frigid air, Jaina realized, was the fire itself. That wasn't going to last long—but long enough for one chance to strike.

The pilot raised a viciously sharp splinter of yorik coral and prepared to drive it down into her, where she lay sprawled at his feet. She reached for her lightsaber again, but it wasn't there. She must have dropped it when she'd fallen.

Before the blow could fall, something moved behind her, well away from where Droma lay slumped against the ravine wall. It caught the Yuuzhan Vong's attention, too, and his eyes momentarily flicked up to look. It was all the time Jaina needed. She struck upward with both feet, forcing the pilot back. His yorik shard went flying, and Jaina was up on her feet in an instant, reaching out with her mind for her lightsaber. It whipped out of the snow and back into her hand. With a vicious *snap-hiss*, it came to life.

The pilot regained his balance and stood, preparing to rush her. Fire still licked at his back and legs, making him a truly monstrous figure. Jaina tensed, ready to cut him down.

But she didn't need to. The alien's stare froze as ice formed across his eyes. Pain and cold couldn't be kept at bay forever, not even by the prodigious Yuuzhan Vong will. With a despairing gurgle, the pilot folded forward into the snow, dead before he hit the ground.

Jaina stepped back, lowering her blade, her breath loud in her helmet. She should have reacted faster than that. Yes, she was still recovering from her crash and the cold had crept as far as her knees, now, but that was no excuse. If it hadn't been for—

She stopped in midthought, remembering what had saved her life. Something had distracted the pilot just as he'd been about to stab her—and that something couldn't have been Droma, for he was only now struggling to his feet in the snow by the flier.

She turned around to look.

Hanging in the thick air before her, the edges of its circular, kitelike body rippling as though in an unseen current, was one of the natives. It was so close she could have touched it, but she resisted the impulse. It looked quite fearsome, with its many-tentacled maw and strange organs pulsing through translucent skin. Hundreds of tiny bumplike "eyes" around the maw seemed to be watching her as closely as she studied it, wondering what it would do next.

In the end, it just wafted gently up into the cloudy atmosphere. When it was several meters away, its elongated tail flexed, and the creature shot over her head with surprising acceleration.

A groan from Droma took her mind away from the strange encounter. He was leaning against the speeder, holding his head.

"I think we should get out of here," he said.

She nodded. "My turn to drive."

Through his suit's visor, she could see a half smile forming below his beaked nose. "Here's hoping we can get the rest of the way without any more problems."

"We've had our fair share for the day, I think," she said, hoisting herself up into the saddle and helping him on behind her.

"Solos *always* seem to have more than their 'fair share' of trouble," Droma commented dryly. "Maybe it's genetic."

"Hey, the universe is the one with the problem," she returned lightly. "It's just the Solos' job to fix it."

The Ryn laughed as Jaina kicked the speeder into life and began winding her way out of the crevasse.

Tahiri ducked. A coufee swished over her head. With a grunt she came back up with her lightsaber in a two-handed blow and drove it into the reptoid's chest. The blue blade stuck out the alien's back for an instant before she withdrew it and stepped away. The alien staggered back with an expression of agonized surprise on its face, then toppled over into the snow.

"Jag, over here!" She hurried up the steep slope with the Chiss pilot following close behind, peppering anyone crazy enough to follow them with projectile and energy fire. At the top of the slope, she paused to collect her bearings, mindful that her silhouette would make an easy target for anyone on either side of the ridge, hurried down the far side.

In the distance, delineated as a red dot on her helmet's display, was an Imperial speeder cruising the far side of the transponder. She tried hailing it by waving her arms.

"Hey, over here!"

"Tahiri, is that you?" Han's voice came loud and clear over the comm. Now that they were in line of sight, conversing was simple.

"And Jag, too. We've lost our speeders."

"I'm on my way." Han changed course, disappearing behind the base of the transponder.

"Come on!" Tahiri grabbed Jag's arm and hurried him down the ridge.

A dark shadow slid across the dimly visible horizon as Han returned with another speeder. The second pilot, Enton Adelmaa'j, sprayed the reptoids coming down the ridge after them, then skidded to a halt in front of Jag.

"Good to see you. We were starting to get a little worried."

"It's not over yet," Tahiri said, pointing. "Here comes the second yorik-trema."

The Yuuzhan Vong lander was proceeding more cautiously than its predecessor, firing plasma bolts into the ground ahead of it. As she watched, one caught a mine. The explosion sent boiling air upward in a dark mushroom cloud. The yorik-trema rolled on through it, unscathed.

Han grunted. "Well, I guess we move to Plan B," he said, waving Tahiri onto the back of his speeder.

Jag jumped on to Adelmaa'j's craft, and together the two speeder bikes raced from the howling reptoids. They split up briefly to locate the other speeders from the party, then regrouped on a relatively clear side of the battle zone. Only one speeder remained unaccounted for, and that belonged to the relay base security chief—a fact that only made Han's scowl cut deeper into his face.

"We can't hide the fact that the base isn't here for much longer," he said. "Especially if Eniknar has gone over. The sooner we get out of here and finish it, the better."

There were no arguments. The communications tech produced a remote timer and keyed a short code into it. He waited a second, then shook the timer and tried again.

"There's something wrong," he said. "I'm trying to arm the charges but the transmission seems to be blocked. The dish must be damaged."

"Or sabotaged, more likely," Han said. He sighed. "Okay, I guess somebody will have to go in and arm the charges manually."

"I'll go," Tahiri said without hesitation.

"And I'll go with her," Jag said.

Tahiri turned to face him. "I can manage on my own."

"I know that," he answered evenly. "But I still need to go."

She nodded, understanding the unstated sentiment. She was still new and untested; someone needed to watch over her until they were certain that she wasn't going to betray them. Which was fine with her. If having him tag along was going to help allay suspicions, then so be it.

They rearranged speeders again while the comm tech explained what needed to be done. The detonator control box was hidden at the base of the transponder. Assuming the box itself was intact, all they'd have to do was input the code into its keypad. The explosion would take out the transponder and anything else within a hundred-meter radius. They would have only a minute to get clear of the blast.

"Got it," Jag said, taking the controls. "We'll meet you back at the base—either on this speeder or the crest of a shock wave."

Han offered a half smile and a lazy salute. "Fly well."

"I always do." The Chiss pilot gunned the engine and sped off toward the transponder.

"When I became aware," Sekot told Luke, "the only person I had to talk to was the first Magister. Jabitha's father, the second Magister, was the one who realized what I was, and who helped me come to terms with my potential. It was he who helped me survive the attack of the Far Outsiders that laid waste to my southern hemisphere; it was he who encouraged me to retool my shipbuilding facilities to the manufacture of weapons and other means by which I could defend myself and the people in my care. When we were next under threat, I wasn't entirely ready, but I *was* able to survive. After a long and arduous journey, I took my charges and myself to safety, revealing myself to them along the way. It was there, after the death of the Magister, the confusion of my birth, and the frantic desperation of my escape, that I finally found time to think."

The being projecting the image of Anakin Skywalker had all the resources of a planet behind it, yet still it radiated uncertainty. It was easy to believe that it was the child Luke's father had once been, enormously powerful, tempted by the dark side but still too young to know what was right or wrong.

"The first thing I asked myself was: where did I come from?" Sekot placed a hand on the lamina surface of the table. "Jabitha's father believed that I arose directly out of the Potentium—that I was a physical incarnation of the life energy he believed filled the universe. To him, that was the only explanation that made any sense, but even then I knew it lacked something. It was a very human response in the face of two incomprehensible phenomena, and it ignored the question of why such living planets had not come into being elsewhere. If intelligence on this scale could spontaneously emerge from a biosphere, why then, in a galaxy of hundreds of millions of star systems, was I the only one? What made me different?"

The intense blue eyes of Sekot's image stared into Luke's without blinking. "I have spent decades examining my being in an attempt to unravel the truth of my self. Anakin Skywalker once described me as an 'immensity,' yet at the same time a 'unity.' All conscious beings could be described as such by the creatures that inhabit them. You all have a multitude of bacteria inhabiting your digestive tracts; from their point of view, you are undeniably immense. And yet at the same time you are also one. The truth of your existence lies on the cellular level, in your genes; I came to suspect that my truth lay on a similarly minute level—comparatively speaking, of course. The people who inhabit my surface are as important to my well-being as the boras, the atmosphere, or the sun. Without them, I would be barren; fallow."

"They're part of your mind?" Hegerty asked, listening with fascination to the words of the living planet.

"Would you say that the microbes in your stomach are part of *your* mind?" The image shook its head. "My intelligence is as far above the Ferroans as yours is above those microbes. They fulfill other needs—needs you would have difficulty comprehending. All you need to understand, for the purposes of this conversation, is that I need them as much as they need me. Without them, it is possible that I might never have existed. Or worse: I might have grown stunted and feeble like the rogue boras that Jacen recently encountered."

The mention of his nephew immediately grabbed Luke's attention. "You know where they are?"

Sekot nodded. "I'm speaking to them now."

Jag kept the transponder between himself and Tahiri and the second yorik-trema. He came in low, relying on the large amount of dust kicked up by mines and energy discharges to give them cover. Only once did they encounter resistance, and the single tsik seru was soon dispatched.

Soon they were ducking through a fence of horizontal girders and into the transponder infrastructure. The exterior framework acted as both shield and support for the large and elaborate antenna structure itself. The detonator control was hidden under the skirt of the antenna, in a cavity too low to accommodate the speeder.

Jag deactivated the repulsor engine and hopped off. Tahiri watched his back while he pulled the machine under cover. Then the two of them scurried beneath the skirt and into the complex beneath.

The base of the antenna was a maze of supports and thick cable conduits leading underground. It was so dark that even his suit's light-enhancing algorithms had trouble coping. They made their way by the shine of Tahiri's lightsaber to the place the comm tech had described. Sure enough, the detonator control was exactly where he'd said it would be.

Jag hunkered down next to it, opening the top of the device with the first of three codes he'd been given. A glowing control surface unfolded, providing him with a small 2-D video screen and a keyboard. It was awkward with his gloves on, but Jag soon managed to tap out the commands required until he had the autodetonation window open before him. The second code gained him access to the timer menu. He typed in a one-minute delay.

"Confirm the final code," he said to Tahiri. "And remember, we only have one chance at this. We get one digit wrong and it'll reset the codes and shut down for good."

Tahiri nodded and began to recite the code to Jag. "Zero-eight-eight-two-three-four-one-zero-three-zero."

"That's what I've got."

He tapped in the digits one at a time while she watched to make sure he didn't mistype anything. Just as he was keying in the second-to-last digit, though, something black shot past his faceplate. He jumped back, reaching for his charric blaster as the glowing controls burst into a shower of sparks. Tahiri was one step ahead of him. Two more thud bugs came darting in; she burned them out of the air with her lightsaber just as a Yuuzhan Vong warrior bore down upon them, waving an amphistaff. Tahiri shouted something guttural in return and met him halfway.

Jag stayed down, not wanting to risk hitting Tahiri with an ill-timed shot in the cramped space, but ready to step in if needed. It was hard to tell exactly what was going on; her lightsaber left sheets of glare in its wake. It looked for a moment as though she was being driven back by heavy blows from the amphistaff, but then, just when he felt sure she was beaten, she ducked beneath the weapon and delivered a lazy-looking slash that opened the warrior up from groin to chin. With a steaming gurgle, the alien fell backward and was still.

Tahiri didn't even appear out of breath when she returned her attention to Jag.

"How bad is the damage?" she asked.

He looked down at the detonator unit. The control surface was blackened and melted; its glow was completely gone. When he touched it, there was no response.

"That can't be a good sign."

"We have to get it working."

He leaned in to examine the unit more closely. "I think it's just the controls that are damaged. The unit itself seems to be functioning. There might be another way to activate it."

Something shuffled out of the darkness toward them. In a heartbeat, Tahiri had turned from Jag, her lightsaber at the ready for another attack. Just as quickly, though, her posture relaxed. It wasn't another warrior, but a Galactic Alliance–issue enviro-suit limned with frost. Steaming blood caked one side. Through the partially fogged visor, Jag made out square, reptilian features, clenched with pain.

"Eniknar?" Tahiri took some of the base security chief's weight onto her as the Noghri almost collapsed to the ground next to them. His lips were moving, but Jag couldn't hear anything.

"His comm is gone," Tahiri said. "You should be able to hear him if you touch helmets."

Jag leaned in to the wounded alien.

"Manual release." Eniknar's soft voice was even more muted than usual, but there was no mistaking the pain he was in. "There's a . . . manual release."

His hands fumbled for the detonator control unit. Around the back was a panel he managed to twist free, exposing several buttons in numerous colors.

"Manual release," he wheezed, falling back against

Tahiri in a manner that suggested all of his strength had been spent. "Coded."

"Will it set off the bombs?"

Nod.

"Is there a delay?"

Shake.

"So whoever sets it off will die."

Another nod.

Jag pulled back, as did Tahiri. They stared at each other over the injured security chief, but before either could speak, Eniknar clutched at the front of Jag's enviro-suit, pulling him closer.

"Me," the Noghri wheezed. "I'll do it. I know the code."

"No," Jag said, breaking free of the Noghri's grip. "You tell us the code, and Tahiri can use the Force to depress the button from a safe distance."

"I don't think we have time for that," Tahiri returned soberly. "And besides, even if we could, we can't fit three on a speeder. One of us would still be left behind."

Jag turned over a number of possibilities in his head, each dismissed as quickly as they came to him.

"How do we even know we can trust Eniknar?" he argued, pulling away from the injured security chief so his objection wouldn't be overheard. "Droma warned us to be careful of him, right? Leia thinks he's a traitor. What if this is a ruse? If we leave him to—"

"It's not a ruse," Tahiri said.

"How can you be so sure?"

Her gaze dropped to Eniknar, seeming to stare into him rather than at him. After a long moment, she looked back at Jag.

"I just am."

"Well, that still doesn't mean he has to be the one who sacrifices—"

"Jag," she interrupted sternly. "We don't have time

for this. From the look of him, I doubt that he's going to survive very long anyway."

Jag sighed. She was right; they *were* running out of time. He leaned back down to Eniknar.

"Are you sure?" he said, offering one last resistance to the plan. "We could try—"

The security chief was already shaking his head before he'd finished. "This way . . . at least . . . I die . . . with honor."

Jag knew it made no sense to argue. The Noghri's strength was ebbing; if he left his decision too long, the situation might be taken out of their hands.

He placed the control unit against Eniknar's chest, and Tahiri taped it in place.

"Twenty seconds," she said through their visors. "Wait twenty seconds, then input the code, okay? That'll give us time to get clear."

Eniknar's eyes were shut as he nodded. "I can wait . . . that long."

They left him there, propped up against a reinforced girder. As Jag gunned the speeder bike off into the darkness, scattering a pack of reptoid ground troops in their wake, he heard Tahiri's voice in his helmet speakers.

"Rrush'hok ichnar vinim'hok," she muttered softly.

"What's that?"

"It's a Yuuzhan Vong blessing," she said. "It means, 'die well, brave warrior.' "

Jag acknowledged the sentiment with a nod of his head, although her ease with the Yuuzhan Vong culture continued to unsettle him. "I guess the others owe him an apology."

"I'll make sure he gets one, when things quiet down."

"A little late, don't you think?"

"Not for those of us who will remember him."

Eniknar's sacrifice didn't sit well with Jag for so many

reasons he had difficulty identifying them all. Chiss culture had a strong aversion to suicide, regarding it wasteful and unjustifiable. Although Eniknar's gesture would save many more lives, it still rankled.

But there was something else that bothered him more. If Eniknar wasn't the traitor as everyone had believed him to be, then who was?

Behind them, the sky lit with a bright, white light, as though an impossible dawn had come to this cold and sunless world.

"Your uncle asks after you," the image with Vergere's face said to Jacen. Saba observed the exchange with senses desensitized to surprise. That Sekot could be in two places at once didn't seem as unreasonable as it would have just a day ago. "I have told him that you are all well, and that no harm will come to you now that the testing is complete."

"Did you test the Ferroanz, too?" Saba asked. She was still smarting at the way she and Jacen had been deceived. The supposed mastermind of the kidnappers, Senshi, smiled serenely at her from where he rested with the Magister against one side of the seeding ground.

Sekot's beaked visage turned to face her. "When I awoke, they were already here. In fact, I suspect it was their arrival that precipitated my awakening—or at least hastened it along. Whatever process I was undergoing to reach full awareness, it needed only their presence to be complete."

"That doesn't explain where you came from," Danni said. The human scientist seemed none the worse for her time spent unconscious at the whim of Sekot. She sat cross-legged on the stretcher, listening intently to Sekot's story. "If you weren't a chance combination of elements requiring just an intelligent, peaceful civilization to jump-start your evolution to consciousness, then what were you? How did you come to *be*?"

"I have asked myself that many times," Sekot said, "and never been able to satisfactorily answer it. Jabitha's father's understanding of the Force was flawed. I know that now. He thought that everything was one in the Potentium, a teaching that has survived among the Ferroans to this day. But the Jedi showed me that evil does exist, and I know that the Far Outsiders stand outside the Force. Where does that leave me now? Did I spring from the Force or somewhere else?"

"We have speculated on this," Danni said. "There are a number of possibilities."

"And I would be interested to discuss them with you another time." Vergere's fringe shivered as she turned to face the human scientist. "It remains, though, that a sample size of one is not enough for either of us to reach a conclusion. The simple fact is that I do not know where I came from. I have not come across any others of my kind anywhere else in the galaxy, and that makes me wonder. Perhaps I did wake once, or many times before, but without the Ferroans I retreated into unconsciousness and forgot those dark periods of my development. I only came into the light when there was someone here to welcome my birth, someone to know me. For without that, could I ever be considered alive?"

Saba was struck by the image of world-minds like orphaned hatchlings, scattered across the stars. What would it be like to grow up alone, never knowing who had spawned you, or who your siblings might be? She couldn't imagine it. Neither could she decide if it would be worse or better than knowing your family and then losing them.

Vergere's alien eyes regarded Jacen coolly, waiting for him to comment.

He did so eventually with a nod. "You're right. It's how we treat others that matters, not where we came from."

"Exactly, young Jedi. I stand by everything I've done since I became alive. I trust and obey my own imperatives."

"Thoze being?" Saba asked.

"The same as any intelligent entity: to live in peace, to grow in knowledge and wisdom, to love and be loved in return." Vergere's smiled was broad and peaceful, belying the words that followed. "And if any tries to rob me of my right to follow those imperatives, I have the same choices as anyone: I can run or I can fight. I have experienced both."

Leia tried Ashpidar for the fourth time, now more worried than before.

"Commander? Are you there?"

"Perhaps Commander Ashpidar is attending business elsewhere," C-3PO suggested.

"I'm not so sure," she said. "It's been far too long. A good commander wouldn't leave her post like this at a time of crisis." She stood after a moment's consideration. "I'm going to see what's wrong."

"Oh, dear." The golden droid's arms flapped like those of a flightless bird. "Do you think that's a good idea, Princess? Perhaps a call to base security—"

"I'd rather check it out myself." She retrieved her lightsaber and a blaster from the passenger area. "It's the only way to be sure."

"As you wish, Princess," the droid said.

Meewalh and Cakhmain, her two Noghri bodyguards, preceded her down the umbilical connecting the *Falcon* to the base.

"Stay here," she said to C-3PO. "Call me on my comlink if you hear anything. If I'm not back in half an hour, or I haven't called you, shut the air lock and wait for Han to come back. Don't let anyone else in, whatever you do."

Leia left him dithering and flustered, reassuring her profusely that he'd do as instructed. She slotted between Meewalh and Cakhmain and walked along the umbilical into the relay base.

The corridors were quiet as she headed to Ashpidar's quarters. The base was on alert, so most of the crew were at their stations, ready in case of an emergency. She passed two of the Ugnaughts and a Sullustan supervisor performing maintenance work on a power router, but apart from that, the base seemed utterly deserted.

Leia took the curving corridor leading to Ashpidar's office at a slower pace, wary of surprises. She didn't know what was making her so edgy, but she couldn't shake the feeling that something was wrong.

The door to Ashpidar's office was, not surprisingly, locked. "Go back and get that engineer," she ordered Meewalh. "Perhaps she can get us in."

While she waited for Meewalh to return with the Sullustan, she tried in vain to listen for anything through the bulkhead. The room on the other side was either empty, or—

She stopped herself short. There was no point heading for such pessimistic conclusions until she had cause to do so. There were a thousand reasons that might explain Ashpidar's silence. Just because she couldn't think of one that held up to close examination at this time didn't necessarily mean there *wasn't* one . . .

"What's the problem here?" the Sullustan asked, striding confidently up to Leia.

"I'm sorry to interrupt your work—" Leia read the engineer's name tag. "—Gantree, but I need to get into this room."

Gantree's response was instantly suspicious. "Why?"

"Commander Ashpidar isn't answering my calls."

"She could be resting."

"At a time like this?" Leia shook her head.

"Then perhaps she's busy elsewhere on the base."

"Have you seen her in the last couple of hours?"

The engineer sighed, her large eyes blinking. "You must understand that privacy on a base such as this is respected by everyone. I can't just—"

"I do understand that," Leia said. "But this is important. I have a terrible feeling that something has happened to the commander. So please, open this door. If my suspicions prove to be unfounded, then I'll take full responsibility."

The Sullustan slowly nodded. "Very well," she muttered, approaching the door and examining its keypad. "But if she asks what—" Gantree stopped, frowning down at the lock. "That's strange."

"What is it?" Leia asked.

"The door," the engineer said. "It's been locked from the outside."

Leia's stomach began to turn over uneasily as the engineer tapped in a long string of codes until the lock finally beeped and the door slid open.

Meewalh went first. Leia followed close behind, her lightsaber drawn but not lit. The first thing she noticed was a smell of ozone in the air. The second was a pair of large feet protruding from behind the desk.

She hurried over to where Ashpidar lay facedown, a web of fine wires wrapped around her horns. The engineer pushed past to examine the body of her commander.

"They tortured her!" the Sullustan exclaimed, tugging at the wires to remove them. "Gotals can't stand intense magnetic fields anywhere near them."

"Will she be all right?" Leia asked, crouching down beside the Sullustan. Gotal physiology wasn't one of her strong points.

"They just knocked her out." Gantree's big eyes looked up imploringly at Leia. "Why would anyone do this?"

"Lady Vader," Cakhmain whispered. "I think you should see this."

She looked up. The Noghri female was examining the safe in the wall of Ashpidar's office. It should have been tightly sealed, but the door was ajar. When Cakhmain swung it fully open, the inside was empty.

Cold rushed through her as she realized what had happened.

"Someone stole the villip."

The Sullustan engineer looked confused. "A *villip*?"

"Eniknar and Ashpidar found one hidden in a maintenance recess a couple of days ago," she explained. "They were trying to find out whom it belonged to when the Yuuzhan Vong attacked. Someone must have used it to lure them here."

"A traitor? *Here*?"

A discomfiting thought struck her. "We thought it was Eniknar because he smelled wrong."

The Sullustan frowned. "What does smell have to do with it?"

"To a Noghri, everything. Usually." She glanced at her bodyguards, but they didn't have the capacity to look sheepish. "The real traitor has been here all along," she went on. "And now he or she has the villip."

Alarm showed on the engineer's expressive face. "They could call the Yuuzhan Vong down upon us!"

Leia nodded gravely. "We have to find a way to stop that from happening."

"Wouldn't they have done it already?

"Unlikely," she said. "They'd need to be able to get away from here first. They wouldn't want to go down with the ship."

"Then they must be heading out on foot, because there are no speeder bikes left."

"And it takes time to put on an enviro-suit." A sense of urgency gripped her; they might have arrived too late to prevent Ashpidar from being tortured for the codes for the safe, but they might yet stop the traitor finishing the job. "Come on."

Gantree hurried from the room close behind Leia. "A roll call would tell us who was missing," she began, flustered by Leia's sudden haste.

"That would only alert them that we're onto them. No, we have to get to them *before* they escape. Which air lock would they use?"

"There's only one designed for suited EVA."

"Take me there."

The Sullustan's short legs propelled her rapidly along the base's corridor, urged on by Leia's certainty that this was the only way to stop the traitor. There wasn't time to move the base to safety—or the *Falcon*, for that matter. If they failed, it would all end here.

The extravehicular air lock was locked when they arrived. Through a thick transparisteel observation window, they saw a diminutive figure working the final seals on an enviro-suit. Leia couldn't make out who it was from the back, but the Sullustan beside her seemed to know automatically. Her hand punched at an intercom.

"Tegg! What are you *doing*?"

The Ugnaught on the other side of the glass didn't respond, except to hasten his efforts. There was a small, vacuum-sealed box beside him, just large enough to contain a villip.

"Why are you doing this?" the engineer went on. "Don't you know they'll kill us all?"

Still the Ugnaught didn't speak, but the look of hatred in the tiny traitor's eyes said it all: Peace Brigade. They were everywhere, their once vague and amorphous resentment and anger finally given shape by the Yuuzhan Vong.

"Can we open the door?" Leia asked.

The Sullustan tapped at a keypad, then threw her hands up in frustration. "He's frozen the controls!"

"Then we have to stop him getting *out*." Leia's palms itched at the closeness of disaster. "Does this lock meet standard safety requirements?"

The Sullustan looked offended at the suggestion that it might not. "Of course! Why?"

"That means the outer lock can't open if there's a breach in the inner lock." She snapped on her lightsaber. "Stand back."

Her bodyguards and the Sullustan moved to the far side of the air lock bay. Leia raised her lightsaber and channeled all her energy along it. She would need every iota of strength she had to drill through a half-meter-thick transparisteel sheet.

Yellow-hot sparks flew in all directions as she brought the tip of her lightsaber in contact with the window. A trickle of molten transparisteel ran down the surface, and she felt the blade sink slowly into it, one centimeter at a time. The Ugnaught looked up and hastened his efforts to escape, but she didn't let herself think about him. His actions were beyond her control right now; she had to focus solely upon the job at hand. She narrowed her awareness down to the blade itself, sending her will in waves down to the very tip as it worked its way through the transparisteel. There she concentrated on breaking chemical bonds, setting chunks of complex materials free, burning deeper and deeper. Her being dissolved in that fire until she seemed no longer to exist. Everything hinged on one incredibly simple task, and she *became* that task. There was nothing else of her left.

An alarm sounding in her ears dragged her reluctantly back to her physical surroundings, thinking she'd made it through the window and thereby activated the breach failsafes. But there was still resistance at the end of her lightsaber. She looked up from the glow of her blade and saw red warning lights flashing, but they weren't from any alarm she had triggered. The exterior air lock was open and the air lock was empty.

She couldn't believe her eyes. It wasn't possible! Yet there it was, undeniable. The Ugnaught had escaped, leaving the door jammed open behind him so they couldn't follow. The same failsafes that might have stopped the traitor now stopped *her*. She couldn't open the inner door while the outer was ajar. All of her efforts had been for nothing. . . . She deactivated her lightsaber.

"Can you move the base without Ashpidar's authorization?" she said, turning to the engineer.

"Yes, but—"

"Just do it. Get it out of here now! It doesn't matter where. I'll get the *Falcon* moving, too, perhaps as a decoy. Any chance at all is better than none!"

Gantree blinked wide, frightened eyes at her. Leia sensed the Sullustan's fear, but she didn't have time to reassure her. If they were going to save the relay base then—

Something clattering in the air lock distracted her. She turned in unison with the Sullustan to see that the Ugnaught had returned. Through the thick, Esfandian air that had filled the chamber it was hard to tell exactly what was going on, but it looked as though he'd tripped headlong over the threshold and now lay sprawled faceup on the floor. As Leia watched, he struggled to his feet, edging away from the open air lock with his back to the window. Seconds later, Leia saw the cause of his fear.

A human-shaped figure in an enviro-suit stepped into the air lock, a glowing violet lightsaber raised, ready to strike.

Relief tightened Leia's throat. "Jaina!"

"I came as soon as I could," came her daughter's voice over the intercom.

"You felt me?"

"Felt that something was wrong. I homed in on you

just in time to catch this little one trying to set up his pet villip."

At that moment, the Ugnaught feinted and made a break for the door. Jaina gestured with her free hand and he flew against a wall, arms and legs spread wide.

Another figure appeared in the door. Leia sensed the two talking to each other, although she couldn't tap into their internal comm system without wearing a suit of her own.

"Droma says there's something going on above," Jaina said as the two of them worked at the obstruction holding the external door open. "Looks like the fighting's started again. We'll let ourselves in while you go check to see if Pellaeon's sent some telemetry."

Leia nodded, her relief at the timely rescue turning once again to worry. Whatever had broken the stalemate, it couldn't bode well for the Imperial forces. They were still outnumbered.

Besides, this wasn't the way the plan was supposed to go. If Jaina and the others had successfully destroyed the transponder tower, making it look as if the relay base had been destroyed, there should be no reason for Commander Vorrik to stick around any longer. He could leave, mission accomplished and honor intact, leaving the Galactic Alliance to sift through the wreckage. So why was he still here?

The crisis with the villip safely averted, her thoughts turned out to the rest of the planet, and beyond. The battle may have been won, but the course of the war was still very much to be decided.

Something anxious and troubling chewed at her stomach. What had gone wrong?

A chill went down Jacen's spine.

"You've decided to fight," he said, trying to fathom the words coming from his former teacher with the same veneration as if Vergere herself were speaking. "Is that what you're telling me?"

"That is not what I said." Sekot turned on him and fixed him with a piercing stare. "I said that I had a choice, and that I have tried both of the options already. I fought off the Far Outsiders. Then, I fled the fire of the inner galaxy, seeking the outer darkness so that I might be alone—so that I might be safe. And for many years I was just that. Then you came to disturb my peace."

"The Yuuzhan Vong came first," he reminded the living planet.

"You both invade my Sanctuary."

"But with different intentions."

The image of Vergere's feathered eyebrows went up in surprise. "You presume a lot, young Jedi," Sekot said. "Without knowing what the Far Outsiders said to me, what they demanded of me, or what they tried to take from me, you seem confident to speak of their intentions."

Jacen bowed his head apologetically. "You're right, of course." He raised his eyes to meet those of Vergere. "Nevertheless, you must have seen something different about us. You allowed us to land, after all; the Yuuzhan Vong you simply destroyed."

"The Jedi have never openly meant me harm, and I have learned much from you in the past. There is much I have left to learn, and you can help with that, under the right circumstances. Many people here remember your kind, and would have been keen to have you here, but for your war."

"We're here in search of peace, not war," Jacen said, injecting every word with as much sincerity as he could muster.

"How can I give you peace?"

Jacen shook his head. This was the question that had haunted him ever since his teacher's death "I don't know," he admitted. "But there has to be something, otherwise Vergere would never have sent us in the first place."

"I could give you weapons to help you fight your war," Sekot said. "The Far Outsiders are invisible to the life flows that the first Magister called the Potentium and that you Jedi call the Force, but that does not make them utter abominations. Ever since their first attack, I have been examining fragments of destroyed vessels, seeking to understand the principles by which they operate."

"Back-engineering their technology," Danni said.

"Precisely. Much that I found was confusing and disturbing, but I took what I could and made it my own. My living ships and weapons bear similarities to those of the Far Outsiders, and few of their weaknesses."

Jacen felt his breath catch in his throat. Was this why Vergere had sent them to Sekot? Part of him was excited by the thought of beating the Yuuzhan Vong at their own game, but it didn't ring true with what he remembered of his teacher. He doubted she had intended for them to find superweapons to help destroy the Yuuzhan Vong. A deeper understanding of their enemy, yes, and perhaps a new weakness, but not another means of wreaking slaughter.

"What's wrong, Jacen?" Sekot asked him. "You don't look pleased."

"I guess I'm not," he said. "I don't think that's why we're here."

"You're not here to get our help in the war?" Jabitha asked.

"We are, yes. But not like that."

"Then how? What else do we have to offer you?"

"I don't *know*."

The image of his teacher crooked one eye higher than the other in a distinctly avian gesture. "I am a force unlike anything you have come across before," Sekot said. "Are you trying to tell me that were I to offer myself as a weapon in your fight against the Far Outsiders, you would turn me down?"

Jacen felt Saba and Danni staring at him, and for a moment two words warred with his thoughts.

Yes—because he was tired of death and destruction and the endless cycle of violence. A military victory for the Galactic Alliance would require the utter genocide of the Yuuzhan Vong species. How could he possibly live with himself if he was in any way responsible for something like that?

And *no*—because he could see no other way to defend those he loved. If there was no other option but military might, he couldn't stand by and watch his friends and family be slaughtered. His conscience would be clear to turn down the offer of such a weapon, he knew, but what was a moral victory if in the end it meant the deaths of trillions?

The weight of the future might rest heavily upon what he would say next, yet Jacen felt incredibly small at that moment. With a word he could change the course of the war, and therefore the destiny of his people.

"Well?" Sekot prompted. "What is your answer?"

"No."

The word seemed to echo in Luke's mind as he imagined generations of children who might not live if the Galactic Alliance failed in the fight against the Yuuzhan Vong—children such as his own son, Ben. He saw every species of the galaxy enslaved to the biological slave machine of Supreme Overlord Shimrra—every cell screaming rebellion, but every limb yoked in an endless cycle of pain and despair. With such images in his mind, could he really afford to turn down the means to the galaxy's salvation that Sekot might bring?

"You *would* accept such an offer?" said the image of

Anakin Skywalker, face tipped forward as though seeking reassurance that he'd heard correctly.

Luke nodded slowly, deliberately. "I would."

But even as he spoke the words, he couldn't help but wonder if, in accepting the offer, he might be straying too close to the dark side, or encouraging Sekot to do so . . .

"Then consider the offer made," Sekot said, smiling broadly.

Behind Luke, the Ferroans gasped as one. This they hadn't expected—and neither had Luke.

"What about all this talk about wanting peace and to be left alone?" Mara asked. She made no attempt to hide her suspicions.

"I still desire those things," Sekot said. "I just know that I cannot have them here, or while the Far Outsiders trouble this galaxy. So my offer is for my benefit as much as it is your own."

"But, Sekot," Rowel spluttered, "what of *Sanctuary*?"

"Sanctuary has already been irreparably shattered," Sekot answered. "You see, the escape of the coralskipper from the moon M-Three was not entirely fiction. One vessel *did* manage to escape my net during the attack, and we must presume that that ship is returning to its masters to report on my whereabouts."

The words provoked a look of both horror and surprise on the faces of Darak and Rowel. Horror for Sekot's decision to help the Jedi, and surprise, perhaps, because even their godlike planet had not been able to prevent one of the enemy's ships from escaping.

Sekot must have seen this in their expressions, too.

"I guess I am not as all-powerful as you think me," it said to the Ferroans. To Mara and Luke it added: "Nor you. Is that a sobering thought?"

Pellaeon observed the demise of the transponder with something approaching satisfaction. The explosion showed as a white-hot dimple bulging up through the dense atmosphere, accompanied by a sharp electromagnetic crack. It was unmistakable, even through the flash and scatter of the battle above.

Now, Vorrik, he thought. *Let's see what you're really made of. Will you turn tail and flee, or have I stung your pride enough to make you stay around, for one final humiliation?*

Kur-hashan seemed to hover, indecisive, as the news sunk in. Pellaeon wondered what was going through the commander's mind. What secret agenda had been confounded? Pellaeon didn't doubt there was one. Expending so much energy to knock out a single communications nexus just didn't make sense. They could have destroyed it days ago simply by pounding the surface of the planet back to molten slag. That they hadn't could only mean one thing: they wanted the base intact.

Pellaeon smiled as *Kur-hashan* began to come about, preparing for all-out attack.

"Send the signal," he instructed his aide. "I think it's been long enough."

Secrets within secrets . . .

Imperial and Yuuzhan Vong forces clashed anew, a thousand bright flashes lighting up the dark world below. TIE fighter hunted coralskipper; capital ships turned their prodigious energies against each other; shields burned a million different colors, dissipating deadly forces in all directions. From the planet below, the skies of Esfandia would be burning bright, as they never had before.

Pellaeon stood firm on the bridge as *Kur-hashan* bore down on him. The hideous, mottled hull grinned like a dreadful death mask. He imagined Vorrik's rage and anticipation building behind it. An infidel might defy the great commander, but victory in the end was assured. As far as Vorrik would have been concerned, it was only a matter of time before his superior forces swept those in his path to the edges of the universe, like dust.

A ripple of worry spread across the bridge. For the briefest of moments, Pellaeon wondered if Vorrik might be right, if he hadn't miscalculated the timing or gotten the message wrong. A thousand and one things could have gone awry, which was why he hadn't shared the truth with anyone but his aide.

Then, just as the grinning skull of *Kur-hashan* seemed to bulge out of the screen at him, a telemetry officer spoke up.

"Hyperspace signatures, sir—dozens of them!"

Pellaeon let out the breath he'd been holding as ships of all shapes and sizes appeared around Esfandia, a rag-tag fleet armed with patchwork cannons and out-of-date missiles. What they lacked in top-of-the-line hardware, though, they more than made up for with surprise and guts. They threw themselves against the warship and its attendant craft, pounding dovin basals and cutting great swaths out of yorik coral. For a minute, it looked as though the alien behemoth might recover its poise, and its control of the situation with it, but with atmosphere and bodies venting in more than a dozen places, and dovin basals failing in great ripples along one flank, the tide quickly turned. A gunboat with unfamiliar markings stitched a line of fiery death down the giant living vessel's spine. Two very unsteady-looking corvettes, working in tandem, took out a yammosk-bearing support ship. A heavily shielded drone freighter spun out of control into *Kur-hashan*'s midsection and blew up as though it had been loaded from stem to stern with high explosives.

"Incoming transmission!" his comm officer announced. "It's from the enemy."

Pellaeon smiled.

Vorrik's hideous visage appeared before him. The commander's bridge was shaking behind him, and the image was fuzzy, as though the room was filling with smoke.

Pellaeon made a gesture to his aide, out of Vorrik's sight.

"I take it you wish to surrender, Vorrik?"

The warrior snarled. "You cannot defeat us, infidel."

"Five minutes ago I would have said the same thing," Pellaeon said. "But now . . ."

"You may kill us, but you will not defeat us! You will *never* defeat us!"

With a roar from the commander, the communication ended. Pellaeon knew what was about to happen. "Full shields immediately!" he commanded. "He's going to blow his drives!"

The order spread among the Imperial and other ships harassing the giant destroyer. Just as *Kur-hashan*'s surviving engines surged forward and something deep in its belly began to erupt, every ship within range shunted all power away from attack to defense. The commander's final gesture was wasted. For all the fury of the dying warship, all the energy expended in one wild rush and all the Yuuzhan Vong lives lost, it did little more than nudge *Right to Rule* slightly off course.

And when the titanic fireball had dwindled to embers, the odds were better than even.

"Transmission from *Pride of Selonia*."

"Put it through," Pellaeon ordered. "My station only."

He turned as a holo image of Captain Mayn appeared behind him.

"Congratulations, Grand Admiral," she said. "I presume you knew all along what was going to happen."

"That Vorrik would self-destruct rather than surrender? No, but it was a good bet he'd prefer to go out kicking. I may not have as much experience with the Yuuzhan Vong as you, but I know their type; I know the way they think. They never bend; all they can do is break, with an eye to the spectacular."

Mayn smiled. "Actually, I was referring to the other ships. Where did they come from? Who are they?"

"Friends of yours, I believe. They told me about Esfandia after Generis. They suggested I come here to avoid another catastrophe. They also said reinforcements wouldn't be far behind, if I needed them. I could summon them by transmitting a code phrase on a particular frequency. When Vorrik attacked rather than giving up the game, I figured the time had come."

"That was quite a gamble, sir."

"You have a problem with the way it turned out, Captain?"

Mayn smiled briefly. "Not at all, Admiral. I might have done the same thing myself, given the circumstances. I'm just trying to work out who these 'friends' of ours are, though."

"I was hoping you could tell me," Pellaeon said. "All I know is that they're calling themselves the Ryn network."

Understanding and puzzlement collided on Mayn's face. "Really? Well, I suppose they could've called in some favors, here and there, but I never suspected they'd have *this* sort of influence."

"So you do know something about them?"

Mayn nodded. "A little. But you might want to talk to Princess Leia and Captain Solo to find out the full story."

With that, Mayn saluted, and the transmission eneded. Pellaeon turned back to his duties, nodding thoughtfully to himself.

"Believe me," he muttered, "I intend to."

"Yes."

Stunned silence fell about the rain-soaked pit in the wake of Jacen's answer to Sekot. He could feel Saba and Danni looking at him, uncomprehending. How could he have said that? their eyes asked. How could he have damned countless millions to unspeakable misery?

He turned away from them both, not wanting their silent accusations. Deep in his heart he knew he'd made the right decision, and two voices in his mind reassured him of that. The first belonged to Wynssa Fel, who had said to him on Csilla: *The weapon at your side seems out of place on a man who professes to hate violence.* The second voice belonged to his uncle: *How do we fight a brutal, evil enemy without becoming brutal and evil ourselves?*

Somewhere between those two statements lurked the justification for his decision. It was the most difficult decision he'd ever had to make, and one he could not explain in a few words to either Danni or Saba. It pained him to think of what the ramifications of his decision might be for the rest of the galaxy, but he wasn't about to back down from the stand he was making. Saying yes to Zonama Sekot had been a show of strength, not an act of weakness.

"After traveling as far as you have to beseech my help," Sekot said, "you reject my offer. Are you sure?"

"I stand by my decision," he answered soberly.

"Jacen . . ." Danni's objection petered out with a bewildered shake of her head.

"Military might is not what we need," he tried to explain. "I cannot countenance destruction as a solution to the threat of destruction. In the long run, such a victory would only bring about our own downfall." He faced Sekot once again. "I'm sorry, but I cannot accept your offer."

The image of his former teacher smiled. "Nevertheless, I have decided to join your cause."

Jacen frowned at Sekot's unnaturally dry image. "What are you saying?"

"I'm saying that you have achieved what you set out to do," Sekot said. "I shall return with you to your war.

Whether or not I can make a difference, of course, remains to be seen."

Vergere's image moved over to where Jacen stood, his mind still numb with shock. To his surprise, the arm Vergere's image placed around his waist exerted a faint pressure, like heavy fog.

"We are done with running," Sekot told him, softly, so only he could hear. "We must find a way to end this war. Perhaps together we can work out which way we must go. Not just for ourselves, but for the sake of all life within the galaxy."

Jacen turned to stare into the eyes of his former teacher. In them he found great intellect and infinite compassion, as well as an ageless, unfathomable wisdom the likes of which he could never hope to achieve. But try as he might, he could find no reassurance in them, and that troubled him more than he was prepared to admit.

"It gives me great displeasure, Supreme One, to report on yet another nest of perfidy, this time in Numesh sector and overseen by the Prefect Zareb."

Nom Anor watched with keen interest as the court of the Supreme Overlord heard of the latest supposed threat to the status quo. The villip hidden in Ngaaluh's robes caught the scene with perfect clarity as she presented her report. He listened with relish, feeling the need for some uncomplicated revenge in order to wash the taste of Shoon-mi's betrayal from his throat.

Shimrra was seated atop his yorik throne, one elbow resting on the throne's arm as he gazed down reflectively upon those gathered before him. The baleful red eyes swept the attentive crowd. There was no sound apart from the shuffling of feet and the soft, creaking contractions of shifting armor, and Ngaaluh's voice, tolling the doom of the former executor Zareb. The planted heretics had been interrogated; their testimony was plain.

"It is with regret that I must deliver this news, Supreme One, but the conclusion is inescapable: you have been yet again betrayed by someone in whom you put your trust."

Shimrra shook his head at the inevitable conclusion. "How is this possible?"

"My Lord, I fear—"

"Not you, Ngaaluh. You have said all you need to say." Shimrra rose to his feet and descended from his throne with calculated precision, red eyes glancing at a different member of his audience with each step. His voice, when he spoke, was like the voice of Yun-Yuuzhan himself.

"The heresy is not a poison gas that sneaks in through the cracks. It is not spirits whispering in someone's ear. It is not a contagion, floating on the wind. No, the heresy is spread by Shamed Ones who are flesh and blood like us. They possess no supernatural powers. Their love of the infidel *Jeedai* gives them no unseen advantage."

Shimrra's posture was one of restrained fury when he reached the base of the steps.

"So, Warmaster, can you explain how these flesh-and-blood heretics are able to corrupt my most trusted servants without being detected?"

The mighty Nas Choka ground sharpened teeth together. "Our investigations continue through all avenues, Great One," he said. "Of prime concern to us is the nature of the traitors Ngaaluh has reported. They are all, you will note, of the intendant caste."

"Indeed." The Supreme Overlord turned to High Prefect Drathul, whose eyes shot hatefully at the warmaster. "Tell me, Drathul, how these Shamed Ones have been able to amass the resources necessary for their existence, let alone to undermine my authority."

The High Prefect shifted uneasily. "I can assure you that the chains of supply are being examined as we speak.

We strongly suspect that some of the knowledge required to divert these resources was obtained from a renegade shaper."

Shimrra's look of disdain required no words. "Master Shaper," he said, turning next to Yal Phaath. "How do you respond to this claim?"

"Such knowledge did not come from our ranks, I assure you, Supreme One." The master shaper locked his grotesquely modified hands nervously in front of him. "Our faith lies firmly in you and the gods."

The Supreme Overlord's expression conveyed perfectly what he thought of that assertion.

"Ah, yes: faith." Shimrra turned lastly to the high priest. Nom Anor wished he could freeze the villip choir on the look on Jakan's face. Watching the warmaster, high prefect, and master shaper squirm had been fine enough, but this was even better.

"This heresy undermines the spiritual center of our mighty people, Jakan," Shimrra said, looming less than an arm's length away from the high priest. "The gods have every right to be displeased at the lack of faith we show in them. Your plans to rid us of this treacherous Prophet show a distinct lack of imagination."

"You may be assured, Supreme One, that retribution is at hand," Jakan pronounced, a slight trembling of his hands the only sign of the terror he was surely feeling. "Such vile blasphemies will not go unpunished."

"Indeed they will not. Our enemies are flesh and blood, after all. They are nothing to the gods but aberrations." Shimrra released the high priest from his stare, and Jakan visibly sagged.

"The question remains, however," said Shimrra, stalking back to confront High Prefect Drathul, "how to explain the spread of the heresy among the higher ranks on Yuuzhan'tar."

Drathul straightened, but remained silent in the face of the Supreme Overlord's piercing stare.

"Perhaps, High Prefect, I am betrayed more profoundly than I ever dared think. Perhaps there is a traitor in my palace, a recruiter for the vile sect that swears allegiance to the *Jeedai*."

Shimrra's voice was low and threatening, and the implications were obvious. Every scar on Nom Anor's head tingled to hear it. He had never hoped it would come to this. Not against the high prefect himself!

"This poisoned kshirrup dares to purvey the Prophet's rot among those closest to me, attempting to turn them against my will. The traitor steals secrets, misappropriates resources, tells me lies, holds a weapon to my throat that I cannot even see. What do you say of that possibility, Drathul?"

The high prefect's name emerged as a low, threatening growl. The audience craned forward to see what would happen next.

"I think it is a possibility, My Lord," the high prefect said in as firm as voice as anyone could muster under the circumstances, "but I assure you—"

"Not another word, Drathul!" Shimrra leaned over the high prefect. "I am observant. I hear the whispers; I sense the hidden eyes upon me. *I know when I am being betrayed!*"

The roar echoed through the chamber. Drathul visibly flinched at the bile in the words. Guards appeared from behind the hau polyp dais, and Nom Anor felt a keen sense of victory sweep through him. Drathul in the yargh'un pit? So soon?

But instead of closing in on the high prefect, it was Ngaaluh whom the warriors surrounded. Staring dumbly at the villip choir, Nom Anor saw the blunt, scarred faces closing in, and it took him a long moment to realize what was happening. It took Ngaaluh just as long, for the guards were almost upon her before she proclaimed her innocence.

"My Lord? What is this?"

"This is treachery," Shimrra said, turning to face her. His burning red eyes seemed to stare right into Nom Anor's frozen heart. "You should know that well enough."

"Supreme One, I swear—"

"Seize her!"

Shimrra strode across from Drathul, growing mightier and more furious in the villip choir with every step. The guards grabbed Ngaaluh and held her tightly. To her credit, she didn't struggle, but Nom Anor felt her fear in the way the villip trembled.

"Your evidence against Prefect Ash'ett was convincing," Shimrra snarled. "Against Drosh Khalii and Prefect Zareb it was watertight. Almost too good, in fact. Wondering, I took the opportunity to question the witnesses you brought here, prior to their disposal in the yargh'un pits. When interrogated *properly*, they told a very different story."

"No—"

"They were planted to deliberately incriminate Ash'ett, Khalii, and Zareb, weren't they, Ngaaluh? *You* are the trusted one who turns against me, not these innocent intendants!"

Behind Shimrra, High Prefect Drathul's face glowed with a mixture of relief and anger.

"My Lord," he said, "this is inconceivable. Ngaaluh's treachery explains much, but for the Prophet to have reached here, into your very court—"

"I did not say anything about the Prophet, High Prefect," Shimrra said, turning. "This traitor uses the trappings of the heresy to accuse her victims, but that does not mean that she adheres to them herself." Shimrra prowled across Ngaaluh's field of view. "No. I sense conspiracies within conspiracies, here. It will take some time—and no considerable effort—to disentangle the truth from the web of lies concealing it."

"I will tell you nothing!" Ngaaluh gasped. The view through the villip shook as her body spasmed. Nom Anor watched and listened in horror as his spy emitted a pained cry, then slumped into the arms of the guards.

There was a commotion. The view shook, and for a moment Nom Anor couldn't tell what was happening. When the villip was still, faces loomed in close, and he realized that Ngaaluh was prostrate on the ground, with people bending over her.

"Poison," one of the guards said. "I fear that she has escaped us, Supreme One."

"It doesn't matter." Shimrra's voice was surprisingly calm. "We could not have trusted the confession of a priestess of deception, even under the most intense interrogation. Her discovery and death is enough to warn the person or persons she served that we are not fools. We cannot be deceived for long."

"The damage she did can be reversed," High Prefect Drathul said. "The lies she told can be rescinded. My intendants' names can be cleared."

"That won't be necessary." Shimrra's reply surprised Nom Anor. "Ash'ett, Khalii, and Zareb will not be wasted. Already reports of heresy are on the increase. Fear of punishment is driving this new purge, and I would not see that undone. One good thing will come of this fiasco. That is a certainty."

The villip continued to transmit as one of the guards kicked Ngaaluh's lifeless body.

"What shall we do with this?" he asked.

"The usual." Shimrra's voice was dismissive. "Whether the Prophet sent her or not, she will serve as a warning to anyone else who would attempt to spy on me and to sow division in my court. Her hidden master will see that I

am no fool. He will know that it is only a matter of time
before I find him, too, and before he shares her fate."

"That time is long overdue," High Prefect Drathul said.

"It will come, faithful servant," the Supreme Overlord
said. "It will come . . ."

Shimrra's voice faded into the background as Ngaaluh's
body was hauled unceremoniously from the throne
room. Nom Anor couldn't tear his eyes from the wildly
swinging view. Muffled grunts and the sounds of heavy
footfalls accompanied the morbid procession through
the palace. There were no exclamations, no questions. A
dead body these days was not an unusual sight.

"Master," Kunra said from the shadows, his voice
tremulous.

"Be quiet," Nom Anor growled. He wasn't in the
mood for a conversation. Ngaaluh was gone, and with
her he had lost his best means of enacting his will on Yuuzhan'tar. Without her, he could no longer observe Shimrra and his court; nor could he tell what plans the Supreme
Overlord was concocting against him. The chance to revenge himself on his enemies had slipped through his fingers, just when he had felt that he had been on the verge
of success.

The rocking of the villip ceased for a moment, and
Nom Anor's eyes, which had been staring blindly at the
villip choir, registered the scene again. Ngaaluh was
swinging back and forth. The guards were counting.
When they reached "Three!" the world whirled and the
body fell.

Ngaaluh and the villip came to rest atop the charnel
pit, tilted slightly to one side. Nom Anor had a perfect
view of rotting bodies piled up in their hundreds. Somewhere in there were the pseudo-heretics he had sent to
their deaths, along with Prefect Ash'ett, Drosh Khalii,
and all the faithful who had been betrayed by Shimrra's

new regime of terror. The boastful Commander Ekh'm Val was in there, too, faceless and nameless, his dreams of glory shattered.

How long, Nom Anor wondered, until the Prophet himself joined them?

"Nom Anor—"

"I said, be quiet, Kunra." He heard a worried crack to his voice, but couldn't hide it. "There is nothing to say."

Together, in silence, they watched the bodies rot. When darkness fell, the view in the villip choir faded to black, but still Nom Anor watched. Hypnotized, he could only stare and think.

How long?

He barely heard Kunra leave to attend to the work of the heresy.

How long? . . .

EPILOGUE

The bridge of *Pride of Selonia* was the quietest it had been for a while, with only a handful of crew members working at stations around where Leia sat at the communications console. For the last couple of days it had been kept busy, along with the *Widowmaker*, mopping up the stragglers of the Yuuzhan Vong strike force that had attacked Esfandia. But now that there was a lull in activities, the crew were concentrating on preparing to return to Mon Calamari for a well-earned break. *Millennium Falcon* was doing likewise, docked for the moment with the *Selonia* while it underwent diagnostic checks and minor repairs. Captain Mayn had given Leia permission to use the bridge's communications facilities to test out the antenna array. While she waited for the go-ahead from Commander Ashpidar, she distracted herself by observing the planet below on the monitors around her.

From orbit, the gray atmosphere of Esfandia appeared unchanged. Bathed only by starlight and the occasional drive flash, the planet had absorbed the recent injections of thermal energy as a lake would absorb a teaspoon of salt, returning to its near absolute zero state within a matter of hours. Glancing at it via *Pride of Selonia*'s instruments, Leia hoped the Brrbrlpp life-forms had returned to their normal ways of life, chatting among themselves and sifting edible motes from the dense air in which they floated. She wondered how long the stories of the battle that had brought bright light to their skies for the first time would circulate, and whether it would encourage an outward surge in their culture.

"Princess Leia." A voice with as much emotion as a droid crackled out of the comm.

Leia put her thoughts to one side. "I'm here, Commander."

"Engineer Gantree has completed her preliminary checks of the antenna array and pronounces it ready for a test run," Ashpidar said.

She didn't have to manufacture her relief. "That's excellent. Tell Fan I'm impressed."

"I shall do so." Even through the wooden tone, Leia thought she detected a flicker of pride. "You can commence transmission when you are ready."

"I presume you'll be monitoring it."

"Only to check signal quality and perform further calibrations."

"Understood. Give me twenty seconds."

Leia closed the comm line and activated the transceiver. She punched in the sequence for Mon Calamari. A signal check came back green almost immediately. *So far, so good,* she thought. Next she keyed Cal Omas's private number, vaguely aware that it would have been close to the middle of the night where he was on the distant water world.

"Here goes nothing," she muttered to herself.

Seconds later, the Chief of State of the Galactic Federation of Free Alliances appeared in the holoprojector.

"Whoever this is," he said, bleary-eyed, "you'd better have a good reason for calling me on my private number at—"

"What's the matter, Cal? Did I disturb your beauty sleep?"

He blinked back sleep, squinting from the holodisplay. "Leia? Is that you?"

"You don't even recognize me?" Leia affected a hurt expression. "It hasn't been that long, surely?"

"It's not that," he said. "Just the holo is kind of fuzzy. Besides which, I'm half asleep!"

"I'm sorry to wake you, Cal," she said sincerely, "but I figured you'd want to know that we've repaired the communications base at Esfandia. Generis won't be far behind."

"This couldn't have waited until morning?"

Leia smiled. He was steadily waking up, and the grumpiness became more of an act with every passing second.

"I'll bet Grand Admiral Pellaeon doesn't take this long to get himself together."

"I'll bet the Grand Admiral *sleeps* in his uniform," Omas said. "Why do you mention Pellaeon, anyway? Is he there, too?"

"Indeed he is," Leia said. "As are the Ryn."

"The Ryn? What have they got to do with anything?" He sighed, knuckling his eyes. "Maybe you should just explain from the beginning what's been going on, Leia."

"It could take a while."

"I plan to be back in bed in ten minutes, so skip the exposition," he said. "Is this transmission secure?"

"No. Not at this end, anyway. But what I'm telling you isn't a secret here. It's common knowledge."

Leia summarized the Battle of Esfandia in as few sentences as possible. Cal Omas nodded throughout. He didn't interrupt to ask questions, and she admired that in him. A good Chief of State had to trust the judgment of those under him—and Cal Omas was turning into a very good Chief of State.

"So you caught the traitor," he said as she neared the

end of the story. "And you repelled the Yuuzhan Vong. That's excellent work, Leia. Did you ever find out why they didn't want the base knocked out? That's the only thing I don't get out of all this."

"Han and I interrogated Tegg when things settled down. The best we can work out is that Vorrik gave instructions for Tegg to send a distress call from the base, once Ashpidar was out of the way. The distress call would read that the base was under attack by Chiss clawcraft— and would end with the base being destroyed, for real. We don't think Vorrik would have left us with an asset like this intact."

"But you *do* think he was continuing that wretched policy of setting neighbors against each other?"

"Sowing confusion and dissent," Leia said, nodding. "Absolutely. It would have taken us ages to clear up the mess, and who knows what damage might have been done? Certainly, given what happened to Luke on Csilla, there are enough factions on both sides who don't want us working together. It wouldn't be hard for a spark like that to create a fire."

"Not this time, though," he said, smiling in approval. "You've done an excellent job, Leia."

She smiled politely and changed the subject. "Is Mon Cal safe to come back to?"

"For now, it is, yes. We've picked up some recon traffic on the outer edge of the system, but nothing has tried to get through. There have been only a few major strikes anywhere, for that matter. Sovv thinks they're regrouping, building up forces for a big push."

"Just like us."

"Exactly. If you're thinking of coming back to check in, now might be a good time to refresh those pilots of yours."

"Understood," she said.

His face took on a serious cast. "I don't want to risk losing one of the best assets I have, Leia. I'd like you *here* in case we need you. There are others I can send to take your place in these communications hot spots. Now you've identified the problem, it won't be so hard to fix."

"Credit where credit's due, Cal," she said. "The Ryn did this for us, and got us out of a nasty scrape. I want them accorded the respect they deserve."

"Maybe so, but Gron isn't going to like dealing with them."

"I wouldn't have thought Marrab would be in any position to dispute an order. After all, his network didn't have a clue as to what was going on. Nor did the other spy networks, for that matter."

Omas nodded. "Believe me, Leia, I take your point."

"Good night, Cal," she said, smiling fondly at him. "We'll talk again soon."

When he was gone, Leia sank back into the seat, using the quiet moment to close her eyes and turn to her thoughts. The peace didn't last long; a few seconds later the comm unit called for attention with a sharp buzz.

Leia leaned forward, speaking into the comm. "Is that you, Commander Ashpidar?"

"It is, Princess," came the Gotal woman's reply. "Just letting you know that the antenna array performed adequately, but we would like also to test it in the other direction, away from the Core."

"I might be able to help you there," Leia said. "Give me a second."

Before she could activate the comm again, though, she heard her husband's voice from behind her. She swiveled around to face him, watching as he made his way over to her, sidestepping the few crew members working around the bridge.

"There you are," he said, coming over to stand beside her. "Captain Mayn said I could find you here."

"Ashpidar has the array working," she said. "We're just testing it out."

He nodded distractedly, as though not really listening. "Have you seen Droma?"

"Not recently." She thought back. "Did he come up with us when we left he base?"

"I'm pretty sure he did. But I was also concentrating on flying at the time, so . . ." The sentence trailed off into a shrug as he stood and made again to leave. "Oh, well, maybe Jaina knows."

"Before you go," Leia said, "I was going to see if I could raise Luke, in case you're interested."

A familiar smile broke through his look of concern. "Sure, why not. Let's see how the old farmboy is doing."

Leia tapped in the codes for *Jade Shadow* and waited as the network searched for the ship's distinctive signature out of the many in the Unknown Regions. It took a lot longer than it had to raise Mon Calamari, but eventually the face of her sister-in-law appeared in the holodisplay, grinning broadly.

"Ah, there you are," Mara said, her expression not hiding her relief. "Finally paid your bills, did you?"

Elegance Enshrined swooped low out of the trees, emitting a hooting cry that made the leaves and branches shake. Thousands of leaping insects and birds cavorting in the airship's wake, gleaming a thousand colors, scattered wildly, thrown into chaos. Thin-limbed climbers responded with hoots and howls of their own as they jumped up and down agitatedly.

Saba, safely ensconced in the ship's gondola, exposed her teeth in a smile. The air was full of sound and excitement. The sun was warm, and Mobus bulged high in the sky like an improbably colored balloon.

The hunt was over. Zonama Sekot had agreed to lend

its considerable weight to the war effort. Much was yet to be decided—particularly how exactly the living planet would contribute—but the essentials were there. Everything Master Skywalker had set out to do had been achieved. They could finally go home.

Home.

The thought held less bitterness for Saba than it had in previous weeks. Despite the obvious differences in climate and topography between Barab I and Zonama Sekot, Saba felt comfortable on the living planet. The air was warm, even when it rained. The constant moisture meant paying frequent attention to her scales and claws to ensure no fungal infections took root, but that wasn't an insurmountable problem. She had certainly visited a lot less inviting planets in her travels.

Jabitha had made it clear that she could stay if she wanted, for as long as she needed. It was an invitation Saba appreciated, and although she hadn't decided one way or the other yet, if she was honest with herself, she had to admit that the offer was a tempting one. Zonama would be a good place to spend time healing—something she hadn't allowed herself to do since the incident on Barab I. Not properly, anyway. The hunter in her had not allowed it. But she could understand now that it was important. When she closed her eyes to think of her planet, she didn't want to see fires raging across its face, but the rugged beauty of its once great mountains and valleys. When she slept, her dreams shouldn't be haunted by the faces of her people spilling from the slaveship, but the faces of all the friends and family she'd had while growing up on Barab I. The time had come, she decided, to stop remembering her homeworld in death, and instead remember it in life.

Not just hunting the moment, she thought, *but hunting the future as well.*

"It's beautiful, is it not?" Kroj'b, the airship's companion, came to sit next her as Elegance Enshrined glided effortlessly toward the landing field.

"This one findz it . . ." She took her time choosing the word, "Exquizite."

"During the Crossings, much of this was destroyed. The boras, the tampasi, the animals." He swept one hand across the view through the gondola window. Danni, Soron Hegerty, and Tekli listened to the man's words, although he directed them to Saba. "It was a terrible time. Many of us hid underground, in special shelters Sekot grew for us. Darkness covered the sky, and every leap through the void made that darkness thicker. The world shook until we feared it would crack." Kroj'b's gaze drifted off to somewhere in the past. "We all lost someone."

"This one iz sorry for your loss."

He smiled toothily in appreciation of her words before continuing. "I remember the day the shelters opened for the last time, and the clouds finally parted. We saw Sanctuary hanging in the sky, and we knew that Sekot was happy. We'd found our new home at last. There were celebrations all around Zonama: dancing, fine foods, drinking—so much *laughter*. It went on for a week, but being only a young boy at the time, it seemed to me a lifetime."

"The thought of going back into the shelterz," Saba said, guessing ahead to the point of the story, "it worries you?"

He shook his head. "I thought it would, but it doesn't."

"Even though you might never be able to return to Sanctuary?" Danni asked from the next bench along.

The airship pilot shrugged. "I figure we've had a good run to remain free of hostilities for as long as we have," he said. "And if Sekot can make the difference that your

Jedi Master believes, then maybe it won't be for too long, anyway. Sekot can win the war for you, and then perhaps we can return here."

"Somehow I don't think it's going to be that easy," said Hegerty, at Saba's rear.

Another shrug. "I guess we'll find out soon enough."

"I have to admit," Danni said, "you're a lot calmer about all this than I expected."

"Yes," Hegerty said. "Certainly more accepting than the likes of Rowel and Darak."

The burly Ferroan smiled at this. "They'll come around to the idea, I'm sure," he said. "What choice do they have? Sekot has made its decision; we must trust in its judgment. If we don't, then perhaps we shouldn't be living here in the first place."

"They're scared," Tekli said. "Most would be after so long of peace."

"I know," Kroj'b said. "But Sekot will protect us. And it won't be like the last time. We've been busy these long years. We have planetary shields built into the mountain ranges that should keep things intact during the jumps, and you've seen how well Sekot can handle itself against an outside attack." He shrugged. "What's there to be afraid of?"

The conversation came to an end as Elegance Enshrined began her final descent to a stretch of wide grasslands. Saba saw Master Skywalker and Jacen Solo standing with Jabitha and Sekot's Vergere persona near *Jade Shadow*. Preparations for the journey would begin as soon as the visitors relocated to another community in the region called Middle Distance. There was still much to organize and decide, but Saba was confident that the most important decisions were now behind them. All that remained was to *do*.

Elegance dropped the last ten meters with a stomach-wrenching lurch. Saba and the others held on for balance until, seconds later, the tall grass of the field was brushing the underside of the gondola. Then they came to a halt, with the airship's body above them rippling in strange and hypnotic undulations.

As the others climbed down the ladder to the ground, Saba held back, staring at the tranquil setting around her. It was green and lush, and the air was both rich and invigorating. Zonama Sekot was indeed a seductive tempter. But she cautioned herself not to become too enamored of the living planet. Beautiful though it was, it held life and death in the same proportions as everywhere else. Its surface teemed with tiny tragedies. It wasn't an oasis from the evils of the universe, by any means. The only thing its controlling intelligence had done was give it purpose and attempt to make it safe from the outside. Nothing more. Sekot—who had more than adequately demonstrated a capacity to be cruel—was the epitome of nature itself.

Jacen told it not to fight, Saba reminded herself, *but still it comes. Is that the action of a peace-loving intelligence? Or is it the next step in its evolution—from easy prey to hunter?*

She shook her head. The concept was too big for her to deal with right now. It would have to wait for another time—for the future, perhaps, to reveal.

She clambered over the side of the gondola and made her way down the creaking vine ladder. When her feet touched the ground, she felt an overwhelming sense of completion. Her hunt was over. She had acquitted herself and brought honor to the memory of her people. Whatever fate had in store for her now, she was confident she was ready to deal with it.

Jaina fumed as *Pride of Selonia*'s chief medical officer examined her skull with his long fingers. It seemed to be taking forever, and was made all the more irritating because of the humming noise he made while doing it. Jaina endured it for as long as she could before pulling away.

"Come on, Doc, can't you just give me a straight answer?" she said, looking up into his large red eyes. "Are you going to let me fly or not? My foot is completely healed."

Dantos Vigos turned away to make some notes in her case file. "One more day."

"What difference is *that* going to make?" she objected. "I'm either ready or I'm not."

"Then you're not," Vigos said. The red eyes turned back to her. "Look, Colonel Solo, I can understand your eagerness to get back to your squadron. But I cannot in good conscience give you the okay to return to duty until your balance has fully returned to normal."

Vigos offered a smile, and Jaina was forced to concede the argument. She knew he was right. After the knock to the head she'd received on Esfandia, her sense of balance hadn't been entirely perfect. That very morning in the *Selonia*'s corridor, the deck had bobbed beneath her feet when she'd least expected it, and she had completely lost her sense of direction.

"Okay," she said with poor grace. "But I'll be back the same time tomorrow."

Vigos nodded his leathery head. "Until then, Colonel Solo . . ."

Jaina left the examination room and headed back to the squadron barracks, grumbling all the way about the injustice of the situation. Her mood wasn't helped any when she got to the squad room to find it empty. Everyone else, it seemed, was out on patrol or helping the Imperials clean up the skies above Esfandia. There was an awful lot of debris floating around, any amount of which could plummet to the planet below and damage the newly repaired antenna array—not to mention disrupting the environment. Now that the Galactic Alliance knew the isolated world was inhabited, extra steps were being taken to ensure that the inhabitants were left in peace.

She took a seat and watched the cleanup operation on the monitors for half an hour or so, occasionally offering suggestions but trying as hard as she could to stay out of Jag's way. He was perfectly capable of running the squadron without her, and she knew she shouldn't interfere. As the orbiting garbage dump slowly took shape, though, swelling in size to resemble a large and craggy asteroid, she couldn't resist buzzing Jag to suggest that they name it "Vorrik's Folly" in honor of the Yuuzhan Vong commander who'd given his life to help create it.

So absorbed was she in her observance of her squadron's activities that she didn't even notice when the door behind her opened and someone stepped in.

"Is this a bad time?"

Startled, Jaina jumped from her seat and turned toward the voice.

"Hello, Tahiri."

The younger woman smiled as she stepped closer. Her pale yellow hair was much shorter than it used to be, and she wore her active-duty combat suit everywhere she went, sealed right up to the neck. She was even wearing shoes, which took a bit of getting used to for Jaina. She didn't know if the girl was attempting to hide her scars with the outfit, or if her combined personality simply liked the uniform. Either way, it made a distinctive sight. Her expression, even behind a smile, was guarded and full of concentration, as though she were feeling her way blind through a very different culture.

Perhaps that's exactly what was happening, Jaina thought. The old Tahiri would have found everything familiar, while Riina would be seeing it all for the first time. There was no longer any separation between the two personalities, but the new persona possessed both at the same time. It would be like the opposite of déjà vu, she imagined.

"What can I do for you?" she asked.

"I wanted to talk," Tahiri said. "If you have time."

Jaina returned to her seat. "It's not as if my schedule is filled at the moment."

Tahiri picked a chair opposite where Jaina had been sitting and perched herself on the edge. All her energy was contained and focused. It made her seem very mature, despite her youthful appearance. Her reopened scars had healed into cold, white lines.

"I came to say that I am sorry," Tahiri said.

Jaina frowned. "For what?"

"There are many reasons. I wish it known that I regret the hardship you went through on my behalf. And I'm sorry, mainly, that they chose you."

Jaina shook her head, confused. "Chose me? Who chose me? For what?"

"They came to you on Mon Calamari. The old me and Riina had different reasons, but they both chose you. If anyone could help them, it was going to be you."

Jaina fought the conceptual complication of Tahiri referring to her previous selves as though they were completely separate identities, and concentrated instead on what she was trying to say.

"I remember when the old Tahiri called me," she said. "She thought Anakin was trying to kill her. Was that Riina talking?"

Tahiri nodded. "Partly—but it was also me, for I was still plagued by guilt. The old me felt as though she had abandoned Anakin by moving on emotionally with her life. She believed she should have done more for him—

or perhaps even died with him." There were tears in the young woman's eyes, but all other emotions were carefully contained. "We were on the brink of mental collapse, sharing one body, some memories, and little personality. Neither wanted the other to survive, but I think Riina knew first what had to be done. Without merging, both would have died, or lost what sanity we had left. As our fragile equilibrium crumbled around us, we threw ourselves at the only person who could help us, trusting her to do what was right, even if she didn't know at the time what that was."

"I think I'm beginning to understand," Jaina said soberly.

"You reminded us of Anakin, Jaina," Tahiri went on. "You were his sister, and are like him in many ways. We felt we could trust you. We felt sure that you would be there for us should we have needed you."

"To end it?"

"Or to rescue us. Either way." Tahiri's expression was grave. "I, the new Tahiri, the person who has inherited everything those two were, am grateful they—we—did choose you. I shall always be in your debt, Jaina, for what you did for us."

Tahiri lowered her head, and Jaina fought to find a way to lighten the situation. She'd seen what debts did to people.

"Listen," she said, "it's really no big deal. Anyone would have done what I did."

Tahiri stood, and nodded once respectfully. "Thank you for your words, Jaina—and thank you for hearing mine."

Jaina studied the young woman before her, wondering exactly who this new person was and how she would turn out. There seemed so little left of the girl who once occupied the body.

"Tahiri," she said as the girl made to leave. Tahiri stopped and faced her. "I just want you to know that, although you've obviously changed, my feelings for you haven't. I still regard you as a friend."

Something shifted behind Tahiri's cool green eyes, and for a moment Jaina thought she might smile.

There was a noise in the doorway, and they both turned to see Han walk into the room.

Jaina stood. "Dad, what are you doing here?"

"What—a father can't come and visit his sick daughter?"

"I'm not sick!"

"Grounded, then. Same thing, right?" Han's smile was wide, enjoying the game.

She smiled in return. "Whatever. What's up, anyway?"

"I was wondering if you happen to know where Droma might be. I can't seem to find him anywhere."

"He came offworld with us," she said, "but I don't remember what happened to him after we docked. What about you, Tahiri? Have you—?"

Her question went no farther, as Tahiri was no longer in the squad room. Jaina assumed that she had slipped out as soon as Jaina's father had begun talking.

Her father's expression mirrored her own surprise. "She can sure move quietly when she wants to," he said. Then, with a little awkwardness, he added, "Is she—?"

"She's fine, Dad," Jaina cut in, anticipating her father's concern.

He nodded, accepting Jaina's reassurance. "I guess I'm still kind of nervy when it comes to the Yuuzhan Vong."

"I understand, Dad," she said. "Really, I do. But Tahiri just needs time to settle in." Then, returning them to the original topic, she said, "You might want to check with the *Selonia* to see if they know where Droma might be. Someone's bound to have noticed him about the place somewhere."

Her father chuckled. "Are you kidding? We're talking about a Ryn here, remember? They're the most ignored beings in the galaxy. That's what makes them such good spies." He shrugged. "But I guess it couldn't hurt."

"What's Mom up to, anyway?"

"Up on the *Selonia*'s bridge, helping test the antenna array."

"Maybe I'll join her; see if she'd like some help."

Her father's smile was wry as he said, "You really must be bored."

"No one at all?" Grand Admiral Pellaeon stared at the image of Captain Mayn of *Pride of Selonia* with undisguised surprise. "There must be *someone* in charge."

"You have to remember that this isn't a fleet as you and I are used to," Mayn said. "It's not much more than a group of individuals working together—albeit a *large* group. There's not much organization to them as far as I can see, and that's reflected in the way they're dispersing. They're not moving out en masse, but in dribs and drabs, when they feel like leaving."

"So who's giving the orders?" Pellaeon asked.

"Most of the ones I've spoken to have said they receive orders through unusual means," she said. "None of them knew about the others until they assembled at the rendezvous where they awaited your signal. Most of them hadn't even *heard* of any Ryn network as such until we explained what we knew. As far as they're concerned, they're just returning a favor someone did for them, sometime in the last year. They seem as much in the dark about it all as we are."

The whole concept mystified the Grand Admiral, and yet at the same time he couldn't help but be impressed by the way the Ryn worked. It was the loosest possible cell system in action: every active member of the Ryn network was in contact with only two or three immediately nearby, but no more; that way, there was no chance of anyone following the trail from the bottom to the top. But there had to *be* a top—or at least a genesis point. They had to have come from *somewhere*.

"Well, we owe *them* a favor now," he said.

"So it would seem," Captain Mayn said. "I guess that's the whole idea."

Pellaeon nodded. "Not only are these people keeping tabs on what's happening in the black spots of the galaxy, but they're helping knit them back together again, too."

"There's nothing like fighting side by side to create a bond between perfect strangers."

"Even old enemies," Pellaeon said with a half smile.

"I have to admit, Admiral, that at first I was . . . wary of you. I felt you might be hiding something from us." Mayn paused. "I just want to say that I hope you can forgive my suspicions. It's hard at times to shake the habit of a lifetime."

Pellaeon's smile widened. "I don't mind what people think of me, Captain, as long as they obey orders."

"I'll happily follow orders, sir, so long as they're good ones."

Pellaeon barked out a laugh. "It's been a pleasure working with you. I hope this isn't the last time we serve together."

"I'm sure we'll serve together again, Admiral. There are still plenty of battles out there left to fight."

Pellaeon's mustache twitched.

"I have visited many systems in my travels," said the image of Vergere. "And of the cultures that inhabited them, none have I seen that did not embrace hostilities to some degree or another."

Luke listened carefully to what Sekot was saying even as his gaze remained fixed on the spectacle of the airship descending to the grasslands. He could see the hide of the giant creature rippling as she slid gracefully through the air. Her entire body flexed, bringing her and her passengers to a near-perfect halt less than a meter above the ground.

"I have seen battles engulf cities, and sometimes entire countries," Sekot went on. "There have even been conflicts that have extended between worlds. It is almost as though the desire for war has spread like a plague through the life-forms of this galaxy."

"Not all sentient life desires war," Luke said, watching as the passengers disembarked from the gondola. "The Jedi dedicate their efforts toward peace."

"From what I have seen, peace does not seem to be the natural state of the universe," Sekot said.

Luke turned at this to face Sekot. "It surprises me that one who's supposed to be as in touch with the living Force as yourself would think this way."

"As it surprises me that one as small as yourself would presume to have such insight into the living Force's moral bent."

Luke faced the image fully now, smiling. "On the first night we came here, Jabitha said something similar to my nephew." The Magister looked up at his words, but didn't interrupt. "She became indignant that Jacen should dare speak for the living Force. The implication was that someone so small in the great cosmos shouldn't dare presume to speak for such a powerful thing. But the fact is, the living Force can choose anyone it wants. Size is not important. Master Yoda was smaller than anyone here, yet he was the wisest person I ever met—as well as one of the most powerful Jedi Masters to ever live. You possess a power, Sekot, that is beyond the imagining of virtually all sentient beings, but that doesn't automatically mean that your connection to the Force is *greater*."

The image of Vergere indicated approval with a smile and a nod.

"You are wise, Master Skywalker," Sekot said. "I think in the days to come, you will supply many answers to the questions I still have regarding the Force."

"This is the beginning of a long journey for us all," Luke returned. "By its end, I think we will have learned much from each other." Then, facing the Magister, he asked, "How are preparations coming along, Jabitha?"

"Preparations are well under way for our departure," she said. "The last three days have seen many changes around Zonama."

"Or not seen," Jacen said, referring to the intense electrical activity that had obscured many locations around the planet's equator.

Jabitha laughed. She and Sekot seemed to have taken quite a liking to Luke's nephew.

"Had you wished to know what we were up to," she said, "then you had but to ask."

"That's okay," Jacen said. "I have a feeling that I wouldn't have understood half of what you were saying, anyway."

Before anyone could reply, the others had joined them. Saba's muscular tail made swishing noises in the grass. Hegerty was holding a satchel full of what appeared to be Ferroan artifacts, judging by the bits and pieces sticking out of it. Tekli's fur was bristling in the gentle breeze, and Danni moved to stand near Jacen, still slightly wary of their Ferroan escort.

Darak and Rowel were being much more civilized to their guests now that Sekot had officially embraced them. Not only had they volunteered to take the four not actively involved in discussions of the future on a tour of the neighboring countryside, but they'd made sure that their accommodations were more than adequate, almost opulent, and that they were treated with deference. It marked a dramatic shift in their relations with the natives, and Luke wondered sometimes whether it was simply a case of being told by Sekot to be polite, or if there might be more subtle forces at work. Perhaps living in the life energies of a planet-sized mind put them more in tune with its thoughts than they realized. Certainly there was no sign of the hostility that had originally greeted the Jedi landing party. Even Senshi had reverted to being friendly, having been set free of Sekot's persuasive influence.

"We went to ruins," Danni told Jacen.

"It's incredible," Hegerty said excitedly. "You won't believe what we found!"

Luke found himself smiling at the gray-haired scientist's enthusiasm, but only half listened to what she had to say about indigenous species versus those introduced by the Ferroans. He couldn't blame her for her excitement; after all, Zonama Sekot was a world filled with secrets and mysteries just waiting to be discovered. It would have been a dream come true for any scientist . . .

"Luke!" Mara's voice broke across his thoughts, and he turned to see her approaching through the tall grass.

"All systems go?" he asked.

"Better than that," she said. "We have contact with Mon Calamari again."

Luke didn't hesitate. Excusing himself from the group, he hurried with his wife back to *Jade Shadow* with Jacen close behind. Being out of contact with the rest of the galaxy hadn't sat comfortably with him the whole time they'd been on Zonama Sekot. Who knew what had happened to the war? To Leia and Han? Or to Ben?

R2-D2 whistled reassuringly as he hurried past to the

cockpit. In the holoprojector flickered the long, aristocratic face of Kenth Hamner. His mouth was moving, but there was no sound.

"I didn't say it was perfect," Mara said, sitting at the pilot's station and fiddling with the controls. "We're getting a data feed, though. It looks like nothing drastic has gone wrong while we've been out of touch."

Luke skimmed through lines of text scrolling down a screen behind Hamner, who had stopped talking, obviously realizing that he wasn't being heard. Luke smiled and nodded to indicate that things were going well at his end. There was little more he could do.

"Wait a second," Mara said, "we seem to have a message coming through on a separate channel." The picture fuzzed out, and was replaced by one that was much crisper—one that caused Mara to smile broadly. "Ah, there you are," she said to the image of Leia. "Finally paid your bills, did you?"

Jacen leaned forward over Mara's shoulder. "Mom!"

Luke's sister smiled with relief at the sight of her son. "Hello, Jacen."

Jacen frowned. "Since when did the *Falcon* get outfitted with a holographic array?"

"Since never," came the reply from his father, leaning in past Leia. "We're on the *Selonia* at the moment. How are things going there?"

"They're okay now," Jacen said. "But with communications down, I was starting to get worried."

"Yeah," Han said. "Sorry about that. The Vong have been keeping us busy."

"They took out the communications relay bases at Generis and Esfandia," Leia explained. "We've just gotten Esfandia up and running again, but Fan Gantree, the engineer here, is still trying to repair the damage. It'll be a while yet before communications are back to optimal."

"Why would the relay bases be targeted?" Mara asked. "It's not as if they're major communications nodes in our war effort."

"I think the Yuuzhan Vong are trying to come between us and the Unknown Regions," Leia said. "Maybe to keep us and the Chiss from joining against them."

"That might be part of it," Luke said.

"Jacen!" Han said. His crooked smile couldn't hide a parent's joy at seeing his son alive and well. "How about you, kid? You been keeping your uncle and aunt on their toes?"

"Always." Luke felt Jacen's hand squeeze his shoulder. "How's Jaina?"

"She got a bit of a bump on her head, but apart from that she's fine."

"And Jag?"

"Busy overseeing our new allies," Leia said.

"You should see these guys." Han put in, "No two ships are the same, there's no central command . . ." Han shook his head disbelievingly. "It's crazy."

"Who are you talking about?" Mara asked, frowning.

"The Ryn," Leia said. Then, with a brief shake of her head, she added, "It's a long story. But they're friends, and they made a difference when it counted. We're glad to have them aboard."

"What about Danni?" Han asked. "How's she doing?"

"She'll be okay," Jacen said. "Everyone's fine. We all love it here. It's going to be hard to leave."

"Where's here, exactly?"

"Zonama Sekot," Jacen said, beaming widely.

"You *found* it?" Leia looked aggrieved that it wasn't the first thing she'd been told. "Why didn't you say so before, Mara?"

"I thought I'd let Luke have the honor."

Mara smiled up at Luke, and a surge of excitement ran through him at the implication of this—something that up until now he hadn't had a chance to fully appreciate. He nodded, smiling. "We really did find it. Against the odds."

"Is it everything you hoped it would be, Jacen?" Han asked.

"It's beautiful, Dad—and more powerful than we dared imagine. It's—" Jacen hesitated, trying to find the right words.

Luke could understand his nephew's difficulty with this. How did you put into words all that the living world represented? Or the impact of standing on its soil, embraced by its life force?

"It's wonderful," Jacen said finally.

"But is it coming back with you?" Leia asked, with an expression that suggested she was afraid of the answer.

"It'll be ready to leave in about a week," Luke said. "I figured we might as well stay until then to work out a few of its mysteries."

"Congratulations, to all of you," Leia said. "That's the best news I've heard for months."

The image flickered, then strengthened.

"Sorry about that," Leia said. "We're still fine-tuning here. We might have to cut this short so they can recalibrate the antennas."

Sad though he was to bring the communication to an end, Luke felt profoundly reassured on one level. His family and home were safe. Leia would have mentioned if there was anything wrong with Ben or if the Maw was under threat. When the antennas were fixed properly, he would patch through to his son's safe refuge and do his best to catch up.

And when the war was over, he promised himself he would make up for the time he'd lost with his son. He knew what it was like to grow up without his father; he didn't want Ben to go through the same thing.

"What about Tahiri?" Jacen asked, a note of seriousness dampening his otherwise buoyant tone. "How is she?"

Han and Leia exchanged a glance. "That's a little hard to explain, too," Leia said.

"She's . . . changed," Han said.

"For the better?" Jacen asked grimly.

Leia nodded. "She's still finding out who she is, but I'm sure she'll get there."

"What name did she choose?" Luke asked.

"She still calls herself Tahiri, but—" Leia stopped suddenly, her eyes narrowing as she studied her brother. "Don't tell me you knew what was going to happen to her."

"I suspected," Luke said. "I thought she just needed time to work things out—and the opportunity to prove herself."

"Well, she's certainly done that," Leia said.

Relief washed through him at the news. "Then all's well that ends well, I guess."

"Seems so," Han said. "We're heading back to Mon Cal now to refit and check in with our esteemed leader. He might have new orders for us."

"And the Ryn have to be integrated into the intelligence network," Leia said. "I don't know how our usual spies are going to react to working with the likes of our new friends, but I'm sure we can bring them around."

"Travel safely," Luke said. "And we'll see you at Mon Cal within the next couple of weeks."

Leia nodded. "May the Force be with you, Luke."

The hologram flickered and died entirely.

"And you, sister," he mumbled to where Leia's image had been a moment earlier.

He sat silent for a long while, holding Mara's hand and thinking about his family, scattered in so many directions across the galaxy. One day, hopefully, he'd see them reunited in peaceful times—if everything went well with Zonama Sekot.

"One step at a time," Mara said, as though reading his mind.

Perhaps she was, he thought. Sometimes it seemed to him that his wife's green eyes could see right into his soul.

"The journey is changing us, Mara," he said. "We're not the same people we were when we set out."

"But that's life, my love," she said. "Without change, then we may as well be dead."

Luke smiled, feeling himself filled with the warmth of her affection. There were so many things he wanted to experience in the future, and all of them were with her. All they had to do was fix the problem of the Yuuzhan Vong and everything else, he was sure, would fall into place.

"Jacen, would you—?"

Luke turned to ask his nephew to make sure Sekot and Jabitha weren't growing restless outside the ship, but Jacen was already gone.

"Do you think we embarrass him?" Luke said.

"Maybe," she said. "Or maybe he's just jealous of what we have together."

Luke was silent for a moment. "Somehow, I don't think so."

Danni was talking to the young Ferroan girl, Tescia, under the eaves of a looming boras. The afternoon sun made the air heavy with heat, but in the shade it was almost cool. There was a pregnancy to the undergrowth, as though it might part at any moment to reveal some strange new form of life.

Jacen paused to lean on a root elbowing out of the ground nearby and listened in.

"And then," the Ferroan child was saying, "I want to see where Anakin came from, and Obi-Wan."

"You mean Coruscant?" Danni asked, glancing at Jacen and offering a fleeting smile before returning her attention to the girl.

"Yes," Tescia said. "It must be the most amazing place!"

"It was," Danni said. "I don't know what it looks like now."

"We'll go there," Tescia said. "We'll go there and get rid of the Far Outsiders and rebuild the world of cities."

"I hope you're right, Tescia." Danni smoothed a stray lock of golden hair from the girl's forehead. "I really hope you are."

The girl smiled up at her new friend, and together they discussed where they'd visit first, when Coruscant was safe again.

Is this the planet speaking, Jacen wondered as he listened, *or a girl brought up on stories of far-off places she never dreamed she would see?*

Whatever the source of the urge, Jacen wondered where he would go if Zonama Sekot helped the Galactic Alliance return peace to the galaxy. There was no easy answer. His memories of Coruscant were a mess of good and bad, spanning his entire life. Part of him was tempted to encourage the tearing down of the city-planet from skyhook to deepest basement, so that something new could be built in its place, but who would decide what should take its place? Who deserved that responsibility?

Jacen was distracted by a low chuckle coming from the undergrowth. He looked up to see the image of Vergere standing near him, her feathery fringe dancing in a virtual breeze.

"Things come and go, Jacen Solo," Sekot said. "We both know that."

"Are you reading my mind?" he asked.

"Perhaps. You still wonder, sometimes, why I woke you first when you arrived here. This, and many other things, you will understand in time."

He stared at his hands for a moment. "I wish you wouldn't appear to me in that form. I find it disconcerting."

"Like this, then?" asked the child who would one day become Darth Vader.

He met the disturbingly blue stare of his grandfather as directly as he could. "Why do you have to take on *any* form? Why can't you just be who you are?"

"Because you couldn't begin to comprehend who I am," Sekot said, returning to the image of Vergere. "There are limits to your understanding—just as there are limits to mine. Mine, however, are an order of magnitude removed from yours. Take no offense, Jacen Solo, but my talking to you now is like you talking to a dust mite that crawled across your skin. Do you believe that such a mite could understand you if you were to speak to it normally? Do you think you would even hear a reply if you listened with your normal ears?" Sekot shook Vergere's head in answer to its own question. "Of course not. In order to communicate between such diverse scales of existence, one or both sides must change. For the moment, I am prepared to make that change."

"Only for the moment?" Jacen repeated.

"We'll see what the future holds." Sekot's expression was concerned, not threatening, yet Jacen felt distinctly unsettled by the conversation. What were they getting themselves into? They were bargaining with a creature literally beyond their comprehension. Who knew what its motives or goals were? Or whether it had some hidden agenda? . . .

"Do you know what it is I crave?" said the living planet through the image of Vergere.

Jacen shrugged. "Peace? Knowledge? A clear conscience?"

"All those things are required for a good life. And all of them have a price."

"That's what you want, then? To pay the price and earn a good life?"

Sekot smiled with Vergere's face. "I think that's what we all want, Jacen Solo."

With those few words, Sekot slowly melted away, and Jacen was left alone to ponder them.

Tahiri was in one of the *Selonia*'s empty holds, exercising. She wasn't hiding as such, but was definitely trying to keep out of the way. It gave her an excuse to work on her technique. Since merging the two halves of her self, she'd been struggling to assimilate more than just ways of thought, speech, and being. The old Tahiri and Riina had fought in very different ways, and she needed to refine the techniques so she could more effectively incorporate both the next time she had to go into combat.

As she sparred with shadows, tossing her lightsaber from hand to hand and kicking powerfully, leaping gracefully, striking the air with unerring accuracy, her mind kept a ceaseless running commentary: Jedi Force leap, *asth-korr* throat hold, Sand People high kick, Kwaad double punch . . .

"Why'd you let him go?"

The voice came from behind her and echoed through the hold. Tahiri didn't break her rhythm even for a moment. She'd known he was coming twenty seconds before he appeared in the entrance.

She performed one last fluid leap and landed firmly on both feet, her body now fully facing Han Solo. Tahiri extinguished her lightsaber, returning the pommel to her belt. She walked casually toward Han.

"Let who go?" she asked, even though she knew who he was referring to.

"Droma!" Han's voice was thick with frustration. "I was getting worried because I hadn't heard from him since we docked, so I started asking around. Captain Mayn told me that a Ryn ship called *Fortune Seeker* docked briefly with the *Selonia* not long ago, and now Jag informs me that Twin Suns escorted that ship to its hyperspace jump point. He didn't know whether or not Droma was on board, of course, but I'm guessing that you do—seeing as you were the one who requested the escort for the ship in the first place. So I'll ask you again: *why* did you let him go?"

Tahiri offered a slight shrug. "Because he asked me to."

Han took two steps into the room. His expression was clouded—hurt, too, although he would never admit to that. He would claim that he was angry at having been deceived. But really, there had been no deception. He just hadn't been told.

"Why you?" Han asked. "Why wouldn't he talk to me?"

That was the core of it, she knew. He was transparent to her. She could see through his reserve with the cold clarity of an alien warrior and read his innermost thoughts with the sensitivity of a Jedi. She felt for him, in her own way.

"Because he knew you would ask questions," she said. "You're too much a part of the system he is trying to work around. There can be only so much overlap before the members of the Ryn network lose the thing that makes them special and become like you: blind in subtle ways, vulnerable when you can't afford to be. For now, you and he must stand apart—until the day that peace comes."

Han shook his head. "Droma wasn't a part of that network. They turned him down."

She smiled at his naïveté. "Do you remember Onadax?"

"Onadax? What's that got to—?"

"Droma gave me a message to give to you," she cut in smoothly. "He said to tell you that he hopes your timing's better next time. And that he still doesn't want your money."

"Timing? Money?" Confusion quickly became realization. "The creep who interrogated me at that bar! *That* was *Droma*?"

She didn't take any pleasure in the way Han had been fooled.

"He encouraged the riot on Onadax to cover your getaway—and his, too. He'd been running the Ryn network through that operation, the bar, for six months. That was about three months longer than he would have liked, he said, but it was necessary to take that much time to make sure everything was running properly; once he was sure it was, he could move on. When you're the head of such a secretive organization, he said, you don't want to sit still too long. Their strength lies in their—"

"Wait a minute," Han said, shaking his head in bewilderment. "The *head* of the organization? Droma? *The* Ryn?"

"It makes sense if you think about it. Your involvement with him gave him a very high standing with all the Ryn. His species has been leaderless for a very long time—not that they want what we would traditionally regard as a leader. They're nomads, born to be wanderers and therefore endlessly exploited. They're *expected* to wander all over the galaxy, so few security people will stop them, beyond the usual harassment. And if someone sees Ryn working, they'll usually leave them alone. The Ryn go everywhere, see everything, and talk endlessly to each other by notes, songs, and rumors carried by trading ships. They're frequent stowaways, so few people would become suspicious at finding Ryn where they weren't meant to be." She shrugged. "What he's done is take what most people regard as being the Ryn's weaknesses and turned them into strengths."

"Who'd have thought?" Han mused with a smile curling one corner of his mouth.

She nodded.

Han shook his head, losing the smile. "I still don't understand why he had to leave so soon. Or why he couldn't tell me all this himself."

She faced his incomprehension squarely. "The more people who know about him and his Ryn network, the greater the risk he runs. The less evidence exists that he runs the whole thing, the safer he becomes. His family won't betray him, and neither will you, but there are people farther removed he can't necessarily trust. The Ryn have learned the hard way not to place their faith in strangers."

"And what about you?" Han said. "I'd have thought you were more of a stranger to him than me."

"Given the reports he'd received from Goure on Bakura, as well as the Ryn on Galantos, Droma offered to adopt me into the movement."

"The fact that you're telling me this now suggests you didn't accept his offer."

She shook her head. "I was tempted, briefly, but I decided against it. For the moment, anyway."

The truth was, it was too early to decide what she was going to do with herself. She was no longer trying to walk two divergent paths simultaneously, tearing herself apart in the process; she was finally walking the one path, and she enjoyed the idea of continuing down that path until she figured out just what she wanted to do—no matter how long that took.

With a sigh, Han's hurt softened and became disappointment. "I would've liked the chance to tell him how good it was to see him again. You know?"

"I do know," she said. "And so did he."

"I don't like the idea of not saying good-bye to my friends. These days you can't be sure that you're ever going to see them again."

"I don't think you have to worry about that," she said. "You'll see Droma again. Maybe sooner than you think."

Han's smile returned, then. He didn't look convinced by Tahiri's words of comfort, but he clearly appreciated them.

"Thanks, Tahiri," he said.

"All wounds heal with time," she said. The words rang with a truth that made her shiver. After so long, she could finally say them with absolute conviction. "All guilt fades, and opposites become one."

"Is that so?" he said with a perceptive look. "Perhaps you should try telling that to the people who made you like this."

She thought about this as she watched Han walk out of the room and return to his ship. Yun-Yammka, the Slayer, hung around her neck in the form of the small silver pendant that she had found on Galantos. It held no significance for her now at all, except as a symbol. It served as a reminder—sometimes grim, more often triumphant—of everything she had endured while finding her new self.

Maybe I will tell them, she thought when Han had gone. *Maybe I will . . .*

"Begun, this Clone War has!"
—MASTER YODA

Turn the page
for a sneak preview
of the very first Clone Wars novel,

STAR WARS: SHATTERPOINT

by Matthew Stover

an original Star Wars adventure
featuring Jedi Master Mace Windu.

ONE

CAPITAL CRIMES

The spaceport at Pelek Baw smelled clean. It wasn't. Typical backworld port: filthy, disorganized, half-choked with rusted remnants of disabled ships.

Mace stepped off the shuttle ramp and slung his kit bag by its strap. Smothering wet heat pricked sweat across his bare scalp. He raised his eyes from the ochre-scaled junk and discarded crumples of empty nutri-packs scattered around the landing deck, up into the misty jade sky.

The white crown of Grandfather's Shoulder soared above the city: the tallest mountain on the Korunnal Highland, an active volcano with dozens of open calderae. Mace remembered the taste of the snow at the treeline, the thin cold air and the aromatic resins of the evergreen scrub below the summmit.

He had spent far too much of his life on Coruscant.

If only he could have come here for some other reason.

Any other reason.

A straw-colored shimmer in the air around him explained the clean smell: a surgical sterilization field. He'd expected it. The spaceport had always had a powered-up surgical field umbrella, to protect ships and equipment from the various native fungi that feed on metals and silicates; the field also wiped out the bacteria and molds that would otherwise have made the spaceport smell like an overloaded 'fresher.

Mace wore clothing appropriate to his cover: a stained Corellian cat-leather vest over a loose shirt that used to be white, and skin-tight black pants with wear-patches of grey. His boots carried a hint of polish, but only above the ankle; the uppers were scuffed almost to suede. The only parts of his ensemble that were well-maintained were the supple holster belted to his right thigh, and the gleaming Merr-Sonn Power 5 it held. His lightsaber was stuffed into the kit bag, disguised as an old-fashioned glow rod. The kit bag also held what looked like a battered old datapad, most of which was actually a miniature subspace transmitter that was frequency-locked to the band monitored by the light cruiser *Halleck*, on station in the Ventran system.

The spaceport's probiotic showers were still in their long, low blockhouse of mold-stained duracrete, but their entrance had been expanded into a large temporary-looking office of injection-molded plastifoam, with a foam-slab door that hung askew on half-sprung hinges. The door was streaked with rusty stains that had dripped from the fungus-chewed durasteel sign above. The sign said CUSTOMS. Mace went in.

Sunlight leaked green through mold-tracked windows. Climate control wheezed a body-temp breeze from ceiling vents, and the smell loudly advertised that this place was well beyond the reach of the surgical field. The other passengers who'd gotten off the shuttle were inside already: two Kubaz who'd spent the de-orbit fluting excitedly about the culinary possibilities of pinch beetles and buzzworms, and a mismatched couple who seemed to be some kind of itinerant comedy act, a Kitonak and a Pho'pheahian whose canned banter had made Mace long for earplugs. Or hard vacuum. Even incurable deafness. The comedians must have been far down on their luck; Haruun Kal's capital city is a place lounge acts go to die.

Inside the customs office, enough flybuzz hummed to get the two Kubaz chuckling and eagerly nudging each other. Mace didn't quite manage to ignore the Pho Ph'eahian broadly explaining to a bored-looking human that he'd just jumped in from Kashyyyk and boy were his legs tired. The agent seemed to find this about as tolerable as Mace did; he hurriedly passed the comedians along after the pair of Kubaz, and they all disappeared into the shower blockhouse.

Mace found a different customs agent: a Neimoidian female with pink-slitted eyes, cold-bloodedly sleepy in the heat. The Neimoidian looked over his identikit incuriously. "Corellian, hnh? Purpose of your visit?"

"Business."

She sighed tiredly. "You'll need a better answer than that. Corellia's no friend of the Confederacy."

"Which would be why I'm doing business *here*."

"Hnh. I scan you. Open your bag for inspection."

Mace thought about the "old-fashioned glow rod" stashed in his bag. He wasn't sure how convincing its shell would be to Neimoidian eyes, which can see deep into the infrared.

"I'd rather not."

"Do I care? Open it." She squinted dark pink up at him. "Hey, nice skinjob. You could almost pass for a Korun."

"Almost?"

"You're too tall. And they mostly have hair. And anyway, Korunnai are all Force freaks, yes? They have powers and stuff."

"I have powers."

"Yeah?"

"Sure." Mace hooked his thumbs behind his belt. "I have the power to make ten credits appear in your hand."

The Neimoidian looked thoughtful. "That's a pretty good power. Let's see it."

He passed his hand over the customs agent's desk, and let fall a coin he'd palmed from his belt's slit pocket. The Neimoidian had powers of her own: she made the coin disappear. "Not bad." She turned up her empty hand. "Let's see it again."

"Let's see my identikit validated and my bag passed."

The Neimoidian shrugged and complied, and Mace did his trick again. "Power like yours, you'll get along fine in Pelek Baw," the Neimoidian said. "Pleasure doing business with you. Be sure to take your PB tabs. And see me on your way offworld. Ask for Pule."

"I'll do that."

Toward the back of the customs office, a large poster advised everyone entering Pelek Baw to use the probiotic showers before leaving the spaceport. The showers replaced beneficial skin flora that had been killed by the surgical field. This advice was supported with gruesomely graphic holos of the wide variety of fungal infections awaiting unshowered travellers. A dispenser beneath the poster offered half-credit doses of tablets guaranteed to restore intestinal flora as well. Mace bought a few, took one, then stepped into the shower blockhouse.

The blockhouse had a smell all its own: a dark musky funk, rich and organic. The showers themselves were simple autonozzles spraying bacteria-rich nutrient mist; they lined the walls of a thirty-meter walk-thru. He stripped off his clothes and stuffed them into his kit bag. There was a conveyor strip for possessions beside the walk-thru entrance, but he held onto the bag. A few germs wouldn't do it any harm.

At the far end of the showers, he walked into a situation.

The dressing station was loud with turbine-driven airjet dryers. The two Kubaz and the comedy team, still naked, milled uncertainly in one corner. A large surly-looking human in sunbleached khakis and a military cap stood facing them, impressive arms folded across his equally impressive chest. He stared at the naked travellers with cold unspecific threat.

A smaller human in identical clothing rummaged through their bags, which were piled behind the large man's legs. The smaller man had a bag of his own, into which he dropped anything small and valuable. Both men had stun batons dangling from belt loops, and blasters secured in snap-flap holsters.

Mace nodded thoughtfully. The situation was clear enough. Based on who he was supposed to be, he should just ignore this. But, cover or not, he was still a Jedi.

The big one looked Mace over. Head to toe and back again. His stare had the open insolence that comes of being clothed and armed and facing someone who's naked and dripping wet. "Here's another. Smart guy carried his own bag."

The other rose and unlooped his stun baton. "Sure, smart guy. Let's have the bag. Inspection. Come on."

Mace went still. Pro-bi mist condensed to rivulets and trickled down his bare skin. "I can read your mind," he said darkly. "You only have three ideas, and all of them are wrong."

"Huh?"

Mace flipped up a thumb. "You think being armed and ruthless means you can do whatever you want." He folded his thumb and flipped up his forefinger. "You think nobody will stand up to you when they're naked." He folded that one again and flipped up the next. "And you think you're going to look inside my bag."

"Oh, he's a funny one." The smaller man spun his stun baton and stepped toward him. "He's not just smart, he's funny."

The big man moved to his flank. "Yeah, regular comedian."

"The comedians are over there." Mace inclined his head toward the Pho Ph'eahian and his Kitonak partner, naked and shivering in the corner. "See the difference?"

"Yeah?" The big man flexed big hands. "What are you supposed to be, then?"

"I'm a prophet." Mace lowered his voice as though sharing a secret. "I can see the future . . . "

"Sure you can." He set his stubble-smeared jaw and showed jagged yellow teeth. "What do you see?"

"You," Mace said. "Bleeding."

His expression might have been a smile if there had been the faintest hint of warmth in his eyes.

The big man suddenly looked less confident.

In this he can perhaps be excused; like all successful predators, he was interested only in victims. Certainly not in *opponents*. Which was the purpose of his particular racket, after all: Members of any sapient species that are culturally accustomed to wearing clothes will feel hesitant, uncertain, and vulnerable when they're caught naked. Especially humans. Any normal man will stop to put on his pants before he throws a punch.

Mace Windu, by contrast, looked like he might know of uncertainty and vulnerability by reputation, but had never met either of them face to face.

One hundred and eighty-eight centimeters of muscle and bone. Absolutely still. Absolutely relaxed. From his attitude, the pro-bi mist that trickled down his naked skin might have been carbon fiber-reinforced ceramic body armor.

"Do you have a move to make?" Mace said. "I'm in a hurry."

The big man's gaze twitched sideways, and he said, "Uh—?" and Mace felt a pressure in the Force over his left kidney and heard the sizzle of a triggered stun baton. He spun and caught the wrist of the smaller man with both hands, shoving the baton's sparking corona well clear with a twist that levered his face into the path of Mace's rising foot. The impact made a smack wet and meaty as the snap of bone. The big man bellowed and lunged and Mace stepped to one side and whip-cracked the smaller man's arm to spin his slackening body. Mace caught the small man's head in the palm of one hand and shoved it crisply into the big man's nose.

The two men skidded in a tangle on the slippery damp floor and went down. The baton spat lightning as it skittered into a corner. The smaller man lay limp. The big man's eyes spurted tears and he sat on the floor, trying with both hands to massage his smashed nose into shape. Blood leaked through his fingers.

Mace stood over him. "Told you."

The big man didn't seem impressed. Mace shrugged. A prophet, it is said, receives no honor on his own world.

Mace dressed silently while the other travellers reclaimed their belongings. The big man made no attempt to stop them, or even to rise. Presently the smaller man stirred, moaned, and opened his eyes. As soon as they focused well enough to see Mace still in the dressing station, he cursed and clawed at his holster flap, struggling to free his blaster.

Mace looked at him.

The man decided his blaster was better off where it was.

"You don't know how much trouble you're in," he muttered sullenly as he settled back down on the floor, words blurred by his smashed mouth. He drew his knees up and wrapped his arms around them. "People who butch up with capital militia don't live long around—"

The big man interrupted him with a cuff on the back of his head. "Shut it."

"Capital militia?" Mace understood now. His face settled into a grim mask, and he finished buckling down his holster. "You're the police."

The Pho Ph'eahian mimed a pratfall. "You'd think they'd hire cops who aren't so *clumsy*, eh?"

"Oh, I dunno, Phootie," the Kitonak said in a characteristically slow, terminally relaxed voice. "They bounced *real* nice."

Both Kubaz whirred something about slippery floors, inapppropriate footwear and unfortunate accidents.

The cops scowled.

Mace squatted in front of them. His right hand rested on the Power 5's butt. "It'd be a shame if somebody had a blaster malfunction," he said. "A slip, a fall—sure, it's embarrassing. It hurts. But you'll get over it in a day or two. If somebody's blaster accidentally went off when you fell—?" He shrugged. "How long will it take you to get over being dead?"

The smaller cop started to spit back something venomous. The larger one interrupted him with another cuff. "We scan you," he growled. "Just go."

Mace stood. "I remember when this was a nice town."

He shouldered his kit bag and walked out into the blazing tropical afternoon. He passed under a dented, rusty sign without looking up.

The sign said: WELCOME TO PELEK BAW.

Faces—

Hard faces. Cold faces. Hungry, or drunk. Hopeful. Calculating. Desperate.

Street faces.

Mace walked a pace behind and to the right of the Republic Intelligence station boss, keeping his right hand near the Merr-Sonn's butt. Late at night, the streets were still crowded. Haruun Kal had no moon; the streets were lit with spill from taverns and outdoor cafes. Lightpoles—tall hexagonal pillars of duracrete with glow-strips running up each face—stood every twenty meters along both sides of the street. Their pools of yellow glow bordered black shadow; to pass into one of the alley-mouths was to be wiped from existence.

The Intel station boss was a bulky, red-cheeked woman about Mace's age. She ran the Highland Green Washeteria, a thriving laundry and public refresher station on the capitol's north side. She never stopped talking. Mace hadn't started listening.

The Force nudged him with threat in all directions: from the rumble of wheeled groundcars that careened at random through crowded streets to the fan of death sticks in a teenager's fist. Uniformed militia swaggered or strutted or sometimes just posed, puffed up with the fake-dangerous attitude of armed amateurs. Holster flaps open. Blaster rifles propped against hipbones. He saw plenty of weapons waved, saw people shoved, saw lots of intimidation and threatening looks and crude street-gang horseplay; he didn't see much actual keeping of the peace. When a burst of blasterfire sang out a few blocks away, none of them even looked around.

But nearly all of them looked at Mace.

Militia faces: Human, or too close to call. Looking at Mace, seeing nothing but a Korun in offworld clothes, their eyes went dead cold. Blank. Measuring. After a while, hostile eyes all look alike.

Mace kept alert, and concentrated on projecting a powerful aura of Don't Mess With Me.

He would have felt safer in the jungle.

Street faces: drink-bloated moons of bust-outs mooching spare change. A Wookiee gone grey from nose to chest, exhaustedly straining against his harness as he pulled a two-wheeled taxicart, fending off street kids with one hand while the other held onto his money belt. Jungle prospector faces: fungus scars on their cheeks, weapons at their sides. Young faces: children, younger than Depa had been on the day she became his Padawan, offering their services to Mace at "special discounts" because they "liked his face."

Many of them were Korun.

A later entry in his journal records his thoughts verbatim:

> *Sure. Come to the city. Life's easy in the city.*
>
> *No vine cats. No drillmites. No brassvines or death hollows. No shovelling grasser manure, no hauling water, no tending akk pups. Plenty of money in the city. All you have to do is sell this, or endure that. What you're really selling: your youth. Your hope. Your future.*
>
> *Anyone with sympathy for the Separatist Cause should spend a few days in Pelek Baw. Find out what the Confederacy is really fighting for.*
>
> *It's good that Jedi do not indulge in hate.*

The station boss's chatter somehow wandered onto the subject of the Intel front she managed. The station boss's name was Phloremirlla Tenk, "but call me Flor, sweetie. Everybody does." Mace picked up the thread of her ramble.

"Hey, everybody needs a shower once in a while. Why not get your clothes spiffed at the same time? So everybody comes there. I get jups, kornos, you name it. I get militia and Seppie brass—well, used to, till the pullback. I get everybody. I got a pool. I got six different saunas. I got private showers—you can get water, alcohol, pro-bi, sonics, you name it—maybe a recorder or two to really get the dirt we need. Some of these militia officers, you'd be amazed what they fall to talking about, alone in a steam room. Know what I mean?"

She was the chattiest spy he'd ever met. When she eventually stopped for breath, Mace told her so.

"Yeah, funny, huh? How do you think I've survived this game for twenty-three years? Talk as much as I do, it takes people longer to notice you never really *say* anything."

Maybe she was nervous. Maybe she could smell the threat that smoked in those streets. Some people think they can hold danger at bay by pretending to be safe.

"I got thirty-seven employees. Only five are Intel. Everybody else just works there. Hah: I make twice the money off the Washeteria than I draw after twenty-three years in the service. Not that it's all that hard to do, if you know what I mean. You know what an RS-17 makes? Pathetic. Pathetic. What's a Jedi make these days? Do they even pay you? Not enough, I'll bet. They love that 'Service is it's own reward' junk, don't they? Especially when it's *other* people's service. I'll just bet."

She'd already assembled a team to take him upcountry. Six men with heavy weapons and an almost-new steamcrawler. "They look a little rough, but they're good boys, all of them. Freelancers, but solid. Years in the bush. Two of them are full-blood korno. Good with the natives, you know?"

For security reasons, she explained, she was taking him to meet them herself. "Sooner you're on your way, happier we'll both be. Right? Am I right? Taxis are hopeless this time of day. Mind the gutter cookie—that stuff'll chew right through your boots. Hey, *watch* it, creepo! Ever hear that peds have the right-of-way? Yeah? Well, *your* mother eats *Hutt* slime!" She stumped along the street, arms swinging. "Um, you know this Jedi of yours is wanted, right? You got a way to get her offworld?"

What Mace had was the *Halleck* on station in the Ventran system with twenty armed landers and a regiment of clone troopers. What he said was, "Yes."

A new round of blasterfire sang perhaps a block or two away, salted with staccato pops crisper than blaster hits. Flor instantly turned left and dodged away up the street.

"Whoops! *This* way—you want to keep clear of those little rumbles, you know? Might just be a food riot, but you never know. Those handclaps? Slugthrowers, or I'm a Dug. Could be action by some of these guerillas as your Jedi runs—lots of the kornos carry slugthrowers, and slugs *bounce*. Slugthrowers. I hate 'em. But they're easy to maintain. Day or two in the jungle and your blaster'll never fire again. A good slug rifle, keep 'em wiped and oiled, they last forever. The guerillas have pretty good luck with them, even though they take a *lot* of practice—slugs are ballistic, you know. You have to plot the trajectory in your head. Shee, gimme a blaster *any* time."

A new note joined the blasterfire: a deeper, throatier *thrummthrummmthrummthrumm*. Mace scowled over his shoulder. That was some kind of repeater: a T-21, or maybe a Merr-Sonn Thunderbolt.

Military hardware.

"It would be good," he said, "if we could get off the street."

While she assured him, "No, no, no, don't worry, these scuffles never add up to much," he tried to calculate how fast he could dig his lightsaber out of his kit bag.

The firing intensified. Voices joined in: shouts and screams. Anger and pain. It started to sound less like a riot, and more like a firefight.

Just beyond the corner ahead, whitehot bolts flared past along the right-of-way. More blasterfire zinged behind them. The firefight was overflowing, becoming a flood that might surround them at any second. Mace looked back: along this street he still could see only crowds and groundcars, but the militia were starting to take an interest: checking weapons, trotting toward alleys and cross streets. Flor said behind him, "See? Look at that. They're not even really *aiming* at anything. Now, we just nip across—"

She was interrupted by a splattering *thwop*. Mace had heard that sound too often: steam, superheated by a high-energy plasma bolt, exploding through living flesh. A deep-tissue blaster hit. He turned back to Flor and found her staggering in a drunken circle, painting the pavement with her blood. Where her left arm should have been was only a fist-sized mass of ragged tissue. Where the rest of her arm was, he couldn't see.

She said: "What? What?"

He dropped his kit bag and dove into the street. He rolled, coming up to slam her her hip-joint with his shoulder. The impact folded her over him; he lifted her, turned, and sprang back for the corner. Bright flares of blaster bolts bracketed invisible sizzles and fingersnaps of hypersonic slugs. He reached the meager cover of the corner and lay her flat on the sidewalk, tucked close against the wall.

"This isn't supposed to happen." Her life was flooding out the shattered stump of her shoulder. Even dying, she kept talking. A blurry murmur: "This isn't *happening*. It *can't* be happening. My—my *arm*—"

In the Force, Mace could feel her shredded brachial artery; with the Force, he reached inside her shoulder to pinch it shut. The flood trickled to sluggish welling.

"Take it easy." He propped her legs on his kit bag to help maintain blood pressure to her brain. "Try to stay calm. You can live through this."

Boots clattered on permacrete behind him: a militia squad sprinting toward them. "Help is on the way." He leaned closer. "I need the meetpoint and the recognition code for the team."

"What? What are you talking about?"

"Listen to me. Try to focus. Before you go into shock. Tell me where I can find the upcountry team, and the recognition code so we'll know each other."

"You don't—you don't understand—this isn't *happening*—"

"Yes. It is. *Focus.* Lives depend on you. I need the meetpoint and the code."

"But—but—you don't *understand*—"

The militia behind him clattered to a stop. *"You! Korno! Stand away from that woman!"*

He glanced back. Six of them. Firing stance. The light-pole at their backs haloed black shadow across their faces. Plasma-charred muzzles stared at him. "This woman is wounded. Badly. Without medical attention, she will die."

"You're no doctor," one said, and shot him.

HEROES

READ MORE ADVENTURES IN

STAR·WARS
I N S I D E R

SUBSCRIBE!

Each year, you'll receive:

- 8 issues of *Star Wars Insider*, each with new fiction by your favorite *Star Wars* authors.
- Membership in the Official *Star Wars* Fan Club
- 4 issues of *Bantha Tracks*, the Fan Club newsletter
- Exclusive membership kit

Go to **starwars.paizo.com**; call (760) 291-1509; or mail check or money order (US funds) to *Star Wars Insider*, PO Box 469078, Escondido, CA 92046-9633.

Just $28.95

($39.95 Canada, $75 Foreign*)

Visit www.delreydigital.com— the portal to all the information and resources available from Del Rey Online.

- Read sample chapters of every new book, special features on selected authors and books, news and announcements, readers' reviews, browse Del Rey's complete online catalog, and more.

- Sign up for the Del Rey Internet Newsletter (DRIN), a free monthly publication e-mailed to subscribers, featuring descriptions of new and upcoming books, essays and interviews with authors and editors, announcements and news, special promotional offers, signing/convention calendar for our authors and editors, and much more.

To subscribe to the DRIN: send a blank e-mail to join-ibd-dist@list.randomhouse.com or sign up at www.delreydigital.com

The DRIN is also available at no charge for your PDA devices—go to www.randomhouse.com/partners/avantgo for more information, or visit www.avantgo.com and search for the Books@Random channel.

 www.delreydigital.com